Hard Ride

FORGE BOOKS BY ELMER KELTON

After the Bugles
Badger Boy
Barbed Wire
Bitter Trail
Bowie's Mine
The Buckskin Line
Buffalo Wagons
Captain's Rangers
Cloudy in the West
Dark Thicket
The Day the Cowboys Quit
Donovan
Eyes of the Hawk
The Good Old Boys
Hanging Judge
Hard Ride
Hard Trail to Follow
Hot Iron
Jericho's Road
Joe Pepper
Llano River
Long Way to Texas

Many a River
Massacre at Goliad
Other Men's Horses
Pecos Crossing
The Pumpkin Rollers
The Raiders: Sons of Texas
Ranger's Trail
The Rebels: Sons of Texas
Sandhills Boy: The Winding Trail of a Texas Writer
Shadow of a Star
Shotgun
Six Bits a Day
The Smiling Country
Sons of Texas
Stand Proud
Texas Rifles
Texas Standoff
Texas Vendetta
The Time It Never Rained
The Way of the Coyote
Wild West

Lone Star Rising
(comprising *The Buckskin Line*, *Badger Boy*, and *The Way of the Coyote*)

Brush Country
(comprising *Barbed Wire* and *Llano River*)

Ranger's Law
(comprising *Ranger's Trail*, *Texas Vendetta*, and *Jericho's Road*)

Texas Showdown
(comprising *Pecos Crossing* and *Shotgun*)

Texas Sunrise
(comprising *Massacre at Goliad* and *After the Bugles*)

Long Way to Texas
(comprising *Joe Pepper*, *Long Way to Texas*, and *Eyes of the Hawk*)

ELMER KELTON

Hard Ride

A TOM DOHERTY ASSOCIATES BOOK
NEW YORK

HARD RIDE

A Forge Book
Published by Tom Doherty Associates
175 Fifth Avenue
New York, NY 10010

www.tor-forge.com

Forge® is a registered trademark of Macmillan Publishing Group, LLC.

The Library of Congress Cataloging-in-Publication Data
is available upon request.

ISBN 978-1-250-16128-4 (hardcover)
ISBN 978-1-250-16127-7 (ebook)

Our books may be purchased in bulk for promotional, educational,
or business use. Please contact your local bookseller or the
Macmillan Corporate and Premium Sales Department
at 1-800-221-7945, extension 5442, or by email at
MacmillanSpecialMarkets@macmillan.com.

First Edition: November 2018

Printed in the United States of America

0 9 8 7 6 5 4 3 2 1

Copyright Acknowledgments

Contents

Hard Ride

MY GUN IS
THE LAW

Sheriff Maury Chance looked out the curtained window into the night. He could see nothing except the glow of distant lamps, but he could hear it well enough. They were throwing a big one tonight down at the Legal Tender. Resentment simmered in him, but there was nothing he could do about it now—nothing legal.

A sympathetic hand touched his shoulder. "Come on over and sit down, Maury. Don't let them get to you this way."

Chance turned away from the window, but the shadow of slow anger still lay in his face. It was a square face, older in experience than in years, with something in it that was always tense, always expectant. Most noticeable were his restless eyes that never missed a thing.

The man who had spoken to him lifted a box from a table and pushed up the lid. "Cigar, Maury? Help take your mind off what happened today."

Chance took it. He reached for his shirt pocket to get a match, and encountered instead the coat of his suit. The suit felt unnatural to him now. He hadn't worn it much the last few years. The most unnatural thing about it was the absence of the gun that usually rode his hip. Thought of the gun made him look for it urgently, before he remembered. He had taken it off in deference to his host. His gun belt dangled from a nail near the door.

His host spoke again. "Like I said, Maury, I regret what happened today. But as a judge, I have to rule according to the verdict of the jury."

Maury Chance nodded. "I understand, Ashby. It's not your fault we can't raise an honest and impartial jury in this town."

Judge Ashby Dyke drew deeply on his cigar, his heavy brows knitted in thought. He was a large man in his fifties, his hair rapidly graying, the first deep lines of age beginning to gully his strong face.

"It's always hurt me when I had to send a man to the gallows," the judge said, "but I believe it hurt me worse today when I had to turn Joe Lacey loose."

Maury Chance frowned. "You don't know how long it took me to get Joe Lacey where he was today. You don't know how many cold camps I made, how many miles I rode, how many times I almost got myself shot. I didn't want to settle for Joe Lacey alone. I wanted to get his big brother Boyd, and Hugh Holbrook, and their whole cow-stealing, throat-cutting bunch.

"But I had to start somewhere, and I started with Joe. I thought if I got him and sent him away, maybe hanged him, it'd scare off a lot of the other riffraff that's been hanging on around here. What was left I could take care of. Now Joe Lacey's loose, and the riffraff is making the most of it."

Far down the street someone fired a gun, a saloon girl squealed, and half a dozen voices lifted high in laughter.

A young woman walked into the doorway that led from the judge's small, comfortable parlor back into the equally small kitchen and dining room. She wiped her hands on her apron and said, "Dinner is ready, Dad."

The judge stood up smiling. "Thelma stayed in that school too long, Maury. She calls dinner 'lunch' and supper 'dinner.' Keeps me so mixed up I'm never sure whether I've eaten or not."

He motioned Maury into the dining room. The sheriff paused

a moment and looked at the judge's daughter. She was a striking young woman, not altogether pretty, but more attractive than a man usually found out here on the frontier of Texas. She had been born in Missouri somewhere, when that, too, had been frontier, and her father had been a struggling young lawyer. She had followed the frontier all her life until her father had sent her east four years ago to attend school, to become the kind of lady her mother had been.

The school had been successful, Maury thought. She had the grace of the grand ladies he had known as a boy and a young man, in the South before the war. He liked the way she wore her black-and-white lace dress. But her manner and her dress seemed out of place here. They were incongruous with the raw town, with that raucous mob he could hear at the Legal Tender, with the hand-polished .44 in his gun belt against the papered wall.

Her dark blue eyes met his, and in them he sensed disapproval. She had a disturbingly frank way of staring at him, as if she could see into his soul and didn't like what she saw there.

Thelma Dyke's slender hands gripped the back of a chair and pulled it out. "Your place, Mr. Chance."

Her lips smiled, but it was a smile without warmth.

Maury bowed. He wished she didn't dislike him, but he never wondered why she didn't. He could see the reason himself, when he looked into a mirror. He could see the bitter lines cut into a face that seldom smiled any more, a face that once had known genteel ways but now was better acquainted with harshness and sudden violence.

As they ate, Maury tried to make conversation with her. "I believe Ashby said you went to school in Boston."

"Philadelphia," she corrected him.

Judge Dyke broke in. "Maury had some schooling in Philadelphia too, Thelma. He took some of his law work there."

That surprised her a little. "Law work? I thought you were only a peace officer."

Maury said, "I used to practice law as an attorney. But that's a long story. You wouldn't be interested."

She didn't contradict him. But Ashby Dyke said, "Sure, she'd be interested, Maury."

"I'll tell her some other day, if she wants to hear it. Not now."

Maury hoped she would never want to hear. It was a hard story to tell, or even to think about.

They ate quietly awhile. Thelma Dyke finally broke the silence. "I should think, Mr. Chance, that it would be a hard transition to make, from attorney to gun-carrying lawman."

He looked levelly at her. "You don't approve of the gun, do you?"

She shook her head.

"Neither do I, Miss Dyke," he told her quietly. "On the contrary, I hate it. I never knew how hard a man could hate until I learned to hate that gun."

"Then why keep on wearing it?"

"Because it's necessary, Miss Dyke. Those law books of your father's are useless out here unless there's a set of guns somewhere to back them up. There are many men here who have no respect for the law, but they do have respect for the gun."

She said, "I suppose you're right. But I can't respect the gun."

"Nor the man who wears it," said Maury Chance.

Judge Dyke broke in. "She didn't say that, Maury. You're in a terrible mood tonight, even for you. She didn't say that or mean it."

Maury managed a smile. "I'm sorry, Miss Dyke."

Hard knuckles rapped on the front door. The judge stood up quickly, then walked to the door and opened it. A thin-framed man in worn clothes walked in. He wore a badge on his dusty vest.

"Maury," he said, excitement rippling in his voice, "things are taking a bad turn down at the Legal Tender. Old Vic said I'd better tell you."

Maury pushed away from the table and walked out into the little parlor. "What is it, Calvin?"

Deputy Calvin Quillan remembered he still had his hat on, and he took it off as Thelma Dyke walked out of the kitchen. "Joe Lacey's down there tanking up on Vic's liquor. He's got a crowd of his friends with him. I guess you've been able to hear that."

Maury nodded.

"He's getting real brave now. He's telling them he's going to hunt you down and make you run. He's telling them that what happened in court today showed that the Laceys have the law hog-tied. He's saying that from now on the Laceys will run this county."

Maury's lips went hard in anger. He clenched his fists and cast a glance at his gun. "I guess I'd better put a stop to it, then."

Ashby Dyke caught Maury's shoulder. "Don't pay any attention to it, Maury. It's drunk talk. It'll wear off and be forgotten tomorrow."

Maury shook his head. "No, Ashby, it won't wear off. If I don't do something about it, that riffraff will get to thinking he's right. There won't be any stopping them then, not until it's gone too far. So I'll stop it now, tonight."

The judge said, "The decent people around here know where you stand, Maury."

"It's not the decent people I have to worry about."

He buckled his gun belt around his waist and reached for his hat. Then he bowed. "My apologies, Miss Dyke, for spoiling the dinner. Maybe I can do better another time."

She said, "Perhaps." But she was looking at the gun, and her eyes said that she hoped there wouldn't be another time.

Ashby Dyke got his hat and reached into a desk drawer. He pulled out a .38 pistol and shoved it into his coat pocket. "I'll go with you, Maury."

"No, Ashby. This isn't your fight."

The judge was adamant. "I turned him loose."

Thelma Dyke tried vainly to stop the judge. When she couldn't, she turned angry eyes on Maury Chance.

"Don't worry, ma'am," Maury said. "It'll be all right."

They walked out into the darkness. It was cool and there was a faint fragrance from the green grass that had risen after the spring rains.

Enough lanterns burned at the Legal Tender to light half the houses in town. The roar of laughter and the harsh voices carried far up the street. Maury Chance and Judge Ashby Dyke walked abreast. Deputy Quillan followed a pace behind them. But as they stepped up onto the porch and shoved through the door, he moved to his place beside them. Small in frame, Calvin Quillan was not small in courage.

A sudden and complete hush fell over the saloon. Maury's gaze swept the room, found Joe Lacey, and stopped there. Lacey set down his glass and began to laugh.

"There it is, boys," he said, "the whole law of Reynoldsville in one package—sheriff, deputy, and judge."

He picked up his glass again and held it high. "Here's to the law, for it won't be with us long." He took a liberal swallow, then wiped his mouth on his sleeve.

Joe Lacey hadn't been shaving for more than two or three years. Drunk or sober, the devil was always looking out of his eyes. He was a good man with a gun, and with a rope—especially on other people's cattle. He wasn't simply a cowboy gone bad; he had been brought up that way. It ran in the family.

Maury started walking toward him. Though his eyes were on Lacey alone, he knew the judge and Quillan were with him. Two paces from Lacey, he stopped.

"You've made some big talk here tonight, Joe," he said evenly. "But that's all it was, just talk. Now you're going to leave and go home."

Joe Lacey said, "I'm not ready to go home yet, Sheriff. You had your chance at me today in court, and all you got was a kick in the britches. Now get out before you get another."

Ice was on Maury Chance's words. "I'm not going, Joe. You are. You've had your laughs. Now go."

Joe Lacey lost all pretense at humor. His eyes glowed with a long-built hatred. "I'll go when I'm ready, Chance. And I'll be ready when I've knocked you off of your high horse. You had your chance at me, and you flopped. Now I'm giving you another chance. Draw that gun, if you're man enough. Kill me if you think you can."

Maury made no move for his gun. Instead he eased a little closer to Lacey. "I won't draw on you."

Lacey's lips drew up defiantly. "I told them you wouldn't. I told them I'd show them what a yellow coyote you really are." Lacey was tasting triumph, and it had a heady, intoxicating flavor.

"Try me, Chance, if there's any manhood left in you at all!"

Maury's voice remained calm but still. "I'm not going to draw because I know I could beat you, Joe. I don't want to kill you and make a martyr out of you. I want to be able to keep hounding you, to put you behind steel bars and make you look like the cheap, common crook you are."

Every word made the red flush of fury grow deeper in Joe Lacey's face. When his hand started to the gun at his side, Maury Chance was ready. With a fast forward stride he grabbed Lacey's hand as it drew the gun. He gripped the gun barrel, gave it a savage twist. Lacey cried out and jerked his hand away, blood running where the sharp trigger guard had chewed into his fingers.

Maury lifted Lacey's gun by the barrel and swung the butt of it at Lacey's face. The outlaw cried out again as he slid back against the bar. His hand went up to his cheek, where the gun had ripped a raw gash.

A long-held fury was driving at Chance. He hadn't wanted it this way, but now he had to show these toughs that he meant what he said. He slashed at Lacey again. The outlaw spun and fell.

Lacey's gun barrel in his fist, Maury whirled on the rest of the crowd. "Anybody else?"

Nobody made a sound. He had taken them by surprise, and now his animallike fury held them cowed.

"Maury, look out!" The cry came from Calvin Quillan.

Maury whipped around, and saw a gun come up in Lacey's hand. But before Maury could change his grip on Lacey's weapon, Quillan stepped in front of him, an old .45 swinging into line.

Lacey's shot roared like a dynamite blast. Quillan heaved backward. A second shot came from Judge Dyke's .38. It whipped Lacey around. The outlaw slumped onto the floor, his shoulder shattered.

Quillan swayed, then began to fold at the knees. Maury grabbed him and eased him to the floor. He glanced at the splotch of blood high in Quillan's chest. A glance was enough.

"Calvin," he said hoarsely, "you shouldn't have."

Quillan tried to speak, but the words wouldn't come. In a moment he was dead.

Maury's burning eyes lifted to the crowd. A knot tightened painfully in his throat. He looked with hatred at Joe Lacey, who was doubled up in a knot, blood spilling around the hand he held to his shoulder.

"I had his gun, Ashby," Maury said to the judge. "Where did he get another?"

"Somebody passed it to him. I didn't see who."

Maury stood up, gripping Lacey's gun as if he meant to crush it in his fist. "Who was it?" he demanded. "Who gave him the gun?"

No one answered. His gaze searched hotly from one face to another. Then he started looking for empty holsters. He found one. He looked up into the man's face. He saw guilt there, and fear.

The man whirled and ran for the door, desperately shoving people out of his way.

"Stop!" Maury ordered.

The man kept going. Maury raised the gun and squeezed the trigger. The man fell like a sack of rocks. He lay on the floor sobbing, holding his bleeding leg. The fury drained out of Maury then. Calmness slowly came back to him.

He turned to old Vic, the man who owned the saloon. "Take care of Calvin for me, Vic."

The whiskered old man nodded. Though the violence had taken place in Vic's saloon, Maury could not look upon the old man as an enemy. Vic stayed neutral, siding no man, blaming no man.

Roughly Maury took Joe Lacey by his good shoulder and jerked him up. "Come on, Joe. You might've gone free today, but you won't get loose any more. You've just hung yourself!"

His blood-smeared face blanched in shock, Joe Lacey was sobering fast. He was crying. "Get me to a doctor. I need a doctor."

Maury gritted, "You'll get a doctor in jail." He jerked Joe Lacey along toward the door, then paused beside the man who lay on the floor, gripping his wounded leg.

"I need somebody to help me get this man to jail, too."

A couple of cowboys stepped out of the crowd. Maury knew them as punchers from Jess Tolliver's Rafter T. They had been watching the excitement, taking no hand in it. "We'll bring him, Sheriff."

Quickly they commandeered a wagon from the street and loaded the two wounded men into it. One of the cowboys took up the reins. Maury kept looking back over his shoulder, expecting trouble to come boiling out of the Legal Tender.

Judge Dyke read his thoughts. "It came too quickly, Maury. They're still in a sort of shock. I don't believe there'll be any trouble."

A woman came running toward them from out of the shadows. She stopped in a shaft of lantern light to watch the wagon come by. Thelma Dyke's face was tight with fear. She looked at Maury Chance first, then saw the judge.

"Dad, are you all right?" The judge nodded, and a sigh of relief escaped her lips. Her shoulders sagged a little. She followed the wagon afoot.

Maury looked back at her once. He was glad he had no one to worry about him, to wonder fearfully if he would walk home tonight or be carried in. If Maury Chance were to die, there'd be no one to mourn him but a few scattered friends. Even they wouldn't think of him long. It was a satisfying feeling.

But sometimes, in the dark of night and in the quiet of his own room, in his sleepless bed, a terrible loneliness moved in upon him like the wail of a blue norther. At such times he would have given his life to have turned back the years for just a little while to know the comfort of his family back home, the mother, the father, the brother, who was four years older than he.

But they were gone now. The brother was lost on the battlefields of Northern Virginia, the mother and father long since buried. There was no one now to care whether Maury Chance lived or died.

The doctor arrived at the jail within a few minutes. He was a gruff little man of short patience who lived alone and seldom shared his thoughts with anyone. If he ever had any emotion other than perpetual cynicism, he kept it well buried.

"Looks like a lot of useless work to me," he grumbled, repairing Lacey's shoulder. "I patch him up and get him healed so you can hang him. Would've been better if you'd killed him in the first place."

"I didn't do it, Doc," Maury said. "The judge did."

He wished immediately he had bitten off his tongue instead of talking. He saw the sudden surprise, then the deep disappointment in Thelma Dyke's face. "Dad, you didn't!"

The judge nodded. "I did. That man killed Quillan, the deputy, and he was about to kill Maury. So I shot him."

She stared at her father as if she still couldn't believe it. Gently the judge placed his big hands on her slender shoulders. "Don't fret over it, Thelma. There's no reason why I should feel sorry about it. I don't."

"That's just it," she said. "Maybe you did have to do it, but you certainly shouldn't act as if it were nothing."

The judge made no reply. Maury Chance moved over beside the young woman. "Don't blame your father, Miss Dyke. He did the only thing that could be done, and you'll realize it when you've had time to think it over. You were brought up on the frontier. Surely those four years in the East didn't make you forget everything you learned as a girl."

Her dark blue eyes leveled on his. "You think I learned to hate guns while I was in the East, Mr. Chance, but you're wrong. I learned it a long time before that. I was just a little girl. Did Dad ever tell you how I lost my mother?"

Pain came into Ashby Dyke's eyes. "Thelma, please."

She went on, "There was a bank robbery in the little Missouri town where we were living. The bandits had a hard time getting out. Bullets started flying everywhere. My mother threw me down onto the floor. Then a stray bullet smashed through a window and struck her.

"We never did know whose bullet it was. It might have been from a bandit, or it might have been from a lawman. It didn't make much difference. She was dead."

Her eyes burned with a quiet hatred as she looked at Maury's .44. "It makes little difference whose hands they're in. Guns make trouble for everybody. Do you think Joe Lacey's friends will forget that Dad shot him? They won't. He's put himself in line for trouble. And what did it? That gun, Mr. Chance."

That whipped Maury Chance. He knew no answer and tried none.

Thelma Dyke's slender shoulders were squared and aloof as she walked out the door with her father and disappeared into the darkness.

Basically, she was right. He granted her that. She was just carrying the idea to an extreme, Maury thought.

Long after she was gone, he found himself still watching her in his mind, still thinking of those proud shoulders, of the ease and grace with which she walked. Most of all, he thought of her face. It could be a pretty face if she smiled. He knew that she must smile a lot. It showed in the little crinkles at the edges of her blue eyes, at the corners of her soft mouth.

But there had never been a smile for him. And he wanted very much to see one.

Joe Lacey's lawyer was late in learning about the shooting. But as soon as he heard, he came on the run. Maury let him into Lacey's lamp-lighted cell. A few minutes later, when the lawyer came out, Maury explained the situation briefly.

"Looks like there's no way for you to wiggle him out of it this time, J.T.," Maury said, with a hint of satisfaction.

J. T. Prosise wasn't exactly a crooked lawyer, but he could teeter on the brim of crookedness as expertly, without falling in, as anyone Maury had ever seen.

Prosise eyed him narrowly. "Are you sure you're not just harboring a grudge because of what happened in court today?"

Maury shook his head. "No grudge, J.T. You did your job, and I can't hold that against you. But I can't forget it, either. I know that next time you'll try to discredit my evidence just like you did today. But next time it won't work. There was a whole roomful of witnesses tonight."

"You had a gun in your, hand," Prosise pointed out. "You had

struck him twice. I think my client would be justified in pleading self-defense."

Maury managed to keep the growing anger out of his voice.
"You can try it, but it won't hold water, J.T. It won't suit a jury."

Prosise smiled wisely. "I think it would suit a jury in this
county," he said pointedly. "Don't you?"

Maury's jaw went hard in anger. Prosise's point was plain
enough. There were too many of Joe Lacey's kind in Reynoldsville, and there would be plenty of them on any jury panel that
might be made up.

"I'm going to convict him, J.T.," Maury said stubbornly.
"This time I'm going to get him."

Prosise only smiled. "We'll see, Chance. We'll see."

Next morning the town was extra quiet. Maury made a tour
of the saloons, just to look around. He found them almost
empty. Old Vic's was like the rest.

"How does it look, Vic?" Chance asked.

Old Vic was polishing glass with a clean white cloth. He took
a long time sizing up Maury, but his gray eyes expressed no
judgment.

"They're waiting, keeping their eyes open," he said. "They're
waiting to see if you try to make it stick. If you could, they'd
start drifting out. They'd know their day was about over. But
you won't make it stick, and they know it. They know you'll
stick by the law, and the law in this case happens to work for
Joe Lacey."

Maury gritted his teeth. "So I'm going to lose. What happens then?"

Vic said, "Some say you're going to die. Joe Lacey's a young,
hotheaded fool. His brother Boyd is just about like him. When
Joe gets out . . .

"But most say it won't happen that way. Most of them are
thinking about Hugh Holbrook. It's Hugh that really runs the
Laceys, and he's a smart man. Talk is that the toughs are going

to run him for sheriff this summer, against you. And they'll run J. T. Prosise against Ashby Dyke. They'll win. There are too many of them not to win."

Maury pondered that, keeping his face blank. "How do you stand, Vic?"

The old man's face was as expressionless as the bare walls of his saloon. "It's not my place to worry about it, one way or the other. But I'm glad I'm not you."

Maury expected it, but he didn't know in what manner the visitation would come. He was considerably surprised, then, when Boyd Lacey and Hugh Holbrook came riding up the middle of the main street in broad daylight. Not a person in town missed their coming. All along the street men stood and stared. But as the two riders reached the courthouse square and dismounted, the spectators began to pull back, to watch from doorways and windows.

Maury had seen them from the window of his office in the jail building. Hitching his gun belt, he stepped out into the doorway and waited.

He caught the hot hatred in Boyd Lacey's eyes, and thought he saw a sudden impulse to try to kill him then and there. But Lacey changed his mind. Like his younger brother, he was a man of impulse. But unlike Joe Lacey, Boyd didn't follow every impulse that came to him.

Maybe the calmness of Hugh Holbrook had something to do with that. Holbrook was a man of cool thinking, of long deliberation, then of positive movement. More than once, Maury had seen a disapproving glance from Holbrook stop the Lacey brothers from launching into some hasty, ill-considered notion.

It was Holbrook's leadership that had built one of the smoothest-operating bands of rustlers and all-around thieves in the Texas Panhandle.

The two men stopped three strides from Maury Chance. "I've come to see my brother," Lacey said at length.

"You can see him," Maury answered, "but I take the guns first."

Lacey started to make some protest, but Holbrook calmly unbuckled his gun belt and held it out. Lacey looked at him, then grudgingly followed suit.

Holding the belts, Maury stepped back inside the doorway to give the two men room. "You know the way, Boyd," he said. "You've been here before."

Lacey's eyes flickered at the insult, and he said something under his breath. A thin smile played on Holbrook's lips.

Where Boyd Lacey was carelessly dressed and left an odor of tobacco and sweat as he walked by, shoulders hunched, Hugh Holbrook carried himself erectly. His military bearing betrayed him. Anyone could tell he had been a soldier—an officer.

He was freshly shaven. His clothes were clean, except for a few dust streaks gained on the ride to town. He was a handsome man, older than forty. When he spoke, it was evident that he was well educated.

An awful waste, Maury always thought when he saw Hugh Holbrook. With the Laceys it was a case of their following their natural bent. They'd never been anything but outlaws. That was all they could ever be.

Who then merited the most contempt, Maury had asked himself many times—the men who were outlaws because it was their nature, or this man who would have been something better, had been something better?

Maury said, "I'm a little surprised you came in this way, Hugh. I'd expected you, all right, but I was afraid it might be different."

Holbrook grinned. "It could have been, but I prevailed on Boyd to do it this way. I've always believed men could talk things out over a calm cup of coffee much better than over the point of a gun."

Maury nodded. "That's sensible. But there's not much to talk out. Yesterday there might have been; today it's gone too far."

"It's never too far gone, Maury. Stop and look at it objectively. If you take this to court, what chance have you?"

"I have plenty of evidence."

Holbrook grinned. "You had evidence yesterday, too. Joe still won acquittal. He'll win next time, and you know it. Where will you stand in this town then? After two defeats in a row you'll be finished here."

Maury's eyes narrowed. "What would you want me to do?"

"Don't ever let it come to trial. Talk your friend the judge into setting a reasonable bail. Let Joe out. Keep putting the trial off. In time the fuss will die down and you can forget about the trial altogether."

Maury said, "I know what you're working at, Hugh. Keep putting the trial off until you're the new sheriff and J. T. Prosise is the judge."

Holbrook's eyes were smug in triumph. "It's not a question of choice, Maury. There isn't any choice. This is the only thing you can do and save your face. Take another whipping and you won't be able to make a stray dog run from you."

Maury stared angrily at Hugh Holbrook a long moment before he answered. Then he clenched his teeth hard and slowly shook his head.

"No dice, Hugh. Sink or swim, I'm going to take him to trial. I'm going to do my best to hang him. If I fail, it won't be because I didn't try."

Holbrook's grin was gone. His eyes had gone the color of gun steel. "Then try your damndest, Maury. I'll see you leave this town like a cur dog, with your tail between your legs."

Anger was still roiling in Maury Chance when he walked into the judge's house. Ashby Dyke put down a heavy law volume and stood up to greet him. Maury told of the visit of Boyd Lacey and Hugh Holbrook.

"We can't get a jury that'll convict him, Ashby," Maury said bitterly. "I know that now. And we can't afford to lose again."

The judge nodded agreement. "I've done lots of thinking about it."

Maury said, "I know of only one way out, Ashby. I've decided to take it. We have a lot of support from the ranches that Holbrook and the Laceys and the rest of this mob have been preying on. Jess Tolliver of the Rafter T was in to see me this morning, as soon as he heard about Calvin Quillan.

"We have only one chance to win this trial, Ashby. That's to clean out this town first—drive out the cow thieves, the gamblers, the small-time crooks, the whole bunch. They outnumber us, but we can do it if we move fast and hit them by surprise. The ranchers are already champing at the bits."

Ashby Dyke frowned, a deep worry in his eyes. "You'd have no legal footing, Maury. We would be nothing better than vigilantes."

Angrily Maury replied. "There is no legal way to do it. And it's got to be done some way, legal or otherwise."

Thelma Dyke walked into the room unseen. Maury turned at the sound of her voice.

"You're a lawyer, Mr. Chance," she said rigidly. "You should have more respect for the law than anyone else has. You should know better than anyone else what happens when you start taking things into your own hands and acting outside of the law."

Maury tried to meet her level accusing gaze, but had to drop his eyes. The color began to rise in his face. "There won't be any law here, the way things are headed. If we can't convict Joe Lacey, we might just as well pull out of Reynoldsville. And we can't convict him the way things are here."

Ashby Dyke firmly nodded his gray head. "That's it exactly, Maury. We can't convict him here. We can't even try."

Maury looked up in sudden alarm. "You don't mean you'd turn him loose?"

"No, we'll convict him. In any county but this one a conviction would be easy to obtain. So I'm going to order a transfer of the trial."

New hope surged into Maury. "Can we get away with it?"

The judge said, "It won't be hard to do. After all, I witnessed the murder of Calvin Quillan. I even shot the defendant. That is more grounds than I need to disqualify myself as judge in the case. And if I am disqualified, the trial will have to be moved."

Thelma Dyke stepped closer to Maury, her eyes pleading. "It's what we need, Maury." She hadn't used his first name before. "We don't want armed mobs running this town, whether they're for us or against us."

"I wasn't going to tell you, Maury," the judge broke in. "I was going to go out and make the arrangements first. I don't want word of this to leak out before we're ready."

Maury shook his head. "No. They'd break Joe Lacey out of jail, or die trying."

"As soon as I arrange a place for the trial, we'll move Lacey. If it's possible, we'll have to do it before his friends know what's happening."

"I hope we can make it work."

The judge said, "It'll be the test of us all, Maury. We have to make it work."

Maury was at the livery stable the next morning to see Judge Dyke leave town on the mail hack that pulled out before sunup. Cautious, they said nothing about their plan. Maury kept his eyes on two saloon bums stretched out in the hay.

"I'll be back as soon as I can," the judge said, as the hack driver swung his team.

"Good luck," Maury called after him. As Maury turned back toward the jail, one of the bums walked out of the livery stable and hurried up a side street.

An hour later, lawyer J. T. Prosise eased into a chair at Maury's table in Oscar Bruton's little cafe.

"Do you mind?" he asked politely. Several other tables were vacant.

Maury shook his head. "Table's big enough. What're you doing up this early?" He thought perhaps he knew.

"Couldn't sleep well," Prosise answered. "Always restless when I have a big case on my hands, such as the Joe Lacey trial coming up."

Oscar came to the table. Maury and Prosise both ordered eggs. When Bruton returned to the kitchen, Prosise leaned back in his chair.

"I've been wondering when the judge would set the trial date. Have you heard him say?"

Maury answered with a negative shake of his head.

Prosise continued, "I understand the judge left town at the crack of dawn today. I'm a little upset that he did so without notifying me. As defense counsel, there are several things I needed to check over with him." Prosise leaned forward, unable to mask the eagerness in his eyes. "Where was he going?"

Maury answered, "I didn't hear him say."

Frowning, Prosise looked down at the table. *He smells a dead mouse in this thing somewhere,* Maury thought.

"Did the trip have anything to do with the trial?" Prosise queried.

"I didn't hear him say," Maury repeated.

He felt Prosise's eyes boring into him, trying to read what was in his mind. But Maury could keep a poker face when he wanted to. Worry rose in the lawyer's eyes, slowly growing into alarm.

Suddenly Prosise slid his chair back, stood, and walked hurriedly out the door. Maury leaned toward the window and watched the lawyer make long strides down the street. Oscar Bruton walked out of the kitchen with a plate of eggs and bacon in each hand, stopped abruptly and stared at Prosise's vacant chair.

"Where did old Long Shanks get off to?"

"I think something happened to his appetite," Maury said.

Just an hour later Maury himself began to worry. Reports reached him that Prosise had left town. At the livery stable a hostler told Maury about it.

"He asked me if I heard the judge say where he was going," the hostler said. "I told him no, he just went off with the mail hack. Prosise up and rented a buggy from me and took out down the road."

"Same way the hack went?"

The hostler nodded. Maury turned and walked back up the street, a worried frown creasing his face.

The days dragged by with a painful slowness while Maury waited for some word from the judge.

Maury saw Thelma Dyke several times during those few days. Usually he met her walking down the street, going shopping or visiting. He found himself watching for her, hoping for a chance to walk a little way down the street with her.

On the fourth morning after the judge had gone, Maury stepped out and intercepted Thelma as she walked up the street with a basket on her arm.

"That looks heavy," he said. "May I carry it for you?"

"It's not, but you may," she answered, smiling.

The smile brought a pleasing warmth to him. He walked beside her, not talking, content with her company.

They passed Jess Tolliver on the street. The rancher tipped his hat. Tolliver still nursed disappointment because Maury hadn't let him organize a posse of his own and clean out the town.

Thelma asked, "Maury, have you heard anything from Dad?"

He shook his head. "No. He thought he would be gone four or five days. I'm not worried." But he was worried.

"Maury," she went on, "I hope you're not sorry you decided to let Dad handle this his way, instead of going along with Jess Tolliver."

"I'm not sorry, Thelma. If it works out—and I think it will—it's better this way."

"No mob, no guns?"

"No mob. But it may take some guns when we move Joe Lacey."

She turned in at her front steps and took the basket. "Maybe not, Maury. Maybe not."

He heard the clatter of horse's hooves, the ring of wheels, and a shout in front of Vic's saloon. A tingle of alarm started in him. He tipped his hat to Thelma and hurriedly turned away.

Out in the main street, he saw Prosise standing in front of the saloon, excitedly talking to a loafer there and pointing westward. In a moment the man swung onto a horse and spurred out. Prosise turned and stared with open hostility at Maury. Then he strode hurriedly toward his own little office, two doors from Vic's.

A buzz of excitement started in Maury. Prosise knew. Everybody would know before they had a chance to move Joe Lacey out.

The news spread over town like fire through tall dry grass. It was only a few minutes until Jess Tolliver hurried up to the jail.

"I just heard the judge is getting the trial moved," he said excitedly. "Is that right?"

Maury nodded. "That's what he left here to do."

Tolliver grinned broadly. "In any other county, Joe Lacey won't stand a chance. I'll take off my hat to the judge."

Maury said, "We had hoped to get Joe Lacey moved before the word leaked out, but Prosise got back before the judge did. We're liable to need some help, Jess."

Tolliver said. "You can have every man on the Rafter T."

"I can use six or eight. You pick them and bring them to me."

Judge Dyke came in with the mail hack at noon. He hurried to the jail.

"I'm sorry, Maury. Prosise tracked me down. He was right there when I made arrangements with the Tom Green County judge to move the case to his jurisdiction. There was no way I could get back before he did."

Reassuringly, Maury laid his hand on the judge's shoulder. "Don't worry, Ashby. We'll make it all right. Jess Tolliver is bringing some good men as deputies. As soon as it's dark, we'll head out."

Worry weighted the old judge's face. "They'll know they're whipped if we get Joe Lacey out of this county. So they'll tear the jail down to get him free."

Impatiently Maury Chance paced the jail office floor, pausing now and again to watch the lowering sun. Nervousness grated at him like a whetstone.

Joe Lacey jeered at him from his cell. "They'll bust me out of this crackerbox jail like it was an eggshell."

Maury would have hurled an angry reply, but he knew it was futile. He mustn't let Joe Lacey rattle him.

Two Rafter T cowboys sat in chairs in front of the door. Behind the building somewhere there were three more. A couple of others, including Jess Tolliver, were out in town, watching and listening. There wouldn't be trouble before dark, Maury told himself. And after dark there wouldn't be a chance for trouble.

At six thirty Judge Ashby Dyke walked up to the jailhouse, nodded at the cowboys in front, and beckoned to Maury. The sheriff cast a nervous glance at Joe Lacey, who lay relaxed in his bunk, whistling softly. Then he stepped out and fell in beside the judge. They walked away from the building, out of earshot of anybody.

Quietly the judge said, "I've got it arranged for the wagon to come at eight thirty. It'll be good and dark by then. Maybe Lacey's friends won't try anything earlier than that." He frowned then. "But they will try. Don't you think so?"

Maury said, "Boyd Lacey won't stand by and let us hang Joe without making a try. Hugh Holbrook's held him back so far because Hugh was certain we wouldn't get a conviction. Now he'll probably drop the reins and let Boyd do what he wants to. He may even help him."

"They'll be in for a surprise when they find Joe Lacey's cell empty," the judge said. "But I wish it were over. I wish we already had him moved."

Confidently Maury said, "We'll get the job done, all right." Then he changed the subject. "Would you go over to Oscar's cafe and order supper brought for us, Ashby? These men had better eat before this starts."

"Supper's already on its way," the judge replied. "Thelma's cooking. She'll be here directly."

Maury smiled at the thought of Thelma. "Thanks, Ashby. We'll all appreciate it."

Thelma came soon, two baskets on her arms. Maury helped her spread the food out on the table. The cowboy deputies came in, filled plates, and walked out again to their places. Maury dished out a portion for Joe Lacey and carried it to his cell, then filled a plate for himself.

Maury ate silently, his eyes on Thelma most of the time. Finally he said, "You've gone to a lot of trouble for a bunch of gun-carrying lawmen."

Thelma's eyes held no criticism. "What you're doing tonight is to stop violence, not cause it."

Earnestly Maury said, "Everything I've done with a gun was meant either to prevent violence or to put an end to it, Thelma. That's all any honest lawman wants."

She was giving him a long, silent appraisal. "I realize that now, Maury." She was silent a while. Then she said, "You told me once you'd explain sometime why you became an officer. You were an attorney once. What happened? What caused the change?"

Maury looked away from her. He studied his nervous hands.

After a bit he said, "I was a little too young for the war. After it was over, I went east and worked my way through law school. It wasn't easy, but I finished. I went home to Virginia then. It wasn't the way I liked to remember it. The war had ruined it for me. So I came west, to Texas.

"You know how it was during the years after the war. There was a country full of Yankee carpetbaggers, trying to rob Texas blind. They ran things pretty much to suit themselves. Then, when the Yanks pulled their troops out of Texas and everybody got to vote again, things started to change. But all the carpetbaggers didn't go. Some stayed and thought they could go on doing as they always had.

"I'd been here two years when I took a land case. A sharp Yankee promoter had swindled a man out of his property. The judges were all Texans again, and I won. But this Yankee swore to kill both my client and me. Well, I'd learned about guns as a boy in Virginia. The sheriff knew it was likely to come to a shooting, and he made me a deputy to protect me, in case it ever came to court. When the Yank came, I was ready for him.

"Texas was wild in those days. Still is, of course, but not like it was then. Anyway, that shooting won me a reputation of sorts. Like a fool, I kept that deputy's badge. There were more shootings. As time went on, I found myself more and more a peace officer and less and less an attorney.

"It finally reached a point that I couldn't stop. Wherever I went, I drew lightning. And finally I wasn't a lawyer any more, I was only a gunman."

In Thelma's blue eyes Maury could see understanding. She said, "The day of the gun is almost over, Maury. One day soon you'll be able to lay yours down, if you want to."

He reached out and touched her hand. "I'll want to, Thelma. Believe me, I'll want to."

Eight thirty. Only a quarter moon was out tonight. Outside

the jail it was so dark that Maury could hardly distinguish the building's bulk against the black sky.

Maury fingered his watch, a current of excitement tingling in him. No reason to be so fidgety, he told himself. But he wished that wagon were here.

For an hour now the noise had been rising in old Vic's saloon. Something was brewing down there. Maury could feel it in the air. It was high time that wagon was getting here, before this night erupted into violence.

The minutes dragged by, and still no wagon. The noise was swelling. Some sort of violence had begun. Maury could hear it, but he couldn't afford to leave here now. He couldn't even afford to send a man to the judge.

He heard the quick footsteps of a man running. Someone burst into the light of the lantern hanging over the front door. It was old Vic himself.

"Sheriff," Vic called excitedly. "Sheriff!"

Maury stepped out of the shadows. "What is it?"

"You'd better get over to my place. They've got Jess Tolliver and one of his cowboys in there. They're beating them half to death."

Maury clenched his fists. What a time for a thing like this! He listened intently, half expecting to hear the wagon. But all he heard was the noise down at Vic's.

"Chuck, Pete," he called. "Come along with me." To the other men he said, "If the wagon comes, you know what to do. We'll catch up with you."

Maury and the deputies struck a brisk trot down the sandy street, old Vic following them. They hit the porch and shouldered through the swinging doors abreast. Maury took in the whole scene at a glance.

One of his deputies lay unconscious on the floor. Two of the town toughs had a half-conscious Jess Tolliver backed up against the bar. They were methodically beating him with their fists, not hard enough to grind him out completely but hard enough to grind him down. A sizable crowd stood watching, making no move to stop it.

Maury gave the deputies a glance that said to cover his back. Then, boiling with anger, he strode forward and grabbed one of the toughs by the shoulder. He spun him around and clubbed him with his pistol butt. The man fell like a rock.

The other man dropped Tolliver and stepped back, defensively lifting his big fists to chest level.

"No you don't, Chance. You don't pistol-whip me."

"You're under arrest," Maury gritted. He swapped ends of his .44, and leveled it at the man. He glanced down at Jess Tolliver. The rancher was bent over painfully, white-faced, his hands tight against his stomach.

Maury looked back at the tough. He knew him. He'd seen him around here off and on for several months. The man would hang around and gamble, but he was a poor gambler and inevitably he would go broke. Then he would disappear. After a time he would be back, fresh money in his pockets. Maury knew where he had been—riding with the Laceys and Hugh Holbrook.

The tough said. "Supposing you do arrest me—and mind you, I'm not saying you can—what'll you do with me?"

"Let you sweat in that jail for as long as it takes Jess Tolliver to get over this beating you've given him."

The tough grinned. "From what they tell me, you aren't going to have much of a jail after tonight. They tell me Boyd Lacey's going to make kindling out of it. And he's going to make hash out of you, Chance."

Gunfire exploded up the street. Maury's heart leaped. The jail! For a second he stood, frozen. Then he whirled and ran for the door. Outside, he saw the flashes where guns were popping on the courthouse square. He heard a sudden ripping sound, a squealing of rusty nails and a splintering of lumber.

Hoofbeats drummed. Men shouted. Then there was a rush of horses into the street.

The two deputies were right behind as Maury Chance made a run toward the jail. The lantern by the jail door had been smashed and the front of the building was dark. But from inside a reddish glow was growing, spreading. They had set fire to the jail.

Horses broke into a run. Again there were flashes of gunfire, as their riders sent last spiteful bullets at the defenders of the jail.

Somewhere at the edge of town Maury heard the horses stop. He heard a man's voice call out, but he couldn't catch the words. There was a volley of shots, the shrill scream of a woman. Then the hoofbeats drummed again.

At the jail, Maury found one of the deputies fighting a crackling blaze that spread across half the floor. He grabbed a blanket from his cot and helped fight the flames.

"What happened?" he shouted. But he could see most of it. A gaping hole torn in the side of the jail, into Joe Lacey's cell. And Lacey was gone.

"The wagon came," the deputy answered, slowing up in his battle against the blaze. "I saw too late that it wasn't our men. They got Jim. I'm afraid he's dead. They clipped Alcorn, too. Had a team of work horses with them. Threw a rope around the window bars and yanked the whole side of the jail out."

In a few minutes they had the blaze under control. A crowd had gathered. Men brought buckets of water to splash over the smoldering floor. The fire died.

Immediately there was a cry to go after the riders. Maury shook his head. "Too dark. All they'd have to do would be to stop, and we'd go right by them. We'd mess up the tracks so badly that we couldn't follow them at all. We'll wait till daylight."

Someone brought in the prisoner who had passed Joe Lacey the gun in the saloon. Wounded in the leg, the man hadn't been able to ride. The Laceys had left him to shift for himself out in the darkness.

They found that the deputy Jim was not mortally wounded after all. And Alcorn had a flesh wound that would soon heal. So, from the looks of it, it wasn't as bad as it might have been, Maury thought.

Someone caught Maury's shoulder. He turned. "You'd better get over to Judge Dyke's house, Sheriff," a man said solemnly. Maury recognized him as the man who lived next door to Ashby.

"What's happened?"

"The worst, I reckon. You'd better go."

The long day with its mounting tension, and the grueling action of the night, had brought a deep weariness to Maury Chance. But he walked hurriedly toward the judge's house, a dark foreboding tightening his stomach.

He stepped up onto the little porch, then stopped in his tracks. On the front porch lay a body, covered by a blanket. The solemn-faced man knelt and pulled the blanket back for Maury to see. Maury's jaw dropped in shock. The judge!

"I heard the shooting at the jail," the neighbor said. "Then a bunch of riders came loping up to the judge's house. Somebody called him. By that time I was standing on my porch. I saw the judge come out his door.

"They cut him down, Sheriff. I saw them in the lamplight that came through the judge's door. It was the Lacey boys. Joe Lacey came in closer then. I could see his shoulder all white where it was wrapped up. He came closer and fired two more shots into the judge's body. He was cussing as he did it. Then they all spurred their ponies and left here in a run. They headed west."

Maury was kneeling beside the body, his eyes burning, his teeth clenched tight. "How many were there?"

"Five. The Laceys for sure, and I'm pretty certain I saw Hugh Holbrook. He rode through the light for a second as they pulled out. The other two I didn't see very good."

Inside the house, a woman was crying. Maury knew it was Thelma. Stiffly he pulled the blanket back into place and stood up. Ice chilling his stomach, he stepped through the door.

Thelma lay on a bed, weeping. Two solemn neighbor women sat beside her. One of them was gently patting her shoulder, but neither woman was trying to talk. At a time like this there wasn't anything helpful that could be said.

Maury walked up beside the girl. "I'm sorry, Thelma," he said, hardly above a whisper.

She raised up, leaned her head against his chest, and gripped his arms, crying. "Maury," she said huskily, a deep bitterness in her words, "I was wrong. You were right. There's only one way to stop them, and that's with a gun. It's the only way they know. I want you to go and get them. I want you to kill them, all of them. Organize your vigilantes. Drive the riffraff out of town, like you said. If they don't go, shoot them!"

Maury stared at her in surprise. But he knew that right now, in her bitterness, she meant it.

Fury crackling in her eyes, she said, "It was my fault. I talked you into waiting, trying it the legal way. Well, we waited. And for what? For this!" Her slender shoulders began to heave. "Go on, Maury. Do it your way."

He squeezed her hand gently. "We'll get them, Thelma. I promise you that. We'll get them all."

In a way, it was a good thing he had the whole night to get ready. Instead of having to take a raw, possibly worthless posse on the spur of the moment, he had time to choose his men. He didn't want to take too many. The more there were, the slower they traveled, the more trouble they were likely to have in closing with Holbrook and the Laceys. He chose five Rafter T men, all of whom he knew and felt he could depend on to do what might be needed when it needed to be done.

At the doctor's office he found Jess Tolliver sitting up on the edge of a cot, one hand against his stomach.

"They kept punching me in the belly," he said tightly. "They meant to cripple me that way. Otherwise I reckon I'm not so bad off."

"Are you still on the warpath, Jess?" Maury asked.

"You're damn right!"

"Then I've got a job for you. The same one you asked for the other day. I'll deputize you and give you the right to organize your own posse from your own ranch hands and the men from the other ranches.

"I want you to round up all the toughs, the gamblers, the known cow thieves, and the rest of the riffraff that hangs around here. I don't want anybody hung and I don't want anybody shot unless it's necessary. But if you have to, go ahead and shoot. I'll back you up.

"I want these men scattered to the four winds. Tell them that if any one of them ever pokes his head into this county again, we'll slip a rope over it. It's come to a showdown, Jess. It's either them or us now, and we can't afford to let it be us."

Jess Tolliver smiled painfully, without any humor. "I'm glad you're turning us loose, Maury. We'll do it right. No hanging and no shooting, unless they force it. But we'll get this place as clean as a hound's tooth for you, don't you worry."

Maury got his five possemen bedded down at the livery stable, with their horses, equipment, and supplies ready for use at dawn. Then he headed back toward the jail in a slow walk, his head down.

He wanted to see Thelma Dyke again, but a visit now would serve no purpose, he knew, except perhaps to satisfy his growing compulsion to be near her. He resisted the urge to go to her. Maybe the neighbor women had gotten her to sleep by now, and she needed sleep.

In the jail the smell of charred lumber was strong, and he moved his cot outside. Lying there sleepless, he had a long time to ponder over what had happened tonight. Somehow they'd gotten wind of the plan to smuggle Lacey out of here. They'd intercepted the wagon and used it to get them close to the jail. That business at Vic's saloon had been a decoy to draw away as many lawmen as possible.

Boyd Lacey hadn't thought this up—Maury was reasonably sure of that. Boyd thought in straight lines. It would have been like him to lead a direct assault on the jail and try to haul Joe Lacey out by sheer force.

No, it hadn't been Boyd Lacey's idea to do it this way. Hugh Holbrook had planned this maneuver. It showed his brand of clever timing, his shrewd strategy.

But the murder of Judge Dyke hadn't been part of Holbrook's plan, Maury theorized. It had been a vicious afterthought, and likely had been done over Holbrook's protest. Hugh Holbrook was not a back-shooter, a killer of unarmed men. There was that much to be said for him.

Maury managed only to doze a little, off and on. When the first sign of light began to rise in the east he was up and watching, his eyes a little raw from want of sleep.

He walked over to the cafe and roused Oscar. While Oscar put on a big coffee pot and prepared to cook breakfast for the posse, Maury went on to the livery stable. In a few minutes the men were up and had their horses ready. They ate silently, sleep still heavy on them.

Outside of town they began circling, each man's gaze on the ground, searching for horse tracks. Presently a cowboy named Pete Ringer let out a whoop. The other riders gathered.

Ringer said, "I've followed it a hundred yards or so to be sure. There are five horses."

Maury nodded and set out in the lead, following the plain tracks. But Pete Ringer was the real tracker in the bunch. They had been riding for about an hour when Ringer suddenly reined up and stepped down. He picked up something Maury's eyes had missed. It was a long strip of white cloth.

"Piece of a bandage, isn't it?" the cowboy asked.

Maury nodded. "Looks as if that heavy binding around Joe Lacey's shoulder might be starting to bother him."

Ringer grunted. "Rubbing, I expect. But it'll bother him a lot more if he takes it all off."

Urgency burned in Maury. The Laceys had a long start, and he wanted to make up for it. But common sense held him down to a stiff trot. If they started running now, the horses wouldn't last out the morning.

The trail led down into a running creek and disappeared. All morning the riders had been working south. The creek ran from northwest to southeast. Maury stared uneasily at the water, wondering which way to turn.

"They've been heading south all the time," a cowboy said. "Looks reasonable they'd take off downriver, pretty much the way they'd been going."

Maury frowned. "Maybe. It's the most logical thing, and it's what the Laceys would do. But Hugh Holbrook's with them."

The fugitives would know that their trail from town was easy to follow to this point, Maury reasoned. They had made no effort to hide it. Riding in the dark, they'd had little chance. But now they were making their first move to throw off followers. And Hugh Holbrook wouldn't do the obvious.

"Well head back up the creek," Maury said.

Followed far enough, the creek would take them back within five miles of town. Chances were Holbrook and his men wouldn't have followed it that far. But then, with Holbrook, you never could tell.

Maury made a sweeping motion with his arm. "Spread out. Pete and I will ride the creek bottom. The rest of you watch for sign where anybody might have pulled out along the banks."

They took it slowly from there, walking some of the time, sometimes managing an easy jog trot where the going was good. They rode a mile, two miles, maybe three, but there was nothing.

Maury felt the eyes of some of the other riders touching him again and again. Their glances told him they thought he'd made a mistake. Maybe he had. Surely by this time someone among the fugitives would have made a slip, and let his horse step far enough out of the water to leave a hoofprint in the mud at the edge.

Pete Ringer finally put the thoughts into words. He said, "It isn't right. There's no sign at all. It isn't soldiers we're following."

"Not soldiers, Pete, but they have a military officer leading them. And you can bet he's kept up a strict discipline."

Ringer shrugged. "Maybe. It won't hurt to follow them another mile. If we don't find anything by then, it seems to me we'd better turn back and not waste any more time."

"Another mile, Pete."

Maury's heartbeat quickened as they rode. It looked bad. Everything indicated that he'd judged wrong. Yet deep within him he had an indefinable certainty that he was right.

They covered most of the mile, and Maury could feel the growing restlessness of the other riders. They were convinced that every step they took was a step away from the fugitives.

Then he saw it. Snagged on a half-buried mesquite limb at the edge of the creek—another strip of bandage. Joe Lacey more than likely had sneaked it off and dropped it while Holbrook wasn't looking.

Pete Ringer's face broke into a broad grin. "You called the turn, Sheriff," he said. "Lead on."

At noon they found where two riders had pulled up out of the creek bed. It was on a gravelly spot, and the men probably thought they could get out without leaving sign. But one of the horses had slipped and fallen. His thrashing had left marks that couldn't be covered up. Maury dismounted and looked past the creek bank, wondering where the tracks would lead.

Ringer was bending over the gravel bar, examining it closely. He called, "Hey, Sheriff, come take a look." He knelt and placed his stubby finger on a rock. "See that stain there? Blood! I told you Joe Lacey would be sorry for taking the wrapping off that shoulder. The fall from that horse must have opened the wound and started it bleeding."

Maury felt his pulse quicken again. "Then these tracks leading off must belong to Joe and Boyd Lacey."

One of the cowboy possemen said, "Well, they're the ones we want the worst. Let's go get them."

The two fugitives had made an effort to stay as much as possible on ground that wouldn't show big tracks. But it was hard to do for very long at a time. And where Maury sometimes couldn't see the trail, Pete Ringer could. They managed to ride fast now, sometimes breaking into an easy lope.

Pete Ringer leaned low over the side of his horse. "Sign's getting fresher. Joe must be wearing out. They're slowing down."

They had trailed the men twelve or fifteen miles, far west of the creek. Maury's eyes were burning, and fatigue had added fifty pounds to his shoulders. It was that sleep he'd lost, he knew. Ahead of them were some cedar brakes where the rolling rangeland suddenly broke into steep slopes, deep washes and brushy draws.

There was no warning. One of the possemen spun and dropped out of the saddle. Immediately afterward came the belated slap of a rifle. In a second all five of the other men were out of their saddles. Maury and a cowboy grabbed the wounded man and dragged him toward a protecting cut bank, leading their horses as they hurried afoot. Two more bullets whizzed over their heads.

They eased the man onto his back. Maury tore the shirt open. The bullet had gone high into the cowboy's shoulder. In Maury's saddlebags were clean bandages and a bottle of whisky he had brought, knowing this might happen. He fumbled the saddlebag open. He had his hand on the bandages when another bullet, meant for him, dropped his horse.

Cursing under his breath, Maury crouched and hurried back to the wounded man. He gave him a long drink of the whisky, noting to his relief that the bullet had gone all the way through. No probing was necessary; that was one good thing. When he had the blood stopped and bandage in place, Maury said, "Think you can hold out awhile, till we take care of our job?"

White-faced, the posseman nodded weakly.

Maury did not have to signal the other posse members to spread out. They had already done it, and they had been cautiously working their way toward the outlaws, keeping on their knees as they edged through the brush. Occasionally an angry bullet searched through the cedar, showering leaves and dust upon the lawmen. But the posse, wisely, were holding their fire until they saw something to shoot at.

On his knees in the sand, Maury worked away from the cut bank, around the end posseman. He began a cautious circle around the bushwhackers. Like an angry hornet, a bullet buzzed by his face, and he dropped to the warm ground. He started crawling then, low against the ground, rifle cradled in his arms. He wanted one good shot at the Laceys.

They stopped firing then, and a new urgency sped him on. They realized they were being outflanked, he knew. They were pulling back. If they got away, all this would have to be done again.

Maury pushed to his knees. "Let's get 'em," he shouted. Crouching, he began to run. He looked toward the other possemen. They were doing the same.

The outlaws were being pushed too hard. They fired a few hasty, ill-aimed shots, for now they were more interested in getting away. One of the men showed himself over the tops of the low cedars as he swung into the saddle. Three possemen's rifles cracked. The man toppled back out of sight.

Maury's heart was drumming. He couldn't see the outlaws

now. One was hit, maybe dead. But the other one might be waiting, gun ready, and that gun might be aimed at Maury.

But a quavery voice called from somewhere in the brush, "Don't shoot any more. I'm throwing my gun away and coming out."

Maury stopped. He held his rifle at his hip and waited. A man stepped unsteadily out of brush, one hand in the air, the other hand inside his stained shirt. Maury's heart dropped into a deep pit. This man was not a Lacey.

He advanced cautiously, half afraid the outlaw would pull the hand out of his shirt and reveal a gun. But when he came closer Maury saw that the shirt was caked with dried blood.

"What about your partner?" Maury asked, carefully checking the man's pockets and boot tops for hidden weapons.

"Dead. You cut him to pieces when he got on his horse."

The outlaw's face was drawn. A sick blue color had spread beneath his eyes. Maury knew the man was running a fever from his wound.

"You got that last night?"

The man nodded. "At the jail."

Maury's lips drew tight. He hadn't known there'd been two wounded men among the five outlaws. That blood spot, then, had been from this man. Not from Joe Lacey.

"What do you think, Sheriff?" Pete Ringer asked solemnly.

Maury looked toward the western sky. "We've lost several hours here. But you can bet your boots the Laceys and Holbrook haven't lost any time. Sun'll be down in a few minutes. We're through tracking for today."

"We could ride back to the creek, so we'd have a fresh start in the morning." Ringer suggested.

"We could, but Dan yonder is in poor shape to ride. We'd better leave him and this outlaw here. Let Curly stay with them. We'll send a wagon back."

Two men were gone now from a posse of five. It would take another man to go after a wagon, and that left only two posse-

men and a sheriff—even odds against the Lacey brothers and
Hugh Holbrook.

Maury put his saddle on the dead outlaw's horse. The moon
was high when the men reached the creek. Maury scooped
creek water into a can and added coffee grounds. Silently they
ate a cold supper and drank scalding black coffee. Maury never
realized how terribly tired he had been until he stretched out
on the ground. He dropped off to sleep without trouble.

Next morning they started riding up the creek as soon as it
was light enough. The tracks would be older now, and the
night wind might have smoothed out any of them that had
been on soft sand. Each time Maury came upon a gravel bar
he stopped and studied it closely. It was a cinch that when the
fugitives left the creek bed they would do it in such a place,
where tracks could not easily be seen.

The close scrutiny finally paid off. Two hours after sunrise,
Ringer found the place. "Angling west now," Ringer said.

They pulled out of the creek bed and headed west. The tracks
were not easy to follow. But as had been the case last night,
there was always enough sign, always enough tracks, to keep
the posse on the trail. It led westward and southwestward,
toward the broken land.

"Headed for the outlaw country, all right," Ringer said.
"They've got the advantage on us there. They've put enough
stolen cattle through there to stock the biggest ranch in the
country. They'll know every foot of it, and we don't."

"Then we'll learn to know it," Maury Chance said grimly.
"We're going to keep riding 'til we find them."

All morning they rode, sometimes losing the trail and hunting an hour before they found it again. Other times the trail
was plain. Now the country was changing. Where it had been
fairly open rolling range, now it was brushy country, cut across
by gullies and ragged slopes.

The time would come when this would be good cow country, Maury mused. It would be good winter range, affording

protection from the howling northers that swept across the open range to the north and east, and there was water enough here.

But it was outlaw country. With men like Holbrook and the Laceys on the loose, a man who scattered a herd into this brush was the same as turning it over to the thieves.

Noon came and went. The sun began its long westward arc. The three lawmen found where the fugitives had stopped to rest. There was a small, hand-scooped pit with dead ashes of a tiny fire. And there was something else.

"What do you make of this, Pete?" Maury asked, pointing to a place where boot heels had dug into the ground, where the sand had been smoothed as if men had sat or fallen on the ground. A couple of tree branches were broken. On one of them hung a small triangular piece of blue shirt cloth.

"Fist fight, looks like," Ringer said, "they've had a falling out."

"It had to be Boyd Lacey and Hugh Holbrook. Joe Lacey wouldn't be in shape to fight."

Ringer searched the ground. "Well, whoever it was, they all rode off together again. Looks like they changed course a little and cut to the south a shade more."

From here on there was little effort to hide tracks.

"Holbrook lost," Maury commented. "He's been leading till now, and he's kept a pretty strict discipline. Now the Laceys are doing it their own way, and they don't care."

"We'll get them, then," Ringer said confidently. "They should've stuck with Holbrook."

They made much better time now that the trail was easier to follow. They alternated between a slow lope and a good stiff trot, riding as fast as they dared to without wearing out the horses that already had put in two days' riding.

Sign was getting fresher. Late in the afternoon Pete Ringer swung down, looked a moment, then climbed back into his worn saddle. "They're traveling slow now. Joe's having trouble, most likely. And they're not much ahead of us anymore. There's a good chance we'll catch them before sun-down."

Sundown came, though, and they hadn't caught up. Darkness crept around them. Grudgingly, Maury Chance reined up.

"We'd better stop here. No use riding blind."

They dismounted and unsaddled, staking their horses. There was no coffee tonight, and Maury missed it. He stretched out wearily on the ground, and in a moment was half asleep.

Suddenly restless, Hodge Isham, who hadn't said six words in the two days, excitedly shook Maury's shoulder. "Come look at what I've seen," he said.

Isham led Maury and Pete Ringer up over a rise and pointed. Ahead, Maury couldn't estimate how far, a pinpoint of light flickered in the brush. Nobody said anything. Nothing needed to be said. Quietly they threw the saddles back onto their horses and remounted, touching spurs gently and reining toward the light.

When he thought they were close enough, Maury pulled up and dismounted. He loosened the cinch and tied the reins to a bush. Ringer and Isham did the same. Maury took off his jingling spurs and tied them to his saddle. He slipped the rifle out of his saddle scabbard and started, the other two men beside him.

They walked a hundred yards. Then they could see it. "Shack," Ringer muttered. "They have a lamp lit in there."

"Pretty sure of themselves," Maury said. He could hear a low murmur of voices, rising now and again in argument.

He thought of crashing into the shack, and the idea set the hair tingling at the back of his neck. It would be like stepping into a hornets' nest. Somebody was bound to be killed. And if they captured the Laceys and Holbrook, they would have them on their hands through a long night.

"We'll wait till morning," he said at last. "We'll get them as they step outside."

They set up a guard shift, one man watching while two men slept. The lamp in the shack went out. Quiet settled over the little clearing in the brush. It was another pitch-dark night. Once, near morning, Pete Ringer shook Maury's shoulder.

"Thought I heard somebody moving around over yonder," he said.

Maury quickly arose. He made a slow, silent circle one way, while Ringer circled the other. They found no one, but they did find where the outlaws' horses were staked. There were only two.

"Holbrook must have slipped away," Maury guessed.

Holbrook had been shrewd enough to know what the Laceys, in their supreme self-confidence, had not been willing to consider—that they could and would be followed. Now, unable to control the Laceys any longer, he must have gone out on his own.

"Time enough for him later," Maury said. "We'll get the Laceys first." They went back to where Hodge Isham was waiting.

About dawn the door was flung open. Boyd Lacey strode outside, gun in hand, and took a hurried look around. "Holbrook's gone, Joe," he said. "He lit out."

Joe Lacey stepped to the door. He looked haggard and drawn. Foolishly, he had removed the tight and chafing bandages from his wound. The dried stains on his shirt showed what the consequences had been.

Boyd Lacey began to stiffen. Some animal instinct was working in him. "Get back in the shack, Joe," he said. "Something's wrong out here."

He began to back toward the door, his desperate eyes searching the brush, his gun raised and ready.

Restless, Hodge Isham made his play. He raised up and fired at Boyd Lacey. Lacey jerked, but his .45 exploded in his hand. Isham bent at the middle and fell on his face.

Maury fired a quick shot at Boyd. A bullet from Pete Ringer's rifle ripped a gash in the door facing as Lacey ducked back inside. The door slammed. There was a loud thump as a bar was thrown into place.

For a long moment, then, there was silence. Maury ran to Isham, but Pete Ringer was there ahead of him. Isham wasn't dead, but it would be only a matter of time. The bullet had caught him in the stomach. He lay in agony, dying a death that might drag on for hours.

No use now in saying that it was Isham's own fault, that he should have stayed down. Pete Ringer's jaw hardened. He clenched his fists and looked toward the shack.

"Anyway, I think Hodge hit him."

Maury waited until his own anger had settled enough so that his voice was steady. He called, "Joe! Boyd! We've got you pinned in. You can't get away now. Come on out and give up!"

He got the answer he expected. A gun muzzle appeared at a window and a bullet droned angrily through the brush. Maury's lips flattened in bitterness. It would be a waiting game, and they didn't have time to wait if they were to get Hugh Holbrook.

But what else could they do? He lay in the sand, rifle to his shoulder, watching for a glimpse of either of the Laceys at the window. Occasionally a gun muzzle appeared long enough to fire a quick shot. Then it would withdraw before Maury had time to answer it.

He had a long time to think, to ponder ways to flush the Laceys out. But he could only figure one way—setting fire to the shack.

That old shack was tinder-dry and would go up like a box of matches. But how to set fire to it? The angry guns of the Laceys wouldn't let a man get within fifty feet. Maury frowned, considering a dozen different schemes. Suddenly he thought of a way that could work.

"Keep them pinned down for me, Pete. I'm going to try something."

He went back to where they had tied their horses, and took the ropes off each of the three saddles. Then he circled to where the Laceys' horses were. He took their two ropes and looped the ends together until he had one rope about a hundred and thirty feet long.

He searched until he found several dead cedar trees. Set afire, they would build to searing flame that wouldn't be easily extinguished. He broke the trees down, stacked them, and tied the end of the rope around them securely. He dragged them as close to the rear of the shack as he could safely go.

Then he started back around to Pete, leading one of the Lacey horses and playing out the rope as he went. He kept jerking up the slack, flipping the rope as near to the shack as he could.

He had only about ten feet of free rope left when he got to Ringer. The red-bearded cowboy stared curiously. "Now what the deuce . . ."

Maury explained, while he whipped the rope closer to the shack, trying to take the bend out of it, trying to get it where Ringer could have a straight pull at it.

"I'm going back around there now. When I get it burning, I'll fire two shots in the air. Then take this horse and pull that rope for all you're worth. Get that burning brush up against the shack."

At the back side again, Maury struck a match to the dead brush. It began to smoke, then broke into flame. He moved to another and repeated. In a few moments the blaze was big and strong. Maury drew his gun and fired twice. He watched the brush pile begin to move, to drag toward the shack.

Twice he thought Pete had struck a snag, that the rope would burn away before the job finished. But the brush began to drag again at the end of the long rope. It piled up against the shack. Then the rope jerked away as the flame burned it in two.

Holding his breath, Maury watched the blaze. Slowly it began to die back as the brush burned away. For a moment he thought it would burn out without setting fire to the dry lumber of the shack. Then the flames brightened. The shack was going!

Crouching, Maury ran back to Ringer. "You did fine, Pete. Now all we've got to do is wait."

It seemed they waited an hour. Flames crackled up all sides of the shack. Brown smoke curled and billowed around it.

"Aren't they ever coming out?" Ringer gritted.

Then the door flew open. The Laceys stepped out together, both wounded but both holding guns. The brothers made a savage, unforgettable picture of fury as they stood side by side before the blazing shack, their hostile eyes searching for a target, defying the death they had lived with so long.

They saw the lawmen and started walking toward them, guns barking, faces twisted in hatred.

It lasted only a few seconds, but it might have been an eternity to Maury Chance. Four men faced each other amid the thunder of guns, the crackling of fire, the swirling clouds of smoke.

Then it was over. Flames billowed and sparks showered as the shack collapsed. The angry crackling of the flames began to die down. Arm lowered but the gun still in his hand, Maury Chance cautiously moved out toward the figures of the Lacey brothers, now sprawled grotesquely in the sand.

He looked down at them a moment, then up at Pete Ringer. He felt no triumph. In him was only revulsion against what he had to do. Looking at Pete, he saw it reflected in the cowboy's eyes. They went back to Hodge Isham. He was still alive.

"He won't last much longer," Ringer said, "but we can't just go off and leave him."

"Stay with him, Pete," Maury said. "Stay till it's over. I'm going after Hugh Holbrook."

Picking up the trail wasn't much trouble. Perhaps Holbrook had sensed what was coming. At any rate, he seemed more concerned with speed now than with covering his trail. It was a good thing for Maury, because he wasn't the tracker that Pete Ringer was.

He spurred into a slow lope. He knew he was risking wearing down the horse, but now that he was this close to Holbrook he felt he had to try to close with him. He slowed sometimes, giving the horse a chance to breathe. Then he pushed him again. There was no way of knowing for sure, but he felt he was closing the gap.

The afternoon wore away. Another night was coming on. Impatience arose in Maury, raw and galling. Then he broke out over a rise and saw his man a quarter of a mile ahead. And Hugh Holbrook saw Maury Chance.

From there on it was a race through the brush, and the men had little to do with it. It was one tired horse pitted against the other, a race to see which horse could hold out the longest. Slowly the gap narrowed. Maury could feel his horse's breath coming harder, and the long strides became more and more labored. But Holbrook's mount, too, was tiring. It was giving out faster than Maury's.

The end came quicker than Maury had hoped. Holbrook's horse stumbled, and Holbrook went rolling in the sand. He came up stunned, grabbing for his gun. The horse struggled to its feet and went trotting off, limping.

Holbrook ran for the cover of brush. Maury spurred after him. He slid his horse to a halt as a bullet screamed past him. He jumped out of the saddle, fell to one knee, got up, and scrambled for cover. He crouched down, watching, listening.

For a long time, then, it became a stalking game, each man stealthily hunting for the other in the thick brush. Occasionally Maury's boot crushed a twig. The snapping of it was like a gunshot to him. He would drop, expecting a bullet to smash into his back. But it didn't come.

It was not long before it would be dark again. Maury felt he couldn't let this go on until sundown. There would be no chance of finding Holbrook then.

He stepped out from behind a thick cedar and suddenly found himself face-to-face with Hugh Holbrook. Each man had his gun lowered. For an eternity they stood staring at each other, neither lifting his gun.

Finally Maury spoke. "You'd better drop it, Hugh. You've come as far as you can go."

"You're by yourself, Maury," Holbrook pointed out. "If I shot you there'd be no one else to hunt for me."

"But you'd have to beat me to do that. I don't think you can do it, Hugh. Do you?"

Holbrook's lips pulled back with a suggestion of a grin. "I can beat anybody in this country." But fear lurked behind his eyes.

"You'd better not try, Hugh."

For a moment a wildness crept into Holbrook's eyes. Maury thought the man was going to try, but he didn't.

"I didn't think you would, Hugh," Maury spoke calmly. "I know the whole story about you. It wouldn't fit."

Holbrook's eyes narrowed, but the fear was still there. "What do you mean?"

"I found out about you a long time ago, Captain Hugh Holbrook Jameson. I found out that you had been in the United States Army, and that you had earned a reputation for shrewd strategy. You were good at sending others out to win. But one day you got caught in the thick of battle yourself, a battle against a superior force of Comanches.

"It was a little too close for you then. There was a big difference between planning a maneuver and fighting it. You took it as long as you could, and then you ran. You'd had a good reputation until then, so they didn't court-martial you, Hugh. They let you resign for the good of the service.

"In spite of that, you could have been a useful citizen, Hugh. You had a great potential. You could have been a real builder out here. But instead, you wasted all that. Why?"

Holbrook was silent a long moment, the gun still in his hand. Finally he said, "I tried, but always the truth came out.

Somebody always discovered it, just as you did. So I took to the gun, Maury, just like you did."

Holbrook grinned ironically, as if remembering a grim joke. "Just like you, Maury," he repeated. "We're a real pair, you and I. I was a good soldier; you were a good lawyer. We've both wasted ourselves. Now it's too late to change."

"It's never too late, even for you. Come along peacefully, Hugh. You've never killed anybody, so far as I know. There's a chance you can get off with a light sentence. A few years and you'll be a free man."

Holbrook pondered a moment, his eye steady on Maury's. Then he shook his head. "No, Maury. My mind would rot in a penitentiary. You know that. It's better to die here, fast, than to die a slow death in a cell."

Maury's lips went dry. He watched Holbrook's eyes, watched for the signal that meant the man was going to make his try. He saw the flicker. Holbrook brought the gun up halfway. Then he stopped. His hand trembled. Holbrook's face fell, and fear shoved into his eyes—open, pitiable fear. The gun barrel wavered, dipped forward, then the gun fell out of his shaking hand.

Maury was holding his breath. He had brought his own gun up and started pressure on the trigger. Now he released the pressure. Stepping forward, he kicked the gun away from Holbrook's feet. Holbrook's trembling legs gave way under him. He fell to his knees in the sand and began to sob.

"Better get up, Hugh," Maury said quietly after a while. "It's a long, long ride back to town."

When Maury Chance had had a bath and a shave, and a change of clothes, he squared his clean brown hat in front of the barber shop's cracked oval mirror and walked out into the street. It was a quiet street now. He had never seen it so quiet before.

To Jess Tolliver and his posse went the credit for that. Like Jess had promised, they had made the place as clean as a hound's tooth. The way Maury heard the story, Jess and his men had accomplished the job through swiftness and surprise. They had done it peacefully. Only one man had been shot, and he had merely gotten a load of buckshot where it would keep him from sitting around the saloons for a while.

Maury stopped a moment at Vic's Legal Tender Saloon. The old man sat on a chair outside the door. Maury had thought Jess probably would force Vic out of town, too. He hadn't, and somehow Maury was glad.

"Looks like business is quiet," Maury said. The old man nodded. "It'll get better someday. The town will grow now, and we'll get a solid class of trade as the country grows."

Old Vic thoughtfully stroked his beard. "Looks to me like you're about out of a sheriffing job. The only thing a sheriff'll have to do around here from now on is collect the taxes."

Maury smiled. "That's the way it should be."

He stepped down into the street again. He headed for the little frame house that had been Judge Dyke's home. On the narrow path he paused to straighten his tie and to take off his hat. He knocked on the door. In a moment Thelma Dyke came. She smiled.

"Come in, Maury."

He stepped inside the door and turned to face her. He had given much thought to what he was going to say to her, but suddenly he couldn't remember a word of it. He stood uncertainly, embarrassment bringing a flush of red to his face.

She was wearing black; that was to be expected. But she seemed to have found herself again, Maury thought. The worst of her grief spent itself while he was gone.

She looked levelly at him. Her eyes were soft. "I heard about all that happened," she said.

He nodded. He was glad he didn't have to tell her himself.

She hesitated a moment, then said, "I didn't mean what I

said the other night, Maury. I was out of my mind in grief. I didn't realize what I was saying."

"I know."

"I'm glad you brought Hugh Holbrook in alive."

"So am I, Thelma. There's no pleasure for me in killing anyone. There never was. There's never been any pleasure for me in carrying my guns."

She made no reply.

She waited, appraising him with her calm blue eyes.

Maury said. "I won't need my guns here anymore, Thelma. I'm going to take them off and hang them up."

She smiled. "I'm glad, Maury. But what will you do?'"

"I've done a lot of thinking. I'm still an attorney. As people begin moving in here and building up this country, they'll need attorneys."

She said, "They'll need judges, too."

His eyes widened in surprise. That thought hadn't come to him.

She said. "The elections will be coming soon. They'll want someone to fill Dad's place. You'd be a good judge, Maury. They'd elect you if you'd run."

He thought, liking the idea but shaking his head.

"I don't know. It's a big job, and it's been a long time."

"You want to get away from the gun. It would be your chance."

He crushed his hat in his nervous hands. The more he thought about it, the more he liked the idea.

"It's a big job for a man to start alone."

Something came into her eyes then, something he'd never seen there before. They were soft, and they were warm. "You don't have to be alone, Maury. I'll be here."

He took an uncertain step forward. "Thelma," he whispered. He touched her arm, then gripped it tightly. He pulled her to him, leaned down, and kissed her gently. He felt the answering warmth of her lips, and her arms circled about him, strong and compelling.

No, he would never be alone again. Wherever he was, whatever he did now, there would always be someone to care, someone whose strength would double his own. It was a good feeling.

SIDESADDLE SWEETHEART

Jay Lockaby was uneasy from the moment he started circling the big, loose-herded bunch of longhorn steers. This was the sorriest looking trail outfit he had ever seen.

It wasn't so much the steers. The cattle looked good enough as they grazed contently on the thick turf of grama grass already half cured by the summer sun. But one thing struck him as strange—they bore no trail brands.

It was the cowpunchers who worried Jay most. Of the four he had ridden by so far, three had been just kids. From the looks of their rigs and their clothes, they were farm boys and runaway youngsters just starting on their first riding job. The fourth was a grown man, but he didn't look like much of a cowboy. Jay had seen plenty of his kind hanging around saloons and swamping out stables.

Up ahead another kid cowboy sat slouched over in the saddle, watching a steer graze farther and farther out from the bunch. The youngster slowly circled around the longhorn. Suddenly he spurred his horse and yelled like a wild Indian. He plunged after the frightened steer and drove the animal deep into the herd. The other steers scattered like a covey of quail. The young puncher trotted back out through the settling dust, happy as a hound dog chasing house cats.

If it had been Jay's own herd he would have ridden over and

given the kid a good dressing-down . . . When he had had his own herds he had done it. But those days were gone.

Maybe a Kansas City businessman like Claude Nickle, having his first experience with a trail herd, wouldn't know how important it was to be able to depend on his men. What Jay had seen so far didn't make him want to sign on here. But a man down to his last dollar, with hunger already gnawing under his belt buckle, didn't have much choice.

He started to ride on by, but reined up as he saw a slender rider spurring toward the youngster. It was a girl on a sidesaddle. A cowboy trailed her.

The girl pulled up in front of the youngster and bawled him out. As the shamefaced boy hung his head, she angrily turned back to the red-haired cowboy who followed her.

"Have you got to tag along behind me everywhere I go?"

The puncher grinned. "I got orders to look out for you."

She tossed her curls angrily, swung around, and rode off. The redhead followed her. Jay watched them a minute, then rode up to the redfaced boy. "Which way's the wagon?"

The youngster pointed off in the general direction which the girl had taken. "Over yonder a ways, other side of the thicket. You starting up to Kansas with us tomorrow?"

Jay eyed the cheap saddle, the boy's brogan shoes, and a limber rope coiled haphazardly against the saddle horn. But he couldn't say much about it. He had had to swap his own good saddle for an old one to get a little "boot" money to eat on.

"Don't know yet. Got to ask them for a job first. Who's the girl?"

"She's Audrey Nickle. Her pa bought these steers. She don't stand for any foolishness."

Jay pondered. He had heard in town that a girl was to go on the trail drive. He hadn't believed it. Who had ever heard of a woman going up the trail?

"I guess Claude Nickle's doing his own hiring," he said finally.

The youngster shook his head. "Oh, no, he's turned that over to his trail boss. Name's Logan Sartain. He's real choosey about the men he hires, Sartain is."

Sartain! Jay stiffened. He breathed the word and felt a sour taste in his mouth. For a moment he thought about turning back. But a man had to eat. He doubled his big fist and rubbed rough knuckles in futile anger across his square jaw.

Jay turned his bay half around and spurred a little harder than he intended to. A real comedown for a man who had once had his own herds. Of all the people in Texas, he had to ask Sartain for a job.

Half a mile beyond the thicket Jay could see the ranch head-quarters. Babb's Lazy B.

He had been hearing about this drive back in town, and it looked like the only thing lazy about husky old Wylie Babb was his brand. Claude Nickle was pretty much of a tenderfoot, they were saying in town. But they were adding that Babb was going to give him an education, the hard way.

Talk was that Nickle hoped to make a fortune buying Texas steers and driving them up to Kansas. Town people had heard that for three days Babb had worn out buckboard teams taking Nickle around to neighboring outfits and showing him their cattle.

The way the town crowd had it, Babb had been careful to show Nickle only those cattle which weren't so good as his own. Naturally Nickle had decided Babb's cattle were the best he could find. He had paid Babb twenty dollars a head, three dollars more than anyone else had gotten.

Ahead Jay saw mesquite smoke curling upward from the far side of a chuckwagon. With the sun already low in the west, a slouchy wagon cook was putting a big coffee pot on the fire. Jay dismounted a safe distance from the wagon and tied his horse to a mesquite. The bay quickly reached up and got a mouthful of the brown mesquite beans. The cook stood by the chuckbox lid, silently watching Jay walk in, spurs jingling.

"I'm lookin' for Sartain."

The cook eyed him irritably. "If he hires any more punchers, I'm going to have to have me three wagons just to haul the grub. Dang kids eat up a can of syrup ever time they come by."

Mesquite brush popped. Jay looked around as three men and the girl rode out of the thicket. He recognized Sartain and felt an old hatred start to work within him. Hard to believe Sartain would be doing honest work. His preference ran to soft jobs, easy money, and painted dance hall women.

Jay glanced at the Nickle girl. She was easy to look at. Her waist didn't look as big around as the crown of a man's hat, the way she sat in her sidesaddle. The little man riding next to her Jay judged to be her father.

The four reined up fifty yards from the wagon to keep from stirring up dust around the cook fire. The red-haired cowhand was quick to swing to the ground and step over to help the girl down. Jay caught the annoyed look on the girl's face when the man kept hold of her waist a moment after she was out of the saddle. She pulled away, and Jay gritted his teeth as he saw the man grin slyly.

Sartain was twenty feet from the wagon when he recognized Jay. He stopped short. His hand dropped toward his gun, then halted abruptly. For a second Jay wished he would try to draw.

"Jay Lockaby!" Sartain breathed. "What do you want?"

Jay managed to keep his voice flat. "I came to sign on with you. If I'd known you was trail boss I wouldn't've come. But I'm here, and I need a job."

Sartain moved up closer. Tobacco-stained teeth bit uncertainly at his lips. Then a hard smile broke over his wide mouth. "You looking for a job from me. That's funny. But we got all the help we need."

Claude Nickle stepped up and studied Jay's face a minute. Jay instinctively liked the man. Green as a mesquite limb, maybe, but he had an earnest look.

"Now, Sartain," Nickle said, "we should be able to use one more. He looks competent."

Sartain spoke up quickly. "You had to watch your expenses when you was engineering, Mister Nickle. It's the same way with cattle. If we go to hiring every run-down cowhand who comes up, you're liable to lose your margin."

Nickle studiously rubbed his chin. "I suppose you're right. But somehow he looks better than the men you've hired for me."

Jay fought down the disappointment. He took off his hat and addressed Nickle directly.

"Thanks anyway. It's kind of late. Would it be all right with you—and the lady—if I stayed here tonight, at the wagon?"

Behind Nickle's back the red-haired cowboy was still pestering the girl. Jay saw her angrily pull away and step up beside her father. Jay wanted to haul off and wallop the cowboy, but he kept still.

"Be glad to have you with us, sir," Nickle said. "With the drive starting in the morning, Wylie Babb is riding out tonight to help the crew celebrate."

Jay caught the silent anger that shone from Sartain's eyes and felt a grim satisfaction.

In the next couple of hours Jay saw every rider who had been hired. Most of them were kids like those he had seen. There were only three grown men! Two looked like harmless rummies. The third was the redhaired one.

Wylie Babb finally came out in his buckboard, with half a case of whiskey to start the hands off on. Jay frowned. If it had been Babb's own herd, Jay knew the ranchman would not have allowed a bottle of whiskey within ten miles of it. In no time at all the two rummies had seen the bottom end of their bottle and were at peace with the world.

Jay took one good look at Babb and decided he didn't like him. The stout ranchman stood there bold as a banty rooster, with his pant legs shoved into shiny black boot-tops and a cigar clamped jauntily between his teeth. He talked easily and laughed aloud. Jay got the idea Babb was the kind who could sell a wagonload of sheep shears to a cow outfit.

Claude Nickle was as excited about the trip as any one of his kid cowboys.

For what Jay suspected was the twentieth time, Nickle went over everything with Babb that might conceivably come up on the trail.

Jay felt his uneasiness increase when he found that Sartain was actually working for Babb. The ranchman had merely lent him to Nickle for the trip. And the woman-chasing puncher, probably the only real cowboy in the crew, was also a Babb man.

The cook took a fiddle out of his chuckbox and struck up a tune. A youngster pulled a battered harmonica from his pocket, slapped it across his knee, and pitched in.

In a little while Audrey Nickle quietly got up and walked out beyond the hoodlum wagon, where a couple of youngsters had put up a small pyramid tent for her. In a minute the red-haired cowboy stood up and walked out away from the wagon in another direction. But Jay knew where he was going.

Slowly Jay stood up and walked out after the cowboy. Once beyond the range of the flickering campfire, he turned back toward the girl's tent. He heard her angry voice above the sound of the music.

"If you don't keep away from me I'll have you horsewhipped!"

The puncher stood facing her, grinning. "Now, little 'un, most girls take it as a compliment when Red Finley starts paying them attention. Most girls don't mind it at all when I . . ."— He grabbed her—" . . . kiss 'em." Finley held her tight and forced his lips against hers while she beat futilely at his arms with her small fists and tried to stomp his toes with her boot heels.

Fire fanned up in Jay as he stepped behind the cowboy. He grabbed the puncher's chin and jerked back. Gasping for breath, Finley turned loose of the girl and lost his balance. Jay stepped in front of the cowboy and drove a hard fist into the man's jaw.

Finley sat down hard and shook his head. He growled angrily and sprang up again, fists swinging. Jay stepped in close and drove a left, then a right, into Finley's stomach. Finley grunted as part of the breath went out of him. He kept swinging, but not so hard now.

Jay tied into him, his fists slashing, pounding into the redhead's face, ribs, and belly. When Finley went down, Jay caught him by the collar and jerked him up again. At last the puncher sagged to the ground, beaten. Jay stood over him, big fists doubled, and fought hard for breath.

The fiddling went on by the campfire. No one had heard the fight. Jay wiped the sweat from his face, picked up his hat, and licked dry lips.

"All right, Finley," he gritted. "Come on over to the wagon and wash your face. You're quitting."

The girl wasn't nearly so nervous as Jay thought she had a right to be. "If I could have gotten my hands on a mesquite club . . ." she said. "I want to thank you, Mister Lockaby. I wish there was some way . . ."

"I'll have all the thanks I need if I can get Finley's job," Jay said flatly. He helped the weakened Finley to his feet. He took out a washbasin and dipped water into it. He made Finley wash the dirt and blood from his face.

"Now you go over there and tell Sartain you're quitting. Don't give him any reasons. Just quit and get out."

Sartain roared angrily at Finley. But the redhead silently pitched his bedroll and saddle into Babb's buckboard and sat down in the darkness to wait for the ranchman to get ready to leave camp.

Jay got a deep satisfaction from the helpless anger in Sartain's face. He walked by Sartain and spoke to Nickle.

"Since you've lost a man, there ought to be room for me, don't you reckon?"

Nickle nodded. "Of course, of course. I see no reason why we shouldn't take him on, do you, Sartain?"

Raw hatred looked out of Sartain's eyes. He hesitated, glaring at Jay. "No, I reckon not." He turned on his heel and tromped off into the darkness.

Chapter Two

The Cook yelled for breakfast long before daylight next morning. Jay threw back his blanket and rubbed his eyes. Sartain had made him stand a double guard during the night to make up for one of the sleeping rummies.

Boyish excitement ran through the young punchers as they wolfed down their breakfast. Claude Nickle's hands trembled, and Jay knew the little man was as excited as his boys. Audrey Nickle seemed the calmest of the lot, except for Sartain and the sour old cook. Jay wondered idly if perhaps she wouldn't prove to be the top hand of the trip.

"I'm a good point man, Sartain," Jay offered as the crew saddled up. "You know I took some of my own herds up north before . . ."

Sartain glared. "Before what?"

Jay eyed him coldly. "You know what, better than I do. You putting me on the point, like you was going to do with Finley?"

Sartain's eyes glowed with triumph, and a hard grin broke on his wide mouth. "You're going to ride drag, Lockaby. You're going to stay back there and tail up the weak ones. You'll chew dust till you'll wish you'd really killed me, that day in Kansas."

Jay clenched his teeth and felt the veins on his temples strain from anger. "I already wish I'd killed you, Sartain. I've wished it a hundred times."

He swung quietly into the saddle and spurred to the far end of the herd.

With a group of inexperienced riders, it took quite a while to get the herd strung out on the trail. But finally the steers were on their way. Far ahead Sartain put a couple of raw kids on the point. One was on each side of the herd, near the lead. If the cattle were to be turned a little to the left, the rider on the left would pull back and give plenty of room, while the rider on the right pulled in close to the steers and shoved them over. The way the young punchers worked it, the trail looked something like the winding track of a rattlesnake.

Most outfits with which Jay had ridden pushed their cattle hard the first few days to get them off their home range and get them trail-broken. Sartain wasn't pushing at all. Jay wondered, and he didn't like it.

It didn't take long for the dust to start choking. Stirred up by the hooves of the steers in the lead, the dust stayed aloft and steadily grew thicker as more and more cattle walked through it. The rummy supposed to help with the drags soon pulled away from the dust, leaving Jay to handle the end of the herd alone.

Audrey Nickle dropped back to the drags and pulled her horse in beside Jay. The sight of her stirred him. He noticed the stock of a carbine in the scabbard which hung beneath her sidesaddle. She choked in the dust, but she didn't try to get out of it.

"There's something wrong between you and Sartain," she said bluntly. "Anybody can tell you're a real cowman. You belong on the point instead of back here. Now, what's the trouble?"

Jay looked straight ahead. "It's something personal. I'd just as soon we didn't talk about it."

She rode along beside him a good ten minutes before she spoke up again. "Do you know any reason why this herd shouldn't be trail branded?"

Jay shook his head. "Every trail herd I ever saw was."

She looked at him worriedly. "That's what I thought. But Babb talked Dad out of it. Said brands at this time of the year might get wormy, and he said extra brands ruined part of the hide and kept the steers from being worth much."

The uneasiness he had felt began working through him again.

"Babb said that? But he even brands his own range cattle at this time of year."

A look of deep concern settled on the girl's face. Jay wondered if she was thinking the same things that flashed through his mind—a worthless crew, a dishonest trail boss, and steers that didn't bear their new owner's brand. Something was in the wind, and Jay didn't like the smell of it.

"Dad's put everything we own into this herd," Audrey said. "We can't let anything happen to it."

About midafternoon Sartain rode back to the drags. "Lockaby," he said angrily, "I think we're short some steers. You've fooled around and let some drop out."

Jay's temper flared. "I haven't lost a head, and you know it."

Audrey Nickle had stayed close to the drags all day. Now she pulled in and started arguing. "I've been back here almost the whole way, Sartain, and no steers have gotten out."

Sartain flashed her an annoyed look. "Then they were left at the bed grounds. Lockaby, you go back and get them."

Jay glared at Sartain through a red haze and fought down a desire to knock him out of the saddle. He knew the trail boss just wanted to get him away from the herd. He wheeled his horse around and struck out over the back trail. As he rode off he heard Sartain suggest that Audrey go up to where her father rode, near the lead.

Jay spurred the lazy horse into a brisk trot. He cursed Sartain for giving him the sorriest mount in the remuda and for sending him off on a fool's errand. He cursed himself for getting tied up with Sartain again.

Half an hour later he heard horse's hooves behind him and reined up. Caution sent his hand quickly to his gun belt as he wheeled around. He felt relieved when he recognized Audrey Nickle loping to catch up.

"You ought not to've come after me," he scolded. "It's bad enough for a girl to be with a trail herd in the first place. And when she starts riding off with a cowboy, people are going to talk."

"I didn't like the way Sartain sent you off," she answered quickly. "He's up to something, and I want to find out what it is."

Jay wanted to grin. Nothing dumb about this girl. "Have you told your dad what you think?"

"I've tried to, but he laughs at me. He's so excited about this trip that he's like a little boy."

Jay liked the earnest look in the girl's blue eyes. "Whatever Sartain's up to, you'll be better off staying close to your dad," he told her flatly. "Now you hightail it back to the herd."

"This herd belongs to my dad, not you," she spoke quickly. "I want to see that it gets to Kansas."

He looked at her and grinned. "You're a regular little fire-eater. But if you get in Sartain's way, he's liable to hurt you."

"Do you think he would hurt a woman?"

Jay wasn't grinning now. "You're not his kind of a woman. He wouldn't mind hurting you, if he thought it was necessary."

She stared at him. "What kind of woman am I?"

That one he couldn't answer. He looked into her pretty face, her clear blue eyes, and groped for words. His heartbeat quickened. A strong urge moved within him. He reached out, gathered her into his arms, and kissed her. She looked surprised, but she didn't resist him.

He turned her loose, his blood warm. She pulled away a little. "You whipped a man for trying that."

Jay looked down at his saddle horn, ashamed. "Yes, and now I feel like whipping myself. You better go back to the herd."

Jay sat there and watched her ride away, a strange tingle spreading through him. He rubbed his rough hands across his mouth and remembered the warmth of her lips. Suddenly he was glad he had joined this outfit. Whatever Sartain was up to, Jay was determined to scotch it.

It was just as he knew it would be. There wasn't a sign of a lost steer anywhere along the back trail. A slow west wind got up as he started making a wide circle of the bed ground. The last place to look would be the thicket where the chuckwagon had stood. Jay rode up to it carelessly, knowing there wouldn't be a steer in it.

A rifle crashed in the thicket, and a bullet zipped past Jay. Panic seized him for an instant as he realized he was caught in the open. He jerked out his six-gun and spurred for the cover of the brush. He snapped off a couple of quick shots in the direction of the rifleman to the east of him. But he knew he couldn't hit anything.

The rifle cracked again. There was a sudden thump, then a groan from Jay's horse as the animal plunged headlong to the ground. Jay desperately kicked his feet out of the stirrups and rolled free. Another bullet searched for him.

Now he was really caught. He was afoot, and it was still thirty yards to the protection of the brush. He bellied down behind the dead horse for cover and wished the ambusher would show himself. But even if he did, Jay knew he was too far away for an accurate shot with the pistol.

The dry grass was like a mat beneath him. It was brittle between his fingers, like tinder.

Tinder. Jay thought a minute, then grinned without humor. The wind was blowing straight from him toward the man with the rifle. If he could start a fire far enough ahead of him to keep himself from being burned . . .

Keeping low, he struck a match on his saddle and pitched it over. The wind snuffed it out before it hit the ground. He tried again, but the same thing happened. This time a bullet creased the cantle of the old saddle. Jay felt in his pockets for a piece of paper and finally found one. He crushed and twisted it into a long wad. He lighted it and let the fire get a good start. Then he rose up a little, hurled the paper forward, and dropped flat. The rifle roared again.

Holding his breath, Jay could hear a faint crackle. Gradually it became louder, and the dry, pungent odor of grass smoke drifted to him. Fanned by the wind, the flames spread out and quickly moved in toward the thicket. Jay eased himself upward and looked over the dead horse's shoulder. Any minute now the fire should flush the ambusher.

Finally he heard a curse and saw a figure jump up and dash for a new place beyond the billowing grey smoke. Jay took advantage of the moment to break for cover of the brush. As he hit the thicket the rifle crashed. But smoke must have been burning the rifleman's eyes.

Jay squatted down under cover a couple of minutes. Then brush rustled as the unknown gunman began to move.

Fire's scorching his hip pockets again, Jay thought. *And this time he doesn't know where I'm at.*

The crackle of flames and the billowing smoke kept moving in. Jay blinked away the sting. The palm of his hand was sticky on the gun.

Suddenly the gunman jumped up with a yelp of pain and plunged forward through the brush. Jay rose up. The ambusher pumped a bullet at him. Jay brought his pistol up and triggered off two quick shots. The man dropped the rifle. He slumped over into the forks of a mesquite, and his hat tumbled from his head.

Jay glimpsed the red hair and knew immediately the identity of the dead man. He knew, too, who had arranged this. Hatred rose in him anew. Then he heard the frightened snorting of a horse. Finley's mount was tied back there in the brush, and the flames were crowding him, Jay knew. He ran back through the thicket to search for the horse. Finding him, he swung into the saddle and skirted out around the flames.

The sun was almost down. Jay knew it wouldn't be long until some of Babb's riders would be out to investigate the fire. Finley's saddle was much better than the old rig he had swapped for, so he didn't go back to get his own.

Darkness caught him before he got back to the herd. Nervousness rubbed him as he rode. But it left him suddenly as he approached the wagon and saw Sartain squatting on his heels beside the flickering campfire, a tin plate of food in his hands. Grim resolve replaced Jay's nervousness. This was the place to settle it—here and now.

He swung quietly out of the saddle and tied Finley's sorrel to a mesquite. Sartain was lifting a steaming cup of coffee to his lips as Jay stepped up into the circle of the firelight. The trail boss's eyes widened. He spilled much of the coffee.

"What's the matter, Sartain? See a ghost?" Jay asked dryly.

Sartain stammered. "Why . . . why, I thought you had quit us."

Jay kicked the plate out of Sartain's hands. "You mean you thought I was dead!" he thundered as the boss jumped to his feet.

Sartain's hand dipped toward his gun, then stopped abruptly as he thought better of it.

"Go ahead, Sartain," Jay taunted. "I passed up the chance once before. Try now and see if I do."

Claude Nickle had excitedly dropped his own plate of food. Now he ventured a step forward, his face a shade lighter than it ought to be. "Now hold on here. What's all the ruckus for?"

Jay answered without taking his eyes off Sartain. "Your trail boss has got some idea for robbing you, Mister Nickle, the same way he once did me. He tried to get me killed today because he knew I was wise to him."

"Don't listen to him," Sartain spoke quickly. "He's covering up. I sent him back today to find some missing steers. He's just now getting back. He's been letting your cattle drop out of the drive so he can steal them."

Rage roared through Jay. He lunged at Sartain and drove a hard right at the stubbly jaw. Sartain turned his head in time for the blow to glance off. Then he jabbed his own left into Jay's ribs. Jay grunted as some of the breath left him. Slowed a minute, he gritted his teeth and closed in with Sartain. They pounded short rabbit punches into each other's stomachs and ribs. Sartain managed to pull back a little and drive a hard fist into Jay's face.

The cowboy went off balance and fell backward. In a second Sartain was on him. The boss grabbed hold of Jay's throat. The cowboy quickly brought up his fists against Sartain's straightened elbows. The boss grunted in pain and turned loose. Jay took advantage of the man's numbness to drive a fist at the side of his face.

Sartain swayed to one side. Jay pushed him over, swung up, and in a second was on top. He started driving his fists into the boss's face.

He stopped numb as he heard a gun click behind him and felt something jab into his back.

"Now hold it right there, cowboy," Claude Nickle's voice said grimly. "You just joined us yesterday, a total stranger. Wiley Babb himself recommended Sartain to me. If you don't let him up I'll blow a hole in you."

Slowly Jay rose to his feet, breathing hard. On the ground Sartain rubbed the back of his hand over his sore lips. He swayed to his feet.

Suddenly the boss's gun was in his hand. The cowboys started ducking for cover. "You've had your last chance, Lockaby," he snarled, shoving the gun forward.

A gun roared, but it wasn't Sartain's. The range boss dropped the pistol. He swayed forward, grabbing at an ugly red streak on his right hand and biting his lower lip painfully with yellow teeth.

"Audrey!" Nickle roared. "Drop that gun!"

She held the smoking carbine steady. "No, Dad. You've got to give Lockaby a chance."

Sartain glared sullenly at her. "Girl, you're going to be sorry you done this."

Jay knew how that sounded to the others; and knew Sartain's meaning was much deeper.

Claude Nickle started moving toward Audrey. "I don't want to have to take that gun away from you, Audrey. Now drop it."

Audrey stood her ground a moment, then started backing up. "Dad, stop it." Then to Jay, "Get out of here, Jay, while you still can."

Jay trotted back into the darkness toward the sorrel horse. As he swung into the saddle he saw Nickle wrest the carbine from Audrey's hands. The man fired quickly and wildly in Jay's direction. A couple of excited kids joined him. Jay leaned low over the horn and spurred out into the darkness.

The sudden movement of hooves to his right told him the shots had frightened the herd. The cattle hadn't stampeded, but they were ready to.

The men at the campfire knew it, too. The firing suddenly stopped. Moments later Jay was out of sight of the campfire. He reined up and listened. There was no pursuit. Apparently the cowboys had lost interest in him and gone to quiet the cattle.

Jay swung down to rest awhile. Hunger stirred within him. With it came helpless anger, and a renewed hatred of Sartain.

"Might as well stake you right here, Sorrel," he said to Finley's horse. "This is as far away as I'm getting till I square up with Sartain."

All the next morning Jay kept far to the left of the herd. By noon his belt was buckled as tight as it would go, and he was weak from hunger. He knew he would have to take a chance and visit the chuckwagon.

After noon he pulled in closer. Luckily the wagon was well out to one side. He waited until a rise hid the herd, then loped in. He kept his hand on his gun as he reined up.

"Don't you go clawing for a gun," he told the grumpy-looking cook. "All I want is a little chuck."

The cook grunted. "Matter of fact, I been looking for you. Knew you couldn't get nothing to eat off out yonder, and you sure wouldn't leave till you got even with Sartain. I figured you'd be back, and I'm glad you are."

Jay looked at him quizzically.

"That girl told me what she's been thinking," the cook went on. "And I think she's right. I been around lots of cow outfits, and I know this one ain't on the up-and-up. What's more, I got a hunch Sartain's about to spring whatever he's got hatching."

"Keep talking."

"He's getting rid of the riders, for one thing. He sent three of the kids out over the back trail on an errand any halfwit would know was a put-up job. And now them two rummies have got drunk and are plumb out of commission.

"Sartain must have given it to them. They didn't have any. Yesterday I searched through their stuff and emptied all their liquor. Fixed it so it would leak out in their bedroll and look like an accident."

Jay grinned. Sartain had hired one good man, whether he had intended to or not.

The cook spat tobacco juice out over the wagon wheel, wiped his moustache, and rubbed his hand on his pant leg. "Sartain don't aim to be out long, either. I went through his stuff this morning. He ain't got enough tobacco to last him a week. And he smokes all the time."

Jay ate a quick, cold meal and loaded his saddlebags with whatever he could find for later on. Then he pulled out again. But he didn't get far from the herd this time.

Chapter Three

The raid came at sundown, quickly and without any warning. It happened just as the cattle were bunched to be bedded down for the night. Watching from a distance, Jay had noticed that the outfit was still short five hands.

Suddenly shots began rattling on the far side of the herd. Even from the distance, Jay heard Sartain's voice bawl "A raid, boys! Run for your lives!"

Twenty riders swept down on the herd from the far side, fir-

ing as they rode. Trail weariness was gone from the cattle in a
second. Panic rippled through the herd like flood water. Then
they were on the run, coming at Jay.

He pulled his horse around and spurred to get out of the way.
Through the dust he saw Sartain fire a couple of careless shots
at the oncoming riders, then topple from his saddle as if hit.

Three frightened kid cowboys were fleeing over the back
trail, spurring hard. A couple of the braver youngsters were still
shooting at the raiders but were too busy trying to keep up with
the herd to do much good.

It was a picture Jay had seen before—dust boiling up to the
frenzied thunder of thousands of pounding hooves—the clatter of horns, excited shouts, and the rattle of gunfire.

Jay managed to pull out of the path of the stampede just as
the first wild-eyed steers went past him. There wasn't any heading them now, he knew, not till they had run down a little.
Anger swept through him, roaring anger that made him grip
his gun with all the strength in his big hand. He could see the
whole scheme now.

Sartain had hand-picked a crew that would give him the least
trouble when Babb's riders came to stampede the herd. Nor had
Sartain died before the guns of the renegades. Jay knew his supposed death had been meant to take the heart out of any of the
crew that might have wanted to fight. Still close to home, these
steers would soon find their way back into their familiar thick-
ets on Babb range. There would be no trail brands to prove they
had ever left, or that Nickle's herd had not been driven out of
the country by outlaws.

A couple of the raiders were loping toward Jay now, firing
their guns and yelling at the steers to keep the big run going.
Jay held his boogered sorrel as still as he could. When the first
rider neared him, Jay brought up his gun and fired. The outlaw
snapped a quick shot at Jay but missed. Jay triggered another
that spilled the man from the saddle.

From the corner of his eye Jay saw the rider get up and

hobble off out of the steers' way, holding a wounded shoulder. Jay went after the next rider now. But the cowboy had seen his intention. He began firing first. Jay ducked low and snapped off a couple of quick shots. The outlaw's horse plunged to the ground. The man rolled into the path of the stampeding steers. He jumped up terrified and started running for safety. A steer brushed him and rolled him over. When he got to his knees another steer hit him.

As Jay turned his back on the cowboy he saw him scramble to safety, half on his hands and knees.

Minutes later the panicked herd had passed. Jay hauled up on his reins and searched through the choking dust for sign of some of the Nickle cowboys. He could still hear sporadic shots. Fear tugged at him. Maybe some of those kids were still trying to shoot it out with the rustlers. But Nickle's force was already cut half in two. It wouldn't stand a chance now.

Where was Audrey? Fear squeezed him tighter as he pushed on through the dust. She must have been with the herd when the raiders struck.

Suddenly Jay got the answer to one of his questions. Claude Nickle and two young punchers materialized from out of the dust. Seeing Jay, they drew their guns and trained them on him. Claude Nickle pushed out a little in the lead. Black hatred showed in his eyes. Sweat rolled down and left tiny lines in the dust that lay thick on his face.

"Jay Lockaby! I knew it was you the minute the raiders came down on us. What have you done with Audrey? Tell me or I'll blast you to kingdom come!"

Audrey missing! Jay's breath came short, and his heartbeat picked up. He tried to explain, but he made no headway. One of the young cowboys said:

"You pull back out of the way, Mister Nickle. Jeff and I'll give him what's coming."

Nickle's voice almost broke. "First I've got to know where he's got Audrey."

He thrust the gun forward and said wildly: "Tell me. Tell me or I'll kill you right where you sit!"

Beads of sweat popped out on Jay's forehead, and his tense hand gripped the bridle reins. Far away he could hear the herd still running. He could hear Nickle's anguished breathing and almost thought he could hear his own heart beating. Then a new sound broke in, the clatter of the chuckwagon. The cook's voice was calling out:

"Nickle! Nickle! Where are you?"

One of the cowboys answered. Moments later the wagon hauled up. The cook sawed on the lines to stop the frightened team. Fear looked out of his own eyes as he pulled up beside the men.

"Miss Audrey's went after Sartain!" he declared, breathing rapidly.

Nickle's mouth dropped open. "You're crazy. Sartain's dead."

"No he ain't. He acted like it to scare your cowboys. I came along with the wagon just in time to see one of the raiders bring him a horse. Miss Audrey seen them, too. She went spurring off after Sartain. I yelled at her to come back, but I couldn't catch her in this kindling heap."

Jay felt the color drain out of his face. "Sartain'll kill her if she crowds him!"

Nickle lowered his gun. His hands were shaking. "You don't know how close I came to killing you, Lockaby."

"We haven't got time to worry about that. Come on!"

Their horses were tired, but the four men's spurs kept the animals going in a long lope after the herd. They spread out so they would miss nothing in the gathering darkness.

Dust still hung thick in the air and choked Jay as he galloped along. He blinked to relieve the stinging of his eyes. Audrey's face kept coming to him, and he remembered her lips. If Sartain did anything to her . . .

A cowboy's shout pulled him quickly to the right. Through

the dust he could see the youngster grab the reins of a loose horse.

"Mister Nickle! Mister Lockaby! Here's her horse!"

Panic grabbed hold of Jay. He slid his sorrel to a stop and looked anxiously at the riderless horse. As the other two riders pulled in, Jay saw the spot on the sidesaddle. He touched it. It was red and sticky.

"Blood! He's shot her!"

They started an even more desperate search then, pushing on through the gloom, scanning the ground ahead of them, afraid of what they would find. It was Jay who found her, or perhaps she found him. He heard her voice calling him weakly. Then he saw her on the ground just ahead of him, trying to push herself up on one elbow.

He tried to call the others, but fear clamped his throat tight. He pulled out his gun and fired three times into the air. Then he swung to the ground and ran to her.

The breath went out of him as he saw the splotch of blood low on her left shoulder. The bullet had gone close to her heart, he realized instantly. Dangerously close.

He gripped her hand tightly, fighting back the dread that rose like a flood within him.

"Dad," she murmured. "Where's Dad?"

"He's all right," Jay answered softly. "He'll be along in a minute."

The three others came riding in from all directions. Claude Nickle jumped out of the saddle and almost fell. His voice broke as he called his daughter's name. Jay yelled at one of the boys.

"Go find that chuckwagon and get it here quick."

The boy hesitated. "What about the herd?"

Jay's lips were tight. "We'll have to let the cattle go. We've got to get her back to town, to a doctor."

The cook dumped his supplies and spread out four cowboys' bedrolls in the wagon to make a soft bed for Audrey. Then they started a weary but anxious all-night ride to town.

On the way Jay told his own story. He told Nickle how he had once driven his own herds to Kansas railroad markets. One day a Kansas businessman offered to lend him the extra money he would need to bring an even larger herd than he had ever brought before. Buying Texas cattle with his own money and money he had borrowed, he got together a big herd and trailed it to Kansas.

Sartain had been one of the cowboys on that drive. He had been a troublemaker all the way up the trail. But he had been a good cowhand, and Jay, shorthanded, had kept him on.

The herd sold all right. Jay banked his own money but withdrew enough to repay his backer and give him a good profit to boot. On his way he was held up and robbed by two masked men. He was positive one was Sartain.

He trailed Sartain all over Kansas, from one saloon and dance hall to another. Finally he had found him in the room of a dance hall girl. The money had all been spent. There was no proof that Sartain had taken it. Still, Jay had known. He had drawn his gun to shoot the outlaw. But somehow he had never been able to pull the trigger.

Paying his debts cost him practically everything he had left, and Jay came back to Texas broke. Since then he had worked for cowboy wages, when he could find work.

Looking at Audrey's ash-grey face in the wagon bed in the light of dawn, Jay wished again that he had killed Sartain that day long ago. He knew that now, no matter what happened, he had that one job to do.

In the front room of the doctor's office, Jay nervously paced the floor. He glanced at the big clock in the corner. Half past two. More than an hour since the doctor had taken the unconscious Audrey into the back room, with Claude Nickle close behind.

A clatter of horses' hooves on the street outside brought Jay's gaze to the window. His breath came short as he recognized the riders. In the lead was stout Wiley Babb, with a cigar clamped between his teeth and looking like he was about to foreclose the mortgage on the state of Texas.

Jay unconsciously dropped his hand to his gun butt as he spotted the man riding close behind Babb. Sartain! Jay clenched his teeth and fought down the impulse to shoot Sartain right then, through the window.

A little way down the street Babb dropped out. He tied his horse in front of the bank and went in. Jay watched Sartain and a couple of other riders go on down to a saloon.

One of the youngsters had stepped behind Jay. "Babb's got him an office in the bank. He's a big shot there. Probably gone to count the money he's swindled Mister Nickle out of."

Jay walked to the door and paused, his hand on the ornate doorknob. "Stay here in case Nickle needs you," he said. "I'm going to help Babb count that money."

He quickly stepped down onto the plank sidewalk and angled across the dirt street. He stopped a moment in front of the bank, wiped his sweaty palms on his pant legs, and pushed through the bank door. He looked around for Babb but didn't see him. He walked up to a slender teller.

"Where's Babb?"

The teller pointed his chin at a closed door. "In his office, but he can't be disturbed now. Say there, I said he can't be disturbed!"

Jay shoved the door open and quickly stepped through. Babb, seated at a desk, almost let the cigar drop out of his mouth.

Jay shoved the door shut.

"What do you want?" Babb asked, plainly a little shaken.

Jay purposely dropped his hand to his gun. "I want the money Nickle paid you for the steers your men ran off last night."

Babb stood up quickly, his face red as a ripe apple. "Now you look here . . ."

Jay pulled out the six-gun and leveled it at Babb's belly. "Your man Sartain shot Audrey Nickle. She may not live. Maybe you'd like to hang for getting her shot."

Some of the color drained from Babb's face. He took the cigar from his mouth and put it in a tray on the desk, his hand shaking. "He told me there wouldn't be any killing," he said weakly.

Jay eyed him levelly, hating the man. "Nickle paid you twenty dollars a head for twelve hundred cattle. That's $24,000. I want it now, to take to Nickle. Add another thousand to help pay for his trouble. That'll make it twenty-five."

Babb stared at him unbelievingly. "Why, you . . . that's robbery!"

Jay slipped his gun back into its holster. "I'm not holding a gun on you. Maybe you'd rather hang."

Babb seemed to wilt. Jay kept talking.

"You were bound to've promised Sartain a good cut out of this deal. I'll just take that myself, to pay back a little of what he stole from me one time in Kansas. Say $5,000."

Babb sat down weakly in his chair, near collapse. He called for someone in the bank. A moment later the slender teller came in.

"Get me $30,000 in cash, Roger." The teller's eyes widened in unbelief.

"Go on and get it," Babb said sharply.

A few minutes later Babb was counting out the money for Jay. Satisfied, Jay shoved it down in his pocket. Then he leaned threateningly toward Babb.

"If you're thinking about trying to get this money back, just remember what I said about that hanging.

"Now then, I saw Sartain go to the saloon a while ago. How long does he usually stay there?"

Babb answered weakly: "All afternoon. He'll stay downstairs and drink a little while. He's got a dance-hall girl upstairs. They call her Prairie Lou. He'll be going up to see her directly."

Jay pulled out his gun again and checked it. "You stay right here, Babb. Move a finger to warn Sartain, and I'll be coming back."

He shoved the gun into the holster, backed out, and closed the door. A moment later he was on the plank sidewalk again. Reaching the saloon, he stopped and looked at the outside stairs which led up to the second floor. He hesitated a moment, then started up. Cautiously he pushed open the door and stepped inside the upstairs hall.

A door opened and a girl stepped out of a room. She stopped and looked at Jay. The smell of her perfume repulsed him. There was too much rouge on her cheeks, and her dance-hall dress was too low in front.

"Where's Prairie Lou's room?" he asked her.

She pointed to a door on down the hall. "That's it, but you better keep away from Lou today. Sartain's in town. He beat one man to a bloody pulp on account of her last week. He said he'd kill the next man he caught with her."

A grin broke on Jay's lips, but there was no humor in it. "He did? Well, Sartain's downstairs. You go down and tell him there's somebody with his girl right now."

Her painted mouth dropped open. "You must be crazy!"

"Never mind. Just go on down and tell him."

He watched the girl walk rapidly down the hall and start down the stairs. He moved quickly to Prairie Lou's door, pushed it open, and stepped into the room.

The heavy odor of cheap perfume was thick enough to cut with a knife. A girl sat at a bureau, brushing her hair as she watched herself in an oval mirror. She put down the brush and stared at Jay.

"I don't know who you are, but if you're smart you'll get out. There's a man downstairs who'll be trying for your ears."

Jay grinned. "I know. I've already sent him word."

He backed away from the door and turned to face it, never letting the girl out of his sight. She watched with eyes opened wide.

"Say here, what are you up to? What do you think you're doing?"

"Just sit down and be quiet," he told her sharply.

Outside heavy boots came clumping down the hall. Jay's heartbeat quickened. Sweat popped out on his forehead and the palms of his hands. He gripped the gun butt tightly. He held his breath as he saw the doorknob turn.

The door pushed open and Sartain stood there. There was a scowl on his ugly face as he grunted, "What the . . ."

Then the scowl turned suddenly to a look of amazement as he recognized Jay across the room. For a moment he stood there staring, his wide mouth open. Then his hand dipped toward his gun.

But even as Sartain's gun cleared leather, Jay was squeezing the trigger.

He knew with grim satisfaction that he had won—that he had finished his job.

The two young cowboys met him almost at the saloon door. Claude Nickle and the cook were standing at the door of the doctor's office, waiting for him.

"That shooting," Nickle said. "We were afraid it was you."

"It was." Jay told the group briefly that Sartain was dead. He reached deep down in his pocket and took out the money Babb had given him. He counted off $5,000 and handed the rest to Nickle.

"There's your herd, all twelve hundred head, plus a few extra to boot."

A broad smile broke out on Nickle's face as he took the money. He blinked quickly and stammered.

"It . . . it looks like my luck's come back to me. Just a little bit ago Audrey came to. The doctor says she's going to be all right."

He paused. "She wants to see you, Jay."

Joy flooded through Jay Lockaby as he stood there. Dumbly he wadded the greenbacks in his hand and thrust them deep into his pocket. He started unsteadily for the door to the backroom. He stopped as he felt Claude Nickle's hand on his shoulder.

"Jay, I'm going to get to Kansas yet. I'll buy more cattle and start again. I'll need you. So will Audrey."

Jay smiled. "I'll stay with you as long as you need me."

His steps stronger now, Jay went on through the door, into the room where Audrey was waiting for him . . .

Kelly Shanklin was a rodeo clown. To the crowds who watched him out in the arena, in his big, baggy jeans, his red-painted face, his ridiculous yellow mop wig, it didn't matter if he wasn't the best clown in the business. He was good enough, and he had plenty of time. He had his mind set that some day he'd be the best, if he didn't slip and let a bull get him.

It was during a rodeo in the West Texas town of Twin Wells that he let a bloody-eyed Brahma get so close to him that the bull's thick black horn caught in the suspenders of Kelly's oversized jeans and almost tore the pants off him. The crowd loved it.

But when the last bull had been ridden and the cowboys were clearing out of the dusty arena, Kelly could see the heavy-built rodeo producer, Charlie Dixon waiting for him at the gate. Charlie was chewing hard on his cigar, the heavy corners of his mouth slanted downward.

Kelly grinned. He knew what Charlie was fixing to say. But before he got to the gate a young cowpuncher grabbed Kelly by the arm and slapped him on the shoulder.

"Sure thank you for drawing that bull off of me the way you did after I got spilled, Kelly. He'd have put a horn in me for certain."

Another puncher scowled at the young cowhand. "You don't have to thank him, Chuck. That's what they got him hired for."

A quick stiffening of Kelly's fingers was the only sign the clown gave of anger. A man got used to taking jealous digs from the likes of Ralph Padgett. But Kelly was warmly pleased by the sudden flush of anger in the young cowhand's face. It was a good thing to have friends.

Charlie Dixon caught up with Kelly as the clown shambled out of the arena. "You like to've overdone it that time, Kelly," he said with thorns in his voice. "I had to grab for my heart pills. What's got the matter with you this year, anyhow? You act like you don't care if you get killed."

Kelly took off his little comic black hat and reamed the sweat from inside the band with the elbow of his red and green polka-dot shirt. "It was a little closer than I figured, Charlie," he admitted. His broad mouth broke into a grin. " But it gave the folks a show. Be some of them back tomorrow, just on account of it."

Dixon grunted. He leaned against a plank fence, watching the crowd file noisily down out of the grandstands and move out toward the parking areas. He chewed on the cigar.

"It's got so you don't think about anything but giving the crowd a good show, Kelly. But by George you don't have to bust up doing it. If you just had somebody to worry about— I sure wish sometimes that you'd married Cindy Baker."

Kelly's grin left him, and his hard gaze drifted down toward the concession stand. Ralph Padgett stood there, his red-striped shirt the brightest thing in the crowd. "You know what happened, Charlie."

Dixon grunted. "But you could've had her back, Kelly. She wanted you."

Kelly's lips tightened. "After Ralph Padgett was tired of her?"

His eyes went again to Padgett, who had one hand around

a bottle of beer and the other around the slim waist of a hard-eyed, softly shaped blonde. Seemed like Ralph's handsome face and smooth talk kept him from having to be by himself.

Probably telling her he was high-point man so far in the saddle bronc contest. Would have been ahead in bull-riding too, if the bull hadn't made an unexpected lunge at the damn clown and dumped Ralph.

Charlie saw what Kelly was looking at. "Still needling you, ain't he? Always got a woman or two around him, generally the fast kind. If they ain't that way to start with, they get that way."

Dixon saw that he had hit a sour note. Kelly was remembering Cindy Baker. "Give me the word, Kelly, and I'll get him run off for good."

Strange, the jealousy a man runs into when he's among the best in his business. Kelly had started his rodeo career as a rider. He never had done anything that he knew of to start Ralph Padgett to hating him. But it had been almost more than Padgett could stand, always being beaten out of top money by Kelly's skill. Then when Kelly had made his start as a clown, Padgett had had to try clowning too. He had flopped on his face.

"No," Kelly said, "don't run him off. He'll dig his own pit some day, and fall into it."

A freckled-faced boy came running up to the arena gate. "Hey, Kelly," he hollered. "You better go see about your mule. Some kids have been trying to ride her, and they've got her tearing things up."

Kelly pelted off through the straggling crowd, his baggy pants billowing out like a ship's sail. Heelfly was a good trick mule, but the little jenny was mean around strangers. Likely as not she'd cave some foolish button's ribs in with her hind foot.

The boys saw him coming. They turned the little gray jenny loose and scattered like a covey of quail. Kelly called to Heelfly, but she had her dander up. She kicked high into the air, then wheeled and took out in a lope down the bull-net fence. She darted under the neck of a startled sorrel horse which was tied to a post. The sorrel snorted and jerked back, snapping the bridle reins. Then it, too, lit out down the long fence.

Kelly heard a girl shout and saw her run after the horse, waving her hands. The little jenny stopped and looked disdainfully after the sorrel, the way a mule does, as if she thought the horse was the craziest animal on earth.

Kelly caught the jenny and gently scolded her. He glanced around at the girl. Before she started shouting at him, he had just a second to note that she was trimly built, fitted snugly into a pair of jeans, and that her hair was brown and done up neatly behind her neck under the broad brim of a gray hat. He noted the welling anger in her blue eyes.

"You'd better do your clowning in the arena from now on," she exploded. "Now you go bring my horse back before I haul off an kick you right in the seat of those big pants." Face burning, Kelly hopped onto the mule's bare back and set her into a high lope with the heals of his oversized shoes. The girl's anger put a feeling of guilt in him, although he knew there wasn't anything for him to feel guilty about. He felt a little foolish, too. He knew how silly he must look, chasing after the sorrel horse on the short-legged little jenny. But he caught the horse in a fence corner and led him back.

He slipped off onto the ground and tipped his comic hat to the girl. "The reins are busted, ma'am. But I got a new pair over here in the trailer. I'll put them on for you."

When he finished tying the reins on with a leather string, he looked up to see an amused smile break across her face. It was as warm as June sunshine, even if she was laughing at him. He could feel color rising again under the greasepaint.

"Sorry to've put you out, miss," he managed. "It was just the kids. Seems like it's natural for kids to want to bedevil a mule."

She nodded. "I shouldn't have flown off the handle at you that way. I guess it wasn't your fault. I couldn't help losing my mad anyway, watching you chase after Streak on that little mule. It was the funniest sign I've seen in I don't know when."

Kelly flushed, then forced a grin like a man caught in a joke. The girl turned away. Suddenly Kelly didn't want her to go, not just yet.

"Say," he called, "I didn't even get to ask you what your name is."

But she didn't hear him. Kelly watched her ride away and wished he could have talked to her longer. His heartbeat had quickened.

He heard footsteps behind him and a contemptuous drawl. "Good looking filly you were talking to, Kelly. Who is she?"

A flinty anger snapped in him as he turned to face Ralph Padgett. He wondered where Ralph's blonde had gone.

"Why don't you stay with your own kind, Ralph?"

Padgett struck a match against the side of Kelly's horse trailer and lighted his cigarette. "Maybe she is. Won't know till I try." He laughed and flipped the match away. "All right, you don't have to tell me who she is. I'll find out for myself, soon enough."

Kelly didn't expect to run into the girl again. He washed off the dust and greasepaint and changed into plain cowboy clothes. Then he went down to the rodeo office, and there she was behind a typewriter, fixing up a list of cowboys and broncs for the next show. She barely glanced at him as he moved in through the door, suddenly awkward.

Big Charlie Dixon caught him by the arm, a huge grin on his broad face. "Say there Kelly, I want you to meet our new office helper, Kathy Lasater. She's Ike Lasater's daughter. You know old Ike, the steer-roper?"

Not taking his eyes off the pretty oval face a second, Kelly nodded. "We met, Charlie, a little while ago."

Recognition brought a quick smile to her soft lips. "The man with the mule!" she laughed.

Kelly swallowed his embarrassment. "If you're a secretary,"

he grinned, "what're you doing with a horse? Have you taught him to type?"

She shook her head. He liked the way the knot of brown hair bounced on her slender neck. "I'm going to use him in the barrel races. I wanted to make the rodeo circuit with Dad this summer, and he said I had to earn my own way."

Kelly kept turning his hat over and over in his nervous hands, trying to think of something else to say. Charlie stepped out of the office a minute. Quickly Kelly said, "Look, Miss Lasater, I don't always look as silly as I do now. I could prove it if you'd let me take you to the rodeo dance tonight."

On guard but laughing, she shook her head.

"You'll be there, though, won't you?" he asked. She finally shrugged. "Maybe, if I finish my work."

Kelly unpacked his best blue suit that night, for the first time in weeks. He hoped the suitcase wrinkles would shake out of it . . .

Charlie Dixon hailed him almost as soon as he stepped through the dance hall door. Kelly shied like a nervous horse, but he knew Dixon could see right through him.

"First time I've seen you at a dance all year, Kelly. Who's the girl?"

Kelly grinned sheepishly. "There ain't any. Just thought I'd come over for a little while."

As he spoke, his eyes searched the big room. His heart skipped when he saw her. She had come after all! He watched nervously as she walked his way.

Charlie snorted. "No girl, eh?" He slapped Kelly on the back and walked off, grinning as if he had caught onto a big secret.

There was a smile in Kathy Lasater's blue eyes. "I finished my work a lot sooner than I thought I would."

It had been a year since Kelly had danced. The last time had been with Cindy Baker. He hadn't even wanted to dance since, but now the steps came back to him easily, and he knew contentment.

The shyness drained away from him as the evening wore on. Kathy's eyes didn't drift away from him and follow the crowd like those of some girls. She didn't give him the feeling that she was just staying with him until she saw something better.

Sitting at a table with her, he found himself loosening up and talking to her about things he hadn't discussed with anyone since he didn't know when. Like his plans for a real side-splitting comedy act to work out for next year's shows. Like his hopes of getting to be the best clown in the business. Like the part of his paycheck that always went to the hometown bank, adding up to buy the old homeplace some day when he had had enough of rodeos.

Kelly was a little surprised how quickly she accepted his invitation next day to another dance. As the weeks passed, the rodeo moved on from one town to another. Seemed like almost every town had a special rodeo dance. Kelly and Kathy always went together.

Charlie Dixon was getting in a better humor with him. "You're starting to show some sense again, Kelly," he said. "Been a long time now since I've seen you try to commit suicide. And the crowd likes you as much as it ever did."

One day Kathy's father, steer-roping Ike Lasater, sought Kelly out. He sat down on a bale of green alfalfa hay and had a long talk with him. By the time Ike got up and started saddling his roping horse, he knew just about everything there was to know about Kelly's past, about his boyhood on the ranch, his hitch in the Army during the war, his rodeo experience.

"Kathy's got so she don't talk about much except you," Lasater said, a smile creasing his brown face. "When your daughter gets that way, you naturally want to find out all you can about the man. Don't mind telling you, Kelly, I'm pleased."

He puffed thoughtfully on his pipe and frowned. "It's not like it was when I found out Ralph Padgett was beginning to play up to her."

Lasater saw the sudden surprise in Kelly's face. "Oh, you

didn't know about that. Well, I just told Ralph that if I ever caught him around Kathy again I'd take the double of a rope to him. She's a right sensible girl. But Padgett operates smoothly, and he's apt to turn any girl's head, no matter how smart she is. He won't get the chance, though, long's I'm around."

But Ike didn't get to stay around much longer. One afternoon he spread a big blocker loop over the horns of a Florida steer and started to head his horse around. The mount's feet slipped out from under him as the steer hit the end of the rope. The whole weight of the big bay's body crashed down on Ike's leg.

"A clean break," the doctor said. "I'm afraid, Mr. Lasater, that you'll have to spend two or three months in bed."

There was some debate about whether Kathy should go back to the ranch with her dad. But Charlie Dixon did some fast talking.

"I'll watch after her, Ike, and see that nothing happens to her. I'd sure hate to lose her now, right in the middle of the season. She's learned how to keep rodeo books and help draw out the bronc and bull numbers for the boys. She's getting right good with the stopwatch, too. Pretty soon we can use her as an official timer."

So Ike agreed and Kathy stayed on with the outfit.

Wherever the rodeo was, it was Kelly's habit to take supper with Kathy. But one day the little jenny went lame toward the end of a show, and Kelly took her to a vet. By the time he got back, after dark, he found that Kathy had eaten.

"Ralph Padgett took me downtown," she said smiling. "You know, I think you all are wrong about him. He's got the nicest manners I've seen in a long time."

Kelly tried to keep the anger in him from showing. "You better watch out, Kathy. Those manners are as false as my clown getup."

There was something in her face that disturbed him. "He asked me to have dinner with him tomorrow, before the show," she said. "That all right with you?"

A sudden feeling of helplessness swept over him. He thought of Cindy Baker. Different girl, but the same story.

"You're your own boss," he said flatly, and turned away.

She looked after him as he swung on his heels and strode away.

Kelly peered between the stout one-by-eight planks of the corral at the humped, black-horned bull which shook its yellow head in rage and pawed up the dirt.

"By George, he's a fighter," bragged Charlie Dixon. "Picked him up at a cattle auction today. He broke down two gates before we could get him out of there."

Kelly grunted, his mind wasn't really on the bull. It was on Ralph Padgett and Kathy, execising their horses together out in the vacant arena.

"Yes sir," Charlie went on. "He'll make them bull riders sit up and take notice. Even got a perfect name for him. See that number on his hip?"

The bull still carried the little cardboard tag which had been stuck on him as he went into the auction yards.

"Number Thirteen, we'll call him," Charlie went on excitedly. "Let the word spread about him, and the crowd'll come from far and near."

Kelly couldn't help being practical. "If he doesn't kill somebody and you have to shoot him," he said.

A short, bowlegged cowpoke names Stubby Miller was the first one to draw Thirteen. Kelly predicted that the bull would throw him within three jumps, so he stood close to the chute gates, to lure the bull away the moment the cowboy hit the dirt.

Old Thirteen lunged out with a bellow that seemed to come all the way up from his belly. The rider on him and the bell tied under him infuriated the big yellow bull into a series of high twisting jumps that reminded Kelly of a Panhandle cyclone. Stubby sailed off and hit the ground rolling.

A man never can explain some of the things he does when he's in sudden danger. Everything would have been all right if the rattled Stubby hadn't paused to grab for his fallen hat. The bull whirled and charged him, head down, horns pointed outward. He hit the cowboy and sent him rolling again. Yelling at the top of his lungs, Kelly jumped in and started slapping the bull in the face with his little comic hat.

The bull jerked back to face Kelly. As he lowered his yellow head again, Kelly could see the Brahma meant business. The clown turned and ran for the red, rubber-covered barrel that he had placed in the arena to attract the bull's attention. Keeping the barrel between him and the bull, he let the big animal take out its rage by slamming the barrel around with its huge head and shining black horns. The crowd roared and clapped hands. But Kelly sighed in relief when the arena director and a helper came out on horseback and drove the Brahma away with bull whips.

"You all right, Stubby?" he asked the cowboy when he got back to the chutes.

"They ought to make me go bareheaded for a month," the puncher gritted, holding his hand to his aching side. "But at least he didn't get a horn in me. That bull will get somebody some day. I pity the man."

Ralph Padgett was standing there listening. "I pity him, too," he said, his hard eyes on Kelly. "Especially if Kelly Shanklin's the clown. He'll get there twenty minutes too late. That bull wouldn't ever have hit you Stubby, if Kelly hadn't had his head in the clouds."

Kelly's fists knotted, but the wouldn't let Ralph bait him into a fight there with the whole crowd still watching.

Stubby's voice was sharp. "Knock it off, Ralph. Kelly done all he could." As Padgett walked away, Stubby grunted, "If I was you, Kelly, I'd let a bull get to him."

Kathy was standing behind the arena fence Ralph was walking toward her. Stubby watched them and added, "I'd do it pretty quick, too."

The show over, Kelly gathered up his equipment, fed and

watered the little jenny, and cleaned the greasepaint off his face. Then he walked over to the pens where Kathy was keeping her horse. He found the girl there as he thought he would, pouring out some oats and putting alfalfa hay in the rack.

She smiled at him and said hello. But it seemed to him that something was missing now, a warmth that used to be there but wasn't anymore.

"It's been a long time now since we went to a dance together, Kathy," he said. "There's one here tomorrow night. What do you say we go?"

She looked away from him toward her sorrel horse. "Not tomorrow night, Kelly. I've already promised Ralph. He's taking me to a big dance over in Morsetown."

Kelly felt his hand squeezing hard on the cedar gate post. He toed a circle in the little scattering of spilled oats on the ground. "You're seeing a lot of him lately, aren't you, Kathy?"

A stubborn set worked into her jaw. "He's always been nice to me."

"It's getting about time for him to stop being nice, Kathy. Only it's liable to be too late when you find out. You don't have to listen to me. You can ask anybody else. Ask Charlie Dixon. Ask your own Dad."

A flush climbed into her cheeks, and her blue eyes were beginning to snap. "You're all treating me like a schoolgirl, like I didn't have sense enough to watch out for myself. Ralph's kind, and he's good. I know he is. And from the way he's talking, I think he's going to ask me to marry him." She lowered her voice and look straight at Kelly. "That's something you haven't done."

That hit him. No, he hadn't asked her. He had wanted to, but he never had found the words to say just the way he wanted, until he had waited too long.

He heard the soft thump of boots and the light tinkle of spurs behind him. He looked around quickly. As he had thought, it was Ralph Padgett. Anger roared upward in him like a flame in a gas burner.

"Don't fool yourself, Kathy," he said. "He won't marry you. He'll never marry anybody, unless he's trapped into it." He whirled to face Padgett. "You listen to me, Ralph. You're not going to do this girl the way you did Cindy, or half a dozen others I know of. You're going to keep away from her. You're going to leave her alone."

Padgett stood still and looked Kelly up and down. "Not very funny talk for a clown, Kelly. She's old enough to do as she pleases. If I'm what pleases her, then I don't see where you've got any say coming."

Almost before he realized what he was doing, Kelly brought up his fist. Padgett went reeling backward. Fury pounding in his brain, Kelly stepped forward to jerk Padgett onto his feet and hit him again. But Kathy rushed by him and threw her arms protectively around the cowboy's shoulder.

"You get out of here, Kelly Shanklin." She was half sobbing with anger. "You haven't got one word of say-so with me. I'm old enough to make up my own mind, and I've done it. Now get away from me and don't come back. Ever!"

Kelly went through the next day in a haze. It seemed like none of his stunts come out right. Even the little jenny didn't do her tricks the way she was supposed to. He guessed he got her cues mixed up. He didn't know. He only knew the crowd was cool. The cowboys sensed something, too.

Riding Heelfly out the gate, he heard somebody say, "If I didn't know Kelly better, I'd swear he was drunk."

Words kept humming through his mind, soft words he had heard from Kathy so long ago, and the angry words she had hurled at him yesterday. The sight of her kept running through his mind and getting mixed up with whatever his eyes happened to be looking at.

Finally it came time for the last event, bull riding. Kelly stood ready and tried to force everything else out of his mind. He did fairly well until it came Ralph Padgett's turn to ride. The bitter taste of hatred had seeped into every part of Kelly. Stubby

Miller's words kept leaping at him. "If I was you, I'd let a bull get to him. I'd do it pretty quick."

He tried to shove the thought away. Why if something happened it would be the same as murder.

Padgett rode until the whistle blew, then slid off. Now was the time for Kelly to run out and lure away the bull. But his hatred had hold of him. He couldn't get his feet to move. The bull turned once and snuffed at the cowboy. Then it whirled away and went on pitching across the arena.

Kelly shut his eyes and swallowed. He took a deep breath and felt the guilt settling heavily within him. It had turned out all right, he tried to tell himself. But what if it hadn't?

When it was over, Charlie Dixon hustled him out behind the corrals. "Whatever's got hold of you, Kelly, you got to shake it loose. You'll get yourself killed, or somebody else."

Kelly broke down and told him about Kathy. Charlie clenched his fists and kicked a rock halfway to the bull corral. "And I promised old Ike I'd watch out for his girl," he stormed. "He ought to shoot me right between the eyes. What do you think we better do?"

Dismally Kelly shook his head. "Nothing we can do. Nothing I can do, anyway. She washed her hands of me. Guess we'll just have to let her take care of herself, like she said."

Ralph Padgett stayed at the same tourist court that Kelly did. Kelly watched him drive away in his car to pick up Kathy and take her to the Morsetown dance. Kelly went on to bed, but he couldn't sleep. A thousand old memories, a thousand torturing thoughts kept working through his mind. He kept watching for Padgett's car to come in again. It never did. When Kelly finally go up at dawn the car was still gone. Kelly leaned his head against the doorjamb, fighting against the bitterness, the desperate anger that welled up in him.

He went out to the fairgrounds to feed the jenny. He thought about going back to town for breakfast, but he wasn't hungry. He ambled around the corrals all morning, his eyelids heavy

from lack of sleep, the anger riding him. Noon came, but still
he wasn't hungry. He bought a hamburger at the concession
stand, ate half of it, and threw the rest away.

Stubby Miller walked up to him. "Kathy Lasater's looking
for you. She's been hunting all over."

Kelly's spirit soared a moment, then sank again. It was over
now. Last night had finished it. "I don't want to see her," he
said.

A couple of times he spotted her coming toward him, and
he dodged away, out of her sight. Once the rodeo began, he
managed to stay in the arena, or close to it. A few times he
looked up at the judge's stand and felt her blue eyes upon him.
Quickly he would turn away, the bitterness heavy in him.

The stunts didn't go any better than they had the day before.
Worse, even. The dark thoughts kept pounding at him, hard as
he tried to push them away.

When at last the bull-riding came, he went into his place almost in a trance. He saw the brindle bull charging at him, but
it was almost as if Kelly's mind was separated from his body.
He couldn't make himself jump aside until it was too late. For
a moment, as he lay there in the dust, fighting to get his breath
back, he thought his leg was broken. Cowboys rushed out and
helped him to his feet. The leg wasn't broken, but it was stiff
and throbbed with pain.

"You better get out of there, Kelly," Charlie Dixon warned.
"You can't dodge bulls on a bad leg."

"I hired out to do this job," Kelly shouted back angrily, louder
than he intended. "Just leave me alone and I'll do it."

He caught a glimpse of Kathy's face. It was white.

He did fairly well with the next two bulls. Then came old
Number Thirteen. With a start, Kelly realized that the rider
was to be Ralph Padgett. Kelly felt hatred seeping through him
again. He noticed a little patch above Padgett's eye and wondered what had hit him. Whatever it was, it was a pity it hadn't
killed him, Kelly thought angrily.

Old Thirteen gave out a murderous bellow as the chute gate swung open. The first jump popped Padgett's neck so that the cowboy's hat flew off. Still bellowing, the big bull plunged forward again. Kelly found himself cheering the bull on, swinging his fists like a man watching a prize fight. The bull jumped, whirled, landed jarringly on all four feet at once.

Padgett was about to come loose, and Kelly could see the fear in the cowboy's wide eyes.

Come on, bull, that's the ticket, Kelly was saying to himself. Throw him. Step right in his belly. He's earned it, every bit.

Padgett came down like a sack of oats. For a second he lay there crumpled, gasping for a breath. The bull turned back on him.

It was time for Kelly to step in. Stubby Miller's words shot back at him again, the words about letting a bull get Padgett. Kelly took a long step forward, and the leg gave way under him.

Sprawling in the arena sand, he saw Padgett defensively throw his hand in front of his face, and saw Thirteen slam that big yellow head into the cowboy's side.

Let the bull hit him, a voiced roared in Kelly's head. Lie there. They all saw the leg give way under you. Nobody can ever blame you.

But Kelly forced himself onto his feet again and moved forward. He pulled off his little hat and sailed it into the bull's face. Old Thirteen jerked his yellow head around and caught sight of the clown. He lowered the head and came charging.

Kelly had just a second to see Padgett scamper away to safety. Then the bull was on him, the black horns shining, the evil eyes bulging. Kelly tried to step aside, but the leg wouldn't move. He heard himself cry out, then felt his breath gust out as the bull hit him. Rolling on the ground, he saw the bull coming again but couldn't move. A horn gouged into his side, and fiery pain roared through him.

He was never quite sure that he saw the horsemen drive the bull away. He felt himself being lifted into the ambulance and heard the shrill siren. He sensed that someone was holding his hand, and that the other hand was small and soft.

He forced his eyes open long enough to see Kathy sitting beside him tears streaming down her cheeks.

He didn't want to be angry with her, but he couldn't help it. If it hadn't been for her—

"You picked your partner, " he managed to say. "Why don't you dance with him?"

"Please, Kelly," she pleaded. " I want to tell you I'm sorry. You were right. I found out last night."

Kelly knew. Cindy Baker had found out, too.

Kathy's voice came to him almost as if in a painful dream. "Ralph was drinking last night. He was drinking from the time we left town. And every time he took a drink, a little of that false front slipped away from him. He started showing what he actually was. By the time we got to Morsetown, there wasn't any more question about the reason he wanted me.

"There wasn't any dance last night. The place where he stopped wasn't a dance hall at all. I tried to make him turn around and bring me back. He wouldn't.

" So I grabbed up an empty bottle from the floorboard of the car and hit him with it. I drove the car around in front of the police station and left it there with him in it. Then I caught a bus and came home."

Kelly felt the bitterness begin to drain out of him. So that was why Ralph hadn't come home. Likely as not he had spent the night in jail. Kelly wanted to grab Kathy and squeeze half the life out of her. But the pain grew worse, and she seemed to melt away into the darkness. He had no way of knowing how long it was before he woke up. He tried to pull himself up on his elbow, but a white-uniformed nurse pushed him back.

"Easy now," she cautioned. "You've just had a blood transfusion."

The words seemed to swim around in his muddled mind. "Transfusion?" he asked, still confused. "Who gave me blood?"

The nurse grinned. "Why that lobby out there was half full of cowboys who wanted to give blood for you. You've got plenty of friends, you know that? But it was the girl who finally gave it. She wouldn't hear to anybody else coming in ahead of her."

The words were beginning to make a little more sense. "Kathy?"

The nurse nodded. "Yes. You feel like seeing her?"

Kelly felt a smile breaking across his wide mouth. The nurse opened the door. Kathy stepped in a little fearfully. Then seeing Kelly's eyes open, she rushed to him. She started to say something but swallowed it, tears sparkling in her eyes. Finally she got it said.

"You can't get away from me any more, Kelly, From now on I'm part of you, wherever you go."

Kelly squeezed her hand. The words were making a lot of sense now.

SENSE OF DUTY

Sam Lunsford hadn't wanted to go to town for Christmas. In fact, he had hoped never to go to Twin Wells again. But bald old Wylie Yount bulldozed him into it.

It happened because late on December afternoon the old bachelor ranchman rode into the Circle Y's south camp and found Sam alone, topping out a raw black bronc in the circular corral. Leaning forward in his saddle, Wylie had opened his wide mouth to bawl something angry at the tall cowpuncher, thought better of it, and sat there tugging irritably at his brown mustache.

He watched quietly as Sam spurred the last jump out of the black, then swung down and tied the thick hackamore rein to a post. Sam put his hand to the small of his back and stretched his long frame to ease the aching put there by the back-snapping ride.

Wylie grunted when Sam opened the gate and walked out. "Not as easy as it was ten years ago, is it, Sam?"

Sam shook his head and came close to grinning. He still lacked a lot reaching middle age, but already the years had begun to carve the first deep lines in his face.

"Now look here, Sam," Wylie said, shaking his stubby finger, "you go to remember you're thirty-five-years old. I hired you to take over my south ranch here, not bust your neck riding broncs. I sent that kid, Mel Pace, out here to do the bronc stomping for you. Even lent him an old saddle."

Grimacing, Sam stretched his back again. "I was afraid that black was too much for the kid, Wylie. Might've hurt him. I figured I owed it to the kid to take the starch out of the bronc myself."

Wylie exploded. "Owed it to him, did you? Won't you never forget about being an inspector for the Cattlemen's Association? You wore a badge for ten years, and now you think it's your duty to take over any risky job you see anybody else doing.

"That's why I talked you into quitting the Association and going in with me. The biggest duty you got from now on is to yourself. You got to quit shoving your neck through the fence for other people all the time."

Sam leaned against the fence and looked through at the bronc, which was still pulling back on the hackamore rein. A bleakness settled over Sam's chiseled face. There was a tightness in his leathery, whiskered cheeks. "I was thinking of my myself, Wylie, when I decided to move way out here, away from people."

Wylie Yount studied the tall cowpuncher a moment, then put his hand on Sam's shoulder. "Look, Sam, for four solid months you've stayed out here. Haven't talked with anybody hardly, or visited any other camp. All right, so the girl did marry somebody else. You don't help yourself none by running away. The sooner you get out into company again, the sooner you'll forget about Verna.

"Now come on to town with me and we'll celebrate Christmas the way a man ought to. What you need is to dance with some pretty women and sniff a little Christmas spirits."

Sam thought darkly of Twin Wells, and he thought of the slim, honey-haired girl named Verna Sherwood. He shook his head and started walking away.

"You might as well quit trying, Wylie. I won't go."

But late the day before Christmas Eve, Sam grudgingly

found himself on the last mile of the town trail, rubbing his rawhide-bound stirrups against those of Wylie and the kid, Mel Pace. The weak winter sun working down ahead of them was only a faint hint of light behind the heavy, gray clouds. Chilling air went through Sam's thick coat, making him hunch over.

Not far ahead he could see the scattering of frame buildings and the railroad shipping pens that made up Twin Wells. Gray smoke curled upward from dozens of tin chimneys and flattened out in the heavy air. The few trees were leafless and bent, surrendered to winter.

It was a lot different from the last time he had seen Twin Wells. The town had basked in the late-summer Texas sun then, the trees in full leaf, the doors all open and friendly.

But Sam had ridden out hoping he would never see the place again. For months he had been waiting for pretty Verna Sherwood to make her choice between him and his friend, young Sheriff Glenn Wilcox. That day she made it.

Not more than half a dozen horses were hitched on the main street now. They stood with heads low, rumps turned to the crisp wind.

Wylie pointed his chin towards Berry's Saloon and grinned, his ruddy face redder than ever from the cold. "First thing to do, I'd say, is to get a little toddy for the body."

The warmth of the small saloon was a welcome thing. The cheery little saloonkeeper stepped out from behind the plain pine bar and rubbed his hands on a stained apron that draped over his belly like a sack over a barrel. Wylie ordered whisky.

The kid looked up at a sign that said no drinks served to minors. He fumbled uncertainly with a coat button. Then he pitched his voice a little lower than normal and said, "I'd settle for coffee, if you got a pot."

The fat little man looked at the kid, then at the sign, and chuckled. "It'll be on in a jiffy, son. Take your coat off and get friendly with that heater back yonder."

Sam said, "That coffee sounds good to me too, Berry."

Wylie grunted. "No way to start a holiday. What's going on around here for excitement, Berry?"

The saloonman tugged at his double chin. "Well, there's a regular Christmas Eve dance tomorrow night. Till then, there ain't much. Not unless you want to go over to Haskell Trigg's poker table at the Blue Chip and help him make his living."

The name made Sam turn around quickly, frowning. "Trigg, you say? Thought he'd've stumbled over a hidden ace by now and go run out of town."

Berry shook his head and looked down at the bar. "Well, Sheriff Wilcox was threatening to run him out, till about three months ago. All of a sudden he let up on Trigg. Since then he's kept his hands off. Been talk about it around town."

Sam felt warm color rising in his cheeks. "What kind of talk?"

Gravely Berry shook his head. "I know you and Wilcox used to be pretty good pardners, Sam. So I wouldn't put much store in the talk I heard, was I you."

Wylie set an empty glass down on the bar, wiped his mouth and turned to Sam. "Didn't you almost get Trigg sent to the pen once?"

Sam nodded. "He's greedier than a wolf. When the cards eren't making enough money to suit him, he started helping get rid of stolen cattle. Somebody shot my best witness, just before the trial."

In the back of the room the kid was admiring a nearly new saddle that had been thrown down in the corner. "Whose sale, Mr. Berry?"

The saloonman rubbed his hands on the apron again. "Feller came in a couple of weeks ago. Sold it to me and caught a freight train back for East Texas."

Chewing his lips, the kid ran his hands fondly over the saddle. It wasn't fancy, but it was stout. "What would you take for it?"

"Just what I gave, fifty dollars."

The kid's face fell. Quietly he walked once again to the stove, still looking back at the saddle.

A rush of cold air chilled the saloon. Sam looked around to see Sheriff Glenn Wilcox push the door shut behind him and stand there unbuttoning his sheep-lined coat. The kid ran to him. The young sheriff caught the boy's shoulders and shook them good-naturedly. It has been Glenn who had picked the kid up as he stepped down off a freight car months ago. He had given Mel a place to eat and sleep and had found odd jobs for him before Wylie finally took the kid onto the Circle Y payroll.

There wasn't anything striking about Glenn's looks. He was ten years younger than Sam, and he still had that boyish expression on his ruddy face. A little red hair peeped out from under his battered, broad-rimmed hat.

Glenn's searching brown eyes fell upon Sam, and the sheriff's mouth dropped open. He managed a quick grin, then hesitantly stepped forward, his hand out.

"Glad to see you, Sam. It's been a good while."

Stiffly Sam took his hand. "Yep. Been pretty busy."

Sam could feel a tension between them. He wished he could loosen up. It wasn't right to greet Glenn like a stranger. As lawmen they had made many a long ride together, slept under the same blanket on the hard ground and even teamed up for a few fights. Glenn couldn't help it that they both loved the same girl.

Finally Sam made himself ask it. "How's Verna, Glenn?"

Glenn looked down at his boots and his cheeks drew in a little. "Better ask her, Sam. I haven't talked with her in nearly three months."

Sam's hands trembled suddenly. "But you married her. You did, didn't you, Glen?"

The sheriff shook his head. "No, Sam. Something came up."

Sam sat down heavily in a rawhide-bottomed chair. A dozen thoughts chased through his mind at once. A half-angry one settled there.

"What did you do to her?"

Glenn's brown eyes fixed worriedly on Sam's a moment, then looked away. "Like I said, Sam, you better ask her. I'll be seeing you."

With a nod at the others, Glenn Wilcox walked back out of the saloon. Sam stared after him, shivering to the breath of chill wind.

A mental image came back to him, a picture of a pretty young woman, a slender woman with honey-colored hair and eyes blue as the sky after a spring rain. Ten minutes later he tied his horse in front a sagging picket fence and walked up onto the plank porch of a weather-grayed, unpainted frame house.

He knocked and heard on old man's voice call from within, "It ain't locked."

Old Andy Sherwood sat at a little table, holding a hand of cards. Across the table from him was another old-timer, jaw bulging from a big cud of tobacco. He nodded at Sam, then went back to this cards.

Verna's father laid his cards on the table face down and stood up to shake hands with Sam. Sherwood's tobacco-stained mustache was in bad need of a trim, and his face was stubbled. He stood in his sock feet.

"Still can't leave the pasteboards alone, can you, Andy?" Sam grinned.

The old man grinned back and spat at a nearby can of ashes. "Age takes away a man's craving for women, Sam, and a bad stomach finally breaks him of whisky. But there's nothing cures an itch for cards."

Sam said, "I'll have to send Mel Pace over here to visit you awhile. The kid thinks he's pretty good at poker." He shuffled his feet a little. "Where's Verna, Andy?"

The old man sat down again and started rubbing his leg as if he had forgotten it needed attention. "She's over to the livery stable, Sam. She's sort of taking care of it for me right now. I have been having rheumatism lately. Can't do much, seems like, without it gets to bothering me."

Sam knew that the main thing bothering the old man was laziness, but there wasn't much point in saying so.

He reined up at the livery barn door and swung down. His hands shook a little as he led the horse in. His heart seemed to swell up inside him as he saw Verna standing there in an old ankle-length woolen dress that she might have used for parties once, when Andy was more provident. She wore one of Andy's old coats with the sleeves rolled up part way.

It's been four months now since he had seen her, four months in which he had tried to forget. But her memory had come back to him a dozen times a day. His heart seemed to beat faster than ever now at the sight of her.

She stared at him, her hands suspended in midair. Then she rushed into his arms and cried, "Sam, Sam, I thought you'd never come back."

He crushed her to him and bent his head so that his gaunt cheek pressed against hers. He felt the wetness of her tears.

"Sam, "she asked, "why did you stay away so long?"

"I thought you and Glenn were married, Verna. I figured we'd all be better off if I didn't come back."

He took his arms from around Verna and she sat down on a bale of hay. She bowed her head. "We didn't marry, Sam." ·

He nodded. "Glenn told me. But he didn't tell me why."

The young woman took a handkerchief from the pocket of the coat and touched it to her eyes. "It isn't easy to tell you, Sam. You always liked Glenn, and you won't want to believe it. But I loved him and I finally had to believe it. Somehow or other, he's gotten tied in with that gambler, Trigg."

Sam remembered the words of the saloonman, Berry. Heavily he sat down on a hay bale beside the woman. "That's hard to take, Verna. I remember the time Glenn caught Oscar Flack stealing cattle, and Oscar offered him a thousand dollars not to take him in. A lot of money, a thousand dollars. But it made Glenn so mad he knocked Oscar right out of the saddle. Glenn's got a real sharp temper, and now and again it makes him do something he's sorry about later. But he's an honest man, Verna."

The girl twisted the handkerchief in her hands. "Men change, Sam. All I know is that Glenn was riding Trigg pretty hard until about three months ago. A couple of times Dad lost money at the Blue Chip, and Glenn made Haskell Trigg give it back to him.

"Then all at once Glenn stopped bothering Trigg. At first people thought maybe Trigg had bowed his neck and thrown a scare into Glenn. They say Trigg's a real gunman, that he could beat Glenn if it ever came to that. They say Trigg's almost as good as you used to be, Sam. Anyway, Trigg got wide open with his gambling. He's won a couple of businesses here in town, and he won all the cattle one rancher had. Glenn didn't stop him. So people have decided that Trigg has bought Glenn out."

Sam tried to roll a cigarette, spilled half his tobacco, and finally let the paper flutter to the stable's dirt floor. "And you've decided the same way, have you, Verna?"

She put the handkerchief to her eyes again. Sam pulled her over so that her head was on his shoulder.

Some love for Glenn must have remained with her, he thought, or she wouldn't be taking it so hard. But right now it was Sam's arms which folded around her. The cold air of the barn chilled his feet and legs. But holding her close, he felt a pleasant warmth in his heart.

The Blue Chip was larger than Berry's saloon, and much more ornate. But it was strictly out for business, while Berry's was as much a friendly meeting place as it was a place to buy a drink. Glancing at the sign outside, Sam saw that an old name had been painted out and Haskell Trigg's name painted on in front of the word "proprietor."

There was nothing flashy about Haskell Trigg. He had squarely built shoulders, a square face and a full black mustache that helped hide any expression that might unintentionally creep out. He wore a black coat and black hat and might even have passed for a minister if he closed his steely, predatory gray eyes.

He looked up from a game of solitaire as Sam walked in. The man's eyes cautiously followed Sam's every step as he walked towards the gambler's table ten feet from the end of the mahogany bar.

"Pull up a chair, Lunsford," Trigg spoke evenly. "Good to see you."

Sam remained standing. He let his gaze rove over the big room. "Looks nice, Trigg. A lot nicer than it ever did when Bomar had it."

Trigg grunted. "Bomar had no pride of ownership. Me, I like to own things. And whatever I own, I want to have in good shape."

Sam looked straight into the gambler's eyes. "Sheriffs too?"

There was not even a flicker in the gray eyes. Trigg reached into his coat pocket for a cigar, clipped off the end with bright white teeth and shoved it into his mouth. "Just what's aching you, Lunsford?"

Sam said, "I want to know what's between you and Glenn Wilcox. Have you got him buffaloed, blackmailed or bought off?"

Not a ripple crossed the dark face, but Trigg bit down on the cigar. " I think you better leave, Lunsford. I wouldn't care to have to fight with you."

Sam doubled and loosened his fists. He knew now that Trigg would spill nothing. "No, you wouldn't want a fight. You know I'd win."

He turned and walked out.

He found Glenn in the sheriff's office, looking over official mail. There was no fire in the pot-bellied heater, and each breath was like an icy little puff of smoke in the chilly room. Glenn sat at the rolltop desk, his coat buttoned all the way.

The young sheriff nodded. "Come in, Sam. Been expecting you."

Silently Sam sat down in a cane-bottomed chair. With stiffened fingers he fashioned a cigarette and lighted it.

After a long silence, Glenn said, "You saw Verna, I guess."

Sam nodded.

The sheriff's face was taut. "She hates me, I suppose."

Sam drew thoughtfully on the cigarette. "You hurt her, Glenn, hurt her bad. But I wouldn't say she hates you."

Glenn went on looking through the mail, but Sam had the idea the sheriff didn't even know what he was reading. Finally Sam dropped the cigarette to the plank floor and ground it under his boot heel.

"We've been friends a long time, Glenn. Want to tell me what's the matter?"

Glenn shook his head. "It doesn't concern you. You'd best stay out."

A thin surge of anger flared in Sam. But he managed to keep his lips closed until the anger had passed. Then he arose on his long legs.

"Since that's how it is, Glenn, I think I'd just as well tell you. I'm still in love with Verna. I'm going to try again to get her to marry me."

The knuckles on Glenn's hands were white, but he kept his eyes fixed on the papers before him.

"Good luck, Sam."

Glenn never looked up as Sam walked out. But when Sam glanced back through the window, he saw the sheriff propping his forehead on his hand.

Verna cooked a fine supper that night. She sliced some thick steaks from a hind quarter of beef that a ranchman had left at the stable as a Christmas present for Andy. She put the steaming meal down on the table in front of Sam, Wylie Yount, the kid and Andy.

Sam sat across the table from Verna. Through the meal he

hardly looked away from her pretty, oval-shaped, worried-looking face, or her long blond hair that tumbled about her slim shoulders. She looked often at him, too, and a couple of times she met his warm gaze with a thin smile.

But it wasn't thin enough that the others missed seeing it. After supper Wylie shoved away from the table. "Andy, what do you say you and me and Mel go out for a friendly hand of poker. Say over to the Blue Chip?"

Andy's gray-mustached face had lighted up at the mention of poker, but it fell a little at the name of the Blue Chip. "Good idea, Wylie. But what do you say we go to Berry's instead?"

The kid chimed in. "Sounds fine. I been wanting to take another look at the saddle over there anyhow."

Wylie pulled Sam over to one side. "Now don't you miss this chance, Sam. Time's running out on you. You don't want to wind up an old bachelor like me."

Sam helped Verna wash, dry and put away the dishes. For a long time then, they sat silently in the living room. Sam was content just to be near her. This was the way he would like to spend the rest of his days.

At last he spoke. "Verna, I'd like to take you to the Christmas Eve dance over at the schoolhouse tomorrow night. That is, if you'd care to go."

Verna looked down at her hands. "I haven't been to a dance since—Yes, Sam, I'd love to go."

Sam arose and put on his coat. At the door he took Verna's hand. "I know I'm probably rushing you too much, Verna. But I want you to know nothing's changed with me. I'm going to get you to marry me if I can."

He pulled her to him. She came willingly. "Have I got a chance?" he asked.

She didn't smile, but her forehead was warm against his cheek. "Maybe, Sam. There are so many things I'm not sure about. Perhaps if you'll give me a little more time—"

She kissed him a warm good night. But a vague worry

gnawed at him as he swung into the saddle and rode toward the hotel.

Early the next morning the Christmas Eve crowd began gathering. Sam visited with old friends, cowboys and cattlemen he had worked with while he was wearing a gun for the Association.

In the afternoon Berry sent for him.

"Don't like to worry you, Sam, and it ain't really any of my business. But that kid that works with you, they tell me he's in a poker game with Haskell Trigg. He won't come to any good down there."

Sam thanked the saloonkeeper and strode hurriedly down to the Blue Chip. The batwing doors had been taken down for the season and replaced with heavy full-length doors that would keep the winter out. Sam closed them behind him. At Trigg's table he saw the kid intently bent over a hand of cards. There was a small stack of chips in front of him. Across the table Trigg sat chewing on a cigar, his black hat pulled low over his gray eyes.

Sam walked across and placed his hand on Mel's slim shoulder. "Better come on, kid. This is no place for you."

Anger was in Trigg's eyes, but he said nothing. Mel did the talking. "Aw now, Sam, I'm doing all right. I started with fifteen dollars and I've run my pile up to almost twice that much. A little longer and I'll be able to buy that saddle over at Berry's."

Sam frowned. "You ought to have enough money saved up anyhow."

Mel shook his head. "I been sending most of my wages home to my mother. Us kids are kind of supporting Ma, you know."

"Well then, "Sam argued, "I'll lend you the money."

Again the boy shook his head. "Thanks, Sam, but there's no use you doing that. I got a winning streak on. I'll have all the money I need pretty quick. Then I'll quit."

Sam glared at Trigg. "There's probably a law against gambling with minors."

Trigg snorted. "Go talk to the sheriff about it. He knows all about gambling. Now move along and let us be."

Sam went straight down the street to Glenn's office. He found the sheriff and told him about the game.

"Sure, "Glenn frowned, "the kid'll get fleeced out of all he's got and probably leave owing Trigg three months' wages. But he's old enough to know better. He went in there with his eyes open."

Angrily Sam said, "All right, I'm going to the hotel to get my gun. I'll stop the game myself, it Trigg's got you bought off."

He was instantly sorry he had said it. Glenn stood up quickly, face red. "You know Trigg hasn't got me bought, Sam. I'll stop the game."

They were halfway to the Blue Chip when they heard the shot. It was followed by loud shouts. Three or four men pushed out of the Blue Chip and started running down the street. Glenn and Sam hit for the saloon in a hard run.

Pushing through the tight knot of men gathered there, they found Mel Pace lying on his back on the plank floor. A cry rising in his throat, Sam dropped to his knees and tore the boy's shirt away to find the wound that spilled blood out across the boy's chest. It was a bad one, but the kid still breathed.

"Tack's gone for the doctor," somebody said.

Raging, Glenn faced Trigg, who stood behind his table, a smoking pocket gun in his hand.

Trigg explained flatly, "The kid lost all his chips and went to complaining that I'd been cheating him. I told him to get out and cool off. He started out, then grabbed a gun from somebody and came back toward me. So"—he shrugged his shoulders— "I shot him. I got plenty of witnesses to prove it."

Sam arose and moved threateningly toward the gambler. "He's just a kid, Trigg. A cocky, eighteen-year-old kid. If you hadn't been greedy and cheated him out of that trifling little roll of his, it wouldn't have happened."

Glenn turned on Sam. "Keep out of it, Sam. I'm the sheriff here."

He whirled back on Trigg. "You've pulled your last dirty deal in this town, Trigg. You're going to pack up and catch the evening train."

Trigg slipped the gun back into his pocket. "I told you it was self-defense. You got no legal right as sheriff to order me out of town."

Face splotched with rage, Glenn ripped off his badge. "Then I'm not talking to you as sheriff. I'm talking as Glenn Wilcox. The train pulls in here at eight tonight. I'm coming down here to be sure you get on it."

The gambler's lips tightened, but there was no other sign of emotion in his face. "And if I don't go?"

Glenn dropped his hand to his gun butt. "Then one of us won't live to see Christmas."

Sudden dread clutched Sam. Glenn wasn't fast enough with a gun. But Trigg was.

Trigg said flatly, "Better think a little, Wilcox. I know a very good story I can tell."

Glenn's face darkened. "Tell it and be damned. But you better be ready to catch that train." He stamped out of the saloon.

Sam stayed while the doctor looked at Mel, then helped carry the wounded kid to the doctor's office nearby. There he and Wylie waited an hour, two hours, three.

Finally the front door pushed open. Verna walked in. Sam knew at a glance that she had been crying. Old Andy followed her, looking like a whipped dog.

"How's Mel?" she asked weakly.

Sam shook his head. "We don't know yet".

A desperate look came into the girl's face. "Sam, won't you please talk to Glenn? I've tried for an hour and it did no good. We've got to stop him some way."

She buried her head against Sam's shoulder. "Oh, Sam," she

cried, "what am I going to do? I'll die if something happens to him."

Sam swallowed. He stroked her honey-blond hair and felt misery settle over him. Now suddenly he realized how much difference there was in their ages. Almost fifteen years.

"You still love him, Verna?" he managed painfully.

She nodded. "I'm sorry, Sam, but that's how it is. Make Dad tell you what he told me."

Andy kept his head bowed. "It's all my fault, the hold that Trigg's got on Glenn. Trigg let me win a little money once, and from then on I couldn't keep away from his poker table. Not even when I commenced losing every time. Then one night I lost the livery stable and every cent I had. More, even. Trigg made me sign a bill of sale.

"I knowed he'd cheated me and I was crazy mad. After the saloon closed up, I broke in and tried to steal back that bill of sale. If I'd had any sense I'd've knowed he'd lock it in a safe. Trigg caught me. He put Glenn over a barrel. Told him he would forget about catching me if Glenn would leave him alone. Even tore up the bill of sale. Said he didn't want a smelly stable anyway. But he said the first time Glenn got to bothering him, he would have me sent to the pen, Sam. And he could've done it, too.

"I was afraid what Verna would say, and I made Glenn promise never to tell her or anybody. If it hadn't been for me, Glenn could've sent Trigg to jail by now. As it is, he's going to get hisself shot, just because an old fool couldn't keep away from a poker game."

Shamefacedly Andy turned to a window and looked out upon the chilly street.

Sam kissed Verna on the forehead. "I don't know as there's anything we can do now, Verna, but we'll try . . . ."

A large Christmas Eve crowd had gathered from ranches all over the country. Two little barber shops were full of cowboys waiting for a shave and a bath. Women shopped in the stores, while children tagged along to see the toys and look wistfully at the hard rock candy.

But by the way the men knotted up in groups, talking and pointing toward the sheriff's office or the Blue Chip, Sam knew the word had spread. There would be a shooting tonight.

Sam argued with Glenn, who sat, with Wylie, in his office polishing his gun with shaky hands. "Trigg's not going to leave, Glenn. He owns too much property here, and he'll never turn loose of it. What's more, you haven't a chance against him."

The sheriff shook his head. "I guess not. But my temper and my quick mouth got me into it. What would people say if I was to back down?"

"Verna would understand, Glenn. She's the only one that ought to count."

Glenn winced at that, but he held firm. Wylie sat still while Sam argued, but Sam could read his thoughts. If Glenn went through with this, Sam could marry Verna.

After a long while the doctor sent word that Mel would live. The news made Sam smile a moment. But he looked back at Glenn and the smile faded. One friend lives and another one dies.

A little before eight, Sam heard the train whistle at a crossing far off in the distance. The color drained from Glenn's face and his hands trembled as he stood up. "It's time," he said.

Sam stood up with him. His heart was pounding, hard. One thought hammered at him. He had to stop this, some way. And there wouldn't be but one way to do it.

"Look, Glenn," he pleaded, "you know Trigg can beat you, but he can't beat me. Let me go!"

Wylie jumped to his feet to protest, but Glenn spoke first. Shaking his head, he said, "It's my fight."

He stepped to the door, then stopped. "If I—" He struggled for words. "Tell Verna I'm sorry."

Pulse racing, Sam said, "Tell her yourself." He crouched a little, then brought up his right fist. Glenn didn't have time to duck.

Wylie looked down wide-eyed at the unconscious sheriff. "Have you gone plumb crazy, Sam?"

"I'm going to put Trigg on that train. You get your horses and gear ready, will you, Wylie? Not a word to anybody."

Wylie was both scared and disgusted. "What if something happens? With a little luck, Trigg might kill you."

"Glenn's my friend, Wylie. I can handle this, and he couldn't. I owe it to him and Verna."

Wylie snorted. "There you go, owing somebody something again." But he walked out to get the horses.

Sam strode up the chilly street to the hotel. There he picked up his gun, strapped it outside his heavy coat and came back downstairs. He moved out into the dark street again. He stopped and turned in at Berry's.

Taking a little roll of money from his pocket, he counted off fifty dollars, most of the roll. "That's for the saddle, Berry. Take it over to the doctor's and tell him it's for the kid. For Christmas."

On down the street, a couple of dozen buckboards and wagons were gathered around the schoolhouse, where the dance was to be. From the church next door came the sound of children's voices singing Christmas songs. Sam sensed that there was almost no one on the dark street. They were all waiting to see if someone was to die. The thought prickled his scalp.

Then he stood in front of the Blue Chip. A cautious glance through the door showed him it was empty. Empty except for Haskell Trigg, sitting at his favorite table. Sam waited a moment, hoping the tingling in his blood would settle. He took a deep breath, then pushed through the door.

Trigg's hands were both in sight on top of the table. They inched backwards as the door opened, then stopped as Trigg recognized Sam. The gambler said nothing for a long moment, his dark face blank.

"Where's Wilcox?" he asked finally.

"He's not coming. I'm here instead."

The square faced held firm a little while. Then a trace of fear rippled across it. "I can't beat you Lunsford."

Sam nodded. "I know it."

The gambler's voice quavered. "Look, Lundsford, I got lots of property here. All I own is right here. I can't leave."

Sam's voice was level. "You got it easy and you're leaving it the same way. Now get up and let's catch that train."

The inscrutable mask was gone from Trigg's face and Sam could sense the battle that went on in the gambler's mind, a battle between greed and fear. In the gray eyes and the way they looked at the saloon, Sam could see the greed, Trigg's determination to hold onto everything he owed.

But another emotion was stronger, and it finally settled. Fear.

Trigg stood up and pushed back his chair. At the door he turned around for one last look at the ornate saloon. Then, tight-lipped, he began walking toward the station. Sam followed two steps behind him.

As the train pulled in. Trigg turned back to plead. "What if I was to split everything with you, Lunsford, share and share alike?"

Sam shook his head. "You're leaving, Trigg. And if you ever come back, I'll kill you."

Trigg stepped up onto the platform of the car. He turned around, his eyes on the darkened town he was leaving, the town which held everything he owned. He was losing it all, quick as the turn of a card. His gaze dropped down to Sam. The gray eyes simmered with hatred for the man who was taking all this away from him.

The train gave a lurch. In that moment Trigg dropped to one knee and jerked the gun out of his coat. Caught by surprise, Sam was slow in drawing his own gun. He saw the gambler's gun barrel come up and was already steeling himself for the white-hot impact of lead.

But the train lurched again and Trigg's bullet went shy. Sam had his own .45 ready now and he squeezed the trigger. Trigg's head jerked back. The gambler slumped forward and tumbled off the car platform.

Sam leaned against a station post, breathing in the cold air to help fight away the sickness that came to him. He looked away from the dead man crumpled on the greasy gravel of the railroad bed.

The sound of the shots must have carried all over town, for as the train ground to a stop he could hear dozens of running feet converging on the station. From the church came the Christmas songs again. Somebody had had the good sense to keep the kids singing.

From toward the Sherwood house he could hear a woman's voice crying out, almost in a scream. Sam stepped away from the station and started toward the voice. He met Verna, running as fast as she could. He caught her and stopped her.

"Let me go," she cried. "I've got to get to Glenn."

"Glenn's not there," Sam told the half-hysterical girl. "He wasn't in it. He's all right".

After a moment she calmed and murmured thanks to God.

"You can tell your dad he's free," Sam said. "Trigg's dead."

Sam caught her chin and tilted it upward. "Now wipe those tears off your face and go over to the sheriff's office. I left a Christmas present there for you."

He kissed her soft lips, then turned her loose. Painfully he watched as she struck out in a run toward the sheriff's office.

Sam went back to the station and explained to a deputy what had happened. "If you need me for anything," he said, "I'll be at the camp."

He paused just long enough to hear one cowboy ask another who had killed Trigg.

"That old bachelor who used to be with the Association," was the answer.

Old bachelor. The words stung Sam as Wylie brought up the horses, and he swung into the saddle.

In front of the sheriff's office, Sam reined up. An ache moved through him as he saw Glenn crush Verna into his arms. But pride was in him too. He looked a moment, then pulled his burning eyes away.

"You're a damn fool," Wylie grunted. "You could've had her yourself."

Sam swallowed. "Shut up, Wylie. Let's get home."

He spurred down the street and out onto the Circle Y trail.

SHE WOLF OF THE BRUSH COUNTRY

Cautiously pushing his way through the thorny tangle of mesquite, Tom Flood almost rode up against the hidden corral before he saw it. His right hand instinctively dropped to his worn gun butt as he pulled the black-legged dun to a halt.

Instant alertness made his pulse beat faster. This didn't belong to any honest ranchman, he knew—not hidden here, miles deep in a thorny jungle of mesquite brush a day's drive from the Mexican border. It was plainly an outlaw setup, like a dozen others he had seen.

Signs showed that it hadn't been many days since cattle had been penned there. They were probably listening to Spanish lingo by now, and healing from the burn of a new owner's brand.

Flood heard the rustle of dry mesquite beans behind him and the faint tinkle of spur rowels. Alarm spun him halfway around in the saddle and made his hand arc upward with the gun. But he knew instantly that he was too late. He let the gun slide back into the holster.

"Git off that horse and keep your hands high!" a gruff voice ordered.

Flood hesitated a moment, his right hand still close to the gun. But what was the use? There might be one man behind him, or there might be ten. He shifted his hand to the saddle-horn, swung his long legs down, and turned around with his hands up.

Two men stood there, and several more were coming afoot through the brush. The man with the gun was about as tall as Flood, just over six feet. His grim face showed the heavy lines of a few more winters, and his belt hung a little lower.

"We been watchin' you prowl through here the last hour or so," he rumbled. His voice made Flood think of a bear. "What are you, a Ranger, or an association man?"

Flood didn't answer as he studied the other. He might be able to outfight him if it weren't for the .45 in the outlaw's big, gnarled hand. But three more men had pushed out of the brush now. He couldn't lick five.

Two men grabbed Flood's arms and twisted them behind his back. The big man grinned in evil anticipation. Shoving the gun back into its holster, he stepped forward.

Flood hardly saw the fist coming. A thousand lights flashed in front of his eyes, and his head rocked back under the sledge-hammer blow. Anger welled up in him. He cursed and struggled painfully to free his arms. The fist plowed into his face again. He felt warm blood trickling down his chin, and grimaced at its salty taste on his bruised lips.

"Search him," the deep voice ordered. Rough hands quickly went through his pockets. He felt the envelope slip out of the inside of his unbuttoned vest

"Here's a letter in a woman's hand, addressed to Tom Flood, general delivery, Del Rio," one of the outlaws said. There was the rustle of paper, then an exclamation. "Hey, it's from old man Cartwright. His daughter must've wrote it for him. He's offerin' this hombre $100 a month. Says all he's got to do is be around with his guns when they're needed."

Through a red haze Flood saw the big man grab the letter and look at it. "Another gunhand, huh? Cartwright's been hirin' a bunch of 'em lately. Thinks he'll run us out of the brush country."

The outlaw threw down the letter and turned scowling to Flood. "Well, this is one he won't git!"

Flood tried to duck, but the two men held him. A big fist drove into his stomach, doubling him over. It felt as if his innards were being ripped out. Another fist smashed into his jaw, and he was seeing flashes again.

Then a woman's voice called out, and the beating stopped. The two outlaws turned him loose. Flood dropped weakly to his hands and knees and shook his throbbing head, trying to clear the darkness from his eyes. He heard hoofbeats as a rider broke through the brush.

"What's goin' on here, Drummond?" the woman's voice demanded.

"Howdy, Zell. We caught one of Cartwright's gunhands snoopin' around," the big man, Drummond, answered proudly.

Flood rose shakily to his feet, struggling for breath. What he saw almost made him fall back again. The woman looked like a dream out here in this wild brush country. Her shirt and riding pants fit tightly around one of the best-shaped figures he had ever seen. Her face was smoothly beautiful, like a statue, but just as hard as one. Wavy blond hair, maybe a shade too light, tumbled down over her shapely shoulders.

Zell, Drummond had called her. Flood realized with a start who she was—Zell Thorn, widow of outlaw Ben Thorn. He remembered when Thorn and another outlaw had gone down in a blazing crossfire just outside the door of the Boom City bank two years ago.

Somebody had warned the law.

Flood remembered the stories about Zell Thorn, half truth, half legend—how she had taken over her husband's outlaw band and ruled a large part of this brush country on the Texas-Mexico border with an iron hand.

The woman was looking him over appraisingly, like she would a fine horse or a good bull. "What's his name?"

Drummond picked up the letter and handed it to her. "Tom Flood, it says here."

Light of recognition flashed in her eyes. "Flood . . . Flood. Say, weren't you sheriff over at Grama Flat a couple of years ago?"

The bitter memory still sent a shudder up Flood's spine. "I was. What of it?"

"They threw you out of there because you wouldn't bring in a friend of yours for murder. Isn't that right?" the woman pressed insistently.

Flood clinched his fists in bitterness as he remembered. He said nothing for a moment, trying to regain his breath. Then he spoke in a voice that stung with long-held hatred:

"He was just a kid, not much over eighteen. I'd about half-way raised him. He got in an argument over a poker game, and he shot a man. It was self-defense. I knew that. But the man had made deep tracks in that town, and his friends howled for a hangin'. I refused to bring the kid in if I couldn't get him a decent trial. They took my badge away from me, hunted him down, and hung him anyway!"

Flood could feel the heat of an old rancor darkening his blood-smeared face, and deep anger was choking him.

"They said I was obstructin' justice. When they buried the kid, they called that justice."

He looked somberly into the woman's eyes. They were as blue as gun steel. "What do you care about all that for? It looks like I got on the wrong side of the firin' line here. Why don't you let your boys drag me off and shoot me?"

The woman smiled a little, and the hard glint faded from her eyes. "I don't think we have to. Maybe you are on the right side after all."

Drummond's heavy jaw dropped. "Now look here, Zell, you ain't gonna' take chances on a Cartwright man. Especially since he just admitted he's been a sheriff!"

"I'm runnin' this outfit, Drummond!" she snapped. Then to Flood she queried, "From the looks of this letter, you haven't got to the Cartwright place yet, have you?"

He shook his head. It still ached. "I was just on my way. Figgered I'd save a couple of days cuttin' through the brush instead of tryin' to go around it."

The woman smiled at him. She was getting prettier every minute. "From the way you were talkin', you aren't too hot on what some folks call justice," she suggested.

Flood eyed her levelly. Bitterness put a raw edge on his voice. "My gun goes to the highest bidder. That's the way it's been the last three years. Cartwright's letter said $100 a month. I didn't ask which way my gun was to point!"

She lifted her hand and put her soft fingers lightly on his bruised face. Flood's raw skin thrilled to their touch.

"If we could offer you a lot more than $100, would you just as soon work with us?" She smiled, and Flood's heart pumped faster.

"You give the orders," he said.

Drummond stepped up angrily. "I ain't lettin' you do this, Zell. He'll put our necks in a noose."

Vengeful fury drew back Flood's left fist and drove it into Drummond's belly. He swung his right, almost from the ground, straight into Drummond's jaw. The outlaw staggered backward and fell in the sand. Anger rumbled in his thick throat. He crushed his fallen hat with his big hand as he struggled to get up.

"That's enough, Drummond!" Zell Thorn snapped, her voice sharp as a coil of barbed wire. "You had it comin' for holdin' him."

At her command, Flood got on his dun horse while she mounted her own animal, a fidgety little bay. She led him through the brush to a small house two hundred yards off. He noticed that it was only a few feet from a narrow, shallow river.

A hundred yards upstream was a larger building, probably the men's bunkhouse.

"You see how we can get cattle into the brush and still keep them under control." Zell pointed out. "We drive them up the river from the north side. We can keep them here till we get enough, then push them on down to where the brush thins out and cut straight across to the Rio Grande. We've got guards posted in the best places. No one has ever trailed us up the river and lived to tell about it."

She led him into her small, unpainted shack. He noticed that it had only one room and a lean-to.

"This used to be my old man's, Zeb Holliday. Cartwright and some of his bunch caught him and his boys and hung them ten years ago."

Her voice was hard. "Ben Thorn and I came back and took it over again four or five years later."

She had Flood lie down on her bed. She brought a dingy white rag and a pan of water. Excitement tingled through Flood as she sat close beside him, carefully wiping the dried blood off his face. He thrilled to the nearness of her.

Zell smiled as she became conscious of his interest. Flood looked hungrily at her full, red lips. He caught her shoulders, pulled her down to him, and kissed her. A hot flame burned through him.

She stood up and smiled down at him. "That was a little sudden."

"I work sudden," he replied.

Laughter danced in her eyes. "And I like it that way. We ought to get along well together."

Later in the day she explained her plans for him. He was to go on to the Cartwright place and take that job.

"Cartwright and the other ranchers are brewin' up trouble," she told him. "Every time they've tried to move cattle to market, we've hit them and taken most of the stock. They've quit tryin'. But they're hirin' gunhands now, like you. It looks like they're up to somethin'. We'll depend on you to find out what."

The hard glint came back into her steel-blue eyes, and it disturbed Flood a little.

"My old man once ruled all that country they're ranchin' on. He made it a refuge for anybody who was on the dodge and needed help. He's dead now. The ranchers killed him. But the day's comin' when I'll take all that land back."

She looked eagerly at Flood. "You'll be one of the most important men in the deal, Tom Flood. You'll be there with them. You can slip out now and again and let us know what they aim to do. Then we'll be ready to stop them."

She leaned over and kissed him again, warmly. He couldn't have refused the job then if he had wanted to.

A shout went up outside. Zell jerked upright in alarm. She ran to the door and peered out. "They got Cartwright!" she exclaimed. She jumped over the one saggy step in front of the door and scurried away.

Flood moved weakly to the door. He saw Drummond pull a slightly hunched, gray-haired man out of his saddle. The old man flopped to the ground in front of the outlaw bunkhouse. Drummond viciously kicked him in the stomach.

Anger roared through Flood as he watched Drummond's cruelty. His body still aching, he moved out and walked quickly to where more than half a dozen outlaws were grouped around the fallen man.

"Pete caught him ridin' up the river, Zell," Drummond was saying. "There ain't much life left in the old devil. Pete put three bullets in him."

Flood choked down a curse as he noted that the bullets had hit Cartwright in the back. The old man's face was ashen, and his eyes were glazed.

Zell looked down at the old man, her cheeks scarlet with hatred. "You thought that by hirin' gunmen you could push us out of the brush, Cartwright. But all I've got to do is send out

word, and inside of a day I can have two dozen good fightin'
men here to help me.

"We've got you now, Cartwright, and we'll get the others.
The day's comin' when all your land will be mine, like it used
to be my old man's. Your beef will carry my brand, and I'll be
livin' in that ranch house. Maybe I'll even have that school-
raised daughter of yours scrubbin floors for me, and cleanin'
out spitoons for my men.

"Yes, that'll all be mine, Cartwright. Zell Thorn's!"

She had had her say. The darkness slowly drained out of her
face. She turned to Drummond. "When he's finished, tie him
across his horse and leave him so the horse'll take him home.
That'll serve warnin' to the rest of them."

She turned and walked back toward her house. Drummond
grinned and pulled out his gun. "I been hopin' I'd git to do
this."

White heat burned in Flood and made him pull out his own
.45. "You're not shootin' him, Drummond!"

The outlaw scowled, his face reddening. "I been with this
outfit too long to take orders from you, Flood."

Flood's hand tightened on his gun butt. "If you think you
can pull a trigger faster than I can, then go ahead and try!"

Drummond stood there glaring at him, his gun leveled on
Flood's chest. His hot eyes raked to the ex-lawman's gun, then
back to his face. Finally the outlaw shrugged and slipped his
.45 back into its holster.

"The old man's done for anyhow," he growled. He turned and
stalked away. But Flood didn't miss the red color on the back
of the outlaw's neck.

He sensed that the old man was going limp. Quickly he knelt
down and felt the weak pulse beat. In a few moments it stopped.
Cartwright was dead. Flood tried to keep from feeling sorry,
but he couldn't. No matter which side he was on, three bullets
in the back was no way for an old warrior to die.

Flood noticed that Zell was watching him from her door. He

arose and walked to her. He sensed displeasure in the way she looked at him.

"Protectin' old man Cartwright won't make you set too well with the boys," she warned him. "And you better be careful about turnin' your back on Drummond."

Two days in and around the outlaw camp gave him time to familiarize himself with the way the Thorn band operated and to study the routes used in moving stolen cattle. When he set out for the Cartwright ranch the third morning, Zell rode with him to where the brush thinned out on the edge of Cartwright range. Her skittish bay shied at every jackrabbit which popped up out of the grass, and every bird which fluttered out of the brush.

"That horse'll booger and run away with you someday just when you need him worst," Flood admonished her with concern.

She laughed. "I like my horses the same way I like my men—with plenty of spirit."

She reined up, and Flood stopped his horse alongside her. "I like you, Flood," she said. "We can do great things together, after we win back all this land."

She gave him a fiery parting kiss, one that made sure he would be coming back for more.

It was a three-hour ride at an even pace to the Cartwright ranch. Flood noted that there seemed to be no cattle between the ranch and the thick brush. C Bar hands probably kept them turned back as a precaution against the Thorn band. Cartwright had been like a man who had built his house on the edge of a cliff, then watched helplessly while the ground beneath began to slough off.

The Cartwright place unfolded ahead of him as he spurred the dun up onto a rise. It consisted mostly of frame buildings, badly in need of paint. They were spread far apart, as Cartwright had had the whole world to build in. To the north of them was a big set of mesquite-limb pole corrals. Dust rose in a swirling cloud as cowhands busily worked cattle.

Flood sloped down off the rise and trotted on into the ranch. A couple or three gunhands lounged in the shade. Apparently they didn't have to help with cow work if they didn't want to. Most gunmen wouldn't want to. Flood picked out the best-kept of the buildings.

This was probably where Cartwright had lived. He heard the sound of a scuffle from inside the house. A girl was crying for someone to let go of her. Anger rose in Flood. Just like some gunhands to molest a woman! He quickly stepped up onto the sagging porch and in through the door. There he saw a slip of a girl fighting a man who was trying to crush her to him.

"Aw, just one kiss," the man was saying. He was obviously drunk. "If I'm gonna' fight and die for this outfit, I at least want to get somethin' worthwhile."

Flood strode forward and grabbed the gunman's shoulder. He pulled him away from the girl and hit him hard. In an instant the girl had grabbed a gun from a holster which hung on the wall. It was the first thing the drunken man saw when he rose off the floor and shook his head clear.

"Now get out!" the girl ordered him sharply. "If we didn't need fighters so badly, I'd run you off the place. You'd better not let my brother hear about this, either. He'd kill you!"

The gunman stood up shakily, glaring at Flood. His eyes suddenly opened wide then as he found that a bottle in his hip pocket had been broken by the fall. He wiggled his foot as if whiskey was trickling down his boot. The crestfallen gunman stifled an oath and shakily hurried out.

The girl turned gratefully to Flood. "Thanks for coming in when you did. Most of the men are out working stock."

Flood felt a warm glow within him as he looked down at her smile. She wasn't so strikingly beautiful as Zell, he thought, but her smile seemed to have something the outlaw queen lacked. Her brown hair, ruffled by the struggle, was still as smooth-looking as silk. And although she was smaller than Zell, her ankle-length cotton dress revealed a fair share of soft curves.

"You aren't one of the new hands, are you?" she queried.

"Not yet," Flood answered. He pulled out the letter and handed it to her. She glanced at it briefly. Sadness crept over her pretty face.

"Dad's gone now," she said quietly, "but my brother and I are keeping the offer just like it says here."

Flood knew it was best to play dumb. "Your father—is dead?"

Her eyes were somber. "We buried him yesterday. That's why we're more anxious than ever to have all the gunhands we can find. We're going to fight the thieves that killed him."

A slow fire burned in her eyes as she looked at Flood. "Every rancher in this country has been rounding up selling stock to drive to market. Always before we've each tried to take them out alone, and the outlaws have grabbed most of them away from us.

"This time we're going out together, and we're hiring all the guns we can get. A lot of the money we get for the cattle will go into hiring more good guns. Then we'll do what the law has never been able to do—push through the brush country and wipe out every outlaw that's in it. That means Zell Thorn and every man in her gang!"

A cold tightness was in Flood's chest as he watched the angry red color in the girl's cheeks. She had plenty of spunk, he knew. Somehow he already regretted that when the showdown came, he would be fighting against her.

Heavy boots clumped on the small porch, and a big man stalked into the house. He was about the same age as Flood. His face was rugged and tanned from years in the outdoors, but his brown eyes were just like the girl's.

"I seen one of them new gunhands weavin' across the yard," he said in a heavy voice. "He wasn't in here, was he, Sis?"

Flood saw a hint of alarm in the girl's eyes. "Why . . . why no, he wasn't in here," she lied quickly.

The big man's face showed relief. "That's good. You can't

hardly trust some of these gun-toters when there's a woman around."

He turned suspiciously to Flood. "Who are you?"

Flood handed him the letter. "Name's Tom Flood. Your dad sent for me."

Cartwright grunted, his eyes narrowed in suspicion. "I thought I seen somebody ridin' in over the hill. How come you be ridin' from that direction? Did you come through the brush?"

Flood nodded. "I figgered I'd save time by cuttin' through it instead of ridin' around it," he answered flatly. He could tell that Cartwright didn't believe him.

"Did you see anybody?" the ranchman pressed.

"Nope." Uneasiness took hold of Flood as Cartwright stealthily eased his hand down toward his gun.

"Where'd you git the bruises on your face?" Cartwright kept on.

The man had seen the marks left by Drummond's fists, Flood realized with a start. He'd have to lie out of this one, quick. "My horse boogered and ran off with me. We hit some low limbs."

The girl stepped forward, frowning indignantly at her brother. "Cut it out, Bryan! He's here to help us. Don't treat him like an outlaw."

Bryan Cartwright scowled. "Why not? I remember hearin' about Tom Flood, the sheriff of Grama Flat. And I know he's lyin' about that runaway. If brush had left them bruises there'd have been some thorn scratches too!"

Alarm began taking an upper hand in Flood now. He had made a bad lie of that one.

The girl argued insistently. "You're acting like a kid, Bryan. You couldn't hope to hire a better man than someone who has been a lawman."

Cartwright's face was dark. "They kicked him out of office,

Betty. And you know as well as I do that the meanest horses are them that's been gentle once but turned outlaw for one reason or another."

His eyes were hot with suspicion. "All right, Flood, you can stay on, but I'll be watchin' you. Don't forget it!"

When Bryan had stalked out, Betty Cartwright looked reassuringly at Flood. "Bryan's always worked hard for anything he ever owned," she said. "He can't like people who have lived any other way. He can't trust gunmen because he's always afraid they'll try to take what he's sweated so long to earn. Because of Dad, and because of your coming in through the brush, he seems especially uneasy about you."

She smiled a little, and the chill began to leave Flood's heart. "Thanks again for helping me," she said softly. "I'll be seeing you again soon."

If Flood hadn't already met Zell, he would probably find himself falling in love with Betty Cartwright, he thought as he stepped off the porch and swung into the saddle.

The rest of the day he helped other ranch hands sort cattle in the pole corrals. Steers, unwanted heifers, and cull cattle were being cut out for market. Flood learned that within the next few days all the neighboring ranchmen were to combine their herds and push north in force.

Zell would be grateful for that information, he knew.

Late in the day Betty Cartwright came out to the corrals to watch. Flood couldn't keep from looking at her every chance he got. Once, when she caught his gaze, she smiled. Flood reproved himself. Zell was his woman, not this Cartwright girl. But he still couldn't keep from looking at her.

Next day most of the C Bar crew went out to help a neighbor. Flood begged off, telling Bryan Cartwright that he wanted to scout over the country, to get acquainted with it. If there was to be a fight on it, he explained smoothly, he wanted to know how the land lay.

Cartwright was plainly suspicious, but he agreed to let Flood go.

The ex-lawman headed north, looking at the trail over which the big herd would likely be moved. The trail grew rocky and hilly a few miles from the ranch. Finally Flood rode upon a valley which was the only convenient pass through a long line of small mountains. It was nearly a half mile through the valley to the flat land beyond—a half mile in which gunmen on the sides of the mountain could snipe at leisure at cowboys driving the herd.

Or, he noted, a band of riders coming through the end of the pass at the right moment could suddenly stampede a herd back toward its drivers and keep the cowboys so busy running that they couldn't fight.

Satisfied, Flood cut back southeast, toward the brush. There was much that Zell should know.

Half a mile deep in the thicket he found the river and followed it on toward Zell's hideout. Sentries stopped him three times before he finally reached the outlaws' bunkhouse and dismounted. Two men sat in the shade, their backs to him. They hadn't seen Flood ride up.

"Drummond ain't spent so much time over at Zell's house since that feller Flood come along," one snickered. "It ain't helpin' his temper none, neither."

Angrily Flood stepped up behind the speaker, put his booted foot in the man's back, and shoved the outlaw face down into the dirt.

"Next time I hear somethin' like that about Zell I'll do worse," he fumed.

Walking on toward Zell's, he reflected sourly that the man had probably been speaking the truth. A pretty woman like Zell, alone among all these rough men, was bound to get plenty of attention. And, he knew, Drummond probably didn't look so bad to a lonely woman.

Jealousy burned within him. He kicked furiously at a rusty

can which lay in the sun. It wouldn't happen again, he vowed. When this was all over he'd take Zell out of this brush country to where she could live like a human. She would be his.

He hesitated as he approached Zell's house. He saw her and Drummond talking to a gaudily-dressed Mexican, who stood leaning back against a heavy-trunked mesquite, thumbs hooked in his gun belt.

"Come on, Tom," Zell called. "I want you to meet Don Diego Fernandez. He buys a lot of our cattle when we get them across the Rio Grande."

Drummond's eyes were sullen as he saw Flood.

Flood disregarded them and shook hands with the swarthy Fernandez. He couldn't help glancing at the Mexican's shiny six-guns. The pearl handles were worn smooth by much handling, but not smooth enough to hide half a dozen notches.

Fernandez nodded at a young Mexican boy who stood timidly by their two horses. "My brother Renaldo and I, we have come with some good news for you," the older Mexican spoke in a heavy accent.

Flood studied the youngster. Not over eighteen, he figured. About like the boy in Grama Flat, the boy the mob had hanged. The brown-skinned lad nervously fingered his saddle, pulling on the leather strings, running his hand over the big Mexican horn.

"I have found a market for many cattle," Fernandez was saying. "A man named Moreno, he ees getting ready to start a revolution down een Chihuahua. He wants many cattle to feed hees men. He has much gold."

The man's dirty-brown eyes shifted constantly from Zell to Drummond to Flood and back to Zell. He grinned greedily. "He weel surely die with hees back to a wall, like all the others who try to overthrow Porfirio Diaz. But hees gold is good. We should get eet before the federales do."

Flood spoke up. "The ranchers are gettin' ready to push their cattle out in one herd. I hear there'll be over three thousand head. What'll Moreno pay?"

Fernandez spoke smoothly. "Oh, he weel buy them from me. When you get the cattle you weel sell them to me and help my men drive them to Moreno. Then I weel sell them to Moreno at a slight profit, a leetle something to pay me for my reesk."

Zell's eyes narrowed. "I suppose you've brought somethin' to pay us in advance."

Alarm showed in the Mexican's eyes a brief instant. Then he grinned shallowly. "Why, yes, I have brought a leetle gold. Eeet weel show that my heart is een the right place."

He reached into the saddlebag and pulled out a couple of small leather sacks. He pitched one to Zell. She untied the string and glanced inside, then she looked up at Fernandez with eyes as sharp as knife points.

"How about the other sack?"

Fernandez licked his lips and held the gold sack to him. "But theees ees for another purpose, senora."

She held out her hand. "The other sack, Fernandez!"

Raw hatred looked out of his dark eyes. He pitched the sack to her.

"What makes you think we'd take the biggest risks and then cut you in for maybe half the gold, Fernandez?" she asked, grinning without humor. "Now that we know who's to buy the cattle, what makes you think we can't find Moreno as easy as you can?"

The Mexican was suddenly like a cornered cat. His muddy eyes darted back and forth over the three, then stopped on Zell.

"Eet ees easy to see why you lead thees pack of dogs, senora," Fernandez seethed. His brown hands eased back toward his guns. "You are a she-wolf. But wolves must die!"

The Mexican's hands blurred as they grabbed at the pearl-handled guns. Flood's chest was ready to burst from tension. Zell wasn't packing a gun!

Flood's own hand dipped downward and came up with a blazing gun. Fernandez jerked back, his sombrero falling off his head. He groaned and dropped his guns. Then he was lying face down in the sand.

The boy Renaldo stared in terror, his face two shades whiter. He rammed his foot into a stirrup and started to swing into the saddle. Before Flood could move, Drummond had pulled his own gun and was pumping bullets into the boy's back. The horse wheeled in terror. Young Fernandez dropped to the ground, rolled over, and lay still.

There was a taste like ashes in Flood's mouth as he looked wide-eyed at the dead youngster. He whirled furiously on Drummond.

"You didn't have to do that! The boy wasn't even carryin' a gun!"

Drummond scowled darkly and spat on the ground. "Bear cubs grow into big bears."

Flood felt Zell's hand resting lightly on his shoulder. "Don't worry about it, Tom. That's just what they'd have done to us when they got us and our cattle down in Chihuahua. Fernandez has had his eye on our setup here quite a while. Besides, nobody'll ever be askin' about those two. They just came too far north of the border."

He looked down at her inviting red lips and at her shapely body. She was trying to smile at him, but it wasn't the genuine kind of smile Betty Cartwright had given him. He kept seeing the Fernandez boy shot down without a chance for life. It made him remember Grama Flat.

"We'll take the cattle to Moreno ourselves," she told him soothingly in her shack. "We'll take all that gold, and we won't split it with anybody. We'll use it to build a cattle empire those ranchers never dreamed about. It'll be ours, Tom, yours and mine!"

She pulled him to her and kissed him fervently, as she had done before. But Flood couldn't thrill this time as he had at first. He was still tasting blood and smelling the acrid tang of gunsmoke.

Flood saw a lot of Betty Cartwright the next few days. She seemed to be arranging it that way. She rode circle like any cow-

boy, helping round up cattle for the drive. Somehow she usually managed to ride close to Flood. The more he saw of her,
sitting straight as a ruler on her sidesaddle, the more he began
to compare her with Zell. In most ways the comparison was
favorable.

One night as he was bending over a battered tin pan, washing up after supper, she came up to him and suggested: "Let's
walk out toward the corrals, Tom. I'd like to talk to you."

He quickly dried his face and put on his hat. He wondered
why he felt so at ease walking beside the girl in the twilight.
He had always been a little nervous, a little strained, when he
was near Zell. Maybe it was like having a good everyday cow
horse and a pretty, high-strung stallion, he thought. The stallion is showy and fun to ride to town on Saturdays. But if the
chips were down, any cowboy would choose his plain old cow
horse for keeps.

"By this time tomorrow we'll be started on our way to market," she said pleasantly as they walked out of earshot of the
house.

"We?" Flood repeated incredulously. "But you're not goin'.
It's liable to be dangerous."

She held her head up proudly. "Zell Thorn will be riding with
her men," she declared. "Besides, a good part of the cattle belong to me. Why shouldn't I go?"

The thought of Betty in the midst of hot gunfire disturbed
Flood deeply. He tried hard to think of some argument which
would keep her at home. Suddenly Betty stopped and turned
to face him.

"You don't seem like a real gunman to me, Tom," she said
quietly. "Maybe you're just bitter and you've convinced yourself
that that's the kind of life you want. But I can tell it isn't."

An uneasiness played through him. Yes, he told himself silently, he had considered it his life the past three years. His guns
for hire—no question asked, except "How much will you pay?"

But the memory of young Fernandez had stuck with him like

a bitter pill the past few days. He had been wondering if that was the kind of life he would continue to lead when this was all over, and he had Zell for his own.

"Tom," Betty said eagerly, almost pleading with him, "when this drive is over, and when the outlaws have been pushed out of the brush country, why don't you stay on here with us? It would be a simple life—no riots, no brawls, no gunfights. But I'm sure you'd like it. I want to help make you like it."

She was close to him now. Her face was beautiful there in the twilight as it turned up beseechingly to his. Her lips were parted a little.

Before he could stop himself, Flood had pulled her to him and was kissing her. It wasn't a fiery kiss like Zell's, but it was deeper, more genuine.

Immediately he was sorry he had done it. He had already made a deal with Zell Thorn.

"You see, Tom," Betty was saying earnestly, "that's what life really should be—a home of your own; someone to come home to after you've done your day's work. Someone to talk to, someone to love, someone to share your life with."

Flood wavered uncertainly. This had gone too far. He wanted to take her in his arms again. But he knew if he did, he could never go back to Zell.

"Come on, Betty," he said curtly. "This is all wrong. We better go back to the house."

There was heartbreak in the girl's eyes a moment. She followed him silently, looking at the ground and biting her lip. When she got home she stepped up onto the porch and ran to the house without looking back.

Flood's heart ached. He cursed himself silently as he headed for the bunkhouse. Somehow he wished he'd never seen the brush country. He wished he had never met Zell Thorn. Bryan Cartwright suddenly stepped out from behind a shed and planted himself squarely in front of Flood.

"I saw you go out walkin' with my sister, Flood," he said

grimly. "I want you to stay away from her, understand? She's too good for any two-bit gun-toter. Especially a renegade lawman!"

Anger mounted quickly in Flood. "Out of my way, Cartwright!"

Cartwright didn't budge. "We're startin' the drive in the mornin'. When it's over I don't want you to come back. If you do, I'll kill you!"

Bryan Cartwright stood there a moment, hand on his gun butt to give his words emphasis. Then he strode past Flood and headed for his house.

Fury boiled in Flood's veins as he turned and watched the man. He could have gunned him down right there. But Bryan was Betty's brother.

In the morning, Cartwright had said. Neighbors' herds had poured into C Bar range for two days now, and they were all being loose-herded a mile north of the ranch. The starting time had been kept quiet. Flood knew he would have to get to Zell's place tonight if the band was to strike the herd before it reached the flat, open country to the north.

The cowhands went to bed early. By ten o'clock Flood was sure they were all asleep. Stealthily he crawled out of his bunk, put on his clothes, and slipped out to the barn. He quietly caught one of the night horses, saddled him, and headed him for the brush country—slowly at first, to avoid waking anyone.

Once he thought he heard someone behind him, and he reined up a moment. There might have been the scuff of a hoof, he wasn't sure. He eased into a slow lope awhile, then stopped again. He heard nothing.

Going was slower as he eased through the brush to the river. There he kept his horse in a steady trot at the edge of the water. As he neared the hideout a coyote howl rose from the brush behind him. But he knew it hadn't been made by a coyote.

Zell, Drummond, and a couple of outlaws were waiting for him under the starlight as he rode into camp. Flood quickly told them about the drive beginning in the morning.

Zell was overjoyed. "Moreno's gold is about to be ours," she exulted. "Drummond, send out men to the other camps. Get all the boys rounded up here. We'll be ready to ride by daylight."

She turned to Flood, grinning with delight. "This is it, what we've been waitin' for. By this time tomorrow I'll own this country, all of it. Those ranchers, what's left of them, will be draggin' it back to where they come from."

She kissed Flood, but he felt no warmth. Shame crept through him like muddy water entering a clean pool. He felt unclean, as if he had rolled in a hog wallow and hadn't taken a bath. He tried to grin with Zell, but he felt as if a part of him were dying—the decent part, or what little was left of it.

"I better get back before they miss me," Flood told Zell dully.

"All right, Tom," she answered, gripping his arms tightly, her face glowing in triumph. "But watch out for yourself when you get to Rock Pass tomorrow. Pull out when the shootin' starts."

Flood tried to kiss her, but it was only a cold peck he gave her. Then he turned back toward his horse.

As he started to mount, Drummond stepped grimly out of the shadows.

"Just a minute, Flood," the deep voice muttered. "I been wantin' to settle somethin' with you. I was the boss around here, next to Zell, for a long time, and I'm gonna' keep on bein' the boss. I was doin' all right with Zell till you come along."

Drummond was close enough that Flood could smell whiskey on the man's hot breath.

"Maybe if I beat your face to a pulp, she'll still think I'm the best man," Drummond snarled.

He swung viciously. Flood ducked and hammered a fist into Drummond's bristled chin. He tried for the outlaw's stomach, but his wrist struck Drummond's arm as the big man lifted it for protection. Sharp pain throbbed through Flood's arm. Drummond's fist sliced against his ribs, and Flood lost part of his breath. Flood drove at Drummond's face again. The big man snapped back as the blow struck. Flood pounded at the outlaw's stomach.

Then the two were swapping vicious blows, pounding, grunting, jarring each other. Flood tasted the sharp tang of blood. His aching head was swimming as he hammered at Drummond's cursing, groaning face and the flabby stomach.

Finally Drummond began to weaken. His fists carried little strength. Flood's breath came short as he drove the finishing blows into the big man's body.

Then Drummond was lying facedown in the sand, struggling vainly to get onto his knees. Flood swayed over him. His bruised fists throbbed in pain and his head ached. He sensed Zell standing beside him, turned and stared at her dully.

She was laughing—laughing at him—Flood realized.

"Fightin' over me," she chuckled, "I'm flattered. Fightin' over me."

For an angry moment Flood wanted to slap her. He fought to get his breath back and tried to figure what to do.

"Glad you enjoyed the fight," he muttered bitterly, then picked up his hat, mounted, and headed back toward the Bar C.

Remorse ate relentlessly at him as he rode. How had he ever let himself get to the point where a woman could twist him around her finger and laugh at him like she would some kid? Zell hadn't been concerned over whether or not the fight had hurt him. She had just enjoyed the show.

The night wind cut at his bruised face and made it burn. He found himself thinking of Betty Cartwright. He wished he could go to her now. Maybe she could ease the pain. Maybe she could help straighten out the confusion that muddled him.

He thought of Zell in the ranch house where Betty now lived. The idea made him clinch his skinned fists in anger. Maybe he had been on the wrong side of this fight from the beginning. The thought wasn't a new one, exactly, but one that he hadn't allowed to come out into the open.

Jogging painfully over the last mile to the Cartwright

headquarters, he mulled it over. It wasn't too late yet. He could still warn the ranchers about the attack that was coming. He could thwart Zell's plan of conquest. Yes, that was the only thing to do.

He slowed the horse to a walk as he rode up to the corral. Inside the open gate he started to swing down from the saddle. Suddenly his heart was pumping desperately, and cold sweat popped out on his hands. A dozen men stepped out of the shadows of the barns and strode grimly toward him. Bryan Cartwright was in the lead.

Flood licked his dry lips and tried to speak. Then he saw Betty coming toward him, along with the men. Hatred and contempt twisted her pretty face. "Traitor!" she breathed in scorn. "Traitor!"

A dozen explanations were in Flood's mind, but all stuck in his throat.

"I was afraid you might pull somethin' like this, Flood." Bryan Cartwright gritted angrily. "I sat up and waited. I saw you slip out of the bunkhouse and saddle up. I trailed you as far as the brush, then lost you. But that was far enough so I know what you were up to."

Someone shouted, "Let's hang him and git it over with!"

Cartwright continued: "We're movin' the herd out now, to maybe git ahead of your outlaw friends. But even if they hit us, we'll have the satisfaction of knowin' you got what was comin' to you."

Dread was like a burning poison creeping through Flood, dulling his nerves, slowing his senses. Desperately he looked at Betty, who stood almost at his stirrup.

"Betty, I've got to tell you . . ."

She didn't give him time to finish. "Bryan was right," she said bitterly, with tears in her eyes. "The only thing to do with a sheep-killing dog is shoot him. And the only thing to do with a renegade lawman is to kill him, too!"

"Let's git him, Cartwright!" someone shouted. "We got a wagon tongue ready, and a rope!"

Flood's horse, sensing the tension, was nervously backing up in slow, short steps. Even with the open gate, Flood suddenly dropped down in the saddle and spurred for the shadow of a barn. Gunshots cracked behind him, and angry shouts cut through the night. Lead whined around him. A couple of bullets burned him as they zipped by.

Bending low over the horn, Flood spurred hard toward the brush. Hooves drummed behind him as some of the men caught up horses and came after him. He cut the horse back to the right, into the dark shadows of a line of catclaw. He reined up a moment, hoping the riders hadn't seen him.

They swept on by, spurring and whipping for more speed. Flood pulled the mount around and swung into an easy lope at a tangent to the right. After a mile or so he was sure he had shaken off pursuit. He cut back toward the thick brush, still in an easy lope.

His thoughts were bitter as he pushed back toward the outlaw hideout. Betty and the ranchers hadn't given him a chance to explain. Maybe they had figured he didn't deserve one. And maybe he didn't, Flood thought.

He found himself wondering why he was going back to Zell. The best thing he could do would be to leave the country, to forget both Zell and Betty Cartwright. But Zell had said she loved him. She had kissed him as if she meant it. Maybe that was why he was going back, to see if it was true.

He ran onto no guards and heard no signals as he splashed through the river, nearing the hideout. They must be all gathered at Zell's, he figured. A glance at the outfit proved he was right. There must have been two dozen men at the bunkhouse, or out in the hidden pole corral, catching up fresh horses.

Flood rode straight to the corral and caught a new horse to replace his tiring one. Then he trotted back to Zell's. Drummond and half a dozen other outlaws were gathered with her in front of her shack, facing the orange—streaked eastern sky.

"What's the matter, Tom?" she frowned, twisting a quirt she

held in her hand. "I thought you'd be out with the ranchers and their herd."

He quickly told her what had happened.

She glared angrily at him. "Now you've fixed things up proper," she cut at him. "They'll know we're gettin' ready to take them. We can't count on them gettin' careless now."

Flood stepped back in surprise. She had never shown anger at him before. She should have been able to see the blood on his sleeve, where one bullet had creased him. But she hadn't asked him about that. She was worried only about hitting the herd.

She turned to Drummond. "We'll get our men lined up on the hills on each side of Rock Pass before the herd gets there. When the cattle get even with us, we'll open up on the riders. We'll have a few men come through the mouth of the pass and stampede the herd back toward the drivers. They won't be able to give us much fight then."

Zell's eyes were like gun steel as she spoke. They gleamed with a lust for blood. "We'll shoot everybody who's with that herd. We won't let a one of them get away. We'll spill so much blood that an army wouldn't dare touch us from now on. Then this country'll be mine, lock, stock, and barrel!"

There was ice in Flood's veins as he stared incredulously at her. She wasn't a pretty young woman now. She was a wolf, a she-wolf, getting set to pounce on her prey.

Flood's nerves were tingling as he saw what he had to do. He glanced backward to make sure there were no outlaws behind him.

"That Cartwright girl'll be with the herd, Zell," he said. "You're not goin' to kill her."

Anger flared again in the woman's eyes. Her knuckles were white on the quirt handle. "Why not? I'd just as soon kill her as anybody else that's with that herd!"

Flood's eyes darted over the outlaws who stood with Zell.

They were all watching him now, watching him like hawks about to drop into a chicken yard.

"I'm not goin' to let you do it, Zell." Flood spoke flatly.

The woman's face was scarlet. She brought up the quirt and slashed it savagely across Flood's face.

Blinding anger choked him as he rubbed the back of his hand across the burning mark and saw the blood.

"You don't love me," he accused. His voice had an edge like a razor. "You never did love me. You just acted like you did so you could use me. When you got tired of playin', you'd have gotten rid of me."

A staggering thought blazed through him then. "I'll bet that's just what happened to Ben Thorn," he said, his eyes narrowed to little more than slits. "You married him to help you get a new foothold in this country. When you were through you found a way to get rid of him."

Hatred smoldered in Zell's eyes. "That's exactly what happened," she gloated. "I had him get us back into this country and work out this organization. We pulled off some good jobs, too. But he started gettin' scared, and he started makin' mistakes. There wasn't room for any mistakes here. So when he went to pull off that bank robbery at Boom City, I made sure the law heard about it. Then I ruled the brush country!"

Flood shuddered. The eyes he had thought pretty glowed like coals now. The mouth which had once set him afire with its kisses was like that of a wolf, with fangs bared. Touching her smooth skin now would have chilled him like touching a rattlesnake.

Revulsion shook Flood, sickening him as he stared at the woman. It was as if he were watching her pretty body and her lovely face decay before his eyes.

Suddenly he realized that he had his gun in his hand. "You're not a woman," he gritted. "You're a black widow spider! I ought to kill you where you stand!"

She snickered at him, laughing in derision. "You ought to, but you can't. You've got too much honor to shoot a woman."

Flood tried to make himself pull the trigger.

"Go on," she taunted. "Pull it! If you don't kill me, I'll kill you!"

Flood knew he could never do it. Gun trained on Zell and the outlaws, he backed toward his horse, stepped into the saddle, and spurred away. Instantly flames licked at him from half a dozen guns.

Flood triggered a couple of shots back at the group. He saw a rider cutting through the brush to head him off. Twenty feet from the man he swung his gun around and squeezed the trigger. The rider leaned back and toppled from the saddle.

Brush popped from three or four points behind Flood. Zell's men were after him. Mesquite branches slapped at him. Thorns clutched at him, ripping his vest and shirt, and burned him like fire. He cut back toward the river, hoping to make better time. Three riders were just behind him as he rode into the edge of the water; their guns spurted flame. Flood aimed and fired once. A rider spun in his saddle. The others reined up to help the wounded outlaw. One of them lifted his gun again.

Flood felt a sledgehammer blow against his ribs. For a second it was as if someone had jammed a hot coal against him. He grabbed at the saddle horn and held tightly as he spurred the horse. Thorns pierced his skin like needles. After minutes of hard riding, he reined up and listened for hoofbeats or popping brush. He heard nothing.

Zell was giving up the chase and getting ready for the raid on the herd, he figured.

Dark fury enveloped him as he thought about her. She had vamped him like she had probably vamped Ben Thorn. But he had been luckier than Thorn. He had found out just in time.

There was no longer any doubt in him as to which side he was on. He had to find a way to defeat Zell's band.

Trying to ignore the pain which wracked him, Flood cut

straight through the brush toward Rock Pass. Within two hours he was in open country, pushing the horse as fast as he dared. One thing was in his favor, he knew. The cattle would be at the pass sooner than Zell expected. The ranchers had pushed their cattle off a couple of hours earlier than planned when they had found out about Flood's duplicity. Flood had not gotten a chance to tell Zell about that.

His side hammered and ached as he swung along in a lope. A few times he had to hang desperately to the horn as moments of weakness overtook him and threatened to drag him from the saddle. But somehow he stuck. And eventually he sighted the ridge of hills that bordered the pass.

He swung around the hills to enter the pass from the far end, where the cattle would come out. Pausing and looking back, he saw a thin line of dust. Zell and the outlaws, coming from the brush!

Flood spurred through the mouth of the pass, which was not a hundred yards wide. Big clouds of dust rose before him, dust stirred up by thousands of hoofs. The point of the herd was not more than three hundred yards back. He squinted and saw Betty and Bryan Cartwright a hundred yards back of the point man, on the right side of the herd.

He kicked the horse and galloped toward them. They saw him and spurred out to meet him.

Bryan's gun was out as the three reined up and faced each other in a swirl of dust "You sure want to die, Flood," Cartwright growled. Flood glanced into Betty's eyes. His heart sank a little as he saw the hatred still burning there.

"I haven't got time to argue," he said quickly. "Zell Thorn and her bunch are comin'. They can't be more than a half mile from the mouth of the pass!"

Bryan Cartwright scowled. "Do you think we'd ever listen to you again? If it weren't for Betty I'd gun you down right here. I'm countin' to five. If you're still in range then, I'll start shootin'."

Flood's lips parted in another protest, but it died in his throat.

He turned and spurred back toward the mouth of the pass. He heard Cartwright yell for his men to look sharp. The only way Flood could warn the ranchers now was to show them what was coming. But it might be too late then.

He reined up in the mouth of the pass and cautiously peered out. Zell and her men were less than two hundred yards away now, spread out in a long line.

His gun against those of eighteen or twenty outlaws! He knew he wouldn't have a chance. But he pulled the gun and checked it. At least this would let Betty and the others know he was telling the truth. He swung the gun up and fired at the oncoming band. He heard the outlaws shout and saw bullets kick up sand at his horse's hooves like raindrops in a tank of water. Something tugged at his sleeve and burned his arm like a hot poker. He fired a couple more shots, then retreated into the pass.

A glance at the herd showed that the drivers were alerted now. Half a dozen men were riding forward to help him.

Suddenly the outlaws poured into the pass. They reined up in surprise as they saw the herd so near, and saw the cowboys coming out toward them. Flood sent a couple more bullets after the outlaws and saw one man drop to the ground.

Lead hailed around him now. He saw Zell Thorn firing at him, her face twisted with hatred. Then the ground began to rumble. The outlaws quit shooting and gestured excitedly toward the herd.

Flood's heart was in his throat. The ranchers were stampeding the cattle toward the mouth of the pass. They were going to push the outlaws out of the way or trample them into the dust! Thousands of hoof beats joined in rolling thunder. Horns clattered as three thousand frightened cattle surged forward.

Zell and her men wheeled their horses and spurred desperately for the outside. Exhilaration raced through Flood. Zell would have little chance to take the herd once it got scattered out over the flat.

As the stampeding cattle neared him, Flood jabbed spurs into his horse's ribs and headed after the outlaws. Some of the ranchmen's cowboys and gunhands were close behind him.

Outside the mouth of the pass, he saw the outlaws were scattering out on the flat, scattering too widely to put up a good battle. Zell was in the path of the herd, fighting her excited horse and cursing her men, trying to get them organized.

Frightened cattle burst out of the pass now, and the outlaws were scattering even more. Dust pitched and rolled in thick clouds and blinded Flood a moment. The pounding wound in his side seemed to be on fire.

Then a big man loomed up out of the dust, his dark face a mask of fury. Drummond!

"Damn you, Flood, you caused this," he fumed. "But I'll git you!"

Flood ducked as flame leaped at him. He swung his gun up and pulled the trigger. It clicked. He heard Drummond laugh in triumph. But the man was suddenly blotted out by a billowing cloud of dust. Flood's lips went dry and his heart was hammering as he moved quickly to one side. He heard Drummond's gun bark futilely.

Flood thumbed one fresh shell into his gun. He didn't dare take time for more. He waited a moment, wondering where Drummond was. He half expected to feel a bullet smash into his back. Then, for an instant, he saw the man's snarling face as the dust thinned right ahead of him. Drummond saw him, too. Flood pulled the trigger a split second before Drummond's white-hot bullet thudded into his arm.

About to fall, Flood grabbed the saddle horn. The dust cleared a moment. He saw Drummond hit the ground on his shoulder and sprawl crookedly in the dirt.

The herd was thundering on by. He remembered seeing Zell in front of it, and he thought of her high-strung bay. Hanging onto the saddle horn, he spurred his mount and swung around the herd, riding for the lead. Here and there he could hear the

crackle of gunfire above the drumming of hooves. He saw cowboys chasing Zell's outlaws and surrounding them. But he
didn't see Zell.

He spurred on through the choking dust, slowly working his
way toward the front of the frenzied herd. Finally he was almost in the open. In front of him, only a couple of lengths ahead
of the running cattle, he saw Zell. She was fighting desperately
at her panicked horse, trying to move him out of the herd's way.

Zell was panicked too, now. She was pulling the pony too
hard. Flood tried to yell to her, to warn her. But in her fright
she jerked at the horse once too often. He stumbled and pitched
her headlong into the path of the cattle.

Zell's terrified scream tore at Flood like a buzz saw. He saw
her there a split second, struggling to get up. Then there was
nothing but the endless waves of running cattle, the tossing
horns, and the deafening thunder of trampling hooves.

Flood pulled his horse away from the herd, terribly sick at
his stomach. The dust was choking him. His wounded arm and
his side were pounding like hammers and burning as if the
devil's own fires were blazing within him.

He dismounted and shook his head, trying vainly to clear it.
It seemed to be spinning, and something was pulling him down,
down, down . . .

He awakened to find a soft hand gently cleansing the wound
on his side. Painfully he opened his eyes. Betty knelt over him,
smiling at him. He found his arm already bandaged. A soft
glow rose within him as he looked up at the girl.

"You were asleep a long time," she said softly.

He tried to grin. "Maybe I was pretty tired."

She put her warm hand on his cheek. "Well, you'll have a
long time to rest when we get you back to the ranch."

Bryan Cartwright strode up. "Wagon's comin'. We'll send
him back in it with the others who were wounded."

His eyes lighted up a little as he saw that Flood had come
to. "Looks like I kind of misjudged you, Flood," he said. "I

guess that even though they took that law badge off your vest, they couldn't take away the one you wore inside you."

He nervously squeezed one of his hands with the other until the knuckles popped. "If there's anything we can give you . . ."

Flood grinned and looked up at Betty. "All I want is a little time," he said. "I think nature will do the rest."

THE BELLS
OF SAN JUAN

It didn't look as if it would be a very happy Christmas for the homesteaders' church in the little town of Hopeful. For more than ten years the pealing of the church bell had brought the faithful to worship on Christmas morning. But this Christmas the bell wouldn't be ringing. It had cracked at Sunday services.

Ranchman Wes Ballard had heard about it, but he hadn't spent any time worrying over it. He had been just barely grown the last time he had set foot in the church. That had been for his father's funeral, ten years ago.

Now Wes frowned and buttoned his heavy coat against the chilly December air as he stood on the ranch's front gallery and watched an old wagon rattle up toward the house. He could recognize the Reverend Andrew McAdam on the driver's side of the seat. The Reverend's daughter sat next to him. Watching them, Wes remembered about the bell.

Wes's younger brother stepped out onto the gallery and looked up at the heavy, gray sky, then down at the approaching wagon.

"Got any notion what that nester sky pilot wants, coming out here on a day like this?"

"I've got an idea," Wes grunted. He felt his temper edge upward as he glanced at the boy and the misshapen cigarette that bent downward from his lips.

"Put that cigarette out before it chokes you to death! And how many times have I got to tell you to quit wearing that six-shooter? One of these days you'll kill somebody!"

Ken jabbed back at him, "You've always told me about how we're going to run the nesters back out of this country some-day. I'm just trying to keep myself in shape. But you're getting to be as much of an old maid lately as Henry Lee."

Wes snatched the cigarette out of Ken's mouth, dropped it and ground it under his heel. "Listen to Henry Lee and you're liable to learn something, Ken. Now you get out to the barn and help him fix his hackamores."

Ken stepped sullenly to the ground. "All right. But don't you let that plow-handle preacher put nothing over on you."

The wagon pulled up in front of the house. The north wind played through the manes of the old team. Tall Andrew Mc-Adam climbed stiffly down from the plank seat, then raised his powerful arms to help his daughter down. He strode up to the gallery steps, peeling off his heavy gloves and smiling genially.

"Evening, Brother Ballard," he said in his Tennessee twang.

McAdam didn't look the way Wes thought a minister was supposed to. But then, McAdam hadn't always been a preacher. He had farmed back in Tennessee for years before he had got-ten "the call." And even now he spent most of his weekdays doing farm labor for those of his flock who were sick, or who for some other reason were behind and needed help.

Wes hesitated a moment, then coolly shook the minister's leather-tough hand. He glanced down at the girl, who stood close behind her father, blowing on her fingers to get them warm. He had seen her around town occasionally.

They called her Ruth. If she had been a ranch girl, Wes would have thought her pretty.

"You didn't come all the way out here in the cold for any

social call," he said bluntly. "Whatever it is you want, we can talk about it better inside, by the fire."

In the big, high-ceilinged parlor the tall preacher looked up at a bell rope which hung down in the center of the room. Hesitantly he reached up and touched the rope, then dropped his arm.

"The bells of San Juan," he said reverently. "Folks tell me they haven't rung for ten years."

"That's right," Wes spoke quietly. "Not since Dad was buried."

Wes looked up at the rope, and for a long moment he fancied he could hear the bells toll again, as they had tolled so many times when he was a boy. He reached up and tenderly touched the rope, careful not to pull it. He let his mind drift back even beyond his own memory.

As a young man his father, John Ballard, had found the bells in the crumbled ruins of an old New Mexico mission called San Juan. Somewhere back in the past, two padres had built the adobe mission to bring the word of God to the Indians. Through the peaceful years they had converted hundreds of redmen.

Then a hostile red horde had swept down from the west. When it was gone the mission was in ruins, the padres dead. Many Christian Indians lay murdered. Others were carried off, never to return.

A reverent man, John Ballard hadn't liked the thought of the bells rusting away. He had loaded them into his wagon and taken them with him. When he later established his ranch, he'd named it San Juan. He'd built a little bell tower, on his house, and made his home a place of worship for other settlers any time a circuit rider came by.

John Ballard had always carried the Book in his pocket, and tried to live by it even when homesteaders began pouring in and plowing up the range he had considered his. No longer having room in his home for all the people who came for Sunday services, he had built the farmers a church in their new town of Hopeful. But he had kept the bells of San Juan.

Then one day there had been an argument over a butchered steer, and John Ballard, friend of the homesteaders, had been shot in the back by a renegade nester.

The Reverend Andrew McAdam was speaking to Wes now. "You've heard about the misfortune that's come to our church, Brother Ballard?"

The man's voice shook Wes back to reality. "I have," he answered quietly. "And I've got a good notion what you're here for."

Wes saw the startled, half-guilty look in the big minister's gray eyes. "But you've wasted you a long, cold ride. I'm not giving you the bells of San Juan."

McAdam swallowed. "Your old daddy was a God-fearing man, Brother Wes. If he was still a-living, he'd want the bells to be in the Lord's service. He wouldn't want to see them rusting away."

"But he's not living, McAdam. Dad tried to be friends. He kept turning the other cheek, and people kept slapping him. They kept taking his land away from him. And when they'd took all they could, then one of your nesters shot him in the back."

McAdam stood in awkward silence trying to work up an answer. Wes felt the bitterness rising in him bringing with it an excitement that made him tremble a little. He glanced at the girl. Her eyes were soft. So was her voice.

"You've been holding your hatred for the farmers too long, Wes Ballard," she said quietly. "You've been blaming them all because of what one man did—one who didn't really belong to the community at all."

Ballard clenched his fists. "Didn't belong? I remember that when the ranchers got together and went to hang him, your dad here got the drop on them with a scattergun. He kept them till the farmers could take the killer off and get him locked up safe in jail."

The big minister held his hands out, palms upward. "But the ranchers was trying to take from the Lord the vengeance that was His," he pleaded. "I wasn't trying to save the killer so much. I was trying save the ranchers. They all realized that a long time ago, Brother Wes. All but you!"

Wes stood firm. "I'm still keeping the bells, McAdam. If it hadn't been for you there's been two or three times those farmers would've left this country. But you'd beg them to hang on, and to keep praying. Then they'd get a good season, and they were here solider than ever before." He paused, then added, "So you see, McAdam, if I help your church, I'm helping the nesters. And I want to see them gone!"

Wes felt somehow exhausted. Silence had long been a habit with him. Now he had said far more than was his custom, and his breath was coming a little short.

McAdam's towering frame seemed to wilt down in disappointment. There was still an argument in his earnest gray eyes, but he couldn't put it into words.

"Come on, Ruth," the minister said finally. "I'm afraid our trip didn't do us much good. The year's been a hard one, and I hate to do it. But we'll have to ask the farmers for money to buy a new bell."

He turned to go. Ruth McAdam had been standing by an old desk that had been John Ballard's. She had picked up an old Bible and wiped the dust off of it. Now she stepped quietly up to Wes and handed it to him. There was a softness in her eyes that made him uneasy.

"Your father had many friends, Wes Ballard. But you've drawn yourself in and made yourself a lonely man, with almost no friends at all. Maybe if you'll go through your father's old Book, you'll learn some of the things he knew."

She smiled then. Just a ghost of a smile, but Wes felt a strange warmth rise in him at the sight of it.

He stepped out onto the chilly gallery and watched the two head back for town in their jostling old wagon. The uneasiness still stirred him. He hadn't put his coat back on, and the dampness quickly went through him. Raindrops began to speckle the steps and the edge of the gallery.

Ken came out of the barn, his gun off, and walked up to the house. "You didn't let that long-legged preacher get away with anything, did you?"

The rain was falling harder now. Wes saw the wagon disappear in the wet gray veil and found himself feeling sorry for the pair in their four-mile ride back to town. He rifled the pages of the Bible absently and hoped his brother couldn't see his disquietude.

"No, Ken," he said. "They didn't get away with anything."

Rain poured down for two nights and a day. Draws were running high.

The rivers roiling, muddy waters spilled over the banks and poured into the streets on one end of Hopeful.

When the rain stopped on Christmas Eve morning, Wes, Ken and Henry Lee scattered out over the San Juan to see after their cattle. Wes and Henry were back by noon, but Ken didn't return. Two hours passed, then three. Still he wasn't home.

Then Ruth McAdam came spurring into the ranchyard as fast as her bay horse could run. She slid to a muddy halt in front of the barn.

"Dad wants you, Wes Ballard," she said breathlessly. Her cheeks were red from cold. "He says you'd best be getting over to Hiram Selby's as quick as you can."

Ken! Wes's blood raced. Without her telling him, he knew Ken had gotten himself in trouble. It had been brewing long enough. And Selby's place was on worthless country the other farmers called Poverty Lane. Nesters there were desperate enough to do 'most anything.

While Wes and Henry quickly flung saddles on their horses, she told them the story. Ken had found the hide of a butchered beef in a draw, washed up by the rolling water. He had met up with a homestead youngster about his own age and given him a beating. The boy had finally told him Selby had butchered the steer, dividing the meat among his beef-hungry neighbors.

Then Ken had ridden over to Selby's, a gun on his hip. And McAdam had found out that a vengeful band of young homesteaders was not far behind him.

It was a hard five miles across the muddy range to the Selby farm. Anxiety set Wes's blood to racing as he saw eight or ten horses in front of the place. He slid his horse to a stop, swung down with gun in hand and hit the little front porch in a run. He slammed his big shoulder against the door and jumped into the room, gun ready.

But he was far from ready for what he saw. Ken lay on the floor, flat on his stomach and helpless as a mouse in a bottle. The big Reverend Andrew McAdam was sitting on him to hold him down. In his hands the minister held a double-barreled shotgun pointed toward half a dozen young farm boys, who stood meekly.

McAdam looked at Wes and grinned broadly. "Glad you got here, Brother Wes. I been preaching to these boys, but they ain't been listening much. I was afraid I was going to have to be giving some of them a dose of stock salt out of this gun."

Relief washed through Wes. Then, uncomfortably, he realized that some kind of thanks was in order. Annoyance rose in him. Now he was indebted to the old preacher, and his daughter, too. But he didn't want to be in debt to anybody, least of all a farmer.

He remembered the butchered beef. "I'll take care of Ken now," he said flatly. "But I got a bone to pick with Selby."

Selby stepped out of the kitchen, his weary, worried-looking wife and two small children behind him.

"All right, Ballard," Selby said, desperation in his voice. "I did kill a steer. My family hadn't had any fresh meat in weeks, and neither had most of my neighbors. It was the first time I ever done it."

Wes was vaguely surprised by the man's bent frame, the temples of solid gray. He knew Selby shouldn't be that old.

"You know I can get you sent to jail," Wes said grimly. "Can you pay for that steer?"

There was no hope in Selby's eyes. "No, Ballard. If I could, I'd've bought it in the first place."

The smallest of the Selby children began to cry. Its mother picked it up and carried it back into the kitchen. The other, a scared little boy, clung tightly to his father's patched pants leg. It struck Wes suddenly that this was Christmas Eve. Yet there wasn't a sign of any Christmas decoration in this lonely little house. Not like the Christmases he had spent as a boy.

He struggled with indecision. He glanced at Ruth McAdam. The soft glow in her eyes brought up the same warmth and the same uneasiness that had risen in him that day in the ranch house.

"All right, Selby," he said, "tell your kids Santy Claus paid for that steer. Only don't kill any more. Come on, Ken, let's go home."

Ken muttered and followed him. As Wes stepped out the door, Ruth McAdam's soft hand caught his arm. Her touch brought up a warm tingle in him. "That was a fine thing you did there, Wes," she said proudly.

He shook his head. "I was just paying a debt."

"A debt?"

"Yes, to you and your dad for helping pull Ken out of that mess. I don't want to owe anything to anybody. This was a way to square up."

Disappointment showed in her blue eyes, then gave way to anger. "So that's all it was, just paying a debt. Well, there's one debt you can't pay off with a couple of sides of beef, Brother Ballard."

She stopped, then added heatedly, "Ever since your dad died you've been living to yourself, feeding yourself on your hatred.

You owe yourself a big debt for ten ruined years. It's going to be a hard one to pay!"

She mounted her horse and drew off to one side to wait for her father. Wes watched her, a tide of emotion swelling within him. Maybe she was right, in a way. It had been a long time since he had found himself really having a good time, the way he had done when his father was alive.

Andrew McAdam stepped out onto the front porch and saluted the three cowboys. "We're having a little Christmas Eve party tonight over to the church, to raise money for a new bell. We want you all to be coming. Bet it's been a long time since you've had an arm around a pretty girl."

Wes looked at Ruth again and felt a deep yearning. Yes, it had been a long time . . .

As they rode back toward the ranch, Ken argued bitterly. "There I was just about to mop up on the whole dadgum bunch when that sky pilot stepped in. And you just stood there watching that heifer make eyes at you. You let them nesters get away with everything!"

"Shut up, Ken," Wes growled.

"I'm not going to shut up. You may forget about that steer, but I won't. I'm going to make them pay for it, you can bet your boots!"

During the ride home Wes kept thinking about the dance, and about Ruth McAdam. Even as he tried to talk himself out of it, he knew he was going.

He knew too, however, that it wouldn't take Ken ten minutes to get on the bottom side of a big fight. He talked Henry Lee into staying home and keeping an eye on the hot-headed boy.

All the way to town the battle went on inside him. He would remember the good times he had once had, and he would think of Ruth McAdam. Then he would curse himself for a fool. But he didn't turn back.

He stopped for a long look at the horses, wagons and buckboards gathered around the church and the schoolhouse next door. He dreaded facing the crowd.

An awful racket of cheering and foot stomping came from inside the little frame church that his father had built so long ago. Children. It must be a Santa Claus party, like so many he had seen. He glanced up at the empty bell tower and remembered the bells of San Juan.

Wes went on to the schoolhouse. There the desks had been pushed aside, and couples were swinging across the floor to the sound of a spirited fiddle. Hat in his hand and heart in his throat, Wes made himself step up on the porch and through the door.

He felt for a moment as if all eyes were on him, and he wanted to run. Then Ruth McAdam stepped out of the crowd. She looked at him incredulously. "Is it really you, Wes Ballard?"

He swallowed. "I kept thinking about that debt. Thought maybe a payment was about due."

She looked up at him, a glowing smile on her face. Then she caught his hand and pulled him out onto the dance floor. Her soft body close to his as they danced set his blood to racing. He was almost afraid to breathe. Never in his life had he felt like this.

As they rested through a dance he watched the farmers slowly file by a collection box and drop in money for a new bell. He knew most of them were giving more than they could really afford.

Ruth danced with him again and again. Wes discovered he was having a wonderful time. He even found himself shaking hands with some of the farmers.

Suddenly alarm began to rise in him. Why had he come? What was he doing? Here he was shaking hands with the people he had vowed to fight. He was dancing to their music, sharing their laughter. He was even falling in love with one of them.

Ruth was looking up at him, happiness shining in her pretty

face. Wes swallowed. A dozen conflicting thoughts passed through his mind.

"I've got to get out of here, Ruth."

Surprised, she followed him out onto the porch. "What's wrong, Wes? You were having a wonderful time. So was I. What's happened?"

He shook his head. "I—I don't know. I'm all mixed up. I guess I just don't belong here."

"But you do, Wes," she pleaded. "For a while there you forgot yourself. You forgot your hatred. These people want to be your friends. You saw that. Please, Wes, try it again."

Once more he shook his head. "I can't. I've got to go home. I've got to think. Good night, Ruth."

Quickly, not daring to give himself time, he stepped down off the porch and strode to his horse. Riding down the street, he looked back once. She was still standing on the porch, watching him.

A new ache pulling inside him, Wes buttoned his coat up tight, touched spurs to his horse and headed down the muddy road in the bright winter moonlight.

He was a mile from the house when Henry Lee came loping out to meet him, reeling slightly in the saddle.

"Go back, Wes," Henry shouted. "Go back and catch Ken. He's trying to git hisself killed!"

Henry leaned forward, one hand on the side of his head. A line of dried blood showed on one side of the old cowpuncher's face.

"Ken's gone to town to rob the nesters of that church bell money," Henry said, his breath short. "Trying to make them pay for that steer."

A tide of anxiety rushed through Wes. "Why didn't you stop him?"

"I tried to, but he hit me upside of the head with his gun barrel. I woke up under a saddle rack."

Wes's blood raced. Shame choked him. "I never taught Ken to steal."

Henry's eyes accused him. "No, but you taught him to hate, and that's as bad. He don't look on it as stealing. He thinks he's getting back something that belongs to the ranch. Your teaching, Wes."

Wes wheeled his horse around and spurred back toward town. The long ride gave him time to do lots of thinking, too much thinking.

The crisp night air brought him the sharp sound of gunshots when he was still a mile from Hopeful. Fear gripped him. He spurred toward the sound and, for the first time in years, found himself breathing a prayer.

Then he saw them sweeping toward him in the moonlight, riding hard along the river bank. One rider was a little in the lead. Ken!

Suddenly Ken saw Wes riding toward him. Instantly Wes realized the boy thought him another pursuer. In desperation Ken reined his horse half around and spurred into the rolling, flooded river.

"Ken! Ken! It's me!" Wes shouted in vain.

Wes got to the river bank just behind the posse. He could see Ken fighting his horse farther and farther out into the churning water. The boy was losing his head. One hand clutched a loose pair of saddle bags and held them to the saddle horn. The other jerked and pulled at the reins.

The pursuers hauled up and watched the struggling boy. Then one rider plunged his horse into the river and began fighting to reach Ken. Andrew McAdam!

Wes spurred into the river twenty feet behind the big minister. He was close enough to see raw fear on the boy's face. Ken's horse was thrashing wildly. Wes's blood turned to ice as he saw Ken slide out of the saddle and into the muddy water. For a moment the saddlebags hung precariously to the saddle horn.

Too far behind to help, Wes knew the decision the minister faced. By moving quickly McAdam could grab the saddlebag and save the money the church had collected for the bell. But the boy would be swept on down the river to drown. If he saved Ken, the money would be lost.

Wes's eyes burned, and he didn't want to look. Then he saw the minister swing out and catch the drowning boy. The saddlebags slid away from the saddle horn and sank beneath the churning brown foam. McAdam started bringing the boy back out of the treacherous, icy water.

On the bank Wes could hear grumbling. "Ought've saved the money and let the outlaw drown," a young man said.

"Hush up, son," came an older voice. Wes recognized it as Hiram Selby's. "That's no way for a Christian to be talking."

Carefully Wes laid his brother down across a little hump on the muddy ground and began squeezing the water out of his lungs. McAdam sat his horse, struggling to regain his breath.

A vengeful handful of young men began moving grimly forward, guns in their hands.

One of them held a rope. Wes reached for a gun, then remembered he wasn't wearing one. McAdam jerked his rope loose from its horn string. His eyes were like a blacksmith's furnace as he faced the angry group.

"Any man who tries to harm this boy will be feeling the wrath of God with the double of a wet rope!"

The little group hesitated, muttering darkly. Then some of the older men, including Hiram Selby, came up and made them move away.

A farmer brought up Ken's horse, which struggled out of the water. McAdam advised, "We better be taking him on into town, to the parsonage. He'll die of pneumonia if we don't git him to bed."

Wes held Ken up to keep him from sliding out of the saddle. He put his own coat over the slim, trembling shoulders. After awhile, bent low over the horn, Ken began to sob.

"He saved me. I stole his money, but he saved me. I—I feel so dirty."

Wes's eyes stung and he closed them. "I know, Ken. I know."

After Ken was put to bed in the parsonage, he lapsed into unconsciousness. His fever rose steadily. Henry Lee came in. Wes spoke quietly to him a moment, and the cowboy left. Wes sat down at the boy's bedside for the beginning of a long vigil.

Toward morning Ken was tossing and turning, murmuring deliriously. All that time Wes sat at his bedside. Ruth was there too, constantly putting wet towels on the boy's head, turning his pillow, whispering confidently to Wes. The minister sat in a corner dozing, his feet in a tub of water that had once been hot.

Christmas dawn came. A stir arose outside by the church. The minister awoke, blinked a few times, and put on his boots to go out and see what it was all about. Just before he reached the door, Ruth felt Ken's brow again.

"Wes," she cried, "I think his fever's going down."

Wes jumped up excitedly, blinking his burning eyes. Forgetting the commotion outdoors, the minister trotted up to the bedside. Wes found Ruth's warm hand in his as they stood there together. Then Ken's eyelids began to flutter and his body began to stir.

Wes felt the tension leave him like a heavy coat sliding off his shoulders.

"Ruth," he said joyfully, "he's going to make it!"

Suddenly the sound of church bells broke through the room. The very floor vibrated to their tone. Ruth looked up at Wes, her eyes wide. Wes glanced at the minister. McAdam stood there, his mouth open, a mist quickly forming in his eyes as he listened, not moving.

"The Christmas bells," McAdam murmured unbelievingly. "The Christmas bells!"

The minister went to the door and opened it. Outside, a happy little group of farmers was gathered around Henry Lee.

Henry had a large set of bells in the bed of a ranch wagon. "Wes sent me for them," he said.

The minister turned back toward Wes, almost choking. "The bells of San Juan!"

Ruth's eyes glowed with pride. Then, without Wes's asking for it, or even hoping for it, she was in his arms. The bells kept tolling. For Wes, they had never sounded more beautiful.

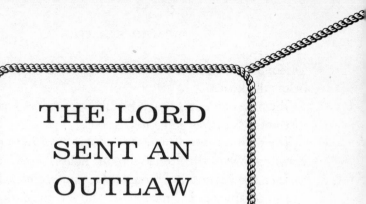

THE LORD
SENT AN
OUTLAW

I never did know for sure just what became of Tom Kincaid. I heard a couple of times that he'd been gunned down by lawmen in one place or another. With every sheriff in West Texas looking for him, all kinds of stories get around about a man like Tom Kincaid. It's hard to tell what to believe.

All I can say is, the time long ago when he showed up on my little Cross S outfit, he looked like the Lord had sent him, guns and all.

I was batching then, working like a slave to get a cow outfit started, and hoping to have a place suitable for a Mrs. Sam Rawlins before much longer. Cutting expenses every way I could, I even broke my own horses. That is, till a little Mexican pony named Chili broke me.

This particular day I had finished the big end of my day's work on my top horse, a sorrel named Sunup. I got out my bronc rig and a dry blanket. It was the fourth or fifth saddle for Chili. The last couple of times all he had done was goat around a little. This time I didn't even bother to tie up a hind foot before I saddled him.

But when I swung into the saddle, all hell broke loose. By the third jump I knew I was done.

Sailing off, I got a glimpse of the mesquite-limb pole corral a second before I came down on top of it. My right leg snapped below the knee.

The pain of it cut through me like a buzz saw. For a minute, it seemed like I was going to pass out.

The sand was hot. It burned my skinned hands as I started crawling toward the little raw frame house.

Then I saw Kincaid. Through a burning red haze I made out a form coming up. I blinked hard, and saw the dark man there on a black horse, looking down at me.

Panic shot through me for a second. I thought it was one of the Jagger brothers. I remembered I'd left my gun hanging on a fence post before I got on the bronc. The Jaggers had been after me ever since I had gotten to the country a day ahead of them and beat them to the best water hole left.

Silent as a statue, the dark stranger swung to the ground, put an arm around my shoulder, and helped me start hobbling toward the house.

I got a good look at him, and I wasn't sure I liked what I saw. His leathery face was grim as a hangman's. His two holsters were tied down. His gun butts looked worn. But his big hands were muscular and rough, not smooth and limber like those of most gunmen I had seen.

Just inside the door he saw the framed picture of Lucy. He froze there a moment, holding me up. He breathed a name, so softly I couldn't make it out.

Finally he put me down on a cot. "Who's the girl?" he asked.

"Lucy Foster," I told him painfully. "She lives on the next ranch. We're goin' to be married."

He stood there looking at me a long moment. His gray eyes were like gun muzzles. Then he leaned over, unfastened my chaps, and felt of the leg.

"Clean break," he said finally. "I'll have to set it."

He went outside and came back with a couple of small boards. Laying them down on the cot beside me, he ripped one of my old shirts into strips, then split my pants leg up to the knee.

He started pulling at the leg. I gripped the cot so hard my hands got numb. At last he was through and was binding the boards to my leg to hold the bone in place. I was so weak I couldn't raise up. Cold sweat stood on my forehead.

"I'll fix you a smoke," he said. He pulled a tobacco sack out of his pocket. A folded piece of paper came out with it and fell onto the cot. As I reached for it he suddenly grabbed it and backed off, his face dark, his eyes dangerous.

Then he slowly loosened up, shrugged, and handed it to me. "Nothin' you can do about it anyhow," he muttered.

It was a reward dodger. It offered a $1000 reward for Tom Kincaid, dead or alive.

My throat got dry as I read on. The description just fitted the stranger here, even to the broad-trimmed black hat with a bullet hole in the crown. Breathing painfully, I handed the dodger back to him.

"Guess you want to keep this, Mister . . . Smith."

His eyes softened a little, but not like they had when he had looked at Lucy's picture. Staring up at him, I remembered stories I had heard about Tom Kincaid, how he came to be an outlaw.

He had once been in love with a girl, the stories went, but another man had won her away from him.

Then the man had deserted her, left her with a broken heart and small-town gossip to ruin her name. Just an average cowpuncher till then, Kincaid had turned into a man hunter. He had found his man and gunned him down. Since then he had ridden the dark trails, alone.

Kincaid turned toward the door. For a moment he paused again and looked at Lucy's picture. Then he went outside. His jingling spurs told me he was headed for the barn.

A while later he came back. "Do you know anybody who'd try to get you hurt?" he asked grimly. I quickly thought of the Jagger boys.

"Somebody stuck tacks between the folds of the blanket you

use with your bronc saddle," he said. "They fixed it so when your weight went into the saddle they'd cut into a horse's back. That bronc's bleedin' in a dozen places."

Anger flared up in me. I started to jump out of bed before I thought of the leg. I told Kincaid about the Jaggers. Ever since I had gotten the water hole, there had been trouble. I had noticed some of my cattle missing, and signs always pointed to the Jaggers.

One day I had caught Hardy and Bascom Jagger on my place, with one of my steers tied down and a cinch ring in a fire, heating to change the brand. We had swapped lead, and I had wounded Bascom. Since then I had dodged bushwhack lead more than once.

To make it worse, Hardy Jagger had been courting Lucy too.

Footsteps sounded on the front porch. Kincaid whirled. His hands darted downward, then back up. Both held guns.

Lucy Foster stepped through the door. Her hand went up to her face. For a moment Kincaid stood there looking at her, then holstered the guns.

"I didn't go to scare you, ma'am," he spoke finally, taking off his black hat.

Then Lucy saw that I was flat on my back. She ran to me. "Oh, Sam, what did they do to you?"

I gripped her warm, soft hand with both of mine. "Horse threw me, Lucy. My leg's broke."

Suddenly I noticed a blue mark on the side of her face, and I sat up quickly. "That bruise," I asked her, "where did you get it?"

"It isn't anything. Just an accident."

Hot blood rushed into my face. I gripped her hand tighter. "Tell me straight, Lucy. Did Hardy Jagger have somethin' to do with it?"

Tears welled up in her eyes. "Yes, he did it. He came over to the place the other night, and asked me again to marry him. I told him I was going to marry you. He got so mad he hit me. I put him out of the house with a shotgun. But as he started to ride away he yelled back that he'd fix you so you wouldn't marry anybody."

She started to sob. "I was afraid he meant it. I kept waiting for some word from you. Today I couldn't stand it any longer. I had to come over and see."

"I'll get him," I said. "I'll get him if I have to crawl over there."

Kincaid was staring at Lucy just the way he had stared at her picture. The hard lines in his face had softened. His eyes seemed to be looking back through the years.

I was so mad I didn't see the anxiety in Lucy's blue eyes. But Kincaid saw.

"You'll stay where you're at," he said firmly. "Get yourself killed and where'll this girl be?"

"How come you're here?" Lucy asked him. "Who are you?"

I spoke up quickly: "He rode up after the accident and set my leg for me, Lucy. He's Tom . . . Smith."

She stared levelly at him. "Sheriff Baldwin came by our place yesterday. He was looking for an outlaw seen heading through this country. The name was Kincaid."

There was a disappointed look in Kincaid's eyes. Lucy saw it too. She added softly: "I want to thank you, Mister Kincaid, for helping Sam. If there's anything we can do to help you . . ."

Kincaid shook his head.

When Lucy started to go, he stopped her by the door, his hat in his hands. "Just one thing I wanted to say, ma'am. I had a sweetheart once. She looked an awful lot like you. I failed her, didn't help her when she needed help most. Don't you worry. I'll see that everything goes all right here."

Next morning Kincaid made me a crutch. He unwrapped the splints and checked my leg. He was so busy rewrapping it that he didn't hear the horseman riding up into the yard. But he heard the jingling of spur rowels as someone dismounted and walked up to the house. Eyes grim, he snaked a pistol out of its holster and stepped quickly into the little back room.

Sheriff Ernie Baldwin whistled a tune as he walked up onto the porch. Seeing me on the cot, he quickly walked in.

"Looks like you stepped in a prairie dog hole, Sam."

I tried to grin, but I was swallowing hard. I knew Kincaid had his gun cocked.

I told Baldwin about my getting thrown off, and that a stranger had come along and helped me.

The jovial lawman's eyes suddenly narrowed. "This stranger, what did he look like? Where did he go?"

"He rode on yesterday, after he had set my leg," I lied. "If it hadn't been for him, no tellin' what shape I'd've been in today."

Baldwin stood there, his gaze sweeping up and down the room.

"Left yesterday, you say?" he mused. "Mighty careless of him to leave his hat."

Something choked me as Baldwin looked at the black hat a minute, then started backing toward the door. "If he comes back to get it, you tell him I'll be passin' by here about noon tomorrow, with a posse. I appreciate him stoppin' to help you, but it won't hurt him to be halfway to New Mexico. You tell him that."

Baldwin stepped out the door. A minute later I heard him spur away. Kincaid came out of the back room, his face hard.

"You heard what he said," I spoke quickly. "You better leave here while you can."

Kincaid nodded. "I'll leave, but not just yet. I promised that girl I'd be sure things went all right here. If I brought you the evidence you need to put the Jaggers away, would you turn it over to the sheriff tomorrow?"

I stammered. "Sure, I would. But there's no call for that. This isn't your business."

"When a man hits a woman like that, it's anybody's business," he replied quickly.

A few minutes later he had saddled his black horse and gone. I didn't know just when I'd fallen asleep or what woke me up. I realized with a start that the day was nearly over. Then as I opened my eyes my heart came up in my throat.

Hardy Jagger stood by my cot, a gun in his hand.

"What do you want?" I demanded.

Jagger snarled. His thick lips lay flat against his teeth as he hit me across the face with the back of his hand.

"You know what we want! Where's that range detective you sicced onto us?"

My face burned like fire. I could taste the salty tang of blood on my lip. "I don't know nothin' about a detective."

Jagger slapped me again. Red flashes darted before my eyes. When the sight came back, I saw Bascom Jagger standing in the doorway. His arm was in a sling.

"He winged Bascom," Hardy gritted. "We caught him after he had shot one of our cows and cut part of the hide off of her, the part with the brand on it. We shot his horse out from under him, but he got away from us afoot, in the brush. While we was lookin' for him, he shot Bascom and took Bascom's horse."

Hardy put both hands on my broken leg. He grinned cruelly as he began to push down, hard. "Tell us where that detective is, and that piece of hide. Else you'll never walk again!"

Black pain cut through me as he put his weight on the broken leg. I choked off a cry that swelled in my throat.

"Tell us, by God, or I'll kill you."

The pain grew worse. I must have passed out. I came to and found the bed and myself soaking wet. Hardy stood there beside me, an empty bucket in his hand.

"Every time you pass out I'll bring you back," he gritted. "Where's that hide?"

He started working on me again. I felt myself go limp. I was vaguely conscious of water being thrown on me again, but I never really waked up.

When I finally did open my eyes again, there was a man sitting beside me, looking down at me in flickering reddish lamplight. Panic climbed up in me again until I saw it was Kincaid.

Weakly I told him what had happened. His face darkened, but he said nothing.

Finally he unrolled a piece of cowhide and handed it to me. It had a brand on it.

"This is nothing but the Bar 8, the Jagger brand," I said.

"Turn it over. Look at the underside."

I turned it over. There, in reverse, was the outline of my Cross S brand. It showed clearly over the more recently-burned Jagger Bar 8. A good brand-changing job with a running iron, or a cinch ring.

I glanced over the room. Everything in it had been turned upside down. No wonder the Jaggers had made such a thorough search.

"They killed my black horse," Kincaid said darkly. "The horse I got off that Jagger went lame. That's why they got here before I did."

I argued with myself a little. Finally I decided: "You take my sorrel, Sunup. He's fast when he's got to be, and he'll take you as far as you want to go. That's the least I can do after you helpin' me like this."

Kincaid nodded. "I hate to take him, but I guess I got to. I can't be here when the sheriff brings that posse." Next morning Kincaid went out, saddled Sunup, and rode back to the house. He stopped in the door and stared a minute at Lucy's picture. Then he gravely turned to me.

"When you get off that crutch, you marry that girl!"

A minute later he mounted and was gone.

I hobbled around a little to get the feel of the crutch, but I wasn't able to do anything. I kept my gun strapped on, afraid the Jagger boys would come before the sheriff did. One thing was in my favor: they wouldn't know the sheriff was coming today.

Just before noon I heard a horse loping up. I worked my way out to the porch in time to see Kincaid pull Sunup to a sliding halt at the barn and lead him quickly into the corral. Then he sprinted to the house, gun in his hand.

"What're you doin' back here?" I asked. "You know the sheriff's comin' any minute! You tryin' to get killed?"

Kincaid's breath was short as he stopped in front of me. "The Jaggers . . . they're comin'."

I kept glancing at the hill, watching for the posse. "I can hold them off till the sheriff gets here. You better clear out while you can."

Then he let the bomb drop. "They got Lucy with them!"

I felt the blood drain out of my face.

"But how do you know?" I asked him desperately. "How you come to see them?"

His eyes smoldered. "I went over to their place to kill them! They were gone, and I took to huntin'. I found them too late."

Just then the two Jaggers rode out of the brush. They had Lucy on a horse in front of them. Hardy Jagger held a gun trained on her back. A crooked smile crossed his rough face, and broadened as he rode nearer.

"You fellers drop your guns or I'll start usin' mine," he threatened. "Since this woman won't have me, she'll be first."

There wasn't much else we could do. Kincaid dropped his gun. I unbuckled my gun belt and let mine fall.

"You know what we come for," Hardy went on. "Bring that piece of hide out here."

Kincaid stood still, his face like a thundercloud.

Jagger reached out, grabbed Lucy's hand, and twisted her arm until she cried out in pain.

"I said git that hide!" he snarled.

Thoroughly sick, I hobbled back into the house and got the hide. Then I remembered an extra gun that was in a holster on the wall. I took it out and held it under the hide.

Working my way back onto the porch, I acted as if I was going to throw the raw leather to Jagger. Instead I dropped it and started to bring up the gun.

But I was too slow.

Jagger's gun barked. A red hot sledgehammer blow hit my

shoulder and spun me around. The crutch and my gun clattered to the porch together. I caught myself on the door facing in time to see Jagger's gun bearing down on me again.

Suddenly Lucy kicked her horse. It lunged forward into Hardy's. The gun exploded harmlessly. In a second Lucy jumped down, grabbed me, and was pulling me through the door. I saw Kincaid scoop up the gun and fire it at Hardy even before it was level with his knees.

Hardy ducked and let fly a wild shot at Kincaid.

Kincaid jumped back through the door. Hardy squeezed off a couple more shots, but they plowed into the wall opposite the doorway.

Lucy was holding onto me tightly and trying to stop the flow of blood from my shoulder with a handkerchief. Kincaid stationed himself by a window. Bascom, his arm still in a sling, jerked his horse around and spurred back for the protection of a wagon on one side of the front yard. He stepped off and fell on his belly behind a wheel.

Hardy swung down and ran for a mesquite tree. His horse stampeded away. Hardy's face showed terror as he glanced back over his shoulder and Kincaid fired at him.

Between shots I thought I could hear the drumming of horses' hooves.

"The sheriff's comin', Kincaid," I yelled. "Get out a back window. We can hold the Jaggers off."

Kincaid didn't seem to hear. He fired at Bascom. Wood splintered from the wagon wheel. Bascom dashed for the mesquite behind which Hardy lay. Kincaid took deliberate aim and squeezed the trigger. Bascom pitched headlong to the ground, rolled halfway over, and lay still.

Hardy yelled his brother's name, but there was no move from the still figure.

Kincaid moved quickly over to my cot and rolled up the blankets, tying them loosely with a short rope. He came back to the door.

"I'm no range detective, Jagger!" he called out. "Do you know who I am?"

Jagger answered with a couple more shots.

"I'm Tom Kincaid, and I'm comin' out to get you, Jagger!"

I thought I could hear the shocked Hardy catch his breath. I saw his head show up a little from behind the mesquite. Kincaid paused a minute, then pitched the roll out the door.

Jagger jumped up and fired wildly at it. His mouth dropped open as he saw the blankets fall to the porch. Then Kincaid stepped out. Fear showed in Jagger's face as he quickly raised his gun. Coldly Kincaid fired, once, twice, and a third time. Jagger dropped his gun. His knees buckled, and he fell forward into the mesquite.

With Lucy's help I worked my way out onto the porch.

My throat went dry as I saw riders come over the top of the hill.

"It's the posse, Kincaid," I yelled. "Get out of here, quick!"

Kincaid was standing on the ground now. He reached out, pulled Lucy into his arms, and kissed her. Then he turned and ran toward the barn. She stood watching him, shock plain in her startled eyes.

Kincaid dashed into the corral, mounted, and spurred out the open gate.

I moved painfully across the porch as riders swept across the yard, shooting at Kincaid. I felt a splint slip, and the bone snapped out of place again. I sprawled off onto the ground.

Blinding pain cut through me as I lay there. I saw Lucy running toward me, and felt her put her arms around my shoulders. I told myself Sunup was too fast—they'd never catch him. I heard myself laughing crazily. Then I knew nothing more.

Like I said, we never did know for sure what ever became of Tom Kincaid. We heard a couple of times that he'd been gunned down by lawmen in one place or another. It always made us feel good to hear new stories about him, because it made us sure that, somewhere, he was still alive and free.

That's all been a long time ago, though. Lucy and I have moved to town now, to end out our days in comfort. Our oldest son is running the ranch.

The splintered wagon wheel stands near the front gate now. On it is a sign that reads:

"Cross S Ranch, Thomas Kincaid Rawlins, owner."

THE MOOCHER

By the time the young man in the faded Levi's and run-over boots had finished his lunch and walked out of the cafe, Kitty Hagen had made up her mind. He was the one she wanted.

The moment he had first pushed in through the door, she had forgotten about the dirty dishes she was clearing off the linoleum-covered counter. She watched him as he hunted a rack for his ill-shaped, sweat-spotted Stetson. Then a gruff voice barked behind her, and she jumped.

"Hey there, Blondie," the proprietor grated in irritation, "you're spilling stuff on the floor."

Color surged into her cheeks as she saw the beets spattered red on the peeling linoleum at her feet.

"I'm sorry, Mr. Pettibone," she said in embarrassment.

"Mop's back yonder by the icebox," Pettibone growled. "Next time watch what you're doing."

He was a fat little man with a sour face and had made her think of a barrel of pickles the first time she saw him.

Quickly she cleaned up the floor, her blue eyes lifting once or twice to the young fellow who had seated himself on the stool at the counter. He wasn't really handsome, but Kitty had always felt a distrust of handsome men. They never got very serious with her because they could always land someone prettier, some girl who didn't have a freckled pug nose and a waitress's soap-reddened hands.

Scowling, Pettibone peeled off his apron and pitched it into a corner.

"You take over for a while, Blondie," he said, his voice curt. "I'm going home to eat."

Her first day there had shown her why he always made sure to go home for his meals.

She returned her attention to the young man who sat reading the menu. His hair was muddy brown, coarse and straight, and some of it hung down over his forehead when his hat was off. His hat-shielded forehead was almost white against the sun-baked brown of his face. His fist looked big and work-roughened as he traced down the menu with one stubby finger. He looked first at the high-priced meals, then at the cheapest ones. His finger came to rest somewhere in between. Kitty smiled.

No spendthrift, she told herself, but no tightwad, either.

His eyes lifted to meet hers. They were dark gray, frank and honest.

"How's the chicken-fried steak?" he asked her. It was always the lowest-priced one, one which cowboys ordered four times out of five.

She wanted to be honest. "No worse than anything else on the menu, and no better."

Pettibone had left a couple in the warming oven, already fried. But Kitty didn't like the looks of them. And with the boss out, she went ahead and fried a fresh one for the young cowboy.

The cowboy was shy. He sat quietly, his big hands folded together on the counter. She felt his eyes upon her when she was turned away, but whenever she looked toward him he was always staring at his hands.

By the time the steak was done, she knew she was going to have to start the conversation herself, if there was going to be one.

"Haven't seen you in here before," she ventured carefully. "You work on a ranch around here someplace?"

He was slow in his answer, slow and a little uncertain. "Kind of. I've got me a little ranch leased out on the divide, twenty miles south of town. I don't hang around town a lot. Costs too much, and I don't like to spend the time."

A quiet friendliness was in his face, but he didn't volunteer any more information for a while. Kitty caught herself glancing at his ring hand. He wore no wedding band. But that didn't necessarily mean anything. Lots of these ranch men didn't. Too easy for a ring to snag on machinery and cut a finger off.

Presently he mustered up courage to point his fork at the plate. "Sure good," he said.

"Thanks," she replied with a smile. "But I don't guess it's anything like your wife can cook."

That was a corny way to ask him, but she had to know.

Her heartbeat quickened at his answer. "I'm not married. Live by myself, do my own cooking. Anything tastes good to me."

She broke into a broad smile. "Well, then, what'll you have for dessert? Some apple pie?"

Pettibone would have cussed a blue streak if he had seen how big a slice of pie Kitty gave the cowboy.

"Made it myself," she said hopefully.

As he pulled on his hat and opened the door, she called after him, "You'll come again, won't you?" Her voice sounded more eager than she had intended it to.

"Sure will," he said, and left.

It wasn't until he was gone that she realized she hadn't learned his name.

She had her hands deep in hot suds when she heard the furtive knock on the back screen. Quickly she dried the dishwater from her hands and unhooked the screen door. The young man who came in had the same pug nose as Kitty, and the same shade of dark blond hair.

"Gerald," she said hastily, "I thought you were supposed to be working with the oil rig crew."

He grinned lazily. "Aw, Sis, I had a little falling out with the pusher this morning. He's got an idea he can get along without me. What you got in the kitchen that a hungry man could eat?"

Alarm quickened her pulse. She glanced at the front door. "Mr. Pettibone may be back any minute. I won't go slipping you free lunches, Gerald. That got me fired from the last two places I worked."

The lazy grin still split his young, untroubled face. "Now, Sis, you know I'll pay for it. That is, if you can lend me a few bucks."

"Didn't you get anything from that oil-field job? You held it three days."

He shrugged. "You know how it is. Social security, withholding tax. And I got in a little game with some of the boys. Fact is, I owe one of them fourteen bucks. Reckon you could let me have that much just till I get me another job?"

Her face flaring red, she slammed a soup dipper to the floor. "No, I will not! You're lazy, Gerald Hagen. You've never worked on the same job two weeks in your life. You sponged off Pa as long as he had anything, and you're sponging off me. You won't get anything this time. You hear? You won't get anything."

But her temper cooled quickly, and remorse began to plague her because of the beaten, puppy-dog look that came into his eyes.

She shrugged her slender shoulders. "I'm sorry, Gerald. You know I didn't mean it. Go on in and sit down. I'll bring you meat loaf lunch, and I'll ring it up on the cash register myself."

She would lend him the fourteen dollars, too, she knew with a hopeless resignation; she had been putting some money aside for a winter coat.

She never had been able to refuse Gerald for long. Sure, he was lazy. Shiftless, some called him. But he was her brother.

At suppertime the cowboy was back.

"Got a mechanic working overtime on my pickup," he explained quickly, as if he felt he ought to justify to her the extravagance of his long stay in town. "I thought I'd like another one of those chicken fries."

Kitty's heart had danced at the sight of him. Now it sagged as she glanced back at Pettibone's sour face in the kitchen. He had had a supply of chicken-fried steaks prepared for an hour, and now they would be flat and tasteless in the warming oven.

"Maybe you'd like a hot beef sandwich better," she prompted. She knew Pettibone would have to fix that fresh.

But Pettibone roared at her from the kitchen. "You deaf or something, Blondie? The man said a chicken-fried steak."

A quick surge of anger warmed her face, and she saw it reflected in the cowboy's eyes.

Other customers came in, but Kitty did little more than take their orders. She stayed close by the cowboy's place at the counter, refilling his water glass, checking the sugar bowl, replacing the napkins. He glanced at her occasionally while he labored at the tasteless meal. His eyes were friendly. But he said nothing.

Once more it looked as if Kitty was going to have to start a conversation herself.

"I guess you have a very nice place."

He looked as if he was glad she had broken the ice.

"Nice enough, I guess. It'll do till I get money enough to buy a place of my own."

"Pretty lonesome out there by yourself."

"Oh, I'm used to it. I've been batching off and on ever since I was old enough to make my own way."

Dreamily she said, "It must be a lot better than drifting from one place to another, never having anything and never hoping for much."

A sudden clatter startled her. She swung around. Fuming, Pettibone slammed his big fist down on the counter.

"You want to get fired, Blondie?" he stormed. "I'm paying you thirty dollars a week to work, not to loaf around and flirt with the customers. If you've got nothing better to do, grab that mop back yonder. This place could stand a little cleaning up."

The cowboy pushed up from his stool, an edge of anger in his sun-browned face.

But Kitty was the first to move. She whipped off her apron and hurled it to the floor at Pettibone's feet. "Yes, it could stand some cleaning up. And it ought to've started a long time ago, you sour-faced skinflint. Well, you can do it yourself, and maybe a little of the soap will splash over onto you!"

Seething, she made one quick whirl through the kitchen to grab her hat and purse, then stalked for the door. Four or five customers watched her, amusement in their eyes.

The young cowboy at the counter stood uncertainly. Quickly he dug up some change and left it on the counter beside the half-eaten steak. Then he grabbed his hat and hurried out.

"Wait!" he called to the girl who rushed on ahead of him, her shoe heels clicking sharply on the concrete walk.

He took off his hat as she stopped and turned toward him. His face was apologetic. "I'm sure sorry, miss. You've lost your job on account of me. I wouldn't have had it happen for the world."

She shook her head, the anger draining out of her. "It wasn't your fault. Maybe it was a good thing. Another day or two and I'd've dumped a tub of dishwater over his fat head."

The young man's mouth cracked into a broad grin.

"I believe you would have, at that. You've got a right smart of temper for a girl your size."

Her anger was gone. Her heart quickened at his grin, and suddenly she was laughing with him.

They began to walk, and before long his arm was locked in hers.

His name was Bill Matthews, she found out. He'd lived around this town most of his life, except for service in Europe during the War. He had saved his money ever since he was a kid, and he'd sunk it into livestock.

"I'm running cattle and sheep, and a few Angora goats to

keep down the brush," he said. "It's not a big outfit right now, but it'll be bigger someday. It takes work and patience. And I've got little use for anybody who won't work."

They turned in at the sagging frame house where Kitty and her brother had each taken a room.

"Kitty," Bill said, holding her hand. She liked the feel of his big rough hand on hers. "I think I know where you can get another job, a temporary one anyway. It beats waiting tables and scrubbing dishes. Can you type?"

"A little, not much."

"Friend of mine has an insurance and real estate agency here. Girl working for him is getting married. He needs a girl for receptionist, clerk, stuff like that till the other girl gets back. I'll talk to him."

His hand tightened on hers. "I like you, Kitty," he said after a long, strained silence. "I'd like to see you again. American Legion is throwing a dance tomorrow night. I haven't been to one in a long time. Go with me?"

She swallowed, trying to keep her face from shining as much as it wanted to. "I don't dance very well. But I'd like to go."

Her hands clasped tightly together, she watched him walk away in a rolling, cowpuncher gait. Her face was glowing now, and she didn't care. Let it shine. Let everybody know.

A lazy voice reached out to her from the sandy porch. "Seems like a pretty nice guy, Sis. Has he got any money?"

Her temper flared. Bill's words flashed back to her. I've got little use for anybody who won't work.

Then her quick annoyance faded. A hundred times she had wanted to explode in Gerald's face, to tell him he was a shiftless loafer, a moocher, a bum, and chase him away for once and for all. But though Gerald was twenty-two, there was still much of a little boy left in his face. It always won her over, and once again she would be the big sister and he the little brother. The angry words would remain unsaid, and Gerald would remain unchanged.

She stood on the porch with him now, an indulgent smile on her face. "I don't know, Gerald," she said. "I didn't ask him."

The next morning the landlady called her.

"Man to see you, Kitty. Be careful you don't let him sell you any insurance."

The man wore a gray business suit, and he held his snap-brim hat in his hands. Kitty could tell despite his town clothes that he had been a cowboy long before he had been a businessman.

"I'm Harper Sloane. Bill Matthews said you were looking for a job, and I'm sure looking for a girl to take one."

She took the job. And she was grateful to Bill Matthews as soon as she walked into Sloane's office. It wasn't elaborate, but it was neat, and it was cooler than Pettibone's kitchen. Nor was Harper Sloane very demanding of his secretary. True to his cowboy upbringing, he didn't stand on ceremony. His business transactions were carried out in a casual manner. What were a few typing errors in a letter? The guy could still read it, couldn't he?

Gerald slacked into a chair in Kitty's room and watched her brushing her blond hair. An expectant glow brightened her face as she looked forward to the dance and Bill.

"This guy Matthews," Gerald said. "Is he really interested in you?" He was tugging thoughtfully at his lips.

Kitty's breath cut short. "I don't know. Maybe."

Gerald went on, "It's easy enough to see that you're interested in him." His fingers drummed on the chair arm. "I'm going to meet him. He might be a good man to know."

Kitty laid down the brush and stared at herself in the mirror. She could see the color rising into her cheeks. Instant fear stabbed her.

"Gerald, you leave Bill alone."

"Now, Sis," he said, "it's a brother's duty to get to know anybody his sister might figure on marrying."

The fear stayed with her as Gerald left the room and tramped down the hall. She remembered that fellow who had had two dates with her in Big Spring, then abruptly had stopped seeing her. Then there was the boy a couple of years ago in Midland. He had liked her a lot, it seemed. But suddenly he would have nothing more to do with her. Maybe it meant something, maybe it didn't. But Gerald had gotten friendly with both of them. She had a lingering suspicion that he had borrowed money from them that had never been paid back . . .

After the dance, Bill drove her home in his pickup.

"It's a little rough, maybe," he said about the bouncing vehicle. "But it's all the car a guy like me needs to have."

He walked around to her side, opened the door, and helped her down. He was a little over-careful about it. He hadn't done this very much, she could tell. A ripple of warmth went through her at the tight grip of his big hand.

"Bill," she said eagerly, "I haven't enjoyed anything as much in ages. Won't you ask me again?"

He grinned broadly. "I sure intend to." He paused. "Kitty, tomorrow's Sunday. What do you say I come in early tomorrow and take you to church? Then if you'd like, we can drive out to the ranch."

Her eyes were shining. "I'll be waiting." His grip tightened. For a moment she held her breath, sure he was going to kiss her. He had intended to, she knew that. But he lost his nerve. So she took matters into her own hands again. She reached up and pulled his head down toward hers.

That was all that was necessary. His nerve came back to him . . .

❖

Kitty liked Bill's ranch as soon as he eased the pickup down over a grade and across a welded pipe cattle guard.

"Those cattle yonder," he said, waving his hand in a long arc, "are good grade Herefords, as good as you're apt to find in this country. And you can't find many Rambouillet sheep that'll shear better than mine, either."

Pride was strong in him. Kitty liked that. She gave the cattle a brief glance. And the sheep. And the goats. But mostly she just looked at Bill.

Eventually he got around to showing her the house. It was old-fashioned, with the roof all working up to one point like a four-sided pyramid. The nearly-bare house was swept and mopped, but the wallpaper was old and yellowed, and the windows could have stood some good curtains.

"The place is little," he admitted, "and it's kind of old. But it's snug, clean, got good plumbing, and doesn't leak when it rains."

He shifted uneasily from one foot to the other. A shy grin tugged at his wide mouth. "Kitty, what I'm trying to say is—well, when I buy my own place someday, it won't be quite like this. I'll build a house just to suit you."

Kitty caught a quick, happy breath. "Bill, is that a proposal?"

Hesitantly, he said, "No—Yes—That is, I meant to make it sound better. But I guess that'll do."

Happily she melted against him. "It'll do fine."

As she expected, Gerald didn't like it much at first. But he warmed to the idea when she began telling him about the ranch. Suddenly she saw the calculating look begin to burn in his eyes, and a chill touched her.

"Say, Sis," he said with a new enthusiasm, "maybe this isn't such a bad idea after all. Like they say, I'm not losing a sister. I'm gaining a brother-in-law."

For the first few nights, Bill came in every night to see her. Kitty was walking around on a big pink cloud. But she began to sense a change in him, an uneasy quiet about him that worried her.

Then, unaccountably, he stopped coming in to see her. The first night she thought something must have happened, or that he was too busy. The second night a real worry began nagging at her as she sat on the dark porch with Mrs. Horton, the landlady. By nine thirty, she gave up.

"It's the ranch work," Kitty said in a strained voice. "Bill has a lot to do." But when she got to her room she closed the door behind her and dropped down across her bed, fighting the tears.

The fourth day she saw him in town, at a distance. But he never came by the office to see her. At home she broke down and told Mrs. Horton all about it.

"Mrs. Horton," she pleaded, "what's the matter with me?"

The old lady shook her head. "There's nothing wrong with you."

"Then why won't Bill come to see me? Why doesn't he tell me what's the matter?"

Gravely the old lady answered, "Because he's too much of a gentleman, that's why. Think a little, Kitty. Can't you imagine who's really to blame?"

Kitty could.

The old lady demanded impatiently, "Then why don't you tie a tin can to Gerald and send him packing? You ought to've done it a long time ago. Bill wouldn't tell you, not in a hundred years. But he's smart enough to know what's bound to happen. As soon as you're married, Gerald will move in on you. He'll sponge off of Bill till Bill gets fed up and runs him off. And then what'll that do to Bill and you?"

Dismally, Kitty shook her head. "I've tried it before, Mrs. Horton. But it always hurt me worse than it did Gerald. He always comes back, and I always give in. I can't help it. He's my brother."

The old lady shrugged her shoulders. "Well, that's the way it is. As long as he hangs around here, mooching off of you and Bill, you can't look for anything but trouble."

In torment Kitty tugged at the handkerchief in her hands until it suddenly began to rip.

Something would happen, she told herself. It had to. Somehow she would find a way to rid herself of Gerald's mooching and still keep a clear conscience.

Harper Sloane's secretary came back from her honeymoon, so Kitty was out of work again. But she didn't have long to worry about it. The day the girl came back, Harper Sloane trotted briskly up to the rooming house where Kitty stayed. His face was heavy with excitement.

"Bill's down at the hospital, Kitty," he said quickly. "You better go see him."

Kitty's face drained of color, and her hand went up to her mouth.

"It's not too serious," Harper explained, "but it's painful. He was climbing up a windmill ladder today, and a rung pulled loose. He landed on his feet and sprained an ankle pretty bad. Darn near broke it."

Kitty found Bill propped up in a chair his face still pale from shock and pain. "It's all right, Kitty," he said. "Doctor says I might as well go on home. But I won't be worth much for a while. I'll even have to hire somebody to take care of the chores."

The idea struck Kitty like the kick of a brown mule.

"Bill," she asked suddenly, "how much money has Gerald borrowed from you?"

He frowned. "Now, Kitty," he said reluctantly, "it hasn't been enough to worry about."

Firmly she asked him again, "How much?"

He hesitated. "Well, I'd say about seventy-five dollars."

A grim smile came to her face. "Don't you worry about hiring somebody, Bill. I'm going out there and take care of you."

"Kitty, you can't do that. A single girl alone on a ranch with a man—you know what people would say."

"I won't be alone," she replied. "Gerald's going, too. He's going to pay back that seventy-five dollars—in work!"

She found Gerald where she expected to, bent over a domino table. "Come on," she said. "I've found you a job."

His jaw fell. Then, cagily, he said, "How do I know if I want it? I haven't even heard what it pays."

Impatiently she grabbed him by the ear and pulled him

away while the other man laughed. "It's already paid you. Now come on."

Bill directed operations from an easy rocking chair in the front room of the old house. First thing, there was a cow to milk.

"Aw, Sis," Gerald protested, "I haven't milked a cow since I was a kid and Pa was a tenant farmer. I've forgotten how."

"You'll remember soon enough," she said firmly. "Now march!"

He did that, and fed the chickens and gathered the eggs while Kitty fixed supper. The only thing Gerald did with any particular enthusiasm was to help clear the supper table of food.

After supper Kitty pointed to the woodbox behind the stove. "It needs filling," she said. "I noticed a woodpile out back of the house, and a good sharp ax."

Gerald's face clouded. "This foolishness has gone far enough, Sis. I'm going back to town."

Her eyebrows arched, and color rose into her cheeks. Her blue eyes snapped. "You'll walk, if you do. It's twenty miles. Start now and you might make it by daylight."

"Bill's got a pickup," he pointed out.

"Yes, and I've got the keys." Her eyes drilled into him. "I want that woodbox filled. You don't get a bite of breakfast in the morning if it isn't full to the brim."

His shoulders sagged in futility, and he went out. A few minutes later Kitty smiled at the solid ring of an ax biting into mesquite wood.

She was up at sunrise and started a fire in the big wood stove. After she had called Gerald the third time, she walked out onto the back porch where he lay stretched in comfort on an iron cot. She caught the cot at one corner and tipped it over, spilling him roughly.

"That cow needs milking before breakfast," she said sharply. "And on your way back, turn out the chickens. Feed them, too."

At the breakfast table, Kitty asked Bill, "What would you be doing right now if you were able to work?"

He glanced sideways at Gerald. "Well, I've started building a new fence out in the horse pasture, cutting off a section for a holding trap. Landowner's giving me credit for it against my lease. Looks like this is going to throw me behind."

Kitty grinned, seeing Gerald begin to flinch. "No, it isn't. You never saw a fence builder like Gerald Hagen."

Breakfast out of the way, Kitty went with Gerald to look over the fencing project. Bill had set thirty or forty posts already, and spots for more postholes were already staked out. Kitty pointed her chin at the posthole diggers.

"All right, Gerald," she said, firm as a rock, "you'd better start earning that seventy-five dollars. The sooner it's finished, the sooner you can leave."

He took hold of the diggers as if the handles bristled with thorns. He made a few experimental jabs at the ground. "Job like this could take a year's time," he said.

"Could," she said, nodding her head, "but it won't. No dig, no eat. I'll be out here to check before you get a bite of dinner."

Bleakly Gerald gripped the diggers and looked up the line past the stakes. It was a quarter mile or more to where the new fence would join the old one. His face fell in agony.

"Aw, Sis, for Pete's sake . . ."

But Kitty had turned around and started back toward the house.

By the end of the day even Kitty was surprised at the number of new postholes that had been dug. Gerald carried new cedar posts from a large stack and dropped them into the holes. He tamped the dirt around them with a shovel handle until the posts set firm and strong. The holes could not be left open overnight, for a horse might step in one and break a leg.

Next morning Kitty went with Gerald to the fencing job. She helped him sight out a straight line and set stakes for more postholes. His back and shoulders were stiff as a two-by-four board when he started. But he soon worked the stiffness away with the posthole diggers.

The days lengthened the line of set posts, and the distance from the old fence became shorter and shorter. Kitty roused Gerald early, and she didn't let him quit until the sun had dipped low and red over the rugged live-oak trees on the high hill to the west. Even then there was wood to chop, a cow to milk, and stock to feed. The dragging days baked a healthy brown on Gerald's face. But always his gaze was on the road to town.

Bill's ankle was mending rapidly. By the end of a week he was walking easily with the aid of a cane.

"Day or two more and I can tend to my own chores," he said.

With Kitty he hobbled out to look at the fence. His face lighted up like a Christmas tree at the sight of the long line of posts, set and ready for stringing of wire. The gap at the end was getting very short.

"Kitty," he said hesitantly, "I guess I've got an apology to make. I reckon I had the wrong idea about Gerald. I didn't tell you, but to be truthful about it, I got a notion he was kind of a deadbeat. I'm glad to find out I was wrong."

Kitty held down the grin that was struggling to get out. "You're forgiven. It's a mistake anybody could have made."

One day Gerald came dragging in at midafternoon, his weary shoulders slumped.

"A little early, aren't you?" Kitty asked, her eyebrows arched ominously.

"It's finished," he said. "Now what about them pickup keys?"

Bill's rocking chair was set in the cool shade of the liveoak trees in the big yard. Kitty sat down on the arm of the chair and looked at him.

"Gerald's leaving," she said. "He's finished the fence job. He says he wants to go to East Texas. He's heard of some good oil-field jobs back there."

Bill pondered. "There are some good oil-field jobs here, too."

She nodded, a smile tugging at her mouth. "Yes. But he wants to go to East Texas."

There was more she could have said. She could have told him she didn't expect Gerald to come back for a long time. The memory of those posthole diggers would serve to fortify his spirit of independence whenever it might begin to lag.

A sadness began to settle into Bill's face. "I'll miss you, Kitty. I've gotten awfully used to having you around."

"Oh," she said quickly, "I'm not leaving."

His eyes widened. "But, Kitty, it's like I told you before. A single girl couldn't stay out here alone. People would talk."

She put her warm hand under his chin and smiled. Her eyes were dancing. "Well, then, what're you going to do about it?"

His grin grew slowly as he pushed himself to a stand and put his arm around her waist. "Do?" he asked, looking into her eyes. "I'm going to phone the minister at the church and tell him to get ready. He's got two cash customers coming in."

THE UNSILENT PARTNER

Doug Corder jerked his pickup truck to a stop in front of Finley's feed store, stepped down into the caliche street and slammed the door. He stood there a moment, looking past the domino hall toward Bandy Blair's real estate office and somehow enjoying the anger that boiled deep down within him.

Once in a while it felt good to be hopping mad at somebody. Hot words had been struggling to get out of him for three years. He had held them back. Now he had just the drive he needed to say them, and he was glad.

He strode past the domino hall, his bootheels clicking sharply on the crumbling old concrete walk. He shoved Blair's door open, then slammed it behind him.

Blair looked up quickly and swung his feet down from the edge of his heel-scarred desk. Doug gave only a glance to the blond girl who sat beside Blair, looking over some papers.

"All right, Bandy," Doug gritted angrily. "Where's the extra cowhands you was going to send out to help us work calves? We've kept the neighbors waiting four days for you. Now the radio's predicting a siege of rain, and we may not get through!"

Bandy stammered apologetically. "Aw now, Doug, I was really figgering on doing that, but one thing came up, and then another, and I clean forgot about it."

He fumbled a cigar out of the pocket of his fresh white shirt and extended it to Doug for appeasement. Doug ignored it and glanced at the girl.

"You mean a blonde came up! One always does."

He saw the fire flash in the girl's eyes. He swung his angry gaze back to Blair.

"Now you listen to me, Bandy. I let you buy in with me on that ranch because you was a veteran, same as I was. But ever since we've been pardners, you've been acting this way."

Doug paused, then went on, his voice even angrier now. "Well, I've warned you before, and I'm serving you final notice now. Either you sell your share of the place to somebody that'll help a little, or I'll cut the ranch right in half and let your part go to hell!"

Bandy stammered. When he was promoting something, he always had a line smooth as the hide on a baby calf. But hem him up in a corner and he couldn't recite the alphabet.

"Aw now, Doug, the fact is, I have been negotiating with a prospective buyer. Name's Tommie Scott. We even drove out and looked the place over."

That sounded good to Doug. "Then you ought to be out working on the sale, Bandy, instead of wasting time with every blonde that comes to town."

Doug glanced back at the girl as he spoke. Her blue eyes blazed, and she stood straight up.

"That's snap judgment, cowboy," she said sharply. "You'd better look before you start tossing out a loop. You're liable to catch something you can't turn loose of."

Doug gave her a good look now. If Bandy wasn't good for anything else, he surely had an eye for women. The angry red in her cheeks made her pretty as a Quarter colt in a hay lot.

"I'm not interested in catching anything but a new pardner," he told her. "Anybody'd be better than Bandy. And he might be all right, if these gold-digging girls would leave him alone."

She knew who he was aiming at. She stepped out from

behind the desk and stood with doubled fists on her slim hips. Sparks danced in her eyes.

"So anybody would be better, you think? You seem to be awfully bad in your judgments. I hope you get a pardner who'll build a fire under you and keep pouring on the wood!"

The color had drained from Blair's face. He was frantically signaling Doug to take it easy. Warmth rose in Doug's cheeks, and he started backing for the door. He'd never in his life won an argument with a woman. He could tell that this wasn't going to be the first time.

"I'll get the cowboys this time, Bandy," he said, one hand on the doorknob. "You rush up things with this feller Scott."

He stepped out of the door, then leaned back in and added to the white-faced Bandy, "I hope you do a better job of picking me a pardner than you have of picking you a girlfriend. I think this one bites."

She picked up a metal paperweight and hurled it at him. He shut the door quickly and heard it bounce off the door facing.

Doug's blood was racing a little. He hoped he'd never run into that girl again. He wished now he hadn't been so angry. There wasn't any call for needling a girl that way. But then, there was only one kind that stayed around Bandy Blair long.

It took Doug all day to find a couple of good cowhands who needed a few day's work and get them ready to go out to the ranch. It wasn't long before sundown when he drove the pickup through the last liveoak grove, over the last cattle guard, and pulled up in front of the bunkhouse.

"You boys know where to spread your bedrolls. I'm going over to my house a little bit. Then I'll be back and we'll get Olen to fix us some supper."

He started for the main house, which was a little way across from the bunkhouse and kitchen. Then he felt his breath leave him, and an oath ripped out of him as he stopped in his tracks.

His trunk sat in the middle of the yard. His clothes, still on hangers, lay on the ground around the front steps. Boots were scattered about. His Sunday hat lay in the dirt, the crown crushed in.

Doug's blood came to a sudden boil, and he headed for the house in a dead run. As he let the door slam behind him, he saw the blond girl standing there in the little living room. She quickly turned her back and finished buttoning a new blouse.

Doug stood slack-jawed a moment, speechless. Than he stammered, "Wh-what're you doing in my house? What do you mean, scattering my stuff all over the front yard? Bandy didn't go and marry you, did he?"

She turned and laughed. It was a triumphant laugh with no comfort in it for Doug. "No, Mister Corder. Bandy didn't marry me. He sold me his half of this ranch!"

The strength left Doug's knees and he wanted to sit down. The anger dropped out of him like a hundred pounds of oats out of a split sack. In its place was a numbness that he knew must have turned his face white.

"Th—then you must be—Tommie Scott."

She laughed again, her voice hard as a rock. "That guess ought to win you a cigar, cowboy. Now I'll thank you to get your stuff away from my house. It's cluttering up my front yard."

Doug backed weakly toward the door.

"One more thing," she said. "This is my house now. See that shotgun in the corner? Next time you come in here without knocking, it's going to be loaded with rock salt. And I'm liable to let you have both barrels right in the hip pockets."

There wasn't a thing to say on top of a statement like that. Doug left.

As he started back across the yard, he felt himself swaying a little. A tall, middle-aged cowpuncher leisurely walked out to meet him, puffing on a straight-stemmed old pipe. He regarded Doug a minute, then finally said, "I was hoping to catch you and give you the news before you went wading in over your head, Doug."

Doug shoved his hands down deep as they would go into the pockets of his Levis and stood there with his shoulders sagging. "This has hit me right between the eyes. What'm I going to do, Newt?"

Newt Hightower puffed on his pipe. "Wait, I reckon, Doug. Not much else you can do. All the paperwork ain't done yet, but Bandy gave her immediate possession."

The puncher gazed toward the main house. "I'm liable to be wrong, but I figger her for a rich city gal. When she's had to do some hard work and put up with some hardships, she'll decide there ain't much sport in ranch life. By then maybe you can buy her out yourself."

They heard a violent argument in the kitchen. A woman's voice barked with the bite of barbed wire, "Now git out of here and stay out!"

Olen Giles came stepping gingerly out of the kitchen and into the yard, looking back as if he thought a snuffy cow was behind him. The fat little cook yanked the flour-sack apron out of his low-slung waistband and wiped his face with it.

"I'm leaving here this minute, Doug," he said in a voice that almost whined. "I've took all I'm going to. That Barker woman the Scott girl brought here just ordered me out of my kitchen."

Doug was almost ready to throw in the towel. "Another woman? Aw, Olen, you can't leave now. I'm going to need all the help I can get."

Olen Giles stared down at his worn-out brogans and continued his flood of self-pity. "Me, who's cooked for cow outfits from Del Rio to Canada. Well, I ain't letting dark catch me on the same ranch with her!"

Newt Hightower just stood there puffing silently on his pipe. Doug pleaded, "Aw, look, Olen, maybe this won't last long. You stay here and help us work cattle. I'll even give you a ten-dollar raise."

Giles looked up without raising his head. "She hurt my feelings awful bad."

"Fifteen dollars."

Giles nodded, his eyes brighter. "Seeing it's you, Doug, I'll stay."

A big woman appeared in the kitchen door. "Hey, you," she yelled out at Giles in a voice like a foghorn, "before you leave, you come back in here and git that spittoon out of my kitchen!"

The first shock was over now, and Doug was beginning to think straight again.

"You said all I had to do was wait, Newt. Well, from now on I'm going to make it so tough for Tommie Scott that she'll be glad to get out of here. And just in case that don't work, I'm going to town right now to see a lawyer. That girl has got to go!"

But Doug didn't get any immediate comfort when he saw lawyer Adam Brite.

"Ordinarily a partner can't sell his part of a business without the other partner's consent, Doug. That's written into most contracts. It's in yours. But when Bandy was in here today to see about the deeds and abstracts, he mentioned some kind of agreement you two had made. He said you signed a paper giving him the right to sell his share without consulting you."

Doug sadly nodded his head. "Yeah, Adam, I got so anxious to get rid of him I signed that paper. I figgered I couldn't get a worse pardner than Bandy. Only I did."

"Well," the lawyer said, looking at Doug over his reading glasses, "it looks like you're stuck. But I'll go through all the contracts and papers. If there's a loophole anywhere, I'll find it for you."

Tommie Scott was up before daylight the next morning when the cowboys were eating breakfast with neighbors who had come over to help. She was right behind them when they went out to the corral to saddle up.

"Catch me a horse, too," she told Doug. "I'm going along."

Doug didn't want to look at her, but he caught his eyes roving over her slim figure, clad in tight Western clothes.

"Can't. We only got one extra saddle, and the cook your cook fired is going to use it."

She grinned triumphantly. "It just so happens I've got my own saddle. So catch me a horse."

Doug thought of a sharp answer, but he didn't use it. He spotted a long-legged gray horse in the remuda and chuckled to himself. That rough-trotting old horse could shake an ant out of a syrup can. Doug sailed out a loop and hauled the horse in.

"Here you go, pardner," he said sarcastically. "We call him Rambler."

"And which horse are you going to ride?" she asked.

He pointed with his chin to a well-made stocking-legged bay. "That bay there, Concho."

Tommie Scott turned to Newt. "Mister Hightower, catch me Concho. Mister Corder can ride Rambler himself."

Doug stood there silently and fumed. Newt glanced first at the girl, then at Doug. There was a trace of a grin on his face as the old puncher swung out a loop and caught the bay. While the girl slipped her bridle on the horse, Newt looked around at Doug again.

"She's got you snagged six ways from Sunday, son," he spoke quietly. "You ain't got a prayer."

By ten o'clock they had the big pasture rounded up and the cattle thrown together in a far corner. While cowboys held the herd, Doug and Newt cut out the dry cows, those that didn't have calves. There was no need to drive them all the way to the corrals.

It was pleasant working. Rain clouds had drifted in, and the air was cool and damp. Doug remembered the predictions of rain, and that worried him.

Occasionally he glanced at Tommie Scott. He had to admit that for a city girl she stuck to her horse like a grassburr. And if she was tired or sore, she didn't show it. Olen Giles, on the other hand, groaned with pain every time his gentle old horse got out of a walk. It had been a long time since the cook had had the seat of his britches shined by saddle leather.

It looked as if the girl just couldn't be discouraged. But Doug saw one more chance.

Over on Tommie's edge of the herd, a snuffy dry cow kept lifting her hornless head up, looking for a way out. It wouldn't be long until the muley would make a break for it. Doug would have let her go, but he saw a wire cut on her hip that would have to be doctored before she was turned loose.

In a minute the cow hoisted her tail and took off past Tommie as if a fire engine was after her. Newt Hightower started to leave the heard and go help.

"Hold it, Newt," Doug yelled, a broad grin on his face. "Let her go. She'll show that girl what the cow business can be like."

For a good ten minutes, every time Doug drew rein a moment, he could hear brush popping and the girl hollering. And every time he heard it he laughed. Finally Newt worriedly rode over to him.

"I think we better go help that girl."

"All right, Newt," Doug chuckled. "Guess she's had enough now. You keep cutting the herd. I'll take Olen with me."

Doug kept chuckling all the way out into the mesquite thicket. Olen trailed, grunting irritably as he bounced along.

But Doug choked off his laughter as he rode into a little clearing and saw her. She sat in the saddle as cool as October, while the cow stood facing her at the end of a rope. She had caught the muley right around the neck.

"About time you got here," the girl said dryly. "I couldn't lead her back."

Doug sat there a minute, his mouth open. He didn't want to believe it. Finally he said numbly, "Heel her, Olen. I'll doctor that cut."

Olen caught the cow's hind feet the third throw, and he and the girl stretched the cow out. Doug knelt on the cow's side and carefully poured medicine into the cut to prevent any worm trouble. By the time he was through, the cow was trembling with anger.

Gingerly Doug slipped Tommie's rope off the cow's head. "Hold those hind feet tight, Olen," he yelled. "Don't let her up till I get in the saddle."

But Olen had been in the kitchen too long. He let his horse step forward, and the rope went slack. The cow jumped to her feet and kicked the rope loose. She shook her head angrily, snuffed and charged Doug.

Heart high in his throat, Doug ran for his horse. But Tommie beat him there and grabbed the reins. She led the horse away in a trot.

"What're you trying to do?" Doug exploded. "Get me killed? Bring that horse back here quick!"

The girl was laughing, and this time it was genuine. "You'll get him back when you apologize to me."

His throat dry, Doug leaped to one side as the cow lunged at him. "Quit kidding and bring me that horse!" he pleaded.

The cow whirled, ducked her head and came at Doug again.

"Say you're sorry for what you said in Bandy's office," Tommie ordered.

Doug leaped aside, but this time the cow caught his knee and spun him around. "I'm sorry!" he yelled. "For Pete's sake, give me my horse!"

"Say I'm not what you thought I was," she laughed.

Doug tried to grab the cow around her head and neck, but his hands slipped off. He went off balance and fell down on his knees in the sand.

"No, Tommie," he conceded desperately. "You're sure not what I thought you was."

Just then the cow caught him in the seat of the pants and bowled him over. Each time he tried to get up, she would butt him with her hornless head and spill him again. Tommie dropped the horse's reins, whipped out a new loop in her rope and expertly heeled the cow. She spurred off quickly and jerked the muley down.

Doug swayed to his feet and staggered to his horse. When Tommie slackened up on the rope, the cow got to her feet, shook the loop off and stood defiantly, jerking her head as she looked first at Tommie, then Olen, then Doug. Finally she turned and trotted triumphantly off into the brush.

Doug was breathing hard. He wiped his sandy, sweaty face with his sleeve and noticed that his shirt was badly ripped. He painfully rubbed a bruised place on his side. When he had most of his breath back, he gritted, "If you was a man, I'd whip the daylights out of you."

"But I'm not a man," she countered. "If I had been, I'd've whipped you yesterday. I guess this about evens us up."

She started laughing again. Olen began to chuckle furtively. Doug looked at his messed-up clothes and his ripped shirt. There was a dull ache in his side. The warmth of anger began to drain out of his cheeks, but he still couldn't see much to laugh at.

"I've had you pegged for a city girl," he said. "But it wasn't any city girl who heeled that cow so slick. Just who are you, anyway?"

She was smiling—a smile that would have looked pleasant any other time. "Been hoping you'd finally get around to asking me that. I grew up on a ranch out in New Mexico, in the desert country.

"When the War came on, my brother John went to North Africa with the infantry and never came back. Later Uncle Sam wanted to buy our ranch as part of a proving ground for new weapons. Dad figured it was one way he could help pay back for John. So he sold. He always figured on buying another ranch. But he died before he ever found a place that suited him.

I liked this country the first time I saw it. I was all set to haggle Bandy Blair down some more on the price when you came in the office mad and jumping at conclusions. You made me see red, and I took Bandy's price right then, so I could start making you squirm."

Laughter danced in her blue eyes. "I guess you've squirmed enough now. I'm willing to call it quits and become a good partner if you are."

She extended her hand. Doug started to accept it, then thought better of it. Shake hands now and he would find it harder to get rid of her if Adam Brite found that loophole.

The smile slowly faded from her face, and she lowered her hand. "If that's the way you feel about it," she said gravely, "I guess the peace pipe can wait."

"I guess it had better," Doug replied quietly. He reined his horse around and headed back to the herd.

Scattered raindrops were falling when he reached the cattle. By the time the crew had the cows and calves moved to the branding pens, the rain had increased to a deluge. Branding-pen wood soaked. Calves' hides were too wet to take a hot iron well.

Disconsolately Doug decided to turn the cattle into a small holdover pasture until it got dry enough to brand. Then the cowboys headed back toward the ranch, and the neighbor help went home.

The second day Doug let the extra men go back to town. The rain kept falling. In forty-eight hours, eight inches of rain had fallen—about four months' normal supply. The pounding rain had long since stopped soaking in. It was pouring off the hill-sides into the draws and out of the draws into the swollen, muddy river. When a rain stopped soaking in, it stopped being useful, to Doug's way of thinking.

He was standing on the front porch, looking vainly for a break in the clouds, when an old green pickup truck came slosh-ing through the puddles in the soaked-up road and pulled to a muddy stop in front of the bunkhouse. An eighteen-year-old boy piled out of it and came trotting up to Doug, the pelting rain bouncing off of him.

"Pap tried to phone you, but your line was out," he said breathlessly. His soaking clothes clung to his body, and his wet hat brim hung down around his ears.

"He says to tell you they got word to him that the river's coming down. It's going to be plenty deep along the river bottoms. He says you better get your cattle out of there and up to high ground."

Alarm rippled through Doug. "I was hoping it wouldn't come to that. I ought to've known better. You get in there and get you some dry clothes, Jakie."

The boy turned quickly away. "Haven't got time. Got to go on and warn the others down the river."

In a minute he was gone. Doug, Newt, and Olen were quickly saddling up horses and loading them into a "boxcar" trailer hitched to Doug's pickup.

Tommie came running out to the barn, slicker over her shoulders. "Where's a horse? Those are my cattle too, you know."

Doug and Newt tried to talk her out of it, but it was no use. Soon four horses were crowded into the long trailer, and the four riders were packed in the pickup.

Half a mile from the river, Doug braked to a stop. "This is as far as we better go," he said. "We'll take the rest of it on horseback."

The ranch had about a mile and a half of river front. The opposite side belonged to another outfit. The rolling river and the pounding rain made a loud, hollow sound that spoke of danger. Water was already more than ankle deep three hundred yards from the river bank.

Doug let Newt drop off first. As the others found cattle, they would drift them out to Newt and let him herd them off to a safe distance. Olen was next. Doug kept Tommie near him. She was used to the desert country. If he didn't watch her, no telling what she might get into here.

The roar of the river got louder and louder as they rode

on. There were many cattle in the river bottoms. They had drifted there trying to find shelter from the storm.

Finally the group had cleared out the first half mile, then three-quarters of a mile. The roar got louder and louder. If the crest came down before they got through . . . Doug shuddered at the thought and spurred his horse up some more.

Then they had gone a mile. The water was constantly rising. Close to the river it was almost to his horse's belly.

Another quarter mile was behind them, and Doug knew the ride would be over any time now. It wouldn't be a bit too soon. The rising water forced him to drift back farther from the river. Luckily, most of the cattle had drifted back, too.

He picked up one straggling little bunch of cattle and drifted them out to Tommie, then on to the worried-looking Olen. One cow kept looking back and bawling.

"Oh, Doug," Tommie cried, "she's got a calf back there some-where. We've missed it!"

The roar of the river had reached a high pitch now. Doug knew the crest was almost on them. "It's too late to go back for it now. The river's just about to come down."

Tommie cut the cow out and let her start back. "Maybe it's too late for you, but it's not too late for me!"

The cow struck out as fast as she could in the knee-deep water. Tommie spurred after her.

"Wait a minute, you little fool," Doug yelled after her. "You'll get drowned."

But Tommie kept spurring.

"Come on, Olen," Doug called. "We've got to go bring her back."

Fear had frozen Olen's pale face as he looked out over the rising water. "No sir, I ain't going out there. I seen a drowned man once. You couldn't raise my wages enough to make me go out there. In fact, soon as we git back to the house, I'm pack-ing up. I ain't staying on this outfit another day."

Olen turned his back on Doug and kept chousing the cattle toward higher ground. Doug wheeled his horse around and spurred after Tommie. He wished Newt was with him. He yelled, but he knew Tommie couldn't hear him.

The crest had come down. Although Doug was two hundred yards from the river bank, his horse was half swimming along. Through the driving rain he could see Tommie just ahead.

She had found the calf floating in the water, struggling to stay up. She was trying to get it onto the saddle with her. But her panicky horse was fighting to get back out of the deep water.

"Hold on, Tommie," Doug yelled. "I'm coming!" But even as he called, he saw her spill out of the saddle and begin floundering in the swirling, chin-deep water.

Doug's heart felt as if it would stop. He fought his horse on through the ever-deepening water. He saw Tommie go under once. As he was about to catch her, she went under again. Finally he grabbed her. His horse shied, but he managed to pull her up behind him.

Choking, she held onto him tightly. The calf was still floating. Doug grabbed hold of it and pulled it across the front of the saddle. Then he started fighting for shallow water.

It seemed like days before they got to solid footing.

The rain was letting up, the danger was past now, but Tommie was still hanging onto him, her soft body tight against his. Doug found that he liked it. Newt came loping up, leading Tommie's horse.

Doug looked back at the swirling water. "We lost our cow somewhere, Tommie. Reckon you've got you a dogie to feed."

In a little while the ranch's second pickup came driving up. Mrs. Barker crawled out from behind the wheel. With her was the lawyer Brite.

"Figgered you all would be needing something warm by this time," the woman smiled, "so I brought out a thermos jug full of hot coffee. Where's that worthless Olen Giles?"

"Last time I seen him he was driving a little bunch of cattle plumb over the hill," Newt chuckled.

Doug sipped the hot coffee. It was worth ten dollars a cup. "Lady," he grinned at Mrs. Barker, "after this, you've got you a job as long as you want it."

Brite impatiently stepped forward. "This is no day for law talk, Doug, but I knew you'd want to know as soon as possible. Bandy's lost that paper. You've got your loophole."

"What do you mean, Adam?"

"Bandy says he's lost the paper you signed, the one that gave him the right to sell half the ranch without your consent. I think he just got scared when I started questioning him and threw it away. Something shady about it. But anyway, you don't have to accept that girl as a partner if you don't want to."

Doug stared down into his coffee cup. He sipped, but the coffee didn't seem to taste good now. He shot a sidelong glance at Tommie. Hurt showed in her blue eyes. Newt looked sad, too.

Mrs. Barker was staring indignantly at the lawyer. "If I'd knowed what you was up to, I'd've dumped you in a mudhole back down the road someplace."

Tommie stepped up squarely in front of Doug. "Well, what's it to be?" she asked quietly. "You can throw my things out into the yard now, if you want to."

Doug smiled. "Yesterday I would have, and I'd've gotten a big kick out of doing it. But you're a real stock woman, Tommie. You proved that. Bandy wouldn't even have thought about doing what you did. Not even Olen would chance it. But you waded in over your head just to save one calf."

He looked over at Brite. "Thanks for coming out, Adam. You'll get a good fee for your work. But I think I'll just keep my new pardner."

Doug extended his hand to Tommie. "This time it's me who's asking you to shake hands."

Her pretty face broke into a glowing smile. She took his hand and gripped it hard.

In a minute the others had turned away and were refilling their cups from the thermos jug. Doug realized that he still had hold of Tommie's hand. But he didn't let go.

"You know, pardner," she grinned, "after this I might even take the salt out of that shotgun."

They looked at each other, both of them still smiling, and all of a sudden Doug's arm was around Tommie. And then, surprisingly, her arms were around his neck.

After a minute, Doug held her at arm's length and stared hard into her shining blue eyes. He grinned. This was going to be quite a partnership. A lifetime one—if the look in her eyes meant the same thing as the hammering in his heart.

As he kissed her, he made a mental note to be sure and remember to thank Bandy Blair.

THE WAY OF
THE WOLF

Booth Walker sprawled in the warm sand beneath the scanty shade of a mesquite and leisurely watched the rider work down off the hill and level out toward him in an easy lope. Stiffly then, because of the rheumatism, he pushed to his feet and squared a misshapen, sweat-spotted Stetson plumb center over his thick mop of gray hair.

His heavy-boned sorrel, hitched to a limb, swung its head around and pricked its ears toward the horseman.

A slow grin broke across Booth Walker's sun-baked face. The turkey tracks deepened at the corners of his gray eyes. Long before Quinn Stovall got there, Booth knew what the message was going to be. It didn't worry him. Calm and patience were a natural thing to Booth. Maybe it was the years of wearing a sheriff's badge that had done it.

"They're coming," Quinn said, spitting a brown stream of tobacco at a rock as he swung a bowed leg across his horse's rump and down. "I didn't think old Delbert would have the gall to come himself. But he is, and he's got three with him."

Booth grunted. His squinted gaze moved toward a wire corral that he used twice a year in branding calves from this part of his W ranch.

The corral was full of bawling cattle, dust swirling thick and brown in the hot, heavy air above them. Beyond the corral, as far as Booth's age-sharpened eyes could see, stretched thirsty grassland, short on forage, shorter on moisture. The only thing showing a sign of green was the scattering of mesquites. They could send their long roots practically halfway to China.

It was August now. It hadn't rained since March. Even then there hadn't been much. From the looks of the brassy Texas sky, it wasn't fixing to rain again any time soon.

A young cowboy took the six-shooter out of his holster and poked a cartridge into the sixth chamber, always left empty for safety.

"You can put that shell back in your belt, boy," Booth said quietly. "There ain't going to be any need for it today."

Behind him another young man squatted under a mesquite, idly sketching cattle brands in the sand, his face frowning in thought. As Booth walked up to him, the man started jabbing at the ground with the stick, his chin set hard as a rock.

As if in answer to the question forming in Booth's mind, Lanny Walker spoke irritably.

"You know I don't like it, Dad. I wish you could've found some other way."

Booth gazed at his son. He wondered if he had looked the same way when he was twenty-two years old, back in—hell, too long ago to talk about. The strong shoulders, the long, straight back, the stubborn pride that flared easily into anger— these were all good things that would help Lanny when this ranch was his. But it took more than those things. It took judgment, too.

Hand on his hip, Booth squatted awkwardly beside his son. "Look here, Lanny, this place is going to be yours someday. You got to learn that there's only one way to handle a freeloader like Delbert Kemp. You know I've tried talking to him. Just as well talk French to a Mexico bull."

The hard set was still in Lanny's jaw.

"I know what's really eating you, son," Booth went on. "It's that Kemp girl. Why don't you forget her? She'll never do you any good."

Lanny poked at the ground so hard he broke the stick. "You don't know her, Dad."

"I know her father, and I knew her mother, too. You're enough of a cowman to realize that a scrub bull and a scrub cow never get you anything but a scrub calf."

Lanny jumped to his feet and stomped away.

Ruefully, Booth watched him go. They had been partners in many ways, yet he wondered why a father must always be in some respects a stranger to his son.

Booth pushed himself back to a stand. A big, dark man with black whiskers and a chest broad as the length of an ax handle stepped up beside him. Worry lay in his deep blue eyes. "You want me to go talk to him, Booth?"

Booth shook his head. "He'll be all right, Sam. Just takes time, is all. Best horses I ever had was the ones that was hardest to break."

He swung his gaze back to the south. He could see the four horsemen now. They had reached the foot of the hill where the heat waves danced, and they were jogging in at a fast trot. Booth knew from the way skinny Delbert Kemp sat forward in the saddle that anger was riding him hard. Booth stepped out a little in front of his crew and stood waiting, his grin set firm. But the humor began to drain away.

"Afternoon, Delbert," he said as the man reined up. He raised his hand in greeting.

"Howdy, Booth," Kemp returned grudgingly. His thin face was splotched with angry red above a scrawny, turkey neck.

Booth's grin widened, but it went no deeper than his face. "Believe I've got some of your cattle in that corral yonder, Delbert."

Kemp shouted, "You know damned well you have!" His

knuckles seemed to swell as he gripped the saddle horn in anger. "You got no call to act so high-handed just because a few of my cows drifted over onto your country."

"A few?" Booth's voice rose a little. "There's more than a hundred head of Cross K cattle in that corral. And they didn't exactly drift, either. They were pushed across a cut fence. Just happened that one of my punchers was riding fence and tracked them down before they got scattered too much."

Booth dropped the last pretense at a grin. His heavy shoulders squared. "It's none of my business how you run your ranch, Delbert. I don't care if you've got too many cattle for your country. It doesn't mean a thing to me if you graze your grass down so short that the first dry spell puts you out of feed and makes your cattle as poor as whip-poor-wills.

"But it's my business when you start trying to slip your stuff through the fence and steal my grass. If it doesn't rain, it'll take all the grass and water I've got just for my own cattle."

His voice began to quicken. "We've free-fed all your stuff we're going to, Delbert. From now on my men have strict orders. If they find any Cross K stuff in here, they'll run the tallow off of it. They'll never give your cattle time to graze. They'll run them till they can't run any more, and then they'll push them back through the fence. Every dollar's worth of free grass you get will cost you five dollars in lost flesh. You better not forget it."

Kemp's Adam's apple was bobbing up and down. He was putting up a big front, like a banty rooster. But Booth knew there was nothing behind it.

Kemp's worthless cowhands knew it, too. A couple of them grinned furtively. The first one that hit town would spread this story in a hurry.

"Still acting the sheriff, ain't you, Booth?" Kemp blurted. "Twelve years out of office and still acting the sheriff."

"I'm protecting what's mine," Booth said. "That's every man's right."

A petty triumph came to Kemp's face. "From what I heard

today, Booth, you're going to need a lot of protecting. They tell me Drake Brannigan's back."

Booth Walker unconsciously took a step backward, his hands suddenly flat against his sides. The grin was on Kemp's face now, though a nervous and lopsided one.

"If he's served out his time," Booth said, "there's no reason he can't be wherever he wants to be."

Kemp nodded. "That's right, there ain't. And it's a safe bet he'd want to be right here, close to you. He spent fifteen years in the pen, remembering every day that you were the one who got him sent up. I'd hate to be you, Booth, even if you have got all the grass."

Booth tried to shrug it off, and he noticed the faint tremor that had come to his lands. "Fifteen years is a long time. Maybe he's changed."

Kemp's grin showed a row of crooked, stained teeth. "Brannigan? Not him. Nothing would ever change him." He hipped around in the saddle and said loudly, in a shallow show of bravado, "Get our cows and let's go, boys."

Booth and his men stood by and let Kemp's hands do all the work of pushing the cattle out of the pen. The cows were mostly longhorn, lank and leggy, of every color. There was one scrawny, cold-blooded bull in the bunch. That was one reason Booth hated so much to see the sorry Cross K stock on his place. With his own land fenced, he was bringing in good-blooded bulls to breed up his cattle. Those stray Cross K bulls always left their cull mark in the next year's calf crop.

Kemp said, "You tell that boy of yours that if he don't keep away from my Sue Ellen, I'm liable to put some buckshot in his pants. I won't have her marrying into family that won't help a neighbor." For the first time Booth noticed that Lanny had stayed back out of sight.

"Don't you worry, Delbert. If my boy was to marry your girl, I wouldn't let either one of them on my place. Your cows are on their way. You better go with them."

Kemp pulled his horse around, but stopped to fling one last hasty remark over his shoulder. "You'll be wishing you'd been better to your neighbors when Brannigan comes around."

Chin sagging a little, Booth watched the procession string out toward the hill to the south, the dust hovering thickly in its wake.

Booth's weather-beaten foreman, Quinn Stovall, stood beside him. His three-day growth of whiskers bristled like barbs on a roll of fence wire. "Maybe Kemp was talking through his hat, Booth. We've heard before that Brannigan was coming, and he never showed up."

Booth said, "No, Quinn, I reckon it's the truth. He was bound to come back sooner or later."

Huge Sam Trenfield moved in front of him. "Look, Booth, what do you say I go hunt Brannigan up and talk to him?"

The ranchman shook his head.

"But, Booth," Trenfield argued, raising his broad, calloused hands, "I know him. I spent ten years in the same cell with him. If there's anybody can talk to him, it's me."

Again Booth shook his head. "It might lead to trouble, Sam. And you got to stay away from that. The first sign of trouble, they'll call off your parole and slap you back into the pen."

Booth limped to the mesquite and untied his big sorrel horse. He let his right hand touch his thigh and remembered how the pistol used to feel there, long ago. He tried to bend the hand as he would have to do to grip a gun. It wouldn't work. The stiffness and the rheumatism had been there too long.

Leading out, he stopped as he rode up to Lanny. A tinge of shame touched him that his own son had ducked out on the showdown—harmless showdown, too. But Booth could understand. Lanny wasn't going to do anything that might bring anger to Sue Ellen Kemp.

"Ready to go, son?"

Lanny swung into his saddle and flicked an irritable glance at his father. "You're running this show."

Booth bit his chapped lip and spurred the sorrel. He hoped he would have a chance to see that Kemp girl. There were a few things he was itching to tell her.

Sitting in the front room of his big frame ranch house, Booth tucked the fiddle under his chin and cut away at some of the old tunes. There was strength enough in the right hand to hold the bow, and his left hand was as good as ever at fretting the strings.

It was funny sometimes, how a man could say on a fiddle the things he couldn't say in words—how he could draw the worry out of him with a tune, and feel washed and clean.

Through the window he could watch his wife, Abbie, in the late afternoon sun, hunting eggs near the barn. Here and there she stopped and bent over stiffly. She put the eggs in the milk bucket she carried on her thick arm. Her pleasant face was hidden from him by the old slat bonnet she wore to protect her from the scorching sun.

Booth heard the horse trot up in front of the house. He put away the fiddle and walked to the door. "Come on in, Sam," he called.

Big Sam Trenfield ducked under the doorway and took off his hat. "I went in to talk to Drake Brannigan, Booth."

"I figured you did."

"I didn't want to make you mad, Booth, but I thought I ought to see what Drake had on his mind."

Booth could read the answer in the worried sag on the big man's face. "You found out?"

Sam nodded. "He still hates you, Booth. He called me a fool for trying to help you. He kept reminding me that it was you that sent me to the pen. He even wanted me to throw in with him. But I told him how you got me paroled, and how you gave me a good job when I got back." Sam twisted his battered old hat in his hands. "He says he's going to get you, Booth. He says he'll take his time, but he's going to get you."

Booth slumped back into his chair. As he had done before, he tried to bend the fingers of his right hand the way he would have to to fire a gun. It wouldn't work. And it never would again.

"There's no point in waiting any longer," he said, his baleful eyes resting on the bad hand. "I'm going to town in the morning."

Trenfield's jaw dropped. "Booth, you can't do that. You can't even fire a gun."

"I'm not going to take one."

Trenfield said, "Then I'm going with you."

"No, Sam," Booth said, "you're going to go back out there with your mules and build some more on that tank. It's going to rain again, some day, and we need all the surface tanks we can build, to catch water. What if you went with me and got into trouble? You want to spend two or three more years in Huntsville?"

"All right, Booth, but at least you ought to take Lanny along with you."

"This ain't his fight. It started when he wasn't much more than a baby."

Booth told himself again he couldn't let anything happen to Lanny. There had to be someone to take over the ranch someday, and Booth had spent twenty-two years raising the boy for that job.

The breeze on an August early morning could be finer than in any other part of the year, before the sun rose to turn loose its dry, furnace fury and put bake-oven heat in it.

Jogging along the wagon trail that wound its way toward town Booth felt pride touch him. There wasn't any doubt about it. He had about the best ranch in the county, except for water.

It hadn't come easy. In the first years after their marriage, he and Abbie had lived in a sagging, unpainted house in town, eaten the cheapest way they could, and worn their clothes till they couldn't be mended any more. Every spare dollar had gone into land and cattle.

In late years, as more state land had gone up for sale, Booth had gotten cowboys to homestead a claim, prove it up for the required three years, then sell their equity to him if they still wanted to. Most of them had wanted to. The place was his now, free and clear, except for a trifling little note here and there.

Even with the worry that crowded his mind this morning, the cowman in him made him ride two miles out of his way. Had to see how much water was left in the Paint Horse surface tank. Satisfaction crossed his face as he looked at the small body of water which meant life to so many of his cattle. It was half full. By George, it had to rain by fall.

A dozen times, in a dozen spots, he had tried to get a windmill on the south half of his ranch. But down as far as the well drillers went, they found only dry sand and caliche. There was nothing to do but depend on the runoff waters he could catch when it rained.

Trotting his big sorrel up to the gate that led out across Kemp's Cross K, Booth leaned forward in the saddle and looked down at the ground. A set of fresh hoofprints trailed west, toward the Kemp house; another set led back. Night crawlers had left their tiny marks across the tracks, showing that they had been made the day or night before. Not much question who had been riding the horse, or what Lanny's purpose had been.

Booth gritted his teeth, then pushed on.

Everybody in town knew where Brannigan was spending his time. He was in Fant Fletcher's saloon.

Fletcher strode out from behind the granite-tipped bar and met Booth at the door. He was a middle-aged man who ran his place strictly for business, and never drank up a drop of his profits. His worried eyes lowered to Booth's belt, then raised again.

"You ain't wearing a gun," he said in surprise.

Booth shook his head and lifted his stiff right hand. "You know I couldn't use one if I did have it, Fant."

Fletcher nodded, frowning. "All right, Booth. But I'll have my shotgun right under the bar. If you get in trouble, I'll give it to Brannigan with both barrels."

"I don't expect there'll be any need for that. I'm hoping I can talk this out with him. But thanks anyway, Fant."

He walked on toward the card tables at the back of the long, narrow frame building. Brannigan was there, flanked by two men. The years had been hard on Brannigan. The flesh was heavy and a little pale on his hard face. His coarse hair, shot with gray, was just beginning to grow out of its close prison cut. But one thing hadn't changed—his eyes. Stabbing at Booth now, they were as flinty as they had been when Booth had clanged the cell door shut behind Brannigan more than fifteen years ago.

A shallow smile broke across Brannigan's face, but his eyes stayed hard. The man stood up to his full six feet and extended his hand. "Howdy, Booth."

Hesitantly Booth put forward his left hand to shake. "Been a long time, hasn't it, Drake?"

The smile dropped away, and the eyes glittered.

"Fifteen years and thirty-three days."

Brannigan turned to his left and nodded toward a tall bean-pole of a man who had been sitting beside him. "Meet Spade Horne. Old friend of mine. We used to make a good pick and shovel team, back in Huntsville. He had a friendlier judge than mine was. He didn't have to stay quite as long."

Booth nodded and put forward his left hand again. Horne just glared at him and eased his own long hands back along the seams of his trousers. He had a death's head of a face, the sallow skin tight as rawhide, the cheeks sunken in beneath sharp, jutting cheekbones. There was the suggestion of a wolf in his yellowish eyes.

Drake turned to the other side and made a sweeping motion with his hand. "You remember Judge Pentecost, don't you, Booth?"

Booth nodded at a shriveled, bald little man. This time he made no attempt at shaking hands. He knew Pentecost, a cheap, crooked little lawyer who never had been a judge and never would be. Somebody had dubbed the name on him as an ironic joke, and it had stuck.

Drake Brannigan eased back into his chair and motioned for Booth to take a seat. Booth shook his head.

"I was hoping you'd see things straight when you came back, Drake," he said. "Ain't any harder to be friends than it is to be enemies. I'll be glad to do anything I can to help you get a fresh start."

Drake's eyelids narrowed. He lighted a cigar and drew on it thoughtfully. "That's easy for you to say, Booth. For the last fifteen years you've been doing mighty good for yourself. Got you a big ranch, they say, and pretty near paid out. But me, I spent those fifteen years behind a high wall, with somebody watching every move I made. Fifteen years carved out of my life, and what have I got to show for it?"

"You got lots of time left, Drake. You can make good use of it, if you want to."

Brannigan studied the burning end of his cigar a long moment, then lifted his eyes. They glowed like the cigar. "I'll make use of it."

Unconsciously he began to tighten his fist. "There was a time when I'd've just come back and shot you right where I found you, Booth. But a man changes his way of looking at things when he's got fifteen years without much else to do. I'm going to get you, Booth, just like I told you I would the day you turned me over to the warden at Huntsville. But I'm going to whittle away at you, a little at a time. I'm going to make it slow for you, the way it was for me. At the end of it, you won't have anything left, not even your pride.

"Maybe by that time you'll come gunning for me, so I can kill you legal. Sure, I'm going to kill you, Booth. But I'll do it when I'm ready, not before."

Booth's face flamed as he listened. His teeth clamped together. He half wished Brannigan would make some kind of play now, so there would be ground for calling in Sheriff Dotson. But he knew Brannigan would be careful. Fifteen years had burned the hatred deeply into him. But it had sharpened his judgment and cunning.

"I'm sorry, Drake," he said quietly. He turned on his bootheel and walked away. Dread began to eat at him, but helplessness was heavy on him, too. He knew there was nothing he could do, nothing but wait for Drake to make his move.

Brannigan chewed roughly on his cigar as he watched Booth Walker move slowly to the front of the saloon and limp out the door. Hatred smoldered in him, and his hand itched on the butt of the gun he wore. For a moment he regretted that he hadn't put a bullet in the ex-sheriff. But all in due time, he told himself.

Spade Horne's eyes accused him. "I don't savvy all this, Drake. You had him right here in front of you. If it was me, I wouldn't make a hard job out of something I could have over within a minute."

Brannigan leaned his chair back and propped his boots up on the table. "Did you ever sit down to a meal that was so good you wanted to eat it slow, to make it last longer?"

Horne shook his head.

"That's where we're different," Brannigan said. "When a wolf kills a rabbit, he does it quick. But did you ever see a cat catch one? He generally plays with it, killing it slow. You've got the way of the wolf about you, Spade. But I'd rather do it like the cat does."

A painted woman in a bright, clinging dress weaved her way back through the saloon, smiling at some of the customers. Brannigan watched her, his eyes burning. A man never knew how hungry he could be for the sight of a woman, until he had been locked up for fifteen years and never given a chance to see one.

He drew on the cigar, musing quietly. Then he turned to Judge Pentecost. "Did you ever look over the deeds that Booth has got to his land?"

Pentecost said, "I've never had any occasion to do so."

"Well, I want you to. I never saw a deed that a smart lawyer couldn't poke holes in. If you find a flaw, we'll jump on it with both feet."

The lawyer's wizened little face twisted into a scowl. "That undoubtedly will take a considerable length of time. It may also take a lot of money. When do you propose to pay me, Brannigan?"

Brannigan's face flared. "You hate Walker, too, don't you, Judge? You want to see him broke just as bad as I do, don't you? Then stop whining about money. You ought to be glad to do it for nothing. It should pleasure you."

Spade Horne leaned forward menacingly. "Besides, if you don't . . ."

Pentecost's tongue flicked nervously over his lips. "Certainly I'll do it, Brannigan. I didn't mean anything. It'll be a pleasure, I assure you."

"That's better." Brannigan rose to his feet. "Come on, Spade. While the judge's handling the legal end, we can start a little digging on our side. We're going out to see a man."

Delbert Kemp's ranch headquarters was a sorry looking place. Drake Brannigan reined in to look it over from some distance. The whole thing, buildings and corrals alike, had been thrown together with cheap, shoddy lumber. The house had never had a coat of paint, and even from where he was, Brannigan could see the lazy sag to the front porch.

He noticed that alongside it was a neat flower bed, but it had wilted into nothing. "Dried up," he said to the lanky Spade Horne, "like everything else around here."

It looked to Brannigan as if the whole country was wilted. All across the Kemp outfit he had noticed that the grass was grazed off almost to nothing. Nowhere had he and Horne been out of sight of gaunt, ill-bred cattle.

"Got a lot more cattle than his country can run," he observed. "Place looks like it was sheeped out."

But in his mind's eye Brannigan was picturing how the ranch might look under different management. "I could make this a good outfit, Spade, if I owned it. And before we're through here, I will own it."

He touched spurs to his dun horse and moved on toward the barn at an easy trot, a thin trail of dust following him. He saw a man sitting in the shade on the barn steps, his legs stretched out lazily, hat tilted over his face.

"Howdy," Brannigan spoke. "We're looking for Delbert Kemp."

The man straightened up. Frowning darkly, the sleep still in his eyes, he pushed back his dirty hat. "What for?" he asked suspiciously.

"That's between him and us."

Nervously the skinny man got to his feet, his Adam's apple bobbing. "Say, ain't you Drake Brannigan?"

Brannigan nodded.

A scared grin forced its way across the man's mouth. "I—I'm Delbert Kemp. What can I do to help you?"

Brannigan smiled to reassure Kemp. "You can do something that'll help us and yourself."

He swung down from the saddle and shoved out his hand. Hesitantly Kemp took it. "I've heard a lot about you in town,

Kemp," Brannigan said smoothly. "From what folks say, it seems you're just the kind of man we need to go partners with on a little deal."

That stirred Kemp's pride, as Brannigan had known it would. Getting over his nervousness, the ranchman grinned foolishly. "Aw, now," he chuckled. "I wouldn't say that." He toed at a little rock that lay in the dust at his feet.

"Let's sit down here and be comfortable," Brannigan continued. He sat beside Kemp on the shady barn steps, handing his bridle reins to Horne. "They tell me Booth Walker gave you a pretty raw deal, Kemp."

Kemp nodded emphatically, his lower lip sticking out. "Yeah, just because four or five of my cows strayed over on him." He began to tell a pitiful, much exaggerated account. Brannigan nodded, listening in great sympathy. He handed a cigar to the skinny ranchman.

"That's why we thought you might like to be the one to help us give Booth Walker what's coming to him," Brannigan said.

Fear sprang into Kemp's wide eyes. "I don't want to get mixed up in no killing."

Brannigan swallowed his contempt for Kemp and rested his hand reassuringly on the man's thin shoulders. "It won't be anything like that. Killing's too good for him." He explained in a general way how he hoped to break Walker, down, a little at a time.

"But we got to have help. And we figure you're man enough to handle the job with us."

Kemp warmed up again. "Well, I have handled some pretty tough jobs in my time. And it'd sure tickle me to get back a few licks at Booth. What're we going to do?"

"I got some ideas," Brannigan told him. "But first, we got to have an excuse for staying out here with you. So you tell it around that I've bought in with you as a partner."

Question arose again in Kemp's eyes. Brannigan quickly

held up his hand. "Won't really be so, you understand. It's just to keep people from getting suspicious. All right?"

Kemp squared himself up to his full height, a proud grin on his face. "Shake, partner."

Brannigan saw the girl as Kemp led him and Spade Horne toward the house. She was out in back, feeding some chickens.

He stopped in his tracks to stare at her. She was young, eighteen or nineteen, but already a woman to quicken a man's heartbeat. Her full blouse fit tightly, and narrowed to a slender waist where it met her split riding skirt. Her high-heeled boots suggested a trim pair of ankles. Brannigan felt the blood begin to stir in him as he let his gaze sweep back over her figure and to the pleasing features of an oval, sun-browned face.

"My daughter, Sue Ellen," the ranchman said. He introduced her to the two men. Brannigan's blood warmed as he shook hands with her. After fifteen years, even the touch of a woman's hand was almost as much as a man could bear.

He watched her later, cooking supper, working about the stove with the lithe step of a dancer, her silky brown hair cascading down about her shoulders. And Brannigan promised himself he was going to get more out of this job than just Kemp's ranch.

Lanny Walker spurred his brown gelding up over the edge of the Paint Horse surface tank and looked down at the brownish water. On the far side a cow had been standing in water almost to her belly. She jerked her head up, the water trickling down her chin. At sight of Lanny she lifted her tail and clattered up over the dump, then disappeared down the far side.

Grinning, Lanny let his horse step gingerly down to the water and drink its fill.

"Lucky there's any water here for you, Snip," he said. "This tank didn't used to hold so good."

Many of the dug tanks in that area had weak bottoms.

They would let the water seep down into the earth instead of holding it. Lanny remembered the day he and a couple more hands had brought a whole remuda of horses over here and milled them around in the muddy tank bottom for more than two hours. That was a method commonly used to pack the bottom of a leaky tank. Since then, the tank had held water fine.

On across the pasture, in the direction of Kemp's Cross K, Sam Trenfield was building a new tank. Lanny slanted over that way.

Under the sun's heat, Sam was laboring behind a stout team of mules. A second team was hobbled out nearby to spell this one. With a long-handled shovel Sam gouged out big scoops of dirt. He hauled them up from the bottom of the tank and dumped them on the edge, where they would serve to dam up the runoff water. The tank resembled a huge bowl, shored up on three sides, the open end facing out toward the draw from which the water would come.

"About finished with this one, aren't you, Sam?" Lanny asked. Trenfield halted the mules. He took off his hat and wiped the grimy sweat from his forehead but missed that which trickled down into his black beard. Sam's sleeve bulged from the thick muscles of his arm.

"I'll be ready to start me a new one pretty quick," he answered. "What brings you over this way?"

"Just looking at the stock. Seems to me there's not as many cattle as there ought to be over on this side of the place."

Trenfield grunted. "Besides which, this side of the place is closest to the Cross K and Sue Ellen Kemp, ain't it?" he asked pointedly.

The color came to Lanny's face as he grinned. "You're not going to start that too, are you, Sam?"

Trenfield shook his head. "I guess you're old enough to know what you're doing. Besides, I've seen Sue Ellen more than your dad has. If it wasn't for her working as hard as two mules, her pa would've lost his ranch a long time ago. She's all right, Lanny. Your dad'll find out one of these days that he's wrong to hold her pa against her."

Lanny dismounted and sat on his spurred heels, idly drawing cattle brands in the dirt. "He hasn't mentioned her the last couple of weeks. Too much else to worry him."

He frowned. "Sam, tell me about Drake Brannigan. Dad won't."

Sam Trenfield drew in a deep breath "Not much to tell. He used to be a pretty tough gunman. Robbed a couple of banks, rustled cattle. Killed two or three men, too, but nobody ever could prove it. It was your dad that finally got him sent up for a bank robbery."

"And now that he's out, he's sworn to get even?"

"That's right. And if I know Brannigan, he will."

Lanny clenched his fists. "Not if somebody gets him first. Dad can't fight anymore, but I can."

Trenfield's eyes suddenly widened. "Don't even think of it, Lanny. You tackling him would be like a cottontail rabbit trying to fight a wolf. Maybe he'll make a slip, and he can be sent back to the pen. That's what we got to hope for. They don't make gunhands like him anymore, and it's a cinch you ain't one, so forget about tangling with Brannigan."

But Lanny didn't forget it. Riding on toward the Cross K gate, he practiced drawing his gun. He was fast, but he knew he wasn't as fast as his dad had once been. And there were those who said Drake Brannigan was faster than Booth Walker ever was.

Two miles into Cross K country, he angled down to a gully that led its winding way out of a clump of mesquite brush. There was where he always met Sue Ellen. They could hide their horses in the gully, if anyone came around. But there was never much danger of their being seen. Delbert Kemp didn't spend any more time a-horseback than he had to. He was too tightfisted to hire enough men, and the wages he paid wouldn't attract anything but the skimmings anyway. His men usually lay down in the shade of a mesquite as soon as they were out of sight of Delbert.

Sue Ellen wasn't there when Lanny arrived, but she came presently. Her pink lips parted in a warm smile as soon as she saw him. She reined up beside him, and he folded his arms about her. For a few moments he forgot about drought. He forgot about Booth Walker, Drake Brannigan, or anything else.

"Will you help me, Lanny?" she asked. "I've found a water hole that's dried up back down the draw. There are a lot of cattle standing around it, and I've got to drift them to another water hole."

Lanny smiled. Too bad, in some ways, that she hadn't been born a man. But he was glad she hadn't.

"Sure, sweetheart. I'll help you. But aren't you afraid somebody'll see you with me, and get your pa sore again?"

She shook her head, her pretty face deadly serious. "There's nobody to see us. Pa fired all the hands. Brannigan's going to get some new ones."

She explained that Brannigan and his friend Horne had moved to the ranch. "Pa says Brannigan's bought a partnership with him, only I haven't seen the color of any money. I wish I hadn't seen Brannigan."

Brannigan. The name sent a chill of dread through Lanny. Now the man was on a neighboring ranch. It made him want to get Sue Ellen away from there as soon as he could.

They rode across the bare, windswept pasture. Presently Lanny said, "I wish we could forget about having to hide from everybody. I wish we could go on and get married, and not worry any more about what anybody else thinks."

Her eyes shining, she reached out and touched his arm. "So do I, Lanny. But we can't. Your dad would hate me as long as he lived. I don't want it to be that way. We'll wait. He's a fair man. He'll be certain to see it our way sooner or later."

Down below the point of a rise, a lone horseman sat watching them. Drake Brannigan's lips drew tight as he saw the young man lean across and kiss the girl. His pulse throbbed heavily, and he vowed that one day the girl would be his.

Old Booth Walker was helping Sam Trenfield pick the site for a new tank. This one would be only about half a mile from the Cross K fence.

Booth grinned as he hunched on his heels and watched Sam's shaggy black dog nosing around in the brush, looking for rabbits. Booth pointed south toward the fence. "See where most of the water will come in from? Kemp's outfit. Water he's too lazy to catch himself."

Sam's white teeth showed through his beard in a wide grin. The big man was pitching his tent, for he stayed on the spot most of the time when he was building tanks. He seldom went to headquarters except to fill his water barrels and get grub or feed for the mules.

"Might be a pretty good place for you to be to watch Kemp," Booth said then. "I know for a fact that there's cattle missing from this south end. Can't find any tracks, but there's a dozen places they could be pushed across in little bunches without leaving enough sign to notice."

There was doubt in Trenfield's deep blue eyes. "Funny, I always knew Kemp was shiftless. But I never would've pictured him as a cattle rustler. Didn't think he had enough guts."

"He didn't have," Booth replied. "But he's got Brannigan with him now. Talk in town is that they're partners. With a big man to back him up, Kemp's got plenty of guts. Let something happen to Brannigan, and Delbert'll fold up like a wet sack."

Trenfield knotted his fists. "You just say the word, Booth, and I'll fold up both of them for you."

Booth's heart swelled. Wasn't often a man could hire anybody as loyal as Sam. But Booth had seen the basic honesty and sincerity in Trenfield, even when the man was sent up for robbery years ago. He had seen Sam's sick wife, the threat of death sinking into her eyes. He had understood the desperation that drove Sam to armed robbery in an attempt to raise money for the kind of doctor she needed. Death had caught up with her too soon, even before Sam's trial. Sam hadn't cared then if they sent him up for eternity.

But Booth had cared, and he had worked hard to get Sam freed.

"Your job's building tanks, Sam," he said. "Dealing with Kemp and Brannigan is mine." He looked up toward the soft hammering of hoofbeats on the dry, short-grazed turf. "I don't know how many times I've told Lanny not to ride a horse so hard," he grumbled, pushing himself stiffly to a stand so his son could see him.

Reining up sharply, Lanny leaned forward in the saddle, his face flushed. "You better come with me, Dad." The words tumbled excitedly from him. "There's trouble down on the Hockley flats."

Booth suddenly felt the color draining from his wide, stubbled face. "What do you mean, trouble?"

"Brannigan's pushing our cattle off of it. Says it doesn't belong to us and he's putting in a homestead claim on it."

Booth didn't spare the spurs. A fast, hard ride westward got him and Lanny to the Hockley country in a hurry. He found his cowboys loose-herding a bunch of his W cattle around what was left of a surface tank. He edged in for a look. The water was low and muddied so that the cattle walked in up to their bellies, but they refused to drink.

Quinn Stovall brought his horse down beside Booth's, the hooves sucking at the thick mud. A thin, sun-dried man, Stovall sat quietly, pondering and spitting tobacco onto the muddy bank. He said, "Reckon we oughtn't've let them get away with it in the beginning, Booth. But Judge Pentecost was with them, and he got to spouting law. I figured we'd better let you talk to them before we lit any matches."

Impatience was pushing Lanny, bringing a blaze to his eyes. "We ought to shove them off so fast they won't know what hit them. We can whip that bunch easily."

But Booth was too old in the business to be carried away. "You did right, Quinn," he said shortly. "Let's go talk to them, then, and find out what this is all about. Lanny, you have the herd ready to push if I give the sign."

He nicked the horse with his spurs and splashed up away from the tank. On the dump he paused again. "Is this supposed to be all the cattle that were on the Hockley six sections?"

Stovall nodded. "They said they brought them all out. Pretty tough bunch Brannigan's got with him."

Booth grunted and put the spurs to his mount again. Stovall sided him.

Brannigan and his men were waiting a quarter mile west of the tank, on the line of the old Hockley homestead. Slow anger burned in Booth as he counted them—five men, besides Brannigan and the Judge. One of them was the tall, cadaverous gunhand named Spade Horne.

Brannigan sat straight in the saddle, a thin smile on his heavy face. He was feeling sure of himself, Booth knew, and the thought worried him. The old Brannigan might have tried to run a sandy like this just in hoping his luck would carry him through. But Booth had an idea the new Brannigan would be plenty sure of his ground before he waded in with both feet.

"I'm giving you two minutes to explain this thing, Brannigan, before I motion my men to start bringing my cattle back."

Brannigan leaned forward confidently, hands cupped on the high horn of his saddle, arms straight. "It won't take two minutes, Booth. The fact is, pure and simple, that the Hockley place doesn't belong to you. You got it by fraud. I've filed a claim on it, and I'm protecting what's mine. Now I'm not even giving you two minutes."

Instinctively Booth eased his stiff right hand down toward

his hip. But there hadn't been a gun there in years. Heatedly he flicked his narrowed eyes toward Judge Pentecost.

"I can see your fine hand in this, Judge." The Judge cringed, looked sideways at Brannigan, then straightened. He made no effort at hiding the hatred in his eyes.

"The answer is quite simple, Walker. This used to be school land that the state put up for sale. Homestead rules, and forty years to pay. But the homestead requirements have never been carried out according to the letter of the law."

"I bought it," Booth protested. "Put up good money for it."

"Bought it after title had been gained by fraudulent methods," the Judge insisted. "I found after considerable study, Walker, that you bought this tract from one Dick Hockley, after you had financed him to homestead.

"But I have discovered that Hockley did not remain the entire three years required under Texas law. He lied to the State officers in making final settlement for the land. I find that he was on your payroll the entire three years. It is my assumption that he lived at your ranch headquarters while he was supposed to be proving up his land. Therefore you were in collusion with him. Should this matter ever reach the courts . . ."

Booth tried to force down the black anger swelling in him. "That's all a lie, Judge. Sure, Hockley worked for me. But he lived on his own land. I paid him to pasture my cattle on it, and I paid him wages to take care of them."

A triumphant gleam came to Pentecost's beady eyes. "Can you prove that by Hockley?"

"Hockley's dead."

Pentecost smiled. "I know that. You have no proof other than your own word, and possibly that of the men in your employ. But a court outside this county might not find your word acceptable, Walker. I advise you to give up, and release this land peaceably to my client, Drake Brannigan."

Brannigan's words came hammering back at Booth from that meeting in Fant Fletcher's. *I'm going to whittle away at you, a little at a time.*

Breathing hard, Booth glared at Drake Brannigan, meeting the outlaw's heavy gaze. "You really think you can get away with this, Drake?"

"My lawyer says I can. And I got five good men to back him up."

Booth's left hand nervously tugged at the leather reins. "We'll see." He reined around and started back toward his cowboys, Stovall riding along beside him.

Halfway between them and the cattle, he stopped and waved his hat in a long arc. His cowboys began to shout at the herd, swinging their ropes. The cows began to move at a trot.

"Tell them to push hard," he shouted toward Stovall. "We'll run right over Brannigan's bunch if they get in our way."

Stovall pointed to the rear. "They're going to get in our way, all right."

Brannigan was spreading out his gunmen, getting ready to make a stand.

A cold, steady fire was eating through Booth. This is as good a time as any, he decided. From beyond a dozen years, the old fight was coming back to him. He wished for good hands, so he could take up a gun. But he had plenty of willing cowboys, and they'd do that for him.

He worked his fist up and down in a pumping motion, the old military signal for speed. The cowpunchers were crowding harder. The cattle labored into a hard run. Pride surged through Booth as he watched his cowboys pushing the fast-moving herd. There was a bunch of riders a man could put his faith in! By the time they reached Brannigan, nothing would stop them or the cattle.

Booth saw the two men spurring hard toward him. For a moment he thought they were from Brannigan's crew, and his face twisted in defiance. But a closer look made him haul up on his reins.

"Stop them cattle, Booth!" Sheriff Dotson bawled through the noise, waving his hands as he kept gigging his horse with roweled spurs. Trailing five or six lengths behind him was Delbert Kemp.

Dotson drew abreast of Booth. His eyes were severe. "I'm telling you, Booth, for your own good, you better stop them cattle!"

Booth swallowed hard. He hadn't expected the law to take a hand in this.

"Just trust me," Dotson went on urgently. "Signal them cowboys to circle that herd."

Rebellion flared in him, but Booth's judgment told him to do whatever Dotson said. He began waving his hat and shouting for the herd to be stopped. He watched until the cowboys began to circle the cattle. Then, wearily, he slumped down in his saddle, glanced sideways at the sheriff.

"I wore a badge long enough to learn that it doesn't pay to argue with the man who's got one," he said. "But I hope you know what you're doing, Dot."

Dotson shook his head. "Can't say as I do, but I'm sure you didn't know what you was about to do, Booth."

Dotson was quiet for a moment, catching his breath after the hard run. He was a man ten years younger than Booth, already graying from years of worry and work. "Delbert here told me a little of what was up. I knew you, and I knew about what you'd do, Booth. So I didn't waste any time getting out here."

Booth frowned. Might have known Brannigan would send Kemp to the sheriff. "It's my land, Dot. They ain't running me off of it."

"I don't blame you. It's pretty plain they're running a fast one on you, Booth. But they'll stub their toe someplace down the line, and when they do, you'll get your place back. Can't you see that Brannigan wants you to go rushing in here half-cocked and get somebody killed? Six sections of land ain't worth the lives of any of your cowboys, or your son, or yourself. So get yourself a good lawyer and start him to work on this. And in the meantime, keep out of Brannigan's way."

Booth shrugged. It sounded sensible. But it sounded slow.

"What am I supposed to do with these cows while I'm waiting? I've already got more than the rest of the place can carry, with the drought on. The Paint Horse and the Hockley place have got the only good water on the whole south side of my ranch. I'll have to throw these cattle on the Paint Horse now. If I was to lose it, I'd sink like a sack of rocks."

Dotson looked down at his horse's thick neck. "Sorry, Booth, that's all we can do right now. You'll just have to make out the best you can."

As Dotson was talking, Kemp slunk off to join Brannigan.

Lanny Walker and Quinn rode up as Dotson spurred west to talk to Brannigan.

"There weren't but six of them, Dad," Lanny said heatedly, accusation in his eyes. "There were nine of us."

Testily Booth said, "You'd've fought them, even though Sue Ellen's old man was siding Brannigan?"

Later he wished he hadn't said it, hadn't let the anger and frustration in him start him to goading his son.

Lanny's eyes held his. There was a trace of anger in them. "He's wrong. Sue Ellen knows that. She wouldn't hold it against me."

Lanny pulled around and rode off toward the herd. Booth shifted his weight in the saddle and glared at Quinn Stovall, the anger still riding him.

"Well, what're you waiting to say?" Stovall calmly jawed his tobacco around and spat a brown stream to one side. "Just waiting for you to give the word about moving them cattle."

Shame touched Booth. "I didn't mean to be so proddy, Quinn. It's just the . . . Shove them east, to the Paint Horse."

Stovall frowned. "Think it'll last till it rains?"

"It's got to," Booth said, and spurred after the herd.

In the gathering darkness, Drake Brannigan hauled up on the bridle reins. He sat his horse in the gravelly bed of a dried-up creek and looked for a moment across the W fence. Irritably he turned in the saddle and peered back through the gloom.

"Come on—get the lead out, Delbert," he said sharply. "Can't you ever keep up with the rest of us?"

Kemp brought his horse into a fast buggy trot and moved up beside Brannigan and Spade Horne.

"I tell you, I don't like this," he said in a whining voice. "If old Booth was to catch me on his land at night . . ."

Brannigan's voice held an angry edge. "You didn't mind seeing us come over to take away his cattle, a few at a time. Now we need you, so stop whining."

He stepped down from the saddle and led his horse up to the barbed wire fence. He pushed on the wires. The staples came out of the posts easily, freeing the wires. He pushed the wires down and held them on the ground with his boot.

"Ride over," he said.

When Kemp and Horne had crossed, he let the wires up and put all the staples in a spot where he could find them when they returned. Remounting, he pulled up beside Kemp. "Now then, which way's that tank?"

He could hear the tremor in Kemp's voice. "I'll lead you."

With the darkness came a full moon, rising and swelling into brilliant blue light that cast long shadows from the three riders. In the still evening air Brannigan could smell the dust that rose under the soft beat of the horses' hooves.

They hadn't ridden more than a mile when their horses shied at the sharp barking of a dog, close at hand. Brannigan jerked up on the reins and dropped a hand to his gun. He held his breath, listening.

"What the hell is this, Delbert?" he demanded in a whisper. "Thought you said there weren't any houses or line camps up this way."

"There ain't," Kemp replied. His voice almost broke in fright. "There's somebody out there, though. Come on, Brannigan, let's go home."

Spade Horne hissed, "Shut up!" Brannigan listened intently a moment for hoofbeats or any sound of men. None came. Finally satisfied, he remounted.

"Stray dog," he said. "Let's go."

Despite Kemp's assurances that he knew just where the Paint Horse tank was, it took more than two hours of circling and hunting in the moonlight to get there. It was Brannigan himself who finally found it.

"These cattle trails seem to be coming together," he said, his eyes on the ground. "We'll follow them in."

When he reached the tank he rode up on the dam and down on the inside. There was something less than half a tank of water left, he saw by moonlight. It was enough water to carry a good many cattle for a while, though.

He looked back at Kemp, the disgust rising in him. If he played his cards right, he wouldn't have to be saddled with Delbert too much longer. There was pleasure in the thought of getting rid of Kemp.

"You sure this is the tank with the weak bottom in it?"

"Yes," Kemp replied in a thin voice. "One of his cowboys told me once that they had the devil's own time making it hold water."

Mouth set grimly, Brannigan reached into his saddlebags. He took out two short sticks of dynamite. He knelt on the bank, fitting caps into the sticks. He picked a spot in solid dirt, as near the water as he could get, and worked one of the sticks down into the dam. He walked thirty yards around the rim and planted the other stick. He struck a match and lighted the fuse. Then he came back in a hard trot and lighted the fuse on the first.

He swung into the saddle and spurred up over the dam. Kemp was already six lengths ahead of him. A hundred yards out, Brannigan stopped and reined around to watch, his eyes wide in expectation.

The earth trembled beneath him, and his horse shied in panic at the twin blasts. Brannigan listened to the splattering of mud on the banks. When all was quiet again, he edged his nervous horse back over the dam. He could see the pits left by the explosions. Dirt and mud had partially refilled them.

"Booth Walker can start counting his dead cattle now," he said to Spade Horne. "If that tank bottom's as weak as they say, those blasts should have cracked it open again. In a day or two the water'll seep down, and there won't be anything left."

He laughed. "And there ain't a thing here to tie us in on it. Booth'll figure out what happened, more than likely. But he can't prove that them two holes weren't made by a couple of pawing bulls."

His hand closed tightly around his gun butt. "I'm doing just what I told Booth I would, Spade. I've taken away six sections of his best land. Without water here, he'll have to throw all his cattle north. Give them a month, dry as it is, and they'll have that part eaten off to the ground. Then Booth'll be where I want him. Sooner or later he'll lose his head and come gunning for me. I'll be ready."

A dog suddenly came charging out of the mesquite, barking furiously. Brannigan's horse reared, almost throwing him. He thought he heard a horse coming.

"There's somebody out there," he barked to Horne. "Circle him, quick."

The man was big Sam Trenfield. Mounted on a heavy bay horse, he made no attempt to get away as Brannigan and

Horne rode up from two sides, their guns drawn. The moonlight was bright enough for Brannigan to see the rage that twisted Trenfield's bearded face.

"You're even worse than I gave you credit for, Drake," Trenfield muttered with hatred. "I never thought you'd go so far as to ruin a man's water."

"You generally fight a man by hitting his weak points," Brannigan replied, the gun steady in his hand. "Water is any man's weak point in this country."

He noted that Trenfield wore no gun. "What're you doing out here, Sam?"

Trenfield explained that he was building a new surface tank. "You almost rode up on my camp. I thought you was fixing to steal cattle, and I followed you."

Spade Horne pushed in impatiently. "What're we going to do with him, Drake? We can't let him go now."

Brannigan narrowed his eyes. "There's only one thing we can do."

He knew Trenfield realized what was about to happen. But he saw no fear in the big man's face. There was only hatred.

Suddenly Trenfield lunged at him. Instinctively Brannigan ducked back, almost losing his balance in the saddle. He tried to swing his gun up, but an iron fist gripped his arm. Another clamped around his throat. He felt himself falling backward off of his wildly dodging horse. He hit the ground on his back, Trenfield's huge build right on top of him. The breath gusted out of Brannigan.

Trenfield's knees were on his chest, crushing him. The two great hands clamped about Brannigan's throat. Pain roared through him as he struggled desperately for breath, his hands flailing weakly. His gun was gone. Trenfield's hate-filled face and the stars above him seemed to be whirling as Brannigan began to fall into a deep black pit of oblivion.

He heard an explosion and knew it was a gunshot. Trenfield's great hands loosened their hold. The big man's weight fell away.

For a moment then, Brannigan had to fight to regain his senses. Spade Horne's figure danced about him. Brannigan's face twisted at the acrid smell of gunsmoke. He saw the wavering image of a gun in the killer's hand.

"Good thing you got him when you did," he breathed brokenly, looking at Trenfield's body crumpled on the ground. "Another few seconds and I'd've been as dead as he is."

Trenfield's shaggy black dog tore wildly into Spade Horne. Furious growls boiled out of the dog's throat. Cursing, Horne struck the animal across the head with his gun barrel, then triggered a bullet into him. The dog dropped, kicked a few times, and was dead.

"Nothing I hate worse than a damned dog," Horne snarled.

Delbert Kemp crawled out of his saddle and staggered up to Trenfield's body. His knees were so wobbly he could hardly stand. He sank to the ground and forced his shaky hand out to touch the body. He looked up, his narrow chin sagging. "He's dead. Great God, you've killed him."

A grim smile came to Brannigan's lips. He suddenly began to see a way to start shoving Delbert Kemp out of the picture.

"We killed him," he corrected. "You're in it, too, Delbert, just as deep as we are."

Kemp's eyes widened in horror. He turned away from Trenfield, his skinny body shaking with sobs. Brannigan watched him try to remount, his foot missing the stirrup three times.

Brannigan looked at Spade Horne and jerked his thumb toward the dead Trenfield. "We can't just leave him here, where they can find him. We got to take him somewhere and bury him."

Horne shrugged. Brannigan knew it made no difference to the tall man whether anybody found Trenfield or not. "They're going to miss him anyhow," Horne said.

Brannigan tugged at his chin. "Maybe not. I'm beginning

to get an idea. Drag that dog off into the brush, out of sight. Then throw Trenfield's body across Delbert's saddle. Delbert can ride behind it. We'll drop by Sam's camp. Then we got to make a fast ride into town." A smile came back to his face. "Booth's going to flinch plenty when they go to hunting his friend for another robbery."

Booth Walker limped around afoot on the dam of the Paint Horse tank. A gray bleakness had settled in his eyes. Mud—that was all that was left. Just mud, where yesterday there had been water enough for many cows. A futile anger simmered in him.

"What do you think did it, Dad?" Lanny asked. There was sympathy and concern in the young man's voice, and a quiet respect for the sadness that was in his father.

"I haven't got any notion, son. I haven't got any notion." He shrugged his thick shoulders. He knew the tank had always had a weak bottom. That was one reason he had wanted to build the new ones, as insurance. But to seep out half a tank of water overnight . . .

For the tenth time he looked down at one of the two new pits. Funny the way the mud was splashed around all over the dam, too. Cattle sometime did that, wading in, then coming out and shaking off the mud. But this time there was so much of it. Almost as if it had been blown out.

Blown out! Booth sucked in a sharp breath.

"Brannigan," he breathed. "I wouldn't put it past him."

Almost desperately he began looking around for sign. But even if there had been any, the thirsty, bawling cattle which had milled around this muddy tank all morning would have tromped it out.

Another thought occurred to him. It wasn't but a couple of miles to Sam Trenfield's camp. If there had been any blasts, chances were Sam would have heard them.

He turned to Quinn Stovall. "You better get the men together and push these cattle over to the north side. Scatter them out among the waterings we've got there. Don't leave any here to starve."

Quinn looked out over the thirsty cattle that gathered around the watering place and the dozen or so that were tromping around in the mud now, bawling as they tried to find clear water.

"That's sure a lot of cattle to put on so little country, Booth. Three or four weeks and there won't be any water left over there, either. Then what'll we do?"

Booth shook his head. "All there is left to do. Pray for rain."

Stiffly he climbed into his saddle. "Come on, Lanny. Let's go talk to Sam."

Riding up to Sam's camp, Booth saw two men walking around, examining the place.

He recognized Sheriff Dotson and a deputy. Dotson stood watching, hands on his hips, as Booth and Lanny trotted in.

"Howdy, Dot," Booth said. Curiosity was prickling him. "What're you doing here?"

"Looking for Sam Trenfield."

"So are we. Ain't he here?"

Dotson shook his head. "No, he ain't."

Booth took in the camp in one sweeping glance. The shovel and the slip were there. So was the camp equipment. But there was nothing inside the tent. And Sam's wagon and one team of mules were gone.

"The little safe was stolen out of Fant Fletcher's saloon last night, Booth," the sheriff said. There was an apologetic tone in his voice. "Tracks showed that one man broke in the back door, carried the safe out, and put it in a wagon. They were big tracks."

He paused, frowning as if he hated to tell the rest of it. "That safe was small, Booth, but plenty heavy. There ain't many men around here powerful enough to carry it by themselves, but Sam Trenfield could."

The sheriff looked at the ground as he finished. "I've accounted for the rest of them. Only Sam is missing. Tracks showed that there was two mules hitched to the wagon. And to finish it off, Booth, Judge Pentecost said he saw Sam in town late last night."

Weakness washed through Booth. He slumped over in the saddle. "Judge Pentecost would lie about the time of day," he said. But he knew there was no use talking.

Even without Judge's word, there was enough evidence right here on the surface to send Sam back to the pen.

Booth felt a quick catch in his throat. "It just doesn't seem possible I could've misjudged Sam so. I'd've trusted him with everything I owned. I know it looks bad, Dot. But I'm going to keep believing in Sam till I hear the story from his own lips."

There was sympathy in Dotson's face. "Don't blame you, Booth. But you'll help us look for him, won't you?"

Booth nodded. "If he shows up, I'll bring him to you."

He pulled his horse around and headed straight for the W headquarters. His head was bowed, and his heart was sick.

Late in the day Lanny Walker managed to slip away from the other cowboys and slant southward. Maybe Sue Ellen would be out on horseback, he thought.

His horse was dry. Lanny worked back to the Paint Horse tank, hoping that with the cattle gone the little water that was left might have settled enough to give his brown gelding a few swallows. There was one small, pot-sized hole that looked fit to drink. Lanny eased the mount to it.

Sitting there, looking around him, he noticed three crows slowly circling over a spot out in the brush. A dead cow or calf, he thought at first. But no one had mentioned seeing one. Curious, he moved over that way when his horse had finished drinking.

Before he got to it, he knew it wasn't a calf. His horse snorted and shied around it.

"Sam's dog," Lanny breathed. He dismounted and shoved aside the branches that had been thrown hurriedly across the shaggy body. He saw the bullet hole in the animal's black head.

A tingling sensation worked up his back as he remounted. A dozen thoughts whipped through his mind at once, making his heart pound. Sam had been here yesterday or last night, or his dog wouldn't have been, and Sam would never have shot his own dog.

Suspicions mounted in him as he pushed through the Cross K gate and headed down toward the gully where Sue Ellen always met him. She wasn't there when he first rode up, but it wasn't long before he heard her horse. He walked out to meet her and caught her in his arms as she swung down from the saddle.

"Lanny," she said, "it's been days since you've been over here."

"You've come every day?" he asked.

"Every day." Her eyebrows lifted. "There's been trouble over there, hasn't there?" she asked, pointing her chin toward the W.

Lanny nodded. "Plenty," he said morosely. He explained some of it.

She sat down, her head bowed, her brown hair tumbling about her shoulders. "And Pa's in it some way; I know he is. He's gotten so scared of Brannigan that he's sick. This morning I saw him with a gun in his hands, aimed at Brannigan's back. He couldn't hold it steady. He laid it on the table, sat down, and cried like a baby. I tried to get him to tell me what was wrong, but he wouldn't talk."

She clenched her fists until they were white.

"Pa's always been shiftless, I know that. But he's still my father. I could kill Brannigan for what he's been doing to him."

Lanny put his arm around her shoulders. "I know, Sue Ellen. He's doing the same to my dad. Dad's changed a lot lately. He's not sleeping, and the worry's beginning to draw on him. Where he used to be easy to get along with, he's getting jumpy and grouchy, cross as an old wolf. But he's like a rawhide rope. He'll stretch just so far, then something's got to break." He smiled at her, and brushed her cheek with his lips. "But let's forget about Brannigan for a little while, Sue Ellen. Let's just talk about us."

He drew her to him and kissed her.

He didn't know how long the man had been standing there. Lanny first saw the shadow that fell across the gully. He shoved away from Sue Ellen and spun around. He had to blink a moment against the lowering sun. But he knew the man who stood there, a middle-aged man with heavy face and flinty eyes, and gun hanging at his wide hip. Drake Brannigan!

"Come on, Miss Kemp," the man spoke gruffly. "You're going home. Your pa'd bust a blood vessel if he was to know where you're at."

Staring at Brannigan, Lanny felt the hatred begin to swell in him. "She's staying with me, Brannigan."

Brannigan frowned. "You're Booth Walker's boy, ain't you?" When Lanny didn't answer, the man narrowed his hard eyes. "She'll do what I tell her, because if she don't, I'll kill you!"

Ice tingled in Lanny's veins. He stared a long moment at Brannigan, the first time he had seen him so close. Sam Trenfield had been right. There was every mark of a killer in the big man who stood before him.

But Lanny's confidence began to grow. Brannigan had no gun in his hand. He would have to reach for it, and that would give Lanny an equal break. He remembered what Sam had said about Brannigan's speed. But Brannigan had spent fifteen years in prison. Maybe time had slowed him. He wasn't a young man any more. Lanny was young, and he was fast. Maybe there was a chance . . .

He dropped his hand. But even before his gun was half out of the holster, he knew Brannigan had beaten him. In the black muzzle of Brannigan's gun, he saw death rushing at him. Sue Ellen screamed.

But the old outlaw didn't pull the trigger. "That was a fool stunt, kid. I could've blown you to hell, if I was a mind to. Next time I will. Now come on out and get what's coming to you."

Turning, Lanny saw another man a few feet farther down the gully. He was a tall, cadaverous man with a wicked grin on his sallow face and a .45 in his hand.

"Why didn't you go ahead and draw, kid?" Disappointment edged his voice. "I'd've shot you down the way I'd kill a dog."

Lanny's blood ran cold. "The way I'd kill a dog," Spade Horne had said. For a chilled moment, as he climbed out of the gully, Lanny remembered Sam Trenfied's dog, shot and hidden in the brush. And he thought he knew now what had happened to Sam.

Brannigan seized Lanny's gun. Before Lanny could duck, Brannigan swung his own gun barrel at the boy's head. It was like a cannon exploding in Lanny's brain. He staggered and fell onto his hands and knees, the world reeling around him.

"Work on him, Spade," he heard Brannigan say.

He tried to dodge, tried to fight back. But he was helpless against the pounding blows Horne delivered. He felt fists driving into his face, his stomach, his ribs.

The last thing he heard was Sue Ellen screaming, "Brannigan, I'll kill you for this!"

Then something hit him across the back of his neck, and he melted onto the sunbaked earth.

Brannigan watched with satisfaction as Lanny Walker fell unconscious. He looked down at his gun. He could have killed the kid. Now he began to wish he had. It had been almost as much as he could stand, watching Lanny Walker hold pretty Sue Ellen in his arms, enjoying a love that Brannigan could never win.

With his toe he gave the boy a shove and sent him rolling back down into the gully. Sue Ellen quickly dropped down beside Lanny. Brannigan could see relief in her tanned face as she realized young Walker was not dead.

"Come on out now," he said roughly, "or we'll go ahead and kill him."

Wordlessly, her face scarlet in fury, angry tears glistening on her eyelashes, Sue Ellen climbed up on her saddle and rode up out of the gully. Brannigan let her take the lead. He fell in a few paces behind her. Spade Horne rode beside him.

"You're letting that girl drive you out of your head," Horne warned. "If you want her so damned bad, all you got to do is take her."

Brannigan didn't answer. Riding along behind her, his eyes glued on her slender form, he felt his heartbeat quickening again.

But all things come with time, he thought. And he kept his distance.

Booth Walker sat bareheaded on the front steps of his house, angrily whittling notches in the wood with a sharp knife held in his left hand. Behind him Abbie Walker sat in her chair, rocking rapidly. Her blue eyes were staring worriedly at things far out across the yard in the noonday sun, past the barns and corrals.

"How do you know they're being stolen, Booth? Without rounding up everything, you can't be certain of a count. Maybe the boys are just overlooking some of them."

Booth shook his head. "They ain't overlooked anything. There's two hundred head gone, maybe three, that ought've been on the south side. And I know Brannigan held out some that was supposed to be on the Hockley place."

There was pain in Abbie Walker's face. Dark circles under her eyes were silent testimony to sleepless nights. Worry had etched the age lines deeper into her forehead. The smile she used to wear as constantly as her apron seldom appeared any more. It had gone when this thing of evil had settled upon them. She had watched the changes in Booth, too, deep changes that were slowly, steadily cutting away the ground from beneath his feet.

"How's Lanny?" Booth asked. "He said anything yet?"

She shook her head. Lanny hadn't said a word since he had staggered in past midnight. Abbie had almost screamed at the sight of the blood on his bruised, swollen face. With Booth's help she had washed away the blood and dirt, salved the wounds, and gotten the half-conscious man to his bed.

Booth tested the keen edge of his knife blade against a new section of the step. "Quinn says he dropped out of the drive late yesterday and rode south. He didn't tell me at the time because he knew Lanny was going to see that Kemp girl. Even Quinn's been helping Lanny slip over there, behind my back."

There was a fleeting suggestion of a smile on Abbie's lips.

Booth added, "When Lanny gets over this, there's going to be an understanding between us. Come hell or high water, he ain't wasting any more time with a daughter of Delbert Kemp!"

The soft thud of hoofbeats made him swing his head to the south. Quinn Stovall came loping in. He didn't pull up until he was almost in front of the house. He swung down and came trotting in as fast as his bowed legs would carry him.

"They've taken some more, Booth," he exclaimed. "Shorty found where they came clear over onto the Murdock section last night. He turned up enough sign to show that they took about forty head. Went to the Cross K with them. They followed that gravelly creek bed to keep from leaving tracks."

Booth jumped to his feet, exhilaration rushing into his broad face that hadn't seen a shave in a week. A man could go plumb crazy, sitting around helpless while an enemy hacked away at him, and not being able to fight back. But here was something a man could sink his teeth into.

"Gather up the boys. They're all around close. Tell them to put their guns on and load up for bear."

Abbie Walker watched them saddle up. She could see the excitement tingling through the men like lightning playing across a herd of cattle in a thunderstorm on the plains. In a way she wished she could stop them. But she knew she couldn't, and she wouldn't try. She would do as she had done so many anxious times in the years behind her—smile and wave goodbye, and hold back the anguished tears until her man was gone.

Maybe now this thing that had been eating at Booth so long would break into the open.

Booth sent one man spurring for town, to get the sheriff. As the old ranchman started to go, he pulled his horse up beside Abbie. He reached out and took her hand, as he used to do, and looked into her strained face. There were no words between them, for words weren't needed.

"You keep an eye on Lanny," he said then, and pulled away. With Shorty and Quinn Stovall in the lead, Booth and his men moved out in an easy trot, making time, yet saving their horses.

It was midafternoon when the riders reached the place where the cattle had been pushed onto the Cross K by way of the gravelly bed of the dry creek. Without hesitation Booth tugged at the barbed fence and noted how easily the staples pulled out of the posts. He pushed the wires down for the men to cross over, and he knew that had been done here many times before.

It was hard to trail the cattle after they got on Kemp's ranch. The place already was so heavily stocked that there were fresh tracks everywhere. But Booth had not forgotten the long training his badge-wearing had given him. He always managed to pick up the sign again. Confident, the rustlers had stopped trying to cover their trail soon after they reached Kemp's place.

Darkness found the punchers still on the trail, miles west of the outside boundary of Kemp's Cross K. They had reached rough country now, browse country. It was state-owned land that no one had claimed. Booth had never found water on it, so he never tried to buy it.

The trail was veering south as the moon rose bright and sharp.

"The herd's some bigger now than it was when it left the W," Quinn Stovall observed.

Booth had noticed that, too. "They've had some more of our cattle hid out, and picked them up along the way. Well, we'll keep following this trail as long as we can see it. Somewhere up yonder they're bound to stop for the night. They can't drive cattle for two nights straight."

Finally they began to hear the occasional bawling of a cow, up ahead.

"We'll move in at an easy walk," Booth said quietly. The old spirit was in him again now. There was a familiarity in all this. He had done it many times before.

They got in close enough to see the cattle in the moonlight, loose-herded on a dry, brushy flat that was studded with mesquite and catclaw. Then a cowboy's horse nickered. Booth saw one of the nightherders whirl around in the saddle, then spur southward. The man was shouting something.

"Take them!" Booth hollered. Hoofs pounded and gun hammers clicked as the men put spurs to their horses. From somewhere up ahead flame lanced out into the night. A half dozen cowboys' pistols answered.

Instantly the cattle were on their feet and running in panic.

"Let them go," Booth shouted again. "It's Brannigan's cow thieves we want right now."

Gunfire crackled in the night. Belching flame spotted the darkness with sudden flashes of burning red and white. Twenty paces ahead of him Booth saw a man buckle in the saddle and fall to the ground. He wasn't one of the W cowhands. Here and there he caught glimpses of other men, fleeing before the sudden rush of cowboys. There was a scream from somewhere as a bullet found its man. Booth reined up to wait, for he had no gun, and couldn't use it if he had.

Presently the shooting died down to nothing. The cowboys

started coming back. As they came, they drove along some of the cattle which had scattered as the shooting began. Booth watched in vain for sign of a prisoner or two. Judas, if they could only catch a thief who would talk, and bring the law's heavy hand down upon Brannigan . . .

But there were no prisoners. If there were any wounded, they had managed to crawl off and hide in the brush. There was nothing to show for the battle but two dead men from the other side.

Many of Booth's cowboys had been scratched and torn by the thorny brush as they had ridden wildly through it in the moonlight. But none had been hit by bullets.

The two dead men had been laid across riderless saddles. Booth dismounted to look at them. He frowned in disappointment, and clenched his left fist. He had hoped he might recognize them as some of the men who had been with Brannigan that day the man had lawed him out the Hockley country. But these two men were strangers. He had never seen them before.

"Say, Booth," one of the hands said, "I found a spring over there, about two whoops and a holler down the draw. It ain't too big, but it'd water a herd like this one. Them cow thieves must've been using it."

Booth rubbed his whiskered chin. A spring—out here! Even then, the cowman in him was plenty alert. A flicker of a smile crossed his face. Maybe this little expedition wasn't going to be a bust after all. He wondered if he might get one of the punchers to file on the land.

"Since there's water and some graze," he said to the men, "I'm going to let you all stay here. In the morning you can start rounding up the cattle. Might be they have the rest of the stuff they stole from us hidden out here. We just as well leave these cattle out here, and set up a camp so a couple of men can watch out for them. It'll be a good place to sit out this drought. I'll send the cook out with a wagon to give you something to eat."

He picked Quinn Stovall to go back to the ranch with him. Riding out, he stopped to look at some of the cattle in the moonlight. He quickly found they weren't all W cattle at all. A good many of them carried the Cross K.

Suddenly Booth broke out laughing—the first time he had laughed in days. He tilted his head back and slapped his left knee so hard that his horse shied.

Quinn Stovall stared at him as if he thought Booth had gone out of his head. Booth exclaimed, "Fine partner Delbert Kemp has got. He's not only stealing our cattle, he's stealing Delbert's, too."

With Quinn to back him, Booth rode directly to the Cross K headquarters. They took the bodies with them. It was way past midnight when they got there, but a lamp was shining in the kitchen. Cautiously the men worked their horses up to the house. Then Stovall said, "That's Sheriff Dotson in there."

Booth relaxed. Dismounting, he tied his horse and walked in, Stovall beside him. In the kitchen sat Dotson, his deputy, Brannigan and Horne, and Delbert and Sue Ellen Kemp. Booth let his eyes rest on the girl. He hadn't seen her in a long time. Pretty, he'd have to admit that. But he'd been involved with two or three girls just as pretty, before he'd finally married Abbie. He'd gotten over them. Lanny would get over this one, too.

"It got too dark for us to follow you," Dotson said. His badge glinted in the flickering lamplight. "Besides, I figured you'd show up here sooner or later, and I decided this was the place to wait. You find anything?"

Briefly, Booth told about recovering the herd. "We got two of the thieves," he said. "We got them tied to their horses out yonder."

Brannigan kept a poker face, but Booth could see the coals burning in Spade Horne's sunken eyes. Dotson lighted a lantern. They went out to look at the dead men.

The sheriff shook his head. "Strangers to me." Quickly he looked back at Brannigan and Horne. "Ever see them before?"

They shook their heads. Booth knew they were lying, and he knew Dot knew it. But there wasn't anything the sheriff could do. A man working for the law had to be careful he didn't stretch any laws himself.

"We'll leave the bodies with you, Dot," Booth said, mounting his horse.

He figured this was the time to drop the gunpowder into the fire. Looking directly at Delbert Kemp, he said flatly, "You know, Delbert, for a while I thought sure it was you and your partner Brannigan that stole my cattle. But I guess I was wrong. I found out they'd been stealing from you, too. About half of them cattle was carrying a Cross K."

Kemp's mouth dropped open. Fury blazed into his eyes as he swung them toward Brannigan. Booth waited hopefully. Maybe Delbert would let slip something in anger that might spill the story. But Kemp had sense enough to keep quiet.

Booth shrugged. He had put a match to the fuse; he would let the powder explode in its own time.

"Good night, folks," he said jovially, and pulled away into the night.

❖

Next morning, early, Booth walked into Lanny's room. His son was sitting on the edge of his bed, weakly pulling a high-topped boot on by its long straps.

"Feel like walking over to cookshack with me for some breakfast?" Booth asked.

Lanny got to his feet, then leaned back against an old dresser, supporting himself with his hand. His head was bandaged. Ugly blue marks marred his face. "Still a little dizzy. But the sooner I get on my feet, the sooner I'll get over it."

Booth rolled a cigarette with his left hand, licked it, and looked directly at his son. "Want to tell me how it happened?"

Lanny's bruised lips tightened in indecision. He said only, "Brannigan."

"How come you were over there in the first place?"

Lanny looked away. "Don't you know?"

Booth nodded. "I reckon. Did she try to stop him?"

"She's just a girl, Dad. She didn't have a gun. What could she do?"

Booth drew long and deeply on the misshapen cigarette. "I can imagine what she did do. She probably laughed with Brannigan when it was over, and told him what a fine job he did. Chances are she did more than that, too. A lot more."

Scarlet flushed Lanny's face. "You're wrong, Dad. Dead wrong."

Booth shook his head. "I don't think so. I was over there last night. I saw the way Brannigan looked at her."

Lanny took a shaky step forward and said, "Stop it, Dad. I won't have you talking about her that way."

Regret weighed heavily in Booth. This was a hard way to have to treat a boy. But a father didn't have a choice, sometimes.

"It'll all be over soon anyway," he said. He told what he had said to Delbert Kemp, and described the anger that had flared in the man.

"Something's got to give now. Maybe Delbert'll get up guts enough to go to Dotson and tell him the whole thing. More likely, Brannigan'll get scared he's going to, and he'll shoot him. Don't matter much which. Either way, Brannigan will be ripe for picking. We can ride over there and clean that place out, and Dotson'll be with us."

Lanny's eyes widened in incredulity. "Dad," he said heavily, "I never thought you'd have it in you to put a man in a spot like that. Delbert won't have a chance."

Defensively, Booth said, "A month ago I wouldn't have done it. But lots of things have changed lately. My conscience is plumb dead, as far as the Kemps are concerned."

"But Sue Ellen! You think I'm going to stand by and let you get her caught in a squeeze like that? If Brannigan kills

Delbert, no telling what he's liable to do to her!" Anger and anxiety strained Lanny's voice. "I'm going to go get her, Dad."

Booth clenched his fist. "And maybe upset the whole thing?" he exploded. "No, you won't. If anything happens to her, it won't be more than she's got coming." His face clouded. His voice demanded obedience. "I've never forbidden you very much, Lanny. But this one time I'm giving you an order that you'd better keep. You're not to leave this place!"

He stomped out. He strode right by the cookshack. The anger in him had crowded out any thought of breakfast. Old Ty Workman limped down off the cookshack steps, picking what teeth he had left.

"Ty," Booth said sharply to the old handyman, "I got a job for you." He thumbed toward the back of the house, where Lanny's room was. "Lanny's still in there. Don't let him leave the place today. If he tries to, and you can't stop him, you come to me!"

Booth and Quinn Stovall went out to ride fence not far from the house. About midmorning they found a bad break.

"Quinn, I wish you'd ride to the house and get that extra wagon. Bring a roll of that new wire with you, and the fence stretchers."

In less than half an hour Quinn returned, still on horseback. "The wagon's gone, Booth. And so's Lanny!" Quinn explained, "He must've slipped out the back way. Old Ty can't see very good anyhow. Lanny got to the barn, looks like, hitched up the team, and took out with the wagon."

"How long ago's that been?"

Quinn shrugged. "No way of telling."

Booth swallowed hard. The first flush of anger drained out of him, and fear took its place. "Come on, Quinn," he barked, swinging into his saddle. "We're going to the Cross K."

Spade Horne sat with his spurred boots on the kitchen table. He was toying with his .45, spinning the empty cylinder and clicking the trigger, the gun pointed at Delbert Kemp. Kemp hunched over the table, his face drawn white as the

frayed tablecloth. His sick eyes bobbed back and forth between Horne's six-gun and the long legal document that lay on
the table before him.

Drake Brannigan stood at the window, watching for Sue
Ellen to come in from the shady front porch, where she was
churning butter. He didn't want her hearing any of this. She
didn't know what had been happening. She had sensed the
tension; he knew that from the uncertainty and the fear that
had been stamped in her face.

Brannigan turned away from the window momentarily to
face Kemp. "It's all legal, Delbert. The Judge wrote it up. You
sign it, and the Cross K is mine."

Kemp's lips trembled. "And you don't pay me a dime. I won't
do it."

"You have to," Brannigan gritted. "If I you don't, Sam Trenfield's body is going to get dug up. Somebody'll find out it was
you who had on Sam's boots that night, and left the tracks in
the alley after we had carried the safe out and brushed away
the sign. We'll be gone, and there won't be anybody left here
to answer for it but you. Did you ever stop to consider what it
feels like to get hung, Delbert?"

Kemp's Adam's apple worked up and down. "What if I sign
it? What'll you do?"

"We'll let you leave the country. Nobody here will ever have
to know where you went to."

Kemp licked his lips. "How can I tell Sue Ellen? She won't
want to go."

Brannigan walked back to the window, letting his eyes rest
again upon the girl. "She ain't going. She'll stay here with me."

Kemp's voice broke. "With you? An ex-convict? A murderer? I won't do it."

But there was only helpless despair in his voice. He would
do it, all right. Brannigan was sure of that. And when it was
done, he would leave the country the same way Sam Trenfield
had. No one would ever know, not even Sue Ellen.

A movement caused Brannigan to shift his eyes to the town road. He saw a wagon coming. He squinted, trying to recognize the driver. Then he cursed under his breath.

Young Walker hauled up his wagon right in front of the house. Sue Ellen jumped to her feet and rushed out to him.

"Hurry up and get your things," he heard Lanny say to her. "I'm taking you away from here."

There was fright in her voice. "Forget about my things, Lanny. Just turn that wagon around and let's go."

Brannigan stepped out onto the porch, hand on his gun, just as Lanny reached down for the girl. "Hold it, Walker," he barked. "You're not taking that girl any place."

Lanny's eyes stabbed at him in hatred. "Get back, Sue Ellen," he said. "Get out of the way."

Brannigan noted that the bruises Horne had given the kid were still there. "You had a pretty hard lesson once already," Brannigan gritted. "That girl is mine. I'll do anything I have to, to keep you from taking her."

Lanny's voice leaped at him. "Would you do what you did to Sam Trenfield?"

Brannigan's heart skipped. He couldn't know. He must be guessing.

The fury that flared into young Walker's eyes betrayed his draw a second before he made it. With his lightning speed, Brannigan beat the kid to it. This time, he told himself, he would make it good.

But even as he squeezed the trigger, he felt the girl throw her body against him. She screamed in rage, grabbing for his gun. Brannigan had no choice. He struck her across the chin, hard, and watched her sprawl out on the porch. He looked back at Walker. The kid buckled at the knees, then plunged headlong out of the wagon.

Crying desperately, Sue Ellen grabbed at Walker. She called his name and turned him over. Brannigan saw then that she hadn't spoiled his shot by very much. The bullet had plowed in deep in the shoulder, close to the heart. Red stain inched across the shirt. Half in panic, Sue Ellen tore strips off the edge of her skirt and tried to stop the bleeding with them.

Brannigan felt Horne's scornful eyes hot upon him. "Go on and finish him, Drake. What's the matter, you gone soft? Shoot him again—or I will."

Brannigan glanced at him, caught the yellow glare of his wolf eyes. He started to level his gun again at Lanny, then looked up quickly toward the wagon road.

"There's no time now," he said. "Two horsemen coming."

He pointed his chin toward the girl. "Take her inside, Spade. Keep her quiet."

She fought like a wildcat, kicking, biting, clawing with her fingernails. But Horne managed to drag her into the house. In a moment he was back again, rubbing his knuckles.

"I shut her up."

Resentment flared in Brannigan. Horne didn't have to man-handle her! But the resentment gave way to a grim smile as Brannigan recognized the two men spurring toward the house in a hard lope. "Booth Walker and his foreman. You keep your hands away from your gun, Spade. I'll call this play."

Walker jerked his horse to a quick stop in front of the un-painted frame house. Stiffly he swung down. For the space of two seconds he looked unbelievingly at the still form of the boy, stretched out on the ground. A choking sound tore from his throat as he hobbled quickly to his son's side. Quinn Stovall stayed in his saddle, hand on his gun. His squinted eyes glittered fire.

"Lanny," Booth cried, kneeling by the kid. His tough old face was broken. "Quinn," he spoke, "he's still alive."

Then his eyes lifted to Brannigan's. Unconsciously his stiff right hand dropped down toward his hip. There was nothing there.

For one tempting moment Brannigan considered killing him right there, with his son. But a new thought struck him. Lanny

Walker would die now. He was bound to, the way he was hit. And what could be harder on Booth than the loss of his son? Brannigan decided to let Booth live a little longer. Let him live in grief and misery. Let his days go bleak and endless, as the days had gone for Brannigan through fifteen long years.

"Help me, Quinn," Booth cried. "He's bleeding to death."

Stovall swung down to Booth's side. He took a big handkerchief from his hip pocket and held it to the wound.

Booth's eyes lifted again to Brannigan. "How come you had to shoot him, Drake? Why couldn't you be satisfied with killing me?"

"He came here looking for Delbert's daughter. He tried to draw on me, and I had to kill him."

Booth demanded, "Where is that Judas of a wench?"

"She's not here."

Booth's eyes fell upon the blood-soaked piece of skirt that lay on the ground.

"She's here," he said brokenly, the bitterness seeping into his voice. "You tell her that if I ever see her again, I'll forget she's a woman. I'll break her neck with my own hands!"

"Come on, Booth," Quinn Stovall said harshly. "There's no time to talk. We got to get Lanny to a doctor."

Brannigan watched until they had gone, hauling Lanny in the bed of the wagon. Then he turned once more to Delbert Kemp. "Come on back in the house, Delbert. We ain't finished our talk."

At dusk Brannigan sat in the old rocking chair on the front porch, idly rocking back and forth. With his hand he reached up and fingered the deed that stuck out of his shirt pocket, and a grin touched his hard face. It was working out better than he had ever hoped.

He had had his revenge on Booth Walker. He would kill him some day, but he would let him live a while longer. He had whittled away at Booth's ranch, taking some of it from him, spoiling most of the rest. Wouldn't be long now until Booth's cattle would begin to starve. Nothing could break a cattleman's spirit quicker than that. Nothing, perhaps, except losing his son. And Brannigan had accomplished that, too.

Now he had title to the Cross K, signed and witnessed. The Judge had gotten the witnesses' names on the deed before he had ever sent it out. In the morning Delbert Kemp would say goodby to his daughter and slink out like the coward he was. But he wouldn't get far. They couldn't leave him living, dangerous as a firebrand in dry grass, likely to break down at any time and sob out a story that would send the law's long arm reaching out here.

Best of all, there was Sue Ellen Kemp. He would have to watch her for a while, but eventually she would give up and accept him. Lanny Walker was gone now. There was no one else she could turn to.

Brannigan breathed deeply of the cool, clean night air, and he was content. From the barn came the clopping sounds of three or four horses, stamping around outside the hayloft, wanting in. He watched the stars brighten against the deepening black of the heavens. They made him remember what an old puncher had told him once, long ago.

"Sleeping outdoors all the time, boy," the old man had said, "you get to where you can tell lots of things by the night sky. Ever see a night when the stars was so crisp and bright that you could almost reach up and pick them? In this country it's a good sign of cloudy weather coming, and maybe a rain. But when the night sky is hazy, and the stars are dull, you can bet you're a far piece from a rain."

A crooked smile came to Brannigan's face. Talking through his hat, most likely. But then, the old man could've been right. The stars were surely bright tonight, almost close enough to the ground that he could stretch out his hand and touch them.

A rain now would do him good, he told himself. Selling Kemp's cattle to that bunch of Pecos thieves had thinned the

Cross K herd down to what it ought to be for the land it was on. Maybe when it rained the grass would have a chance to come back. He would have money in his pockets then, big money. Sue Ellen couldn't afford to turn up her pretty nose at him.

The heavy clump of boots on the porch disturbed his thoughts. Spade Horne stomped around beside him and sat down, hanging his long legs off the edge. "That girl ain't made any move to get away this afternoon, not since I caught her coming out the window and clipped her with my fist. You want me to watch all night, too?"

Irritation edged his voice. Brannigan knew Spade would just as soon shoot the girl and Kemp too, and be done with it. There was too much of the way of a wolf about him.

Brannigan gritted his teeth. There would come a day when he would have to get rid of Spade Horne. Spade and his hankering for blood would get them hung if ever the cards fell wrong.

"You go on to bed, Spade. I'll watch out for the girl."

When Spade had gone back into the house, Brannigan eased out of the rocker and worked his way quietly across the star-lit yard to the barn. He opened the door of the saddle shed and walked back to a corner that was sunk in darkness. Seating himself on an empty saddle rack, he looked toward the open door and the dim shaft of moonlight and starlight that fell in upon the wooden planking. He rolled a cigarette and leaned back to wait.

Sue Ellen came before long, quietly leading a horse on a rope. The rope had come from her room, he guessed, and she had snared one of the horses at the hayloft. Warily she tiptoed in through the door. She slipped a bridle from a nail on the wall and eased her saddle and blanket off a rack near the door.

Silently Brannigan got to his feet and moved up behind her. She didn't sense his presence before he grabbed her wrist. In sudden fright, she screamed.

"You can drop that rig," he said quietly. "You're staying here."

He had meant to turn loose of her wrist. But with her free hand she swung the bridle. He ducked his head in time to keep the steel bits from smashing into his face. They glanced off his ear, driving a crashing pain through his head. In reflex he twisted her wrist. She cried out again.

She was fighting him just as she had fought Spade Horne, kicking at his shins, stomping at his toes, struggling desperately to twist her arms loose from his grasp. And with every breath she was crying in helpless anger.

Something broke loose in Brannigan. He hadn't meant it to happen. But the weeks of watching her from a distance, hungering for a touch of her skin, a smile from her lips, had kindled a slow fire in him. Now, fighting with her, feeling the pressure of her body against his, was more than he could stand. His wall of patience tumbled, and he was pressing her back against the barn wall, crushing her wrists in his hands, forcing his lips upon hers. His love of her was a roaring fire in him.

Suddenly his senses rushed back to him. He heard the click of a gun hammer, and a frightened yelp, "Let her go, Brannigan!"

He whirled. In the door stood Delbert Kemp, a shotgun wavering in his trembling hands. The light struck Kemp in the right way to expose the wildness of his eyes. There was fear in his face, abject fear that threatened to crumble the man to pieces. Yet with it was a driving hatred that somehow was holding him together—for how long, there was no way to know.

Brannigan felt a chill touch of fear on the back of his neck, clammy and sickening. He dared not move, for he knew the terrified Kemp, his nervous finger on the trigger, was a more deadly enemy right at this moment than Booth Walker had ever been.

The girl pulled away from him.

"You and Horne and Judge have stolen everything I own,

Brannigan," Kemp blurted in a broken voice. "You made me help murder Sam Trenfield, and you've made me a thief. But you'll not take my daughter. I'll kill you first!"

The shotgun leveled. Brannigan leaned heavily against the wall, ice at the pit of his stomach.

Then Spade Horne was behind Kemp, his .45 drawn. He shoved the barrel of the gun into the small of Kemp's back.

Suddenly Kemp wilted. A smothered cry of terror ripped from his skinny throat, and he let the gun sag, then drop clattering to the wooden barn floor.

Brannigan shouted, "Don't shoot him, Spade."

But the thrill of spilling blood was in Horne's sallow face. He pulled the trigger. Kemp dropped to the floor like a sack of grain.

For a moment Brannigan was swallowed up in rage. "Damn your heart, Spade, I told you not to shoot!"

Coolly Spade Horne shoved the gun back into his holster. "We was going to kill him anyway."

"But, you bloodthirsty fool, not right in front of the girl."

Horne's simmering yellow eyes shifted past Brannigan and settled on the girl, huddled against a saddle rack, sobbing in grief and terror.

"Now that she's seen it, Spade," he said flatly, "we'll never be able to trust her out of our sight." His voice was venomous as a snake. "So we got to kill her too!"

Another chill ran down Brannigan's back. The sadistic killer had had it all figured out, he realized. He had stacked the cards so they would fall this way. Brannigan looked at Sue Ellen, slender and pretty and warm. He wanted her alive.

"You won't kill her, Spade." There was ice in his voice. He took a step toward Horne. The tall man reached once more for his gun. Brannigan leaped at him, bowling him over backward, pinning the long hand to the rough board floor with his knee. Then Horne jerked the hand free, and it closed around Brannigan's throat. They rolled back and forth on the splintery floor, grunting in fury and exertion and pain, sweat soaking their clothes.

Suddenly Horne jerked free and jumped shakily to his feet. He balanced himself against a saddle rack. "She's gone!" he cried.

Brannigan pushed himself up to a stand. In a glance he saw that all the guns were still where they had fallen. She had darted out past the two struggling men, and hadn't taken a chance on being able to grab a gun.

"We got to find her," Horne exclaimed, desperation in his voice. "If she gets to the law . . ."

They searched in vain through the semidarkness. There were a hundred pools of blackness which could hide her even as they walked close enough for her to reach out and touch them.

Horne's anger burst from him in a torrent. "You're a fool, Brannigan, a woman-crazy fool. Even afoot, she can get to town by morning, and have the sheriff on our tails before we're out of the county." He cursed. "Now the whole scheme's shot to hell. You had all you could ever ask for—a ranch signed over in your name, a potful of money, a chance to live high the rest of your life. And you spoiled it all because you lost your head over a girl."

Despair swept through Brannigan. He sat weakly on the ground and rested his head in his hands. He knew Horne was right. He wouldn't stand a chance now.

There would be no getting away, not this time.

He realized he had left too many weak links in the chain. Sooner or later, they'd catch one of those Pecos cow thieves. Maybe all of them. They would talk. And when Sue Ellen told what she had heard, the law would squeeze the truth out of Judge Pentecost. That one couldn't hold his tongue for long. He'd spill the story about what had really happened to Trenfield.

Then Booth Walker would come looking for Drake Brannigan. Even if the law gave up the hunt, Walker never would. One day Brannigan would ride around a hill, and Walker would be there waiting for him, gun loaded and ready. That crippled hand wouldn't hurt Walker then, not when he had the blood lust burning in his eyes.

Spade Horne had already caught a horse and was throwing a saddle on him. "Well," he spoke impatiently, "are we getting out of here?"

Brannigan gazed up at him a long moment. The feel of death was already upon him. And with that final desperation came an old hatred, surging back to him. Directly and indirectly, Booth Walker had brought all this upon him.

"Yes," he said, "we're going. But we'll ride out by way of the W. I'm going to settle my account with Booth Walker. I'm going to pay him in full!"

It was much later than Booth Walker usually stayed up. But there was no use trying to sleep. He paced back and forth across the kitchen floor, the strike of his boots echoing through the empty house.

He wished he had remained in town with Abbie. But he had stayed as long as he could stand it. He had left Quinn Stovall there to come and fetch him if there was any change in Lanny's condition. Booth was alone here, except for old Ty Workman snoring out yonder in the bunkhouse.

The loneliness and the worry bore heavily upon Booth's shoulders. His eyes were bleak as he paused now and again to step out onto the back porch and gaze up at the starry skies. There was no sound except a coyote howling somewhere out across the draw, and the steady tick-tock of the clock.

Booth would listen for a few moments, then start pacing again. A dozen half-smoked cigarettes lay on the floor beside the woodbox, where he had flipped them in distraction.

Once he sat down with his old fiddle and tucked it under his chin. He tried to drain some of the sickness out of him with music, as he had been able to do so many times before.

But he laid the fiddle aside. He was too old to break down and cry. And for once the music was not strong enough to cry for him, to wash away the grief.

A new sound came to him. He stopped and listened. The rapid pounding of a horse's hooves. A chill worked down through him, and he leaned on the doorjamb for support. His newest cigarette dropped unnoticed from his fingers.

It's Quinn, he thought. *Come to tell me Lanny's dead.*

But it wasn't the voice of a man that hailed him from out of the darkness.

"Booth Walker!" Sue Ellen cried. "Booth Walker!"

He heard the sound of her small boots, striking the front porch. The door slammed, and she rushed into the kitchen. Her face was drained almost white.

"They're coming to kill you, Mr. Walker," she exclaimed. "Drake Brannigan and Spade Horne!"

Numbed, Booth didn't get what she said. Staring at her, he could see only the body of his son, crumpled in front of the Kemp ranch house.

"Get off my place," he said.

"Can't you hear?" she demanded. "I said they're coming to kill you!"

But Booth heard only the echo of his own words, uttered in fury this afternoon. *Tell her that if I ever see her again, I'll forget she's a woman. I'll break her neck with my own two hands!*

He started walking toward her, his left fist clenched at his side.

What she did then brought him up short, in astonishment. She slapped him, hard, across the face. She brought up her hand and slapped him again.

He jerked his head back. Eyes wide, he raised his hand to his burning cheek. With the sudden fire of pain, his senses returned to him.

"I didn't mean to act that way," he murmured then. "What was it you said?"

Quickly she told him. "You'd better get a gun, then blow out this lamp. They can't be far behind me."

The gun rack was in the living room. Booth took out his pistol and tried it in his right hand. It wouldn't work. And he knew he could never shoot straight with his left hand.

His eyes fell upon the old double-barreled shotgun. He took it out of the case and held it. With both hands, he knew, he could manage. And if he wavered a little, it wouldn't matter. The scatter of the shot would take care of that. He would have to get close. But closeness held no fear for him. There was room for little emotion in him now but the consuming hatred that swelled in his heart.

Two barrels—two men.

Carefully, deliberately, he rammed two cartridges into the breech, then closed the gun. He reached into a drawer, took out five or six more cartridges, and shoved them into his pocket.

He blew out the lamp and moved toward the front door. "You better stay in here till it's all over," he told the girl.

"No," she said, "I'm going with you."

As they sat on the porch, waiting, she told him all that had happened. She didn't cry. There was pain and grief in her voice, but there was strength in it, too, strength and a hate-driven determination.

"After I slipped out of the barn, I hid in the shadows. They walked by me a dozen times and didn't see me. I heard them say they were coming here. Soon as they were gone, I caught a horse. I made a wide circle to get around them. Then I rode as fast as I could."

Listening to her, looking at the strong profile of her face against the stars, Booth began to wonder if he might have been wrong. There was a power in this girl that didn't come from her father. It didn't come from her mother, either. There must have been some stronger souls among her ancestors, he thought. Maybe Delbert and his wife hadn't been typical of the strain.

Brannigan and Horne weren't long in coming. He heard the hoofbeats as the horses came out of the draw, and then stopped.

"They're going to slip up afoot," Booth whispered. "They think they'll catch me asleep."

It seemed like half an hour before he discerned a movement among the deep shadows of the yard. Tension grew within him. Carefully, staying in the black of the porch, he moved away from the girl. An electric tingle began to play up and down his spine. He clutched the shotgun tightly, and felt the sweat begin to pop on his hands.

Then, suddenly, there the man was, right at the edge of the porch. He stopped, peering through the darkness. There was no mistaking that tall, angular body. Another few seconds, Booth knew, and he would be seen.

"I'm right here, Horne," he said. Instantly Horne brought up his .45. Booth tried to squeeze the trigger of the shotgun. It was clumsy, holding it with both hands.

The gun exploded, just as a slug drove high into Booth's left shoulder and hurled him backward with the force of a sledgehammer. Blinking at the grinding pain, he saw Horne drop.

Booth sank to the sandy porch floor. The shotgun was still in his hands. There was slack in both triggers. He cursed himself for a clumsy fool. He had fired both barrels.

He realized it wouldn't take Brannigan many seconds to find him. In desperation he tried to break open the gun at the breech, tried to fish the extra cartridges out of his pocket. But he lay stiff and helpless, the wound a roaring furnace in him.

He was finished, he realized. He couldn't reload the gun— couldn't fire it if it was loaded.

But he felt gentle fingers upon his whiskery cheek. "Lie still," Sue Ellen whispered.

She took two cartridges out of his pocket and reloaded the shotgun. She stepped down off the porch then, hiding the gun behind her, pointing the muzzle downward.

Brannigan's voice broke through the darkness. "Walker! Walker! Come on out!"

Sue Ellen's voice was steady, and hard as flint. "Walker's dead."

Booth thought he could hear Brannigan gasp. "Sue Ellen!"

"Walker's dead," she repeated. "So's Horne. There's no one left but you and me."

Booth imagined he could hear a footfall. Brannigan said, "Come on, Sue Ellen. Let's get away from here. Horne won't threaten you anymore. Come away with me, Sue Ellen."

"You still want me?"

Hope rode high in his voice. "I've always wanted you."

Her voice lowered. "I'm here, then. I'm waiting for you."

Booth knew he could hear the footsteps across the silent yard. They were slow at first, wary. They grew faster. He could see Brannigan then, in the starlight, walking eagerly toward the girl who stood there alone and evidently helpless, her arms flat against her sides.

He caught the sudden movement of Sue Ellen's hands. He heard Brannigan's sharp cry, almost lost in the thunder of the shotgun.

Even Ty Workman's deaf old ears had heard the shooting. He came and helped Sue Ellen support Booth Walker as they pulled him back into the house. By the time Quinn Stovall got there, Sue Ellen had the bleeding stopped and a bandage wound tightly across Booth's sagging shoulder.

First Quinn had to know what had happened. Then he said, "Lanny's going to make it. The doctor says stopping the blood in time was the only thing that saved him."

Booth leaned back in his easy chair. Relief washed through him, leaving him clean of worry for the first time in weeks. Things had to get better now. Nothing could ever happen that could be worse than what they had put behind them. He forgot the throbbing pain that lanced through his shoulder. It was all over now. He was happy.

Sue Ellen's shoulders began to shake with dry sobbing. There were no tears left in her. But she had to cry.

Booth watched and said nothing. Best to let her get it out of her system. She would be all right then. There was iron in her. She would make a good wife for Lanny, when the boy was well again . . .

The drought broke in October. The rain came slowly at first, its gentle fall soaking straight into the thirsty earth. Then, when the first needs of the dry soil had been met, the rain began to drive down in torrents. Draws swelled with muddy water. Rivers and creeks ran again. The surface tanks Sam Trenfield had built were filled and overflowing, from the Hockley place to Paint Horse. A green hue returned to the range.

It was too late to make much grass before winter. But with luck, the cows would pull through in fair flesh. They could bear their calves and regain their fat as spring came again to bring new life to the flats and the rolling hills.

When the rain stopped for a while, Booth saddled up to make a circle on horseback with Quinn Stovall. The doctor had told him to keep off of horses, but doctors didn't know everything.

They climbed their horses to the top of one of Sam Trenfield's dams and looked at the water lapping over the edge.

"Sam would've been tickled to see this, Booth," Stovall said.

Booth nodded. "You bet."

The town had turned out big to give Sam a decent funeral, after the Judge had broken down and told the whole story and showed where the body had been left in a shallow grave. Booth had been glad for that. It helped make up for a little.

Booth pointed his chin southward, toward the Cross K. "What say we trot over yonder and see Lanny and Sue Ellen, Quinn?"

Quinn frowned. "Reckon they been married long enough to want any company?"

Booth grinned. "No, I guess not." He paused. "They'll make

a good ranch out of that outfit, soon as Lanny's able to get out and work. They make a fine pair."

Quinn nodded. "Guess it's in the blood."

"Yep," Booth replied, "like I always said, it's all in the breeding."

He eased down off the dam and reined his sorrel back toward the ranch house, the soft mud splattering. "Let's go home, Quinn. Shoulder's beginning to ache a little. Must be the medicine that crazy doctor's been making me use."

WET WEATHER

The main trouble with West Texas was that it didn't rain often enough. And when it finally did rain, it forgot to stop.

Such were Snip Wheeler's sour thoughts as his horse splashed along in mud and water hock deep. Cold rain poured off Snip's flattened hat brim and ran down his black slicker in a hundred rivulets. His toes squished in water-filled boots.

Fine time for old John Leatherwood to have one of his spells, Snip thought dismally. It had been raining more than a day when the attack had hit Snip's gray-haired partner. Alone, John had staggered to the cabinet and reached for his medicine. But the bottle had slipped from his shaky old hands as he had tried to work the cork out.

When Snip returned from the barn he'd found John lying on the floor, hand on his heart. The precious brown medicine lay spilled, mixed with a hundred pieces of glass.

A swallow of whiskey had brought color back to the old man's face after Snip had put him on his cot. Then Snip had saddled the wet, snorty rustling horse and ridden the twenty miles to town. When he got there he found that the doctor himself was sick.

Now Snip was most of the way back to the ranch, with two

bottles of medicine in his saddlebags and damp cold in the marrow of his bones.

He squinted as he spotted a strange form on the trail ahead. The driving rain obscured it until he rode near. Then he saw that it was a wagon, covered by a tarpaulin stretched over wide hoops. It was pointed the same direction he was riding.

A girl's voice shouted at two big gray horses hitched to the tongue. They pulled and strained, their big hooves sinking deep into the mud. But the wagon was mired almost to the axle. It hardly budged.

What would a girl and a wagon be doing this far out, and in weather like this? Snip asked himself as he rode to the front.

She didn't look bad, not bad at all. She was not much over twenty, he judged. Scarlet in her cheeks showed she was mad, and probably had been ever since the wagon had gotten stuck. Red hair hung to her shoulders from under a water-soaked hat.

"You haven't got as much chance as a raindrop on a hot stove of getting the wagon out of that hole," he advised. "You better take it easy and let them horses rest a little."

"Maybe if you'd tie onto us and let your horse help pull it might get us out," she replied sharply.

Her tone cut under his skin. "It wouldn't help you none. There's a dozen places ahead just as bad. You'd get stuck again. You better get on one of them horses and let me take you on into the ranch."

She lifted her chin. "I will not! All I know about you is that you're a rude cowboy that won't even help a girl get a wagon out of a mud hole."

Anger stung Snip. "All right, Red, suit yourself. There's a sick man at the ranch who needs attention. I haven't got time to fiddle around and argue with some redheaded female."

He wheeled his horse around and touched the spurs to him. He had splashed along about fifty feet when the girl called, "Wait!"

He looked back in time to see her climb down off the wagon

seat and step into the mud, her slicker flopping. She started un-hitching the team.

"I can't stay here!" she shouted. "Wait a minute."

Snip did some hot talking under his breath as he rode back to the wagon. Wherever there's trouble there's usually a woman in the middle of it. This wasn't any country for women. He'd seen one try it, and he still tasted the bitterness sometimes.

Without a word he helped her get the harness off the two horses. She crawled back into the wagon and brought out a couple of bridles, a blanket, and a sidesaddle.

"Hurry up," Snip said irritably. "Old John could die while I'm standing here waiting for you."

Her brown eyes flashed an answer that didn't need words. "Saddle that dark gray," she snapped. "I'll gather up a few things to take along."

He tried to give her a foot lift as she started to get into the saddle. "I don't need any help from you," she told him. "Just lead the way."

And lead it he did. He tried to set a pace that would jar some of the independence out of her as she rode along, leading the second gray. But she kept right up with him.

His anger began to wear away. He didn't get much practice at being mad, and he couldn't stay that way long. After a while he sneaked a glance at her and had to catch himself to keep from chuckling. She seemed to have plenty of spunk, he had to admit. A lot more than Vivian had had.

The led horse's hooves slipped as he hit a slick spot. As he struggled wildly for footing, the reins fell from the girl's hand.

Quickly Snip wheeled around and caught them. He looked at the girl's face and she looked at him. He suddenly felt like laughing.

"Lose a horse, ma'am?"

She came near to smiling then. "Looks like we kind of struck sparks for a while," she said. "I was just too mad to see straight."

The new brightness in her face made Snip feel warmer, even if he was half soaked. "My name's Snip Wheeler, Red."

She tried to frown. "My name's not Red. It's Susan Applegate."

Snip laughed. "Susan Applegate? That makes you sound like a nester's daughter."

A little of that red color spread in her cheeks again and her eyes were defiant. "Is that so bad, being a farmer's daughter? If it is, cowboy, you'd better give me back that horse and go on your way. Because that's just what I am!"

"I—I didn't mean to make you mad again, Red," he said hastily. "Come on. We better hurry up and see what we can do for John."

As they rode on in Snip found out she was an East Texas farm girl. Her father and mother were in another wagon and had been a little in the lead. The family was headed for new farmland her father had located up in the Panhandle. Somehow, in the rain, she had turned the wrong way and gotten lost from the other wagons.

It was a cinch this was the end of the line for her until the rain stopped and the ground dried up a little.

Old John was in pretty good shape, they found. Good enough shape that his wrinkled, weather-beaten face broke into a broad grin as he saw the girl come into the house with Snip. First time the salty old man had grinned in two weeks.

He raised up on one elbow, his cot-springs groaning in protest. "By George! Don't tell me you went and got married after all the things you said to me about women, Snip." He grinned. "And in so short a time!"

Snip's face stung as the girl glanced at him a minute.

"Not married by a long shot," she said quickly. "I'm just glad that the fellow who's spoken for me has at least got some manners."

Spoken for! That disturbed Snip a little. He told himself it didn't really make any difference. No woman was ever going to snag him like Vivian had caught brother Henry. But Snip started wondering what kind of man Susan Applegate had gotten.

The first thing Snip knew, the girl had a fire going in the unhandy iron "bachelor" stove and was whipping up a hot meal. She knew how to make herself useful, all right. But right away she was giving advice, just like Vivian.

"You ought to get you a good cookstove, Mister Leatherwood," she told old John. "This bachelor stove does more dancing than cooking."

Snip decided he'd do some man a favor and break her of giving advice. "We've always got by just fine with that stove," he told her quickly. "If it don't suit you, you can go back out to that wagon and try cooking on a campfire with wet wood."

Old John's big gray mustache bristled. He opened his mouth to roar at Snip, but the girl beat him to it.

"I was talking to Mister Leatherwood, Mister Wheeler. If you don't like the things you hear, you can go sit out in the rain!"

Shame crept through Snip. He looked down at his big hands and felt his face sting.

There wasn't any good reason for him to keep needling her. But he kept remembering his brother Henry—and Vivian. Snip and Henry had originally set up this place together and had gotten along pretty well in a dugout. Then Henry had married Vivian. He had built this house for her and bought her all the things he could afford.

But Vivian was a city girl. She couldn't be pleased. She had nagged and criticized, asked for things she couldn't have. Finally Henry had given up, sold his share of the ranch to old John and moved to town.

So there Henry sat now, behind the counter of a general store. Like a square peg in a round hole, he was always longing to get back to the range. But because of Vivian he never would.

This raw country just wasn't made for a woman, Snip told

himself again. But as he watched the girl's slim figure working at the stove and listened to her talking to old John in a
voice as pretty as the birds that sang at sunup on a cool spring
morning, he felt envious of the man who was to marry her.

Snip marveled at the way Susan bossed John Leatherwood
around and made the old man love it. Nobody had ever told
John anything. People merely made suggestions, and careful
ones at that, or got a good cussing-out. But Susan even had him
thinking about getting a milk cow.

The rain abated a while the next morning. Snip went outside to look around. He soon sensed that someone was behind
him. He turned and saw Susan Applegate standing there looking at an open space on one side of the house.

"Ever think about planting a garden, Snip?" she said.

Giving advice again, just like Vivian, he thought darkly. "A
garden?" he said. "What kind of a clodhopper do you think
I am?"

A scarlet tinge crept into her cheeks. "I was just thinking
about John," she said evenly. "All you ever eat out here is beans,
bread, and beef. Some green vegetables would be good for his
health—and for that matter, for yours."

"Old John's lived many a year on beans, bread, and beef," Snip
retorted, "and he's done right well. I'm not going to have my
hands turn the shape of a hoe handle."

She turned to go, her face flushed. "I didn't mean anything.
Just a suggestion."

She paused on the steps a minute. "I've also been thinking
how good it would be if you had some chickens. You could build
a chicken house with the scrap lumber you've got piled under
your woodshed. You'd be surprised how good the eggs would
taste of a morning."

Snip wanted to feel disgusted. But a new kind of tingle went
through him as he watched her step primly up onto the porch
and into the house.

He turned and tromped on out to the barn, mud sucking at

his boots. He found that he was sorry for what he had said to her. Look out, Snip, he told himself. You're getting to where you like her. If you're not careful, you'll wind up behind a store counter, too.

He wondered if that would really be so bad. But then—she was spoken for.

He could tell it was going to rain some more. He put out feed for the rustling horse and the two grays, and opened a gate so they could wander out into the small foot trap. He checked the latch on a second gate. It would be too bad if they got out into the big pasture. The outfit would be left afoot and it might take days to catch a horse.

Snip eventually found himself at the woodshed, looking at the lumber that had been left over from construction of the house and barn.

A chicken house wouldn't be so very hard to build.

He was washing up after supper that evening when old John finally asked the question that had bothered Snip ever since Susan had come here.

"Who's this feller you're promised to marry, Susan?" the ranchman asked flatly. "I hope he's not as hardheaded as my pardner's been the last day or two."

Snip looked up quickly as he sensed Susan smiling at him. It made him feel warm and uncomfortable.

"Snip's not so bad, John," she said. "He's proved he can listen when something's said that's worth listening to. He's been out at the woodshed most all day, building a chicken house."

"But who's the man you're going to marry, Susan?" Snip pressed quickly, wondering if she sensed how much he wanted to know. "What is he, a ranchman, a storekeeper?"

Susan's smile didn't seem quite genuine now. "His name is Lester Green. He's on his way to the Panhandle with us. He's taking up some farmland close to the place Papa is putting in, and . . ."

"Are you in love with him?"

Her face reddened. "Look here, Snip Wheeler, I consider that my business, not something for you to . . ." She broke off.

Wiping his trembling hands on a towel, Snip slowly moved closer to her. "I said, are you in love with him?"

She looked down at the floor. "It's been sort of expected ever since I was a little girl. Our dads always kind of took it for granted."

A bitter taste was in Snip's mouth.

"Well, there's a cud for you to chew on.

"She comes here giving us advice and acting spunkier than a sackful of wildcats. But she lets people shove her into marrying somebody she doesn't really want, just because it's always been expected!"

Snip's hands trembled as he rolled his sleeves and buttoned his cuffs.

Her voice was husky. "It's not just that. He's solid and dependable, and a good farmer. Maybe if you were that way . . ."

She broke off as tears welled up into her stricken brown eyes. She whirled away from Snip and ran out the door. He stared after her, an ache in his throat.

John Leatherwood stomped angrily over to Snip in his sock feet. "You knuckleheaded idiot!" he growled, his face flushed. "You make me so mad I could spit from here to the woodshed. That girl's been watching you all day and wishing you'd say something nice to her. Now git out there and ask her pardon before I have another stroke!"

Snip walked out the door, a knot drawing up inside him. Susan stood by the corner of the house, dabbing at her eyes with a handkerchief. Snip slowly walked up behind her and gripped her arms tenderly. She pulled away from him and took another step forward, still keeping her back to him.

"I didn't mean to hurt you, Red," he said softly. "It was just that, well, I like you. I hate to see you making a mistake."

She still didn't face him. She dabbed at her eyes again. "You haven't acted like you like me."

He stepped forward and turned her around to face him. She didn't try to pull away. Her tear-filled brown eyes looked straight into his face.

"You don't know how hard I tried not to like you, Red. But I couldn't help myself." His voice was low.

He pulled her to him and started to kiss her soft-looking lips.

Then a man's voice called, "Susan!" Snip turned quickly. He saw a large, hulking man in overalls swing down from a big bay work horse.

"Lester!" Susan cried.

Lester Green shuffled quickly up to the couple. His ruggedly handsome face reflected more annoyance than pleasure at finding the girl.

"Susan," Lester said, half reproachfully, "I been hunting every place for you. I found the wagon early this morning. How come you didn't stay with it?"

"Why, why," she said uncertainly, "Mister Wheeler brought me here to get me out of the rain. He and his partner have been taking care of me."

Lester stared darkly at Snip. "Kind of looked that way."

He put his arm around Susan's shoulder and carefully pulled her away. "I figgered you'd be all right," he went on. "I didn't see much use in coming back till the rain stopped. But your pa and ma kept a'worrying. They wanted me to come look for you. You got to try to please the old folks, you know."

Snip glared at him. "You don't seem to've worried none."

Lester glared back. "A woman's got to learn to take care of herself, wherever she's at. But maybe this time it's a good thing I came along."

He started walking toward his horse, pulling Susan along with him.

"Get your horses, Susan, and let's go."

"But it's getting late," she protested, "and it's going to rain some more. You just go back and tell the folks where I am, so they won't worry."

Lester looked at the dark rain clouds and frowned. "Reckon you're right." He glanced hostilely at Snip and said, "We'll both stay here."

Snip grimaced as if he had tasted something bad. He wanted to kick Lester right in the hip pockets, but he said, "Sure, sure. Go in the house, Red, and see if you can find him something to eat. We'll turn his horse out with the others."

He saw Susan grin as she turned back toward the house. Anger began riding him, and sank its spurs deep. Snip walked to the barn with Lester. While the farmer unsaddled, Snip put out some feed for the big bay. As they left the corral he carefully made sure the gate's sliding bar was in place.

While Lester was at the table, wolfing down cold biscuits and beef, Snip sat in a rawhide-bottomed chair, gritting his teeth and clenching his fists in his pockets.

Susan looked at him with a cheery light in her brown eyes. "What were you going to say to me a while ago, Snip?"

He growled, "I was fixing to say I hope the rain quits."

It was raining straight down again the next morning when Snip got up.

John's deep coughing had awakened him. Somehow the old-timer had caught cold. Snip glanced at Lester, rolled up in some blankets on the floor, and hoped the hard pallet made the farmer sore. He heard Susan moving around in the kitchen.

Snip wanted to go in and talk to her. But Lester's coming had made him feel grouchier than a wagon cook. He thought maybe he'd better stay away from Susan until he was sure he could keep from arguing with her.

Snip put on his slicker, pulled his hat down tight, and walked out into the rain. It was pouring so heavily he could hardly make out the woodshed. He was almost to the barn when he saw that the corral gate was open.

A startled oath ripped out of him. He broke into a trot, mud gripping at his boots and almost pulling them off. Snip swore darkly under his breath as he looked at the open gate, then trudged back to the house. He let the front door slam behind him.

Lester was up now. He and Snip glared hostilely at each other a minute.

"You didn't go back out to the barn and leave the big pasture gate open, did you, Lester?" Snip demanded.

"I ain't been out of the house."

Old John coughed, then asked, "What's the matter, Snip? Horses out?"

Snip nodded angrily. "Yeah, and I'd sure like to know how it happened."

Susan stood in the kitchen door, holding a skillet. She gasped as if she had suddenly remembered something. She said, "I'll bet . . ." then cut the sentence short.

"You'll bet what?" Snip pressed quickly.

"Well," she said hesitantly, "I should have thought to tell you. Old Rambler, that big dark gray, is bad about opening gates sometimes."

Snip felt like stomping the floor. "So now we're all afoot! If you'd just told me, I'd've wired the gate up. What if John gets sick again? It's twenty miles to town, every step of it in mud a foot deep."

Her face was flushed. She waved the skillet at him. "You don't have to start yelling at me. I'm sorry!"

"Sorry? If John gets pneumonia you will be sorry! And I'm getting sorry I ever stopped at that wagon!"

He saw scarlet flash into her face. Her cheeks were suddenly tight and her lips grim. Anger rippled through him as he turned back to the door. Lester glared at him but didn't say a word. Old John's coarse voice roared at him to come back. But Snip stalked off the porch and out to the woodshed, rain pouring down on him.

The cold rain sobered him quickly. This was the end of it, he told himself. He hadn't meant to yell at her that way. But he had been on edge since Lester had come, and now losing the horses

had made him fall off the deep end before he had time to realize what was happening.

It was better this way, he tried to convince himself. He hadn't
had any business thinking about winning Susan.

But an ache cut through him. He knew he didn't want to
lose her. He had been trying to compare her to Vivian when
there hadn't been any comparison. Vivian had always asked for
things she didn't need—high-priced clothes, expensive furniture, good times. Susan's suggestions had all been good ones—
garden, chicken house, milk cow—things to make country life
better, things that cost little but labor.

Well, he'd try again in a little bit, when they'd both had time
to simmer down a little. Maybe if she saw him working on the
chicken house again . . .

The rain made a terrific din as it beat down on the low woodshed roof. Snip sawed and hammered for perhaps a quarter
hour. He stopped once, thinking he heard someone call. Hearing nothing above the sound of the rain, be started working
again.

The second time he knew he was being called. He dropped
the tools and trotted back to the house. Old John stood in the
doorway, his face dark.

"You knucklehead! I been trying to call you for ten minutes.
I couldn't git Lester to go out and git you." John put his hand
on his chest and coughed, then continued.

"You ought to've knowed better than to talk to Susan that
way. She's as hardheaded as you are when she's mad, and she's
plenty mad now. She went out in the rain, hoping to find them
horses."

Alarm tingled through Snip. "She's liable to get lost! She'll
die of pneumonia!"

John coughed again. "If she does, it'll he your fault. You made
her so mad she stomped out of here without even taking her
slicker."

Snip whirled on Lester, who was standing behind John. "Why didn't you stop her?"

The farmer's eyes were dull. "She said she was through with me because I didn't take a poke at you for talking to her that-away. She's got a mind of her own," he added flatly. "If she don't want to use it, it ain't my worry."

Snip turned on his heel and headed for the door, anxiety tugging at him.

John caught him by the shoulder. "Just a minute before you git away. I want you to know it wasn't Susan's fault them horses got out.

I slipped out there and opened that gate myself after everybody was asleep."

That was the closest Snip had ever come to bursting a blood vessel. "You! Why you dim-witted old hellion! So that's where you caught cold! You trying to kill yourself?"

"No Snip, just trying to make sure that girl stayed here till you got up enough gumption to ask her to marry you. And if you don't, I'll find me an ox yoke and bend it over your thick skull!"

Snip hit the rain in a fast walk. She'd head straight east, he figured, the way the ranch buildings and corral faced. That was a good way to start, anyhow. The rain still poured down. A couple of hundred yards from the house he began calling her.

Mud tugged at his boots. Water seeped in and chilled his feet. He slipped once and went down on his knees. Dirty, silty water flowed around him, carrying with it mesquite leaves, grass litter, and twigs.

He kept calling, but there was no answer. He trudged on, slowly zigzagging back and forth through the ankle-deep water. The rain slacked off.

Finally it was thin enough that he could see a little distance ahead. Then he spotted her. She was struggling along aimlessly, sinking deeper at every step. Snip called her. She turned and saw him, then kept walking away from him. Snip trotted after her as fast as the mud would let him. Finally he caught her. She was soaked. Her hat brim hung loosely around her head. Her red hair was wringing wet.

"Let the horses go, Susan," he pleaded. "You'll die of pneumonia out here."

Her lips were tight. "You wouldn't care as long as you got the horses back."

He gripped her arms and pulled her close to him. She pulled back stubbornly, shivering from cold.

"Please, Susan," he kept on, "I didn't mean what I said a while ago. I've acted mean to you because I was trying to convince myself I didn't want you. But all I've done is prove that I love you."

He held her tighter, desperately. "You're not going off to the Panhandle. You're staying here. I'll finish the chicken house. I'll get a milk cow. I'll even plant that garden, Susan, if you'll marry me!"

She looked up at him as if she could hardly believe what she heard. Her face slowly began to loosen up, and a smile gradually came.

It seemed like an hour before she finally put her arms around him and cried, "Oh, Snip, it took you long enough to get around to that!"

The rain slacked off to nothing as they slowly walked back to the house, arm in arm. They stopped at the barn a minute, and Snip shut the corral gate.

"The horses'll come up for feed sooner or later. If the gate's shut, they'll wait around till we can catch them."

Then he put his arm around Susan's waist and they walked on toward the house. The clouds were breaking in the east and a rainbow was forming. Susan glanced up at the rainwater that still dripped off the roof.

"You know, Snip," she said, "an awful lot of good drinking

water goes to waste off that roof when it rains. Now if we dug us a cistern . . ."

Snip shrugged his shoulders and grinned. "Uh-oh, here we go again."

```
┌─────────────────────────────┐
│                             │
│     WHEN HAPPY              │
│     LOST HIS               │
│     LAUGHTER               │
│                             │
└─────────────────────────────┘
```

WHEN HAPPY
LOST HIS
LAUGHTER

Most places Happy Lane had ever worked, he had rolled up his bedding and moved on after about six months. But the redheaded young cowpuncher had been at Gill Thorpe's Cross T Ranch more than a year now, and there wasn't any sign he figured on leaving. Gill was a fine ranchman to work for.

But two babies were the main cause of Happy's staying. One of them was a cute little feller about eighteen months old, just toddling around good, with big brown eyes and a way of catching hold of a man's finger and smiling at him and making him feel like he owned Texas with a fence around it.

The other one was a cute little girl about eighteen years old, with big brown eyes and a way of catching a man's heart and making him feel like he wasn't worth two cents.

It just didn't tally out, he had been telling himself for months. If anybody else had ever made him as miserable as Patty Thorpe did, he would have put a couple of counties between them.

But every time a notion of leaving the Cross T pushed into his mind, Gill's little boy Scooter would come toddling along. There wasn't anybody could resist that sandy-headed button.

Either that, or he would see Gill's sister Patty tripping around, or hear the music of her voice. Miserable or not, it looked like Happy was hooked.

Now he was spurring along through the Cross T horse pasture, pushing a little bunch of broncs over the brow of a sandy hill and onto the sloping trail that led squarely through the gate of the ranch's biggest corral. Down below him he thought he could see the cause of about half of his misery.

Just walking up to the front of the rambling frame ranch house was Dodd Casey's black-legged dun. Happy always noticed horses first. He didn't even have to look at the young rider.

Another horseman was with Dodd. He was riding a good, deep-chested streak-faced bay. After looking over the horse, Happy glanced at the man in the saddle. Sheriff Blair Rice. Fit company for Doleful Dodd, Happy thought. Dodd was the kind who would shy at a jackrabbit. Having a badge-toter around probably gave him a feeling of security.

Closing a gate on the spooky broncs, Happy peered through the dust to see Gill Thorpe come out of the house, little Scooter hanging onto his hand. Gill was in his mid-thirties and was the kind of man a cowboy was proud to work for. He stood tall and straight, proud as an eagle. He never raised his voice. He didn't have to.

Patty came out onto the little ranch-house gallery. Happy heard the trill of her greeting to Dodd.

He didn't need a mirror to know his ears were red. He swallowed hard and tried to think of a good joke to cover up his feelings as he swung back into the saddle and moved toward the house.

He had gotten along fine with Patty until Dodd had come along and leased a little ranch across the river, and put on it some cows his dad had given him. Dodd was the kind who could see the black edge of doom in the prettiest sunrise, if he ever got up that early. But his serious manner had somehow or other captivated Patty.

Happy saw the disappointed drop in Dodd's long jaw as the red-headed puncher came riding up from the corral. Happy nodded at him and told himself gleefully that Dodd must feel like a housecat meeting a hound dog before he got to the bird cage.

The cowpoke turned to the sheriff and grinned. "Howdy, Blair. Haven't seen your smiling face out here since you was running for election."

Color rose in Rice's pudgy cheeks. Happy shot a sideways glance at tall Gill Thorpe and saw him choke down a grin. Gill had been sheriff in this county just as long as he had wanted to run. He had beaten Blair so many times it didn't do to tell. Rice hadn't been able to get elected until Gill had quit the badge business and bought himself a ranch.

Dodd spoke up, his voice nervous. "This isn't any time for your bad jokes, Happy. We've got bad news for Gill. Awful bad."

As far as Happy was concerned, that was the only kind of news Dodd ever brought. He wanted to remark that if a man could make a living just by worrying, Dodd would be the richest young feller in the county.

But he could tell by the way Patty's brown eyes were snapping that she was already irritated with him for his interruption. He kept quiet and tousled little Scooter's sandy-colored hair.

Sheriff Blair leaned forward in the saddle, his face serious as an undertaker's.

"Like I started to say, Gill, we got word that Morty Bowen was shot down trying to bust out of the penitentiary. He was old Fount Bowen's youngest boy, you know. Fount's blaming you because you was sheriff when Morty was caught and sent him up.

"There's some as says that old Fount ought to've been sent up, too. But the point is, we've found out the old warhorse is over in the rough country, trying to get some of them no-count relations of his stirred up. They got their sights set on you, Gill. Thought I better let you know."

A vague uneasiness began stirring through Happy. He

glanced at Gill, but Gill's head was bowed so Happy couldn't see his face. He knew Gill was looking at little Scooter. Gill's strong jaw was set to one side, the way it always was when he worried.

Rice spoke again. "I'll deputize a few men and send them out if you think you need them, Gill."

Happy looked hopefully at Gill. That was a good idea, he told himself. No telling what old man Bowen was liable to do. But Thorpe shook his head.

"No thanks, Blair. That'd make the old scorpion worse than ever. Best thing's to try and reason it out with him. I did it once before."

Blair nodded and started pulling his horse away. Happy thought disgustedly that he could see relief wash across the sheriff's face. Rice was glad he didn't have to do anything that might give old man Bowen a grudge against him, too.

"You coming, Dodd?" the sheriff asked.

Dodd looked at Patty. "I think I'll stay awhile, Blair. Thanks."

Happy frowned as jealousy started welling up in him again. He knew doggone well he wasn't as good-looking as Dodd. His red hair had a mind of its own and wouldn't comb worth a plugged nickel. Happy's mouth was a little too wide, and there was usually a silly grin on it. He was twenty-two years old now, but his deep tan still didn't hide a few freckles that had been with him ever since he had been a barefooted kid back in East Texas.

Jealousy and a little dread were all mixed up inside him. He fished for a joke to cover them up.

"If the Bowens are coming, Gill, guess I better teach Scooter to throw rocks."

Gill looked squarely at him. The frown on his face faded out, the jaw relaxed, and a slow grin started. Finally he chuckled, "Happy, if a hundred Comanches had you surrounded and out of ammunition, I think you'd laugh at their warpaint."

But if the joke made Gill feel better, and relaxed Happy

himself, it didn't do much for Patty. When Gill went back into the house to talk to his wife, Martha, Patty shook her finger under Happy's nose.

"That's just what's the matter with you, Happy. You never know when to be serious. Gill has real trouble on his hands. You didn't hear Dodd joking about it."

Happy felt irritated at the pleased smile on Dodd's face. He wanted to remark that the biggest joke about Dodd was Dodd himself. But it looked like Happy's chances with Patty were already bad enough.

Scooter's tiny hand gripped Happy's. The boy pointed toward the corrals, where the fighting broncs were working up dust. "Horsie. Horsie."

Some of the hard feelings drained out of Happy. Warmly he picked up the kid. "Good thing you reminded me, Scooter. I got to top out a couple of them widow-makers."

He handed the boy to Patty. "Better watch him. If you don't he'll get right out there among them broncs."

Happy rode a couple of the broncs he had been on before. Because it was the third or fourth saddle for them, they didn't give him much fight. He finally tied them to the outside of the plank corral fence. Then he roped out and hackamored another bronc, a stout, stocking-legged black that watched him with eyes rolling and muscles trembling. He had sacked this horse out once, but he hadn't been on him.

Skillfully he tied up one hind foot and held his saddle blanket across the horse's back a few times, getting him used to the feel of it. Presently he left the blanket in place and started feinting with his saddle until the horse stopped dodging. He swung it up over the blanket. Gingerly he reached under the skittish bronc's belly and cinched up the saddle.

When he got through, the black had a hump in his back big as a watermelon. A good sign there would be plenty of fight in him. Happy liked that idea. Might help bounce out some of the pent-up resentment he felt toward Dodd.

The bronc didn't disappoint him. He came undone like a bale of alfalfa with the wires cut. He heaved upward, then plunged down squarely with a jolt that rattled Happy's teeth. One rear hoof hit Happy's spur and set the rowel to jingling. The black tried a back-twisting spin.

Once or twice Happy had to grab the saddle horn. There wasn't any disgrace in it, long as a man was by himself.

Suddenly he realized he wasn't by himself. His heart bobbed up as he saw Scooter toddle between the two boogered broncs tied outside and start crawling under the corral fence.

"Get back, Scooter!" he yelled. But he knew hollering at the boy was a waste of time. Let Scooter see a horse, and he wouldn't stop until he got to it. Even if it was a wicked bundle of gouging white teeth and threshing sharp hoofs.

Desperately Happy kicked his feet out of the stirrups and let himself go slack in the saddle. In an instant he was sailing off the black's side. The ground jarred half the breath out of him. A hoof glanced off his shoulder. Instantly he got to his knees and shoved himself toward the boy. He tried to yell, but his mouth was full of sand.

He grabbed the kid and rolled him back under the board fence just as the pitching bronc brushed him again, slamming him against the raw planks.

Weakly Happy crawled over the fence. Squatting on his heels, he brushed what sand he could from the sobbing boy's rumpled clothing and wiped Scooter's nose. For a moment he felt a little like spanking the kid.

But crimineezer! It wasn't the button's fault he liked horses. And he wasn't old enough to understand they weren't all gentle like old Soapy, the pet.

Happy heard hurried footsteps scudding toward him. Martha Thorpe grabbed up her little boy. Gill Thorpe's strong face was a shade white.

"We saw it out of the window, Happy. That sure was fast thinking."

Embarrassed, Happy swallowed, then grinned. "Aw, there wasn't any thinking to it. I just got throwed off, and I hustled Scooter out of there so he couldn't see how red my face was."

Gill rested a hand on Happy's shoulder, then turned and followed his wife and Scooter back toward the house.

Happy remembered he had left Scooter in Patty's care. Painfully he got to his feet and limped out to see where she was.

He saw her sitting in the shade of a chinaberry tree with Dodd Casey. Doleful Dodd was talking serious as a summons-serving lawyer. She was listening to him with her brown eyes wide and entranced. Watching them, Happy realized they had forgotten all about Scooter.

He started back toward the corral, angrily toeing up dust with his scarred boots. He noticed Dodd's black-legged dun where Dodd had left him, tied to a young chinaberry in front of the house. Dodd was often giving Happy advice on how to ride broncs, especially if Patty was around. But Happy had observed that the horses Dodd rode were always dog-gentle.

A furtive grin broke out over Happy's wide mouth. He slipped the bridle off the dun's head and gave the horse a gentle slap on the rump. The dun trotted out onto the trail home. Happy limped back to the horse corral and let himself go into a spasm of laughter.

About an hour later Dodd let out a yelp that even stirred up the chickens. Innocently Happy went back to the house, most of his limp worn off.

Gill Thorpe was rubbing his lantern jaw, an amused twinkle in his eyes. "Reckon he got tired of standing there and rubbed the bridle off."

Dodd was wringing his hands. "But what can I do? I'm afoot."

Happy butted in with a poker face. "We got an extra saddle out in the barn. And there's a couple of pretty gentle horses among my broncs."

Dodd eyed him warily, then glanced at Patty. Happy knew

Dodd wanted to be sure they were gentle. But he wouldn't say anything with Patty listening.

While Dodd stood behind him, bridle in his hand, Happy thoughtfully looked over the penful of broncs. He bit his lip to keep from grinning. He considered roping out Cherokee. The sorrel was almost broke. But he was a fool about his ears and hard to put a bridle on. Happy didn't want to scare Dodd away. Not yet.

Well, there was Rooster. Rooster wasn't too much trouble to saddle up. But he still took a notion now and again to spill somebody.

Putting the saddle on for Dodd, Happy saw the little hump rise under it. Yes, sir, today Rooster had the notion. Holding down his mirth, Happy handed Dodd the reins and stood back to watch him get showed up.

Rooster came unwound before Dodd ever got settled in the saddle. Dodd kept a strangle hold on the horn for about two long jumps, then sailed off with a loud bawl and spraddled out like a bullfrog.

Happy couldn't stand it. He leaned against the fence and guffawed. Outside, Gill Thorpe was chuckling. Little Scooter clapped his hands and shrilly signified his delight.

But Patty's face was red. Quickly she opened the gate and rushed in to Dodd. "You clown," she yelled at Happy, "can't you see he's hurt?"

Happy gulped. Doggone it, he hadn't meant to hurt Doleful. He had just wanted to whittle him down to size.

"It's my back," Dodd breathed as if in great pain. Happy lifted him up, and Dodd groaned, "I won't be able to ride now."

Patty was murmuring sympathetically to him, taking time now and again to flick an angry glance at Happy. She put her hand on Dodd's smooth cheek. "Take it easy. Looks like you'll have to stay here with us."

Happy let go of Dodd, and Dodd almost fell again.

"Stay here?" Happy said. He stomped once, good and hard. Talk about taking one step forward and falling back two!

They fixed Dodd a cot in the living room. When Happy went in for supper he saw Dodd lying there contentedly. Patty sat in a chair beside him, rolling him a cigarette. Happy hardly tasted his supper.

Dodd's life of ease and comfort went on the next day. He still claimed his back hurt him. Patty had to hold onto him to help him get around. For a man supposed to be in pain, Dodd sure wanted to get around a lot, Happy thought suspiciously.

But Gill didn't give Happy much time to fret about it, or to worry about old man Bowen, either. He sent him out to look over a bunch of cattle on the south end of the ranch. It took almost half a day. On his way in, Happy swung through the back side of the horse pasture and pushed the broncs in again.

Coming off the hill and down toward the corral, he reined up so sharply that his horse slid his hind feet in the sand. Way down yonder on the trail came some horsemen. For once Happy paid no attention to their horses. He gave the men an anxious glance, then socked the spurs to his horse. He pushed the broncs into the corral in a hard lope.

Gill Thorpe stood out in front of the barn. With him, holding his hand and shrieking merrily at the horses, was Scooter. Dodd Casey was there, too, with Patty. Dodd leaned on a cane he had found somewhere.

Happy's heart was pounding now. Excitement bubbled in him. He strained for breath. "Bowen's coming!" he yelled before he reached Gill. "Old man Bowen and three others."

He turned his horse loose with the others in the corral and trotted anxiously toward Gill. "Looks like they're loaded for bear. I saw sunshine reflect off of a gun."

Dodd's face drained white. "A gun?" He stammered, "We— we can't get caught in the open. We've got to have cover."

He dropped the cane and started running toward the house without help. There was almost no trace of a limp or weakness about him. Watching him, Happy half forgot Fount Bowen a moment. "That two-bit, loafing, no-good faker!"

He looked at Patty as much as to say, "I could've told you how he'd turn out." But he didn't say anything. From the stricken look in her eyes, he knew she didn't need anyone to rub it in.

Fount Bowen and his men were in plain sight now. Happy's pulse throbbed. "Maybe we better go get us some guns, Gill."

Gill shook his head. "I got a rifle in the barn, if we need one. But I'd rather talk the old mossyhorn out of it."

He glanced at his sister. "Take Scooter and get to the house, Patty."

Her lips trembled. "Be careful, Gill." She looked at Happy, her brown eyes sick. "That goes for you, too, Happy." She ran toward the house, carrying the boy.

Old Fount Bowen pulled up a good thirty feet from Gill and Happy. He held up his hand to signal his men to stop. Bowen had been a big man before age had trimmed away the flesh, leaving only a big frame in his grimy, loose-fitting clothes. Even at the distance the old man's eyes were like flint, glaring balefully out from under a floppy wide hat brim. What little breeze there was fluttered his dirty beard.

The three men with him spread out. All were younger but cut from the same cloth as old Fount. Happy felt panic building up in him. He wished for a gun. But he wondered miserably if he could use one, even if he had it.

Gill's quiet voice was steady. It calmed Happy a little. Gill pointed with his square chin to one lean rider who was the image of the old man.

"Fount's oldest boy, Nort," he said. "He's the worst of the pack. Killed a couple of Rangers, but we never could prove it. The witnesses disappeared."

The old man held a carbine across the pommel of his saddle. "You done heard about Morty, I reckon," his voice ground out.

Gill nodded. "I did, Fount. I was sorry to hear it."

The old man chewed a moment, then spat a brown stream of tobacco juice. "I bet you was. You just wished the rest of us was dead, too."

He leaned forward, his gnarled old hands like liveoak knots on the carbine. "I notice you got no gun, Gill. You better git you one."

Happy's heart thumped. He hardly dared breathe. He glanced sidelong at Gill. Thorpe's jaw stood out, but if there was any real fear in him he didn't show it.

"Now look, Fount," Gill said evenly, "I know how you feel, and I'm sorry. But what's done is done. There's no need of us fighting."

The old man spat again. "I didn't come here to talk, Gill. I'm giving you one last chance to git you a gun."

The old man raised the carbine. Happy wanted to turn and run, but his legs felt paralyzed. Gill was still motionless, his face rigid.

A shot thundered from the ranch house. The old man's horse dropped. Bowen's hat flew off and went rolling across the sand as he hollered, and one of the men with him spurred in to pick him up.

"What fool . . ." Gill started. He grabbed Happy's arm and began running back toward the barn. "The gravy's spilled now."

Somebody fired from behind him. Gill stumbled and sprawled on the ground. Blood spurted out onto a pant leg.

Seeing the blood, Happy froze for a moment. The barn was nearest, and there was a gun in it. But Gill had to have help quick or he would bleed to death. Happy couldn't help him and shoot, too.

Quickly he helped Gill up onto his one good leg. Gill's arm around his shoulder, Happy started across the hundred-yard space to the house. He was grateful for the chinaberry trees the last owner had planted there.

Bowen's men started firing at them, but Happy kept moving as fast as he could with the wounded man hanging onto him. Once he felt a slug rip at his sleeve and burn his arm. Others sang by him, or shot up geysers of sand at his feet. But Bowen's men were too busy hunting positions to shoot with care.

It seemed a week before Happy got to the house. Patty exposed herself to fire to hold the door open for him. Instantly Patty and Martha Thorpe went to work on Gill's wound. Little Scooter was shrieking in fright. Dodd Casey stood trembling at a window, shakily trying to reload a rifle.

For a moment Happy's anger overrode his fear. "Gill could've gotten killed because of your itchy fingers on that gun."

Dodd's voice was as wobbly as his hands. "I—I thought Bowen would shoot him—maybe kill us all."

The shooting was sporadic, but the bullets came often enough to show that every one of the four men was in action. Every time one of them fired, Dodd would fire back wildly. The fear hadn't completely left Happy, but he got enough control of himself to hold his fire until he saw a target. That wasn't often.

Once his bleeding had stopped, Gill asked weakly for a gun. They didn't let him have it.

Happy knelt at his boss's side. Thorpe's face was drained pale.

"Gill," he spoke haltingly, "it's all my fault. Me, and my punk jokes. If Dodd hadn't shot at the old man, you might've talked that bunch out of it. Anyway, you'd've had a chance to get a gun. And if I hadn't turned Dodd's horse loose and got him on that bronc, he wouldn't've been here in the first place."

He blinked hard, and he saw the way Patty was looking at him. "If we get out of this, I'll never pull another joke again as long as I live."

Patty picked up a pistol and took a stand at a window. Happy got to his feet and went back to his own place.

Looking across the yard, he picked out the men's positions. He thought about the rifle in the barn, and wished he were there. If he were out yonder and someone else was firing from the house, they could make the Bowens' positions untenable.

But it was more than a hundred yards to the barn, a distance it would be hard to make now that the four enemies were settled and ready. He moved toward the door once, prepared to try and run for it. But cold, clammy fear settled in his stomach. He couldn't make himself go out.

He settled back, trembling, and called himself a coward.

Of a sudden he got a feeling something was wrong. He listened. He couldn't hear Scooter's frightened cries any more.

"Where's Scooter?" he demanded excitedly. There was a quick, frantic search for the boy. Then Martha Thorpe all but went into hysterics.

Happy looked out the window again and sucked in his breath. Out by the corrals was Scooter, getting ready to climb under the fence and into the pen with the excited broncs.

His knees almost buckling under him, Happy realized what had happened. Panicked by the gunfire, the child had gotten out the door unnoticed during the excitement. He had headed for the next best place he knew, the horse corral. Happy watched the frightened horses plunging back and forth as each new shot was fired. In another minute Scooter would be under those hooves.

There wasn't any choice now, no question as to whether it could be done. Tensely Happy reloaded the pistol he held and dashed out the door.

Bullets cut at him as he dodged out among the trees. His high heels weren't made for running, but he thought at the moment that he was doing better than a jackrabbit. One man raised up from behind a bush. Happy fired at him and kicked up dirt in the man's face.

Panic rushed through him as he saw Scooter get up on the inside of the pen with the horses. Reaching the fence, Happy grabbed the top and swung himself up. He heard a slug strike the planking. Burning splinters bit into his hand.

A second later he dropped to his hands and knees on the other side. Scooter squealed as the black plunged toward him, eyes rolling. Jumping up, Happy grabbed the kid and pulled him out of the way.

Bullets still sought him. Happy realized that one of them could hit the button. He sprinted toward the side door of the barn. Opening it, he shoved Scooter inside and jumped in after him. He closed the door from the inside. A couple of bullets ripped through.

"Keep down, Scooter," he yelled at the sniffling boy. Desperately he searched for the rifle Gill had said was in the barn. He found it, with a handful of cartridges lying beside it.

The Bowens had swung their fire to the barn, apparently realizing how Happy's being there had endangered their positions. Carefully sighting out the door, Happy squeezed off a shot at the nearest man. He missed. He tried again. The man went down, gripping his shoulder and squirming.

Out behind an overturned wagon not far from the house was Old Fount himself. He was partially exposed to Happy's fire. If he moved out of Happy's way, he would show himself to the house. Happy sent a couple of slugs whining in after the old hellion. Even at the distance he could hear Fount curse.

There was a third man beyond Bowen. The thought came to Happy that the fourth man had disappeared. Happy wondered vaguely where he had slipped off to.

Probably on the far side of the house now, he decided.

He aimed carefully and squeezed off another shot at Bowen. Fount cried out in pain. Happy lowered the rifle. His heart sickened at the thought of killing the old man, no matter how badly he might deserve it. The oldster was yelling something. The third man got up cautiously, then ran toward him. A moment later Patty opened the door and motioned to Happy.

Thoughtfully he looked at Scooter. The barn was probably still the safest place for the kid right now, he told himself. He shut the door and left the wailing button locked in.

With the help of the third man, Fount was dragging himself out from behind the wagon, gripping a wounded arm. "We give up. Dammit, don't shoot no more," he hollered as Happy came up holding the rifle.

Happy glanced at the man he had wounded in the shoulder, then back to the oldster.

"There was four of you. Where's the other one?"

Bowen scowled. "I'll let him tell you."

Happy ducked as he heard Patty's frightened voice shout "Look out, Happy. Behind you!"

He whirled to see a red flash and a plume of smoke from behind a chinaberry. A hot slug whirred by his head. He brought up the rifle and fired at the tree.

Nort Bowen staggered out, his lank frame bent. He dropped his gun and fell on his face.

After that it was all over. Weakly Happy dropped to his knees in the sand. The fear that had gripped him so long was gone. Exhaustion crept into its place. Nausea turned Happy's stomach over. The first time in his life he had ever shot at anybody. Now he had killed a man, and spilled blood from a couple of others. He wanted to crawl off somewhere and be alone.

Old Fount had had a stomachful of fighting. The loss of a second son was more than he could stand. He was ready to go back to the rough country and to remain there.

Dodd Casey was more than glad to take a horse and go to town for the sheriff and a doctor for Gill, just so that he could get away.

Sick at heart, Happy dragged himself off to the corrals and sat moodily in the sand. All right, Happy Lane, he told himself in revulsion, make a joke about this. You're so doggone good when it comes to joking to keep from showing you're mad or worried or embarrassed. Make a joke now. But he couldn't do it.

Patty came out to him presently and knelt beside him at the corral fence. She put her small hand on his shoulder.

"Happy," she said softly, "I want you to know I'm ashamed of myself. I thought because Dodd took everything so seriously that he had his feet on the ground. I thought you were still just a kid. I was wrong about that. Maybe you do joke and cut up. But I think now that down under it all, you're more grown up than Dodd ever will be."

Her words, the earnestness in her eyes, made Happy feel better. She slid her hand down from his shoulder and put it on his own hand.

He felt his face turn warm.

"I heard what you told Gill a while ago. But don't ever quit joking, Happy. I want you to keep laughing, from now on."

She kissed him lightly on the cheek, then smiled. Happy swallowed hard. He felt the heaviness begin to pull away from him.

The sickness settled.

His heart felt easier.

Suddenly he remembered something. Scooter!

"Crimineezer! I left Scooter locked up in the barn."

He jumped to his feet and ran toward the barn. He jerked the door open. Scooter stepped out uncertainly, tears streaming down his plump cheeks.

His wide brown eyes looked accusingly at Happy.

Happy couldn't stand it anymore. He grabbed the boy up and broke out in wild, uncontrollable laughter. Scooter didn't know what it was all about, but he started laughing too. Then Patty joined in.

The last of the sickness left Happy. It didn't belong there. Nothing belonged but laughter.

And he had a feeling he would have that from now on.

There could be no doubt about the sudden volley of gunfire that echoed from the ragged mountain pass to the south. For more than an hour the sixteen soldiers in grey had watched the mirror flashes on the high points. They had seen the blue-clad Yankee cavalry patrol trot into the defile.

The rattle of gunfire tapered off. For a terrible ten minutes there was silence, a quiet as awesome as had been the screaming sound of death at Valverde on the Rio Grande, or Apache Canyon in the Gloriettas.

Lieutenant Miles Overstreet, Confederate States of America, unfolded his spyglass with trembling hands and trained it on the pass. He stood tall, a lean, angular man in dusty grey, with futility weighing heavy on his shoulders. His hand-sewn uniform was frayed and stained from a thousand miles and more of riding and fighting and sleeping on the ground. A thousand miles since San Antonio. A thousand miles of sweat and thirst and blood.

The Indians came then, fifty-odd of them, riding northward in single file. The clatter of their ponies' bare hooves on the rocks came clear as a bell on the sharp morning air. Exultant yelps ripped from red throats like the cries of demons in a child's nightmare. Behind them the red men led a dozen riderless horses. Not wild mustang Indian ponies, but well-bred mounts of the U.S. Cavalry.

Overstreet's leathery skin stretched even tighter over his jutting cheekbones. Despite the knife-sharp chill left from the night air, a trickle of sweat worked its way down through the streaked dust and the rough stubble of whiskers. He lowered the glass and looked at the remnant of his command. Fifteen men, flat on their bellies in skirmish line.

"Load up," he said. "We're next."

For this was New Mexico Territory in April of 1862, torn by civil war, with white man against white man, and red man against them all. Less than a year ago, fiery Colonel John R. Baylor had led his Second Texas Mounted Rifles up from captured Fort Bliss to take New Mexico for the newly formed Confederacy. Then had come General Henry Hopkins Sibley and his huge Brigade. The men were ill-clothed, ill-fed, poorly armed. But through eight months of struggle and privation they had ridden to one victory after another—Fort Fillmore, San Augustine Springs, Valverde, Albuquerque. At last they had raised the Confederate flag over Santa Fe itself and envisioned a daring sweep across to California, to the gold fields, to the open sea.

Then came disaster in one flaming day at Glorietta Pass. Grim men in tattered grey turned their faces southward toward Texas, the sweet taste of victory now bitter ashes in their mouths.

Men like Miles Overstreet, who had known the dream and now stood awaiting the futile end of it. Wasted under a savage onslaught that no one had even considered.

He listened to the click of captured Yank single-shot carbines as his men prepared for a battle that could end but one way. He saw one soldier flattened out in fear, without a weapon.

"Vasquez," Overstreet called to a dark-skinned trooper from the brushy cow country below San Antonio. "Give Hatchet back his gun. His little mutiny is over."

His men! The thought brought an ironic twist to his cracked lips. Cowards, deserters, scalawags. The sorriest soldiers in Sibley's Bridgade, and Major Scanling had saddled him with them.

A thousand times he had cursed the day he stole a victory right under the pointed nose of the glory-hunting major. Scanling's lips had smiled as he read the commendation. But his eyes never masked the anger that simmered in him. Scanling transferred Overstreet then. Gave him these men, prisoners all, to relieve their guards for action.

"We need a good officer like you to handle them," he had said, his yellow eyes gleaming. "Take them. Delay the federals long enough for the main body of troops to get away. Hold every pass as long as you can, then drop back and hold another. We're buying time with you—with you and these miserable scum who call themselves soldiers. Go on, Overstreet. Go on and be a hero."

He had hated the major then, and his hatred swelled a little more every time he'd been forced to use his own gun to keep half the men from running away. Now, this looked like the end of it.

Beside Overstreet, young Sammy McGuffin rose on his knees and lowered his head in prayer.

"Better flatten out there and spend your time getting ready for those Indians, son," the lieutenant said curtly.

The boy looked up in surprise. "You don't believe in prayer, sir?"

"I believe in a man taking care of himself."

The Indians stopped three hundred yards short of the Confederates' position. They shouted defiance and waved muskets and Yank guns and showed the fresh scalps that dangled beneath the firearms. Then they wheeled their ponies and galloped away into the morning sun, shouting their victory to the mountains.

Overstreet stood watching openmouthed, hardly believing, hardly daring to believe.

Sammy McGuffin's high-pitched voice spoke out, almost breaking. "They're leaving. They're letting us live. But why?"

The answer came in a gravel-voiced drawl from a thick-shouldered, middle-aged Texan with a stubble of black beard coarse as porcupine quills. Big Tobe Wheeler said: "That's the way with Indians, boy. To them killing is a sport, kind of. Without they really got their blood hot, they'll generally kill just enough to satisfy their appetite. They'll count a few coups and have them a victory to brag about in camp. They'll pull out before they start to taking a licking theirselves.

"Maybe tomorrow they'll get the itch again and come looking for us. But not today."

The trooper named Hatchet was already on his feet and making for the horses. "Well, they ain't going to be finding me here."

Overstreet yelled at him, an edge of anger in his voice. "You hold up there, Hatchet. You'll ride out when the rest of us do."

Hatchet turned and glowered at him with eyes the light blue of a shallow stream, disturbing eyes that never stopped moving. As was his habit when he was angry, he gripped his right arm with his speckled left hand. The faded grey sleeve showed where a sergeant's chevrons had been torn away. Hatchet was a thief. He had lost his rank after he had left a battle to hunt for loot in a bullet-scarred town.

"Look here, Lieutenant, you know we're whipped. Between them damn Yankees and the redskins, we ain't got a chance. Now let's hightail it like the rest of the brigade, and get back to Texas with our hair."

Overstreet's long back was rigid, and his lips were drawn tight. "We're heading for Texas like the rest, Hatchet. But we're going like men, not like whipped dogs. Any time we get a chance to take a lick at the federals, we'll do it. Try to run away again and I'll gun you down."

Deliberately he turned away from Hatchet's silent fury, half expecting a bullet in his back. One day that bullet might come.

And if it did, he knew that probably every man in the outfit would swear he had died by enemy fire.

"Mount up," he ordered his scalawag band. "We're moving south."

He rode out in the lead, tall and straight in the saddle, just as he had once ridden with the Texas Rangers, before Secession. He held his shoulders squared. But within him was a certainty that Hatchet was right. Wasted, gone for nothing, were all those hard miles they'd fought. All those days they'd ridden until their tailbones were numb and their dry tongues stuck to the roofs of their mouths. All those men they'd lost. Good men, fighters. They'd died bravely, most of them. But they'd died for nothing.

A dull ache worked through his shoulder, and for the hundredth time his mind dwelt on the angry words of that girl in the makeshift hospital in Albuquerque. Shafter, her name had been, and she was a Union supporter all the way. A refugee from farther south, someone had said. Her name was American, and so was her speech. But proud Spanish blood showed in her raven hair, her piercing brown eyes almost black, her oval face in which even her hatred pointed up her strong-willed beauty. She was helping in the hospital only because wounded Yank prisoners were being treated there along with the Texas soldiers.

Always he remembered the sharp odor of the nitric acid before it was swabbed onto his wound to cauterize it, and he remembered the caustic words she had spoken after he had half-fainted from the searing agony.

"Remember this well," she had said. "It wouldn't have happened if you *Tejanos* had stayed home. This is Union land. Maybe you've taken it, but you'll never hold it. You were beaten before you started."

She was right. They were beaten. It was a painful thing to run away, leaving so much unfinished, so much hope unfulfilled. Yet it might not be so bad, he thought, if they could win just one more victory, one more triumph as a final gesture. With all his soul he longed for that one last chance.

From his fifteen men, there were two whom he trusted more than the rest. Before riding into the pass, he sent Vasquez and big Tobe Wheeler up on either side to scout for ambush. When they hipped around in their saddles and waved their hats, he moved on in.

They found the Union soldiers heaped like bloody rag dolls, scalped and mutilated. At a glance Overstreet knew the Indians had stripped them of guns and ammunition. A few months ago the sight would have made him turn away, sick at his stomach. Now he only grimaced and rode on in.

His grey eyes sought out the body of the commanding officer. Spotting captain's bars on the shoulder of a bullet-torn uniform, he swung down and knelt beside the dead man. There might be papers.

Inside the coat pocket he found an envelope, the corner stained a sticky red. Opening it, he became aware of the one-time sergeant methodically searching the pockets of the Union soldiers.

"Hatchet," he thundered, "do you even have to rob the dead?"

The trooper's pale eyes flitted over him, then away. "They must've been trading post Indians, Lieutenant. Leastways they knew what money's for. They ain't left a two-bit piece in the whole bunch."

"Get back on your horse, Hatchet," Overstreet ordered.

He took the letter out of the envelope. Reading it, he felt his heartbeat quicken. There was a sudden eager tingling in his fingertips.

He had hoped for another chance, all but begged the devil for it. Now here it was, delivered by a bloody band of paint-smeared savages. He read the letter again, half afraid his imagination had run away.

But it hadn't. This was an order for the Union captain to take a detail of cavalry and proceed to the Walton Shafter ranch west of the Rio Pecos. There he was to prepare for shipment a store of rifles and ammunition which had been hidden by Union forces fleeing northward from Fort Stanton the year before.

A train of ten wagons will be dispatched on the 10th instant, and should reach the ranch within two days after your arrival. Shafter, his daughter, and household should also have returned by this time. The family abandoned its ranch and took away its cattle upon the approach of the secessionists.

You will render all possible service and show utmost courtesy to them. Shafter was a loyal scout for the forces of General Kearney fifteen years ago. The family has been of much aid in this campaign.

I do not have to tell you how badly any and all munitions are needed if we are to successfully push the rebellious Texans from our borders.

Martin Nash, Colonel, Commanding

Overstreet clenched his fists, crushing the order. Ten wagons of munitions . . .

Not enough to wage much of a war, but enough for one good battle, if judiciously used. And who could say? It had taken just one battle, that awful fumble at Glorietta Pass, to turn back the grey tide that had all but engulfed New Mexico. Ten wagons of munitions. Pitifully little. But who could say they might not halt the retreat, and launch the grey legions on a new drive that could carry all the way to California?

A quivering trooper named Brinkley spoke up and penetrated the spell.

"For God's sake, sir, can't we get out of this place? My flesh is crawling like a barrel of snakes."

Overstreet led the men on beyond the grisly scene in the pass. He reread the letter as he rode, and wished the Yank colonel had been more specific in locating the ranch. But probably the captain had known.

A name leaped out at him. Shafter. "Shafter, his daughter . . . should have returned." He remembered the dark-haired, dark-eyed girl in the hospital. Shafter had been her name, too. The same? It couldn't be. The haunting beauty of her face had been with him ever since he had left Albuquerque. But he knew he would never see her again.

South of the pass they stopped to breathe the horses. Trooper Brinkley took off his coat, a worn grey coat with a big blue patch on the right elbow. "How long to Fort Bliss, sir?" he asked. "A week? Ten days?"

Overstreet fingered the letter. This was as good a time as any to break the news. Watching sullen anger swell in many of the men's eyes, he told them about the Yank colonel's order. He had expected some trouble, but he hadn't expected it to come so suddenly. Eyes wide with fright, Brinkley swung into his saddle and started backing his horse away.

"Not me, Lieutenant. I wouldn't stay in this country for ten wagons of gold."

He touched spurs to his horse's sides. Another soldier leaped into the saddle and clattered after him.

Overstreet reached for his holster and brought up the Colt Dragoon he had used with the Rangers. He fired one shot, just over the men's heads.

The two soldiers hauled up short. They came back, their faces sickly pale even beneath the dirt and whiskers.

"Take their guns away, Vasquez," Overstreet ordered the dark-skinned trooper. "They'll go to Fort Bliss when the rest of us do."

He felt Hatchet's washy eyes upon him. "You're a long way from home, Lieutenant," the trooper said casually, so casually that Overstreet felt a chill work down his back.

He remembered a hellish afternoon a week ago when they

had turned back a Yankee troop in a rock-strewn canyon. A bullet had whipped by his ear and into a boulder, burning his face with rock dust. It hadn't come from Union guns. He had whirled and seen Hatchet lowering a carbine. But with all that shooting around them, what could he ever prove?

The coldness still on him, he cut short the rest stop and pushed the men on. They rode in stolid silence, the talk long since burned out of them. Before sundown they stopped to cook a light supper, then moved on a few more miles to a dry, fireless camp.

A pink tinge was creeping over the east when big Tobe Wheeler shook Overstreet's shoulder. "Two men gone, sir."

The lieutenant leaped to his feet and quickly looked around him in the cold semidarkness.

Wheeler rubbed his bushy jaw. "Brinkley and Thallman, sir. Shorthanded like we was, we had to let Brinkley have a gun to stand guard last night. We put Thallman with him to see he didn't run away. But the way she looks, I'd say he talked Thallman into going with him."

Wheeler's rough face twisted in a scowl. "Worst of it is, sir, they took a lot of our rations along with them. And we got little enough as it is. You want to trail them?"

Overstreet clamped his teeth together and choked off an oath. "Let them go. If we caught them, we'd have to waste two more men on guard duty. Get the men up and let's move out."

He drove his right fist into the palm of his left hand. What else could he expect, with the men Major Scanling had given him?

So the troop moved on, riding from the time the peach color broke in the east until the last red had faded from the western sky. Every time they passed a settlement or ran onto a brown-skinned settler, Overstreet sent Elijio Vasquez to inquire in Spanish about the Shafter Ranch. For three days the answer was only a shrug of the shoulders.

Then one day they came upon a Mexican herding a small

band of sheep. Vasquez turned away from the man, his weary face split by a gleaming smile.

"He say it is to the south, not far from the Rio Pecos. He say Shafter and his herd have pass this way, not many days ago."

Overstreet saluted the herder and headed south, his men behind him. The herder never gave the soldiers more than a passive look, such as he might have given a freight outfit with a string of mules, or a line of ox-drawn *carretas*. War was an old, old thing to these people.

The troopers quartered east. Watchfully they crossed canyon after canyon, ravine after ravine, that snaked out in search of the alkaline flow of the Pecos. At last the men drew rein and looked out across the turbulent brown water that etched its way between the mountains and the dreaded Llano Estacado, the Staked Plains.

There had been considerable Indian sign, so the detail sent its outriders far to the flanks, and Overstreet allowed no hunting for fresh meat.

Presently Wheeler came riding back in. "Settlement ahead, sir. Trading post seems to be all there is to it. Looks more like an Indian camp than anything else to me."

Overstreet climbed up on a low point and unfolded the spyglass. No sign of Yankee troops. There was only one long, L-shaped adobe building, with a small storehouse behind it. Out to one side was a brush corral with a number of Indian ponies in it. Scattered all about was the litter and filth of years of careless camping.

More than once, along the border, Overstreet had gotten the sudden sense of dread that crept over him now. Frowning, he folded the glass and rejoined the command. "Vasquez, you and I will go in alone. The rest of you men will stay out of sight. If you hear trouble, come on the run. If you don't, come in ten minutes."

As an afterthought he handed Wheeler the spyglass. Then the two men in dusty, torn grey rode into the settlement. A wariness kept stirring in Overstreet. He could see it in Vasquez's face, too. Vasquez had nerves like the steel in the long bladed knife he wore in his belt, and that he had plunged hilt-deep into the shoulder of another trooper at Albuquerque because that trooper had molested a girl whose skin was brown like that of Vasquez.

A dark, portly man stepped out of a middle door and stood hesitantly in front of the rude adobe building. Hands shoved into the waistband of incredibly dirty trousers, he studied the men in grey. Then he looked at their horses. Overstreet knew the man would give his eye teeth for the two mounts.

"Ask him first if there've been any Yankees around here yet," the officer said to Vasquez. The soldier spoke in quick, fluid Spanish. The trader's reply came back in chopped Spanish, accentuated with hand signals and a quick shaking of the head.

Vasquez turned to the lieutenant. "He say no, no Yankees. He say the men in grey are always his friends. Also, he ask if we are alone."

Overstreet realized suddenly that something in the man's face wasn't Mexican at all. The eyes were blue. And now that he looked closer, he could see the sun strike a reddish tinge to the matted beard and the hair which showed under the broad-brimmed sombrero. The discovery set needles to prickling his skin.

He became aware of almost a dozen dark men stepping stealthily out of doors all along the lengthy adobe building. A few were Mexican, but most were Indians. They were armed, and they formed a wide, tight circle around the two soldiers. Overstreet fought back a panicky urge to draw his gun. It would never clear the holster.

One of the Indians was wearing a soldier's grey coat with a blue patch on the right elbow. Short hair rose on Overstreet's neck. Brinkley's coat! The two deserters had not gotten far.

The trader switched to English. "Ain't no cause for alarm, Lieutenant. All of us here are good friends of the South."

As he talked, his mouth broken in a mirthless, yellow-toothed smile, the trader was walking toward the two soldiers. Suddenly he reached out and caught the reins of both horses, right below the bits.

Vasquez whipped out an oath and grabbed for the knife at his belt.

"Hold it, Vasquez," Overstreet barked. He could see the yawning chasm of death in a dozen gun muzzles.

Still smiling, now triumphant, the trader said, "If I was you, I'd step down easy. Was I to give the signal, my boys'd cut you in two. They like to see the blood run."

Anger and fear mixed in the blood that pounded through Overstreet's veins. Throat dry, he started to obey. Just as his right leg swung over his horse's rump, he saw sudden excitement hit the Mexican and Indians like a cannonball. The trader's smile vanished. He let go the horses.

The Rebel soldiers had ridden in quietly and ringed the post. All of them had guns in their hands. A quick murmur rippled through the motley trading post bunch as they weighed the proposition, whether to drop their guns or stand their ground. At last one wrinkled old Indian lowered the ancient muzzle-loading pistol he held, and the others followed suit.

Relief washed through Overstreet as his men rode in. The scare had left him momentarily weak. The black-bearded Wheeler was in command, sitting his horse with all the pride and arrogance of a Yankee sergeant. He saluted the lieutenant, then motioned for the Mexicans and Indians to line up.

Overstreet turned to Vasquez, who seemed to have taken a quick grip on his nerves. "Call everybody out of the building, into the yard. Tell them any man who hesitates or runs will get a bullet through him."

Three more Indian bucks, a couple of slatternly squaws, and a disheveled Mexican woman came out of the building and joined the line.

"All right, men," the lieutenant said with vengeance in his

voice, "search every room. If anything goes wrong, don't hesitate to shoot."

It was then that Sammy McGuffin pulled his horse up beside the Indian wearing the grey coat.

"Look," he shouted, pointing his finger. "He's got Brinkley's coat on."

Evidently thinking he was being pointed out for death, the Indian desperately lunged at Sammy's horse. He grabbed the carbine from the boy's hand. It exploded, and the kid jerked, crying out in pain. Dalton Corbeil shot the Indian.

Tobe Wheeler grabbed the boy and held him in the saddle until two troopers jumped down to ease the whimpering lad to the ground. The wound was a raw, gaping hole well inside the left shoulder.

Watching the wound being bandaged, Overstreet asked Wheeler, "Think he can ride?"

Wheeler nodded. "He'll have to, I reckon. A couple of them redskins slipped away during the excitement. Even afoot, it ain't going to take them all week to find help."

Searching the post, the soldiers found only a couple of cases of old muzzle-loading guns, a little gunpowder, a roomful of Indian trade goods, mostly rotten whisky, and a nose-pinching stack of buffalo robes.

Overstreet nodded toward the hides. "There's no buffalo here, Wheeler. I'd bet these were traded from the plains tribes across in Texas."

The thick-bodied soldier drawled, "If you was to ask me, sir, I'd say this is what they call a *Comanchero* post. A dirty bunch of Indian traders that'll swap guns, whisky, captured women and children, or anything else, long's there's a profit in it. It'd suit me fine to cut the throats of the whole bunch before we leave here."

The lieutenant caught a short, banty rooster of a trooper named Duffy gulping a long swig of the trader's whisky. The little man choked, and tears welled up into his eyes. "Terrible stuff, sir," he wheezed, the whisky still searing his throat. "Should be against the law, the making of it. Will you have a drink with me?"

Overstreet shook his head. "No. And if I catch you taking another drink of it, I'll make you walk till your drunken brain explodes. Dump that stuff out, all of it."

The soldiers piled up all the guns, powder, and trade goods. Overstreet told them to take out what they could use.

"Then set fire to the rest of it."

The fat trader's mouth dropped open. His hands began gesturing violently. "For God's sake, Lieutenant, you wouldn't go and leave us here unarmed, would you? We got enemies."

Overstreet gritted. "From the looks of your red-skinned cronies here, I'd say you ought to have friends enough to protect you."

He frowned at the trader then, and an idea came to him. "What's your name?"

The red-edged eyes smouldered. "Bowden. Pate Bowden. What difference does that make to you?"

Overstreet reached forward and grabbed the man's dirty collar. "Do you know where the Walton Shafter Ranch is?"

The fat man nodded. "I ought to. What few troubles I have, that's where they come from."

Overstreet snapped, "Then get your saddle. You're riding with us."

The trader started to argue, but Wheeler poked him in the belly with the muzzle of a carbine. Bowden turned to obey. As he saddled a fat pony in the corral, he flicked his hate-filled eyes at Overstreet.

"I promise you this: you won't get far; my friends'll be on your trail before the dust settles; your scalps will be drying on a pole by this time tomorrow."

Overstreet angrily grabbed the man by the grimy collar again and shoved him roughly back against his horse. "If you think you're going to lead us into an ambush, you'd better forget it.

You'd die with us, because we'd slit your throat like we'd butcher a beef. Remember that. Now let's go."

They put the wounded boy into his saddle, and one trooper rode beside him to give him support. The detail moved out. Three soldiers rode ahead, pushing all the Indian ponies before them. Overstreet turned back once to look at the dark smoke that curled upward into the hazy sky. He got a grim satisfaction from the dismay in Bowden's greasy face.

He knew the trading post Indians wouldn't follow afoot, and they certainly wouldn't go to the Yankees. But they might bring another kind of help—dark-skinned savages with paint-smeared faces, muskets and shortbows, lances and scalping knives. The thought made Overstreet spur harder.

Far into the night they rode, then slept in a fireless camp with no warm rations. All night Sammy McGuffin whimpered in painful half-sleep. Before daybreak the troop was up and moving again, watching the back trail for any sign of pursuit.

It was a long ride, a hard ride. Sitting wearily in the saddle, Overstreet let his mind wander back through the years to other rides he had made. They had been long rides, too, and he had made them stirrup-to-stirrup with his father. The distance hadn't mattered much to him as a boy, for always there had been something new to see. And always there had been that commanding fire in old Jobe Overstreet's eyes.

Jobe Overstreet had been a circuit rider, with a black coat over his shoulders and the Book in his pocket, and he had ridden the length and breadth of the frontier to bring the Word to scattered settlers who hadn't seen a church in years. It had been a hard life, one that would have left a weakling of a boy by the wayside. But it had been worth all of it to thrill to that grand fever in his father's voice as he would stand above the gathered crowd in a clearing or on a hillside or along a creek bank.

But gradually, somehow, there came a change. Young Miles Overstreet found other activities more to his interest. He made fewer and fewer of those long rides beside old Jobe. That impassioned voice no longer sent a thrill tingling down his spine, and doubts began to crowd out the faith that had dwelt so long with him.

He would never forget that day he rode up to the little log structure that passed for a home and told his father that he had joined the Texas Rangers. It had been painful to watch the bitter disappointment etch itself into his father's lean, brown face.

"Don't be too soon making up your mind, son," Jobe had said with patience. Not until then had Miles noticed how completely grey his father had become.

"Tis a sad thing to see a man turn away from the Book and take up the gun. The gun brings misery and death to the body. But the Book, boy, the Book is food and drink and life for the soul."

But Miles had been young and bold and high of heart, and he had ridden away. The quick glance he took over his shoulder was the last look he had ever gotten at his father. That look was burned into his mind, his father standing like a great oak, his broad shoulders sagging a little, his head bowed in prayer.

Soon afterward Jobe Overstreet had gone down toward the coast to give comfort to the dying in a yellow fever epidemic. But the fever fastened itself upon him. And as the epidemic itself died away, Jobe Overstreet died, too.

The news had struck Miles like a thunderbolt. That a man who had spent his life serving his Lord should have to die in suffering when he had been on a mission of mercy . . . Miles Overstreet's faith had ebbed away, and it had never returned.

In midafternoon he began to notice that Bowden was leading them slightly to the east again. Worry began pulling at him, and he sent outriders a little farther away to watch for sign that anything was wrong.

It wasn't long in coming. Vasquez spurred in, waving his hat excitedly. "Indian camp, sir," he shouted breathlessly. "About a mile ahead. Forty men, maybe fifty. This man," he motioned toward Bowden, "he try to make us ride right into them."

Fury pulled Overstreet around in the saddle to face the trader. "You misled us, Bowden. You remember what I told you?"

The pudgy cheeks drained color, and the blood-rimmed blue eyes widened. Suddenly Bowden spurred the pony and clattered down the rocky slope, trying recklessly to make the Indian camp. Half a dozen troopers raised their rifles.

"Don't shoot," Overstreet yelled. "You'll have the whole camp on us."

He spurred after Bowden. The fat Indian pony wasn't much match for a well-bred cavalry mount, even though the bigger horse was tired from day upon day of riding. Overstreet reached his long arm around the trader's neck and pulled him out of the saddle. Then he dropped him and watched him roll and thrash among the sharp rocks. He swung down and jerked the trader onto his feet, drove a fist into the wide mouth and sent Bowden rolling again.

Out of the corner of his eye he saw Vasquez catch the trader's horse and start bringing it back.

Overstreet stood with fists doubled and watched blood trickle down the fat chin. "I meant what I told you back at the post, Bowden. You're going to lead us to Shafter's. I'll tie a rope around your neck and drag you through the rocks if I've got to. But you'll lead us, and lead us right."

No words passed from Bowden's bruised lips, but his blackening eyes told of the hate that seethed in him. Stiffly he mounted the pony and headed out again, a little west of south.

They had to make another dry, cold camp. Lying rolled up in his dirty blanket, sleepless, Overstreet let his thoughts wander again. They dwelt mostly upon the girl in Albuquerque. There was pleasure in remembering her dark eyes, the beauty of her face. In his imagination even the harshness was gone from her words, the only words she had spoken to him. Strange, how it was that sometimes even the thought of a woman could bring comfort to the worry-crowded mind of a man.

They came in sight of the Shafter place the next morning.

The ranch headquarters had been built along a creek that evidently ran at some times of year and held water in deep holes the rest of the time. In a small irrigated patch stood traces of last year's corn crop. Last year had been a dry one in New Mexico, poor for forage and poorer for crops, unless they had had some irrigation.

All the buildings were of the inevitable adobe, set close together as in a fort, with open space all around and a stout cedar picket fence on all sides to slow up any attack. The main building was in a hollow square, with a Mexican patio in the middle. All rooms evidently opened into the patio, for there were only windows along the outer walls.

Out back was a cedar thicket. Nearby, but outside the fence, were two small adobe outbuildings and pole corrals.

Overstreet noted with satisfaction that there were only three or four horses around. Scattered up and down the creek were cattle grazing upon the short green grass that had begun to rise.

"No sign of Yanks, Wheeler," he said.

At his signal, the men moved into double file and struck up a trot. At the rear was Vasquez, acting as guard for Bowden.

"Straighten up in those saddles, men," Overstreet ordered. "At least we can look like soldiers."

Wheeler spurred to the front and opened the gate that led through the tall picket fence.

Three men stepped out of the archway that led into the patio. They stood waiting, regarding the soldiers in quiet hostility. Two were Mexicans. Warily Overstreet watched the rifle one of them held in his hands. The third man stepped forward into the yard with the dignity of a soldier proud of his service. He was not a big man, but Overstreet got the idea he was as sturdy as an oak. He wore an old deerskin shirt and plain black trousers. Overstreet noted that the man's right arm hung stiffly at his side.

The stiff-armed one spoke quietly, and the Mexican reluctantly laid down the rifle. The lieutenant raised his right hand in salute. The man at the archway raised his left in the sign language signal for peace.

"Mister Shafter?" Overstreet asked. The ranchman nodded his grey head, his sharp eyes never leaving the officer's face. "Lieutenant Miles Overstreet, sir, presenting his compliments."

The ranchman's tone was civil but not friendly. "Get down, Lieutenant, you and your men. I reckon you're hungry. We ain't got much, but what's here, you're welcome to it."

"That's kind of you, sir," said the lieutenant. "But first, we've got a wounded man here. We don't have any medical supplies. We'd hoped maybe . . ."

The old scout had taken two long steps toward the boy McGuffin. He saw the blood on the lad's uniform and called without waiting for Overstreet to finish speaking.

"Linda! Linda! Come out here. There's a man needs help."

A girl stepped out into the patio and through the archway. Overstreet blinked and stiffened in the saddle, words stuck in his throat.

It was the girl from the Albuquerque hospital!

Quickly she moved up beside the tanned scout who was her father. She looked at Sammy and said impatiently, "Don't all you *Tejanos* just sit there like a bundle of feed. Somebody help me get this boy inside."

Woodenly the lieutenant swung down from the saddle. Wheeler and another man lifted Sammy off his horse. The girl led them into the patio and through a big door to the left. Overstreet watched her, hardly conscious that his mouth was open, and that he held his hands stiffly in midair. Shafter had to speak twice before the officer caught his words.

"My daughter, Lieutenant."

Overstreet nodded and tried to force his startled mind to something else. He let his gaze sweep over the buildings. "How many people are there here, sir?"

"No Union troops, Lieutenant. You don't have to worry about that."

"How about your own people?"

"A handful. My daughter and me. Half a dozen hands and three of their women. We just came back from up north to get the ranch fixed up. We brought a few cattle with us. The main herd won't come till the grass is up good."

He shrugged his shoulders in the manner of one who has spent much of his life among the Mexican people. "So you see, Lieutenant, there's not much here to plague your mind. I'll get the *cocinero* to fix some beef for your men, and you can move on."

He led Overstreet into the bare patio and turned back just before stepping under the shady *portales*. He pointed his chin toward the trader Bowden, sitting his horse belligerently at the rear of the troop.

"I don't know why you have Bowden with you, Lieutenant. It's none of my business. But there's one thing I'll ask of you. I don't want that man to set foot under my roof."

Overstreet had to grin. Here was a man he was going to like, even though Shafter was a Union supporter.

"Bowden is our prisoner, Mister Shafter. He tried to get us killed by Indians."

He was pleased by the grim look in Shafter's eyes that said the trader was getting what he deserved. "He ought to hang," commented the ranchman. "He's a *Comanchero*, and about as bad as the worst of them."

Again Overstreet looked at the closely gathered ranch buildings. "You're a long way from help here, sir. How've you managed to keep your hair?"

Shafter turned and gazed out across the ragged spread of mountains and the valley that was beginning to show a cast of green as the spring sun had edged northward. His blue eyes were proud.

"A man this far out can't look to governments for much help, Lieutenant. He's got to make his own treaties. But I've been living around Indians ever since I came west to trap beaver.

That's been thirty years ago. I've been making my own treaties and keeping them, even when armies weren't able to."

Overstreet followed him through a thick, adobe doorway and into a parlor. It was a fair-sized room, about twenty feet square, with a big Navajo rug covering the dirt floor. Taking up most of one side of the room was a big open fireplace, upon which this morning's coals still smoldered warm. Overstreet ran his fingers over a solid, handmade table that must have come from Santa Fe. The other furniture was the same, crudely designed but strong and well finished.

Through another door he could hear voices. He stepped up to it and watched Linda Shafter and a middle-aged Mexican woman working over Sammy McGuffin, talking to each other in soft, quiet Spanish.

Overstreet's heart picked up as the girl's dark eyes lifted to his briefly, then dropped again to her task. The same black hair, the same slender, softly rounded form that had quickened his breath in Albuquerque, and dwelt in his mind ever since. It was the same beautiful oval face, the skin smooth as fresh cream.

The lieutenant fingered the rough brush of beard on his face and looked regretfully at the dust and grime on his frayed uniform. He wished the girl hadn't had to see him this way.

Presently she was finished. Freshly bandaged, Sammy McGuffin lay quietly, his eyes closed. Overstreet wondered whether he had fainted or gone to sleep. Whichever it might have been, it was merciful.

Overstreet stood before the girl, hat crushed in his hand. "What do you think, ma'am?"

She was washing her hands in a pottery bowl. "He'll live, if you'll let him rest a few days and get a chance to mend."

He shook his head. "I'm afraid we can't, not long. We've got to be moving south."

Her eyes met his. He knew how he looked and knew what she thought of him by the thinly veiled dislike he saw there.

"If you don't want to kill him," she said, "you'll have to leave him here."

He stared at her incredulously. "You'd let a Texas soldier stay here, and you'd doctor him?"

"We'll help any wounded man who needs attention. Even a Texan."

Overstreet wondered. But he knew from the look in her eyes that she meant it, and that her father backed her up. That made it harder to do what he had to do.

"I can't tell you how grateful I am, ma'am. That's why I hate this so much. We've got to search your place."

A thin line of anger momentarily crossed Shafter's thin, wind-cracked lips. Then he nodded and said in the Mexican fashion, "My house is yours, Lieutenant."

Overstreet took a flashing glance at the girl. There was a flush of anger on her face, and her arms were folded tightly across her breasts.

"Mister Shafter," said Overstreet, "please call all your people together outside there, in the patio."

Shafter stepped to the door and spoke in Spanish to the two Mexican hands. They separated and returned quickly with two other men and three women.

"Two men are out on horseback," said Shafter. "They'll be back by noon."

Overstreet stepped in front of his men. "Now search every room of every building. You know what to look for. Bring along any guns you find. But don't touch anything else. Do you hear me? Nothing else."

As the soldiers disappeared into the buildings, Overstreet turned to the angry girl. "I hope you'll understand, Miss Shafter. In war we have to do a lot of things we hate. This is one of the things I hate most. It embarrasses me, and it humiliates you. But you're on one side of the wall, and we're on the other. We can't take any chances."

His words did nothing to allay her resentment. So Overstreet tried to dismiss it from his mind. After all, she was a Yankee girl. But the regret stayed with him.

By ones and twos the men straggled back. With them they brought perhaps a dozen guns of all makes and kinds. Anxiously Overstreet searched each face that approached him. But he knew without asking that the gun and ammunition cache had not been found.

Finally all the men were back but one. The missing trooper was Hatchet.

Overstreet heard a rattle in a room to his left. He remembered that he had seen Hatchet go into a door on the right.

Fresh color washed into Linda Shafter's cheeks. "That's my room he's in," she said sharply. "I'm telling you, Lieutenant, I will not have him prowling through my things."

She whirled around so fast that her skirt sailed a little and half wrapped itself around her legs as she quickly stepped forward and pushed through a door. The lieutenant heard her gasp, then shout angrily, "Put that down! It's mine!" He heard something crash and heard her cry out in pain.

With two long strides Overstreet reached the door and shoved in. The slender girl was picking herself up from the floor and leaping again at Hatchet. Angry Spanish words were tumbling from her lips. She grabbed for a box Hatchet held behind him. He pushed her away savagely.

"Get away from me, you wench, or I'll really hurt you."

Overstreet barked at Hatchet in a voice sharp as a spur rowel. "Stand back there, Hatchet. Whatever you've got in your hand, give it to that girl."

Hatchet whirled on the lieutenant. His wide nostrils flared. "Maybe you can tell us what to do in the field, Overstreet, but this ain't the field. What I've found, I'll keep for myself."

Out of the corner of his eye Overstreet saw the lithe young woman reach into a slat bonnet which hung from the wall. She swung around with a gun in her hand. It was an old-fashioned horse pistol like Overstreet had seen so many times as a boy.

And who'd have thought to look in a bonnet hanging from a peg on the wall?

"Now, you thieving *Tejano*," the girl snapped at Hatchet, "you put down that box."

Hatchet's stubborn, bearded chin was low. "You ain't got the nerve to shoot anybody. But I'd break your arm." He moved toward her.

"I told you to stand back, Hatchet," Overstreet said again. "That's an order."

He stepped toward Hatchet. The girl swung the pistol around to cover him, too. "You promised us, Lieutenant. I'd just as soon shoot you as any one of your sticky-fingered renegades."

Overstreet stopped. So did Hatchet. The lieutenant swallowed hard. One nervous twitch of her finger could kill either of them as completely as a Yankee cannonball. And fire in her dark eyes showed she would do it.

She didn't see Wheeler step up behind her. Like a bullwhip, his hand snaked out and jerked the pistol from her fingers. She whirled on him as if to beat against his big body with her little fists. Then she broke down and began to sob. Wheeler looked down on her in embarrassment and pity and looked as if he wanted to run.

Overstreet snatched the box from Hatchet's hand, put it on a table, and opened it. Inside was a string of pearl-white beads, a broach that appeared to be of gold, and a couple of sparkling rings.

"They were my mother's," the girl said.

Overstreet handed her the box and put his hand on her shoulder to comfort her. But touching her set his blood to tingling, and he drew his hand away.

"My apologies, ma'am. Whatever else may be wrong with us, we're not thieves."

Outside, he let his anger spill in torrents. "What have I got to do to make you learn that we're fighting Yankee soldiers, not civilians, Hatchet? Every settlement we've been through, you've tried to loot it. I almost wish you hadn't lost your sergeant's rating before you were sent to me. I'd like to have ripped those chevrons off your sleeve myself."

To Wheeler he said, "Hatchet's under arrest. Disarm him. Find a good place that one man can guard and put him and Bowden in it."

Later Overstreet faced Shafter and his daughter under the shady patio portals. "I wish I could repay you the trouble we've caused you."

Linda Shafter's eyes still held a spark. "I wish you could just hurry up and leave."

The lieutenant flinched. "So do I. But first we're going to get the Union munitions that you have hidden here."

Shafter straightened and clasped his stiff arm with his good hand. The girl caught her breath quickly. Then the old scout dropped his hand and said, "Somebody's lied to you, Lieutenant. We don't know anything about any munitions."

Overstreet shook his head. "I don't intend to get harsh now, after what you've done for us. But you know and I know that there are ten wagonloads of guns and ammunition hidden somewhere about the ranch. One way or another, we're going to find it."

Shafter folded his good arm across his chest. "Even if there were any munitions, Lieutenant, we wouldn't tell you."

The lieutenant smiled. "If you did, sir, I wouldn't respect you. But we'll find it ourselves."

He went back into the parlor and looked around. He knew his soldiers had searched every building. It appeared the cache must be somewhere out on the ranch, not at the buildings. He turned on his heel and felt the Indian rug sink into the dirt beneath his foot. A sudden hunch hit him. He stepped back, pulled up a corner, and rolled away the rug. He saw nothing but the dirt floor.

Impatiently he shoved open a door in the thick adobe wall and went into the next room. He looked under two smaller rugs there. Nothing. But in the third he found what he sought. Half buried beneath the dirt was the knotted end of a rope. He pulled it up until the slack was gone, then began to tug on it. He could see a big block of dirt rise a little. He called for help.

With big Tobe Wheeler and another trooper helping him, he lifted the trap door and set it back on its leather hinges.

Even without looking into the musty tunnel, he knew he had found the cache. Carefully he lowered himself through the door, then dropped to the bottom. Wheeler came after him, while the other trooper waited above to help them get out.

"An old getaway tunnel, I'd bet, sir," Wheeler said. "Put there to give folks a chance to light out in case they had to. I'd bet a man a quart of good corn whisky that it comes up in the thicket we seen behind the house."

Exhilaration was in Overstreet like the warmth of Mexican wine. He stood there a moment, almost afraid to look. The dust tickled his nostrils, dust that had lain undisturbed for months, now stirred up again by troopers' boots.

"What I mean, sir," Wheeler called enthusiastically from up ahead, "she's full of powder, percussion caps, and the like. A regular little arsenal, she is."

Overstreet's heart pounded as he worked through the gloom, surveying the huge cache. It was all there, rifle boxes that seemed never to have been opened—keg upon keg of powder—case after case of cartridges and percussion caps.

What a battle could be fought with all this! The thought of it prickled Overstreet's skin.

As he stood there, memories came back to him, sobering memories of men he had known, men he had led. Many of them lay dead, way back yonder in an alien land, dead for a cause most of them probably had not even understood. Since Glorietta it had looked as if those deaths had been in vain. Now, maybe they hadn't been.

He knew that this, properly, should be a time for prayer. He wished once again for the faith that had meant so much to him as a boy, the simple but rock-firm faith of his father. But that faith was gone, faded behind the helpless agony of yellow fever, and the sickening glut of war-spilled blood.

He did not bow his head, and he spoke to no one in particular. But standing there in the dusty gloom, he vowed that he would give his own life, if he had to, to insure that those deaths had not been for nothing.

He set up guard posts at each end of the tunnel. Resignedly, Shafter watched. He kept his good arm folded across his chest, the fingers nervously tugging at the sleeve of the stiff arm. There was a thin play of anger along his lips.

"All right, Lieutenant, so you've found it. What can you do with it?"

"We'll take it with us, if we can. If we can't, we'll touch it off. One thing for certain, Mister Shafter, it'll never kill another Confederate soldier."

A half smile touched Shafter's age-nicked mouth. "You can't pack it out of here on your backs."

Overstreet leaned his angular frame against an adobe wall. "It won't hurt to tell you now, sir. A train of ten Yankee wagons is due here most any time, to get all of this. They'll get it all right, but they'll be working for Jeff Davis."

Shafter dropped his arm. Color splotched his face, and his blue eyes hardened. Linda Shafter stepped forward, her pink lips tightened.

"They won't give up the wagons easy, Lieutenant. You know that. Men on both sides will die, fighting for them. Then, if you win, you'll take the munitions and use them to kill more soldiers. Don't you think there's been enough killing already?"

Overstreet shoved away from the wall and stood straight again. He looked levelly into her pleading dark eyes. He could feel regret rising in him, and he fought it. "There's been too much killing, ma'am. But it's not right to the men who've died if we give up so long as there's a thread of hope left in us."

He tipped his hat and started to walk away. He turned back,

his throat tight. "I'm afraid we'll have to keep a watch over you from now on. That is, unless you give me an oath that you won't try to get away or send any signal."

The girl's eyes were defiant. "You know we won't do that. If we get a chance, we'll certainly send a warning."

Overstreet bowed gravely. "It's your choice. I'm sorry."

Walking away, he heard Shafter say to his daughter, "He's a soldier, Linda. Secessionist or not, he's a soldier."

A dozen times in the hours that followed, Overstreet walked out to the guard stationed on a rise a few hundred yards north of the buildings. He would take the spyglass he had lent the man and use it to scan the shimmering horizon.

"Haven't you seen anything yet, Tillery?"

"No, sir, nary a sign of wagons so far."

Overstreet would walk back to the buildings, kicking up dirt with the toes of his boots, impatiently drumming his fist against his leg.

Again and again his thoughts turned to the girl, and he found pleasure in them. He told himself she was with the enemy, that he was drawn to her only because it had been so long since he had been near a woman. But he felt again of his scrubby beard, and he went looking for a razor and soap.

Later he visited Sammy McGuffin in the room where the wounded lad had been placed on a rough frame cot and a corn husk mattress. The thin face was drawn and white. Sammy tried to rise onto one elbow as Overstreet entered.

"Better lie down and take it easy, Sammy," the lieutenant said.

Sammy shook his head. "I'll be all right, sir." He paused, his pained face strained with worry. "About those wagons, sir. Think they'll get here today?"

Overstreet shook his head. "I wish I knew. It'd be worth a ton of Yankee gold to get those wagons here before night. Every hour we have to wait means that somewhere back yonder some Yankee column is getting an hour closer to us."

Overstreet saw how the boy's hands trembled. "It's apt to be a pretty hard fight for them wagons, ain't it, sir?" Sammy was struggling to control his frightened voice. The lieutenant nodded. "Maybe." The voice quavered. "If we lose, sir . . . we'll go to some Yankee prison. They'll go and throw us in a dungeon someplace and leave us to rot."

His voice broke, and the boy sobbed. "I'm afraid, sir. I don't want to go to prison."

Overstreet put his hand on the slender shoulder. "Don't worry, Sammy. You won't be a prisoner."

Darkly he arose and walked outside. He had intended to leave Sammy here where he could rest and receive attention. But now he knew that whatever the cost, he would take the boy along.

The sun was slanting down toward the tops of the mountains to the west when the guard came trotting in, sweat cutting streaks across his dusty face.

"Wagons, sir. Coming now, maybe a mile off. Counted twelve of them. There's an advance guard of a couple of men, riding this way."

Overstreet started shouting orders, excitement rising in him. "Move all the horses to the thicket, out of sight. Put all the civilians in a room together. Deploy around the building, with guns on the ready."

The civilians were moved into the parlor. Overstreet went with them. "We're going to try to work this so there won't be anybody killed," he said. "Best way you all can help is to stay quiet and still."

A glance outside showed him the two Union riders almost at the outside gate. Hands sweaty, Overstreet drew the Colt Dragoon. "Step into the patio gate so they can see you, Mister Shafter. Don't try to make any signals. No use in getting somebody killed."

Shafter stood in the archway. The lieutenant kept back but managed to watch the two federals cautiously riding up. Both drew rein. One, a big noncommissioned officer, held a saddle carbine in front of him. The other, dressed like an officer, had his hand on the butt of a pistol, still in the holster.

Hardly breathing, Overstreet whispered, "Shafter, wave them on in. Tell them it's all clear. Remember, one wrong move and they'll die."

He could see color rise on Shafter's neck. But the ranchman lifted his good hand in greeting, Indian fashion. "Howdy. Get off and come in."

The Union officer's eyes suspiciously roved over the yard and patio. "You're Shafter, I presume." Shafter nodded.

The Yankee captain finally relaxed and swung down to the sand. The corporal slipped his carbine into its saddle scabbard in courtesy, then followed the officer's example.

Shafter stepped back into the room. For an instant his hot eyes touched Overstreet's, and the lieutenant could see shame and anger in them. Stepping into the room, the officer blinked against the semidarkness. His eyes suddenly widened, and his hand dipped toward the holster as he saw Overstreet.

"Hold it, Captain," Overstreet said sharply, shoving the Colt forward. "You're my prisoner."

The blue-clad corporal was caught right in the doorway. He crouched there, looking out at his horse as if gauging how long a jump he would have to make to reach his carbine.

"Get it out of your head, soldier," the lieutenant said. "A dozen rifles are aimed at you. You'd never make it to your horse."

The soldier stood trembling, more from anger than fear. Outraged, the captain raised his hands as Overstreet stepped toward him and slipped the pistol out of the holster. "What do you want here?"

"The same thing you do, the Union munitions. We're taking your wagons, Captain. Signal them in."

Already the wagons were in sight. Overstreet could count them. Red color blazed across the federal captain's face.

"They'll stop out there until I give them the word to come in. I won't do that."

Bluff it out with him, Overstreet told himself. "You will if you don't want to see your men killed, Captain. We're ready to kill, if we've got to."

But the captain didn't bluff. "It would be far better to lose a few men here than to let you take those munitions and kill a lot more."

Overstreet looked at the big Union noncom and knew what he had to do. "Wheeler," he called, "bring a couple of men, and run."

To the drawling Wheeler he said, "The corporal's about your size. Think you could persuade him to lend you his uniform for a little while?"

The Yankee captain bristled. "Listen to me, soldier. If you put on that uniform, even for a minute, it makes you a spy. It makes you liable for hanging."

A half grin appeared under Wheeler's black moustache as he answered in his gravelly, lazy voice. "If you want to hang me, Captain, you'll have to wait your turn. There's folks back home already got first rights on that privilege. That's why I had to leave Texas in the first place."

He led the big Yank non-com into another room. Overstreet heard the sounds of a short scuffle, then a powerful blow. A moment later Wheeler came back dressed in dusty blue. "Reckon I was a little the biggest."

All of a sudden Overstreet was jubilant. It was going to work. "Now get out there and stand by that gate. Wave them in. If they ask any questions, you're part of the advance detail that got here two days ago. Shut the gate as the last wagon comes through. Then watch out for your neck."

At the gate Wheeler waved the hat he had taken from the Yankee corporal. The wagons had halted, apparently according to orders. Now they began to move. Overstreet could hear the shouts of the army mule drivers.

His heart was pounding high in his chest as the first wagon came through the gate, then the second and the third. Each wagon had a driver and three spans of mules. They kept rolling.

He heard a startled shout behind him. The enlisted man who had come in with Wheeler. "Look out, sir!"

The Union captain had made a quick dash for the door. Hardly having time to think, Overstreet raised his pistol and swung it down at the officer's head. With a sigh the captain sank to the Navajo rug that covered the dirt floor.

Linda Shafter ran to the man. Turning him over, she said something in Spanish. One of the Mexican women quickly brought her a vase of water and a cloth. Wiping the captain's unconscious face with cold water, the girl looked up. Her black eyes leaped at Overstreet in fury. Her lips trembled with words unspoken. The lieutenant knew their meaning even though he didn't hear them, and they brought pain to him.

The twelfth wagon moved into the big enclosure. Overstreet saw Wheeler shut the gate, then sprint away to cover.

Swallowing hard, the lieutenant stepped to the door. "All right, men," he called. "Move out."

The grey-clad Texans stepped outside almost simultaneously. There was a second of shocked silence among the few Yankee horsemen and the teamsters. Then all shouted at once. Carbines and pistols whipped out. A driver popped his whip at his mules and swung them around toward the gate, only to haul up short as he saw it was closed. He jumped down to unfasten it, but was driven back by a whining slug from Wheeler's carbine.

Half a dozen wild shots were thrown by the Yankees, but their targets were too elusive. Overstreet's bold voice carried above the confusion. "Throw down your guns. You haven't got a chance. We've got your officer."

Grudgingly the soldiers began to comply. They swung down to the ground and started forming a line, hands held up even with their shoulders. Within two minutes the wagons were taken.

Overstreet wondered about the two extra wagons and found them to be carrying forage and rations for the troops.

Pausing now, he realized that his heart was pounding like a steam engine. Somehow, they had done it. The worst scalawag detail in the Sibley Brigade. Hardly a man in it worth his hide and tallow. But they had captured twelve Yankee wagons and a cache of munitions.

How far would it be now to safety? A hundred miles? A hundred and fifty? A hard race at best. But the lead had been won.

Quickly he counted the Yankee soldiers. Twelve mule drivers, one for each wagon. A mounted escort of ten men, not counting the officer and non-com. A short detail for such a job. But probably it had been kept short in confidence that the advance detail would furnish escort enough on the trip back. Somewhere, a Union officer had mistakenly discounted the Indian threat.

To his men, Overstreet said, "Half of you take those mule drivers and get the teams unhitched from the wagons. Take them to water. See that they get feed and rest. There'll be little enough of it once we get started."

There was a rattling of trace chains, the stamping of hooves, the harmless cursing of mule drivers as the animals were freed from the wagons and led away in harness. Overstreet turned to the rest of the men.

"Now, you'll line up those wagons by hand, tongues facing out toward the gate. Hurry up. We don't aim to lose any time."

In a quarter of an hour the wagons had been lined up side by side, the tailgates toward the square adobe main building. Under guard, the mule drivers came back. With the guard detail was Wheeler, still in blue.

"What do you say, Lieutenant, that I take a little spell and get back in me decent clothes? Every time I take a look at the yellow stripe down the legs of these pants, I start seeing red."

The trooper's drawling complaint brought a smile from Overstreet and drained some of the tension.

"Hop to it, Corporal. As far as I'm concerned, you're a corporal from now on."

Overstreet took a quick look to the west. The sun had dipped almost to the tops of the mountains, and thin clouds were purple against the red fire of the sky.

"We're going to start loading those wagons now," he said to his own soldiers and to the prisoners. "We'll load till night if we've got to. We'll be ready to pull out of here in the morning, no matter what."

He put part of the Union soldiers to work lifting the gun cases, the powder kegs, and the boxes of percussion caps up out of the tunnel. Other Yankees picked up the munitions at the trap door and carried them out to load them on the wagons. The only pause was a short mess period for prisoners and guards alike to eat a warm meal cooked out of rations found in the Union mess wagon.

With darkness, the men put up lanterns and candles and worked and sweated and cursed on in their flickering orange light. One by one, the wagons were piled high and the canvas covers laced tightly over the hoops.

Overstreet let the Union captain watch with him. Terrell Pace was the officer's name. He was fifteen years out of Vermont, ten years out of the Point, and two years in the bitter cold and blistering heat that took their turns in the New Mexico Territory.

"You don't have a chance, Overstreet. You're substituting courage for common sense, and it'll kill you. If you're thinking of heading west and striking your own troops, forget it. Most of Sibley's Brigade is on the other side of the Rio Grande, working its way back down to Fort Bliss in Texas. Canby's Union troops are following on this side. Federal soldiers would pick you up long before you reached the river."

Stubbornly Overstreet said, "We're going south. We might get help at Fort Stanton."

Pace smiled. "Try again, Lieutenant. There's a good chance Fort Stanton, too, will be in Union hands before you get there."

A new worry gnawed at the lieutenant. He hadn't realized the situation was so bad. There was a chance the captain was lying. But Overstreet knew it was a slim chance, not one he could depend upon.

There was only one course then, he realized darkly. They would have to remain on the Pecos side of the divide and by-pass Fort Stanton. They would have to try to take their wagons across the Guadalupes and come into Fort Bliss from the east. And in all that tortuous route, they could expect no help. No help except from God.

He wondered suddenly why that thought had struck him. It had been a long time since he had even considered asking help from God.

He heard a shout from inside the patio. Hatchet's partner, Dalton Corbeil, came running out to him, eyes wide with excitement.

"Lieutenant, Tillery's hollering for help. Says one of Shafter's Mexicans is gone."

Keeping Captain Pace in front of him, Overstreet hurried to the building and pushed into the room where he had left the civilians under guard. He found the guard Tillery still half in a daze, rubbing the back of his head. Overstreet saw a triumphant gleam in the dark eyes of Linda Shafter. A thin smile creased the wrinkled face of the old army scout. Overstreet quickly counted the civilians and found that one was gone.

"I'm sorry, sir," the guard said, pain glazing his eyes. "I thought I'd made friends with Shafter, and I relaxed too much. Somebody hit me over the head.

"I finally managed to pull up on my feet again, but by then one of the Mexicans was gone."

Angrily Overstreet stepped toward the cripple-armed old ranchman. He saw victory in the squinted blue eyes. "You'll never make it now, Lieutenant. I sent Felipe Chavez, one of the best men I have. You'll never find him out there in the dark. But he can find his way. It won't take him long to catch a loose horse. And as soon as he can locate any Union troops, the army will be on your tail."

There was a roar from the Texan Corbeil. He was whittled from the same block as his friend Hatchet. Grabbing the scout by the leather shirt, he pulled him off his feet and drove his fist into the old man's stomach.

Overstreet grabbed the soldier's grey coat and tried to pull him back. "Damn you, Corbeil, stop it! Do you want me to throw you in the same place I've got Hatchet?"

Corbeil's face was red all the way up from his collar. He had a gun in his hand. "We ought to hang him, that's what we ought to do! Just let me go. I'll put a bullet in him."

Overstreet wrenched the trooper's gun away. "It won't do, Corbeil. In his place you'd have done the same thing, if you'd had the guts. But you're like your friend Hatchet, and most of the others in this sorry outfit. You've only got the guts when you've got a cinch.

"Now get out of here. And tell Wheeler I want him."

Corbeil paused at the door, his eyes brimming with rage. "Just remember what Chaney Hatchet told you, Lieutenant. You're a long way from home."

With the Union captain's help, Overstreet lifted the old man up and put him on a bed. Linda Shafter glanced at the lieutenant a long moment. He thought he could see a softening in her eyes.

"Thank you, Lieutenant," she said hesitantly. "I think he'd have killed Dad." Her lips quivered as she picked up her father's hand.

Wheeler came in. Overstreet said, "We can't waste another minute, Corporal. Speed up the loading of those wagons."

Wheeler frowned. "I'm afraid the men are working about as fast as they can already."

"They've got to work faster. Put all our own men at it too, except those you have to have for guard."

"Do my best, sir," Wheeler said.

Overstreet motioned to the Mexican men who were still in the room. "You go along with Wheeler. He'll put you to work. And Wheeler, send for Hatchet and that trader Bowden, too. Let them lend a little muscle."

There was a trace of a grin on the Union captain's face. "Looks as if you outsmarted a whole detail of federal soldiers, only to be defeated by one smart old scout, Overstreet. Why don't you quit?"

A coldness worked through the lieutenant. "We won't give up, Pace, until we're in Fort Bliss or until we've blown every last pound of powder sky high, so you'll never get a chance to use it against us."

Within an hour the last wagon was loaded, and the getaway tunnel was empty. A choking veil of dust hung in it. The men who climbed out were grimy and tired.

Overstreet looked to the east. Not a sign of light there yet. But it wouldn't be long until the sun started pushing back the darkness from above the mountains. He put the Yankee cook to preparing breakfast. He dispatched the teamsters, under guard, to harness the mules and bring them to the heavy wagons. Then he went into Sammy McGuffin's room. Linda Shafter was there. The boy turned his head to look at the officer, but he no longer tried to rise. The soreness had worked all through him.

"Think you're ready to go, Sammy?"

The girl whirled around in protest. "You can't take him out in one of those jostling wagons. You'll kill him!"

Fear rose in Sammy's high-pitched voice. "I'm all right. I can travel. Please don't leave me here for them Yankees to take."

Overstreet tried to smile. "We won't leave you, Sammy."

Outside the room the girl anxiously caught the lieutenant's wrist. Her touch brought excitement to him. "If you're really going to take him, you'd better start praying for him. He'll need it."

"I made him a promise, and I won't abandon him as long as

he's so scared of the Yanks. As for the praying, I reckon I'll let you do that. Nobody's ever answered any prayers of mine."

Watching the mules being hitched to the wagons, Overstreet noticed that the short, squatty Duffy was wobbling a little. At first he thought it was merely fatigue and knew there was reason enough for that. But he became suspicious and called Duffy over. The trooper's eyes were glazy, and his breath fairly stank with the smell of liquor. Somewhere he had found a bottle. The lieutenant snatched it from his shaky hand and hurled it to the ground, smashing it.

"Wheeler," he said sharply, "when we start out, tie Duffy's wrist to the tailgate of one of the wagons. Let him walk until he sobers up."

When all the mules had been hitched up and the men had eaten, Overstreet had everyone gather in front of the patio archway.

"Captain Pace," he said, "I'm just going to take along your teamsters. That's as many as my men can watch anyway."

The captain frowned, as if he couldn't believe it. "You mean you're leaving the rest of us here, free?"

Overstreet nodded. "The rest of your detail, Captain. They'll be afoot. But you're going with us."

Answering the sudden angry question in the officer's eyes, the lieutenant went on, "Without your leadership, I don't think your men will do much to hurt us."

Overstreet stopped next in front of the portly Indian trader. There was an almost unbelievable stench of liquor and tobacco, buffalo hides, grease, and sweat about the man.

"I'd like to hang you, Bowden. Satan himself knows you deserve it. But chances are the Yankees will hang you soon enough anyway. I'm going to have to let you go."

A dry grin broke across the man's flabby, bearded face. But there was murder in the evil blue eyes. "Did you ever scalp a man, Overstreet?"

The lieutenant shook his head. A chill played down his back.

"A bloody business," Bowden said. "But you don't know how much satisfaction there can be in it when the man's somebody you hate."

He paused to give his words emphasis. "I'm going to get your scalp, Lieutenant!"

Even in the near-darkness, Overstreet could see raw hatred burning in the trader's face. That chill hit him again, and he turned away.

"All right, men," he said, "mount up."

Captain Pace stepped in front of him. "I'll try once again to put some sense in your head, Lieutenant. The army will never let you get this train of munitions to your lines."

"They'll never take it," Overstreet said grimly.

"Perhaps not. But if they see they can't, they won't hesitate to blow it up, so you Rebs can't use it. A few bullets in the right place would blast the whole wagon train halfway to the moon."

The lieutenant froze. He realized Pace was right. "Even if it meant killing you and your mule drivers?" But he knew the answer.

"Yes. There are only thirteen of us. But who knows how many would be killed if you got this train to your lines?"

Overstreet rubbed his face hard. If only there were some way . . . Something that might make the Yankees hold back, to avoid a battle with this train . . .

He looked around, and his eyes rested on the girl, Linda Shafter. Strange that at a moment like this he could think only of her beauty, the warm thrill that had swept over him at her slightest touch.

Then the idea came. The only thing that might hold the Union troops back. Under any other circumstances it would have been a cowardly thought, even a despicable one. But this was war. This was a win-or-lose struggle for ten wagons loaded to the top with munitions, worth more right now than its own weight in Yankee gold . . .

"I'm sorry, Miss Shafter," he said, "but I'm going to have to ask you to come along with us. You'd better get some things together."

She gasped. Old Walton Shafter stormed out of his place like a wounded bear. "She's my daughter, Overstreet. I won't let you do it."

The lieutenant's voice was edged with regret. "I'm afraid you don't have any choice, sir. Neither do I. If I did, I wouldn't think of taking her."

Captain Pace swore. "You intend to buy your protection with a woman's life, Overstreet?"

Overstreet shook his head. "Not my protection, Captain. The protection of this train. Any Yankee troop that catches up with us now will be plenty careful how it shoots at these wagons."

He could feel the old scout's anger upon him like the furnace heat of an August west wind. He turned away to see that his men were on horseback, including Hatchet. The Union teamsters were up on their wagon seats. Sammy McGuffin had been laid carefully on a pile of blankets in the mess wagon. Overstreet pointed to a lead wagon.

"Climb up, Captain."

A moment later the girl came out with a bag under her arm. Old Walton Shafter folded his good arm around her.

"I know there's no use me begging you not to take her, Lieutenant. So I'll just give you a warning. If any harm comes to her, Texas isn't big enough to hide you. Wherever you go, I'll hunt you down. Don't forget that, Overstreet. Because I won't."

The man's eyes were like muzzles of a double-barreled shotgun. They put a chill under the lieutenant's skin.

"No harm will come to her, Mister Shafter, not unless it's from the Yanks. I promise you that. And as soon as we figure we're out of the danger area, I'll send her back, with Captain Pace and his men as escort."

Helping the girl up onto a wagon seat beside a middle-aged Union teamster on Sammy's wagon, Overstreet felt the keen throb that passed through him at the touch of her skin. But her stabbing anger was like a whip when she turned her flashing eyes upon him for a moment.

He swung into the saddle, lifted his arm, and brought it down in a forward arc. "Forwa-a-rd . . . ho-o-o!"

Mules strained in the traces, and one by one the wheels of the loaded wagons began to turn. In a jangling of chains, a popping of whips, the train moved out the gate a wagon at a time. Outside, they made a right turn, and the tongues pointed south toward Texas.

As he prepared to follow, Overstreet had all the remaining soldiers and civilians herded into one small outbuilding. He left Vasquez to guard them.

"Stay here three hours," he told the dark-skinned trooper. "By that time we ought to be far enough on our way that nothing they can do afoot will hurt us."

Then he reined around and followed in the thin, lingering dust of the wagon train. The sun, just beginning to break through the haze over the mountains, sent long, ragged shadows reaching far out across the broken ground. Sharp morning air brought steam rising from the laboring mules and the nose-rolling horses.

Overstreet felt rather than saw Wheeler rein in beside him.

"Well, sir," the trooper said, "looks like we're on our way—to hell or to Fort Bliss, whichever comes first."

From the time the light of dawn fanned out across the endless, rough-hewn distance, Overstreet was continually turning in the saddle, anxiously looking over his left shoulder for dust, for horsemen, for men afoot. Each time he faced back toward the moving wagons, a thin smile would come to his lips. But soon the worry was dragging at him again, and he had to look back once more.

Shortly before noon Vasquez caught up, easing his horse along in a sensible, strength-saving trot.

"Any trouble?" the lieutenant queried.

Vasquez smiled, showing a broad row of gleaming teeth beneath his trimmed black moustache. "Only the fat one, the *Comanchero* Bowden. He is try to climb out a window. I put a bullet close to him, close like a glove. Ay, what *maldiciones* he is heap upon my poor head."

The trooper sobered. "I think he is a man to fear, Lieutenant. More *malo* than even the Yankees."

At noon Overstreet halted the train at a little water hole to rest and water the mules and to let the soldiers eat a hasty meal of hard tack and cold Yank bacon. He detailed Wheeler to check the load on every wagon, to make sure it was riding properly.

From up the line in a few moments came the sharp echo of argument. He saw Chaney Hatchet with his back to the end gate of a wagon, shaking his fist at Wheeler.

"What's the matter here?" the lieutenant demanded.

Hatchet swiveled to face him. There was a flash of defiance in his washy blue eyes as he angrily gripped his right arm with his left hand. "I just told Wheeler I'd already checked the wagon, and he could move on."

Instantly Overstreet guessed what was the matter. "What're you hiding in that wagon, Hatchet?"

Splotches of color showed through the dirty stubble on Hatchet's flat cheeks. "Nothing, Lieutenant. I just said everything's all right here, and I don't like being made out a liar."

Lips suddenly tight against his teeth, Overstreet stepped forward. "Move aside there, Hatchet. I'm checking that wagon."

Hatchet caught his shoulder and jerked him back, but not before the lieutenant had glimpsed the little black box wedged between two rifle cases. Flame heat whipping through him, he whirled on the trooper.

"So you slipped back into that girl's room and stole her jewelry box again."

Quick as a jackrabbit, Hatchet leaped upon the wagon and grabbed the box. He jumped down again, his speckled right hand hovering just above the pistol strapped to his waist. "It's mine, Overstreet. I'm keeping it if I've got to blast you to Kingdom Come."

A shadow of fear lurked in Overstreet, but he couldn't afford to show it. He tried to keep his voice flat as he stepped slowly forward.

"You know you can't shoot me, Hatchet. You'd be stood up against a wall, or hung to a tree limb. Hand me that box and get your hand away from that gun."

The washy eyes reflected indecision. Overstreet tried to take advantage of it by jumping at Hatchet. But the thief darted aside, bringing the pistol up out of the holster and leveling it at Overstreet's body. The lieutenant stopped short, his heart pounding. But Hatchet wavered, and Overstreet knew the man was not going to fire.

He grabbed the pistol, roughly tore it from Hatchet's fingers, and hurled it to one side. A sudden desperate fury exploded in the thief's shallow eyes. With an animal roar of anger, Hatchet sprang upon Overstreet. He dropped the box. The beads gleamed white on the rocky ground, and the rings rolled away.

The first rush threw Overstreet off balance. He fell on his back, knocking some of the breath out of him. Instantly Hatchet was on him, driving his fists at the lieutenant's face. Overstreet threw himself to one side, rolled over, and sprang to his feet. He dodged just as Hatchet scooped up a fist-sized rock and hurled it.

He charged in again, twisting his whole body in a bone-crushing drive at Hatchet's ribs. Hatchet bent at the middle and roared in pain. But somehow he managed to hit Overstreet a hard belt to the side of the head. The lieutenant faltered, blinking his eyes against the spinning flashes of light that exploded in his brain. Hatchet hit him again, and he lurched backward against a wagon wheel.

Braced momentarily, he caught his balance and lunged forward. His drive carried him into Hatchet and on. Hatchet stumbled. Overstreet started plowing hard blows into the man's face and stomach. Fury guided his fists, pounding, crushing, hammering until Hatchet folded and sank weakly onto his face.

Overstreet stood there breathing hard, his fists still gripped so tightly that the fingernails bit into the flesh. He wiped sweat from his face and saw the smear of red on the grey sleeve.

"Take his guns away, Wheeler," he said at length. "And see that he never gets them back this time."

He stopped a moment, watching Linda Shafter carefully pick up the jewelry and put it back in the box. Her glance met his, then fell away, and a flush crossed her cheek. Overstreet swallowed, lurched toward his horse, and fumbled the canteen loose from his saddle. His throat washed clear, he leaned against the horse for support and looked across the saddle. He could feel almost all eyes upon him.

He signaled with his hand and said sharply to Wheeler, "Head them out again. Hasn't everybody seen enough?"

He poured water into one hand and tried to wash his face, but the water trickled out between his fingers. A hammer was driving nails through his brain. He sat down upon the ground and put his wet hand to his forehead.

He heard the canteen lid rattle, then felt the comfort of a wet cloth against his burning face. He looked up at Linda Shafter. She was bent over him, carefully wiping his face with a soaked handkerchief. Her fingers on his cheek brought a sudden warm contentment to him. He watched her, almost forgetting the pain, letting his mind give way to wonder.

She saw the question in his eyes. "I owe it to you, don't I? After you fought for me the way you did?"

He shook his head. "That fight started a long time before either of us ever saw you."

He flinched as the cloth touched a cut on his cheek.

"I didn't mean to hurt you," her quiet voice said apologetically. Her dark eyes met his.

"Didn't you?" he asked softly. "You should have, after all the trouble I've brought on you."

She didn't answer. She finished washing his face, turned away, and walked back to her wagon. Sitting on the ground, Overstreet watched her, still feeling the stir of excitement she had aroused in him.

The train kept rolling until darkness closed in upon it. It was rolling again by the time the reddening suggestion of sunrise rose in the east. As the hours dragged by, the lieutenant kept pausing to look back over his shoulder. But his eyes no longer spent so much time searching over the broken back trail as they did watching the lithe, slender figure of Linda Shafter, sitting on her wagon seat beside a blue-clad mule driver, or kneeling in the back of the wagon beside the wounded Sammy McGuffin.

Then, in midafternoon, a sudden flicker of light snapped his gaze to the top of a mountain far to the left. He reined up sharply and watched. It came again. He looked back and saw an answering flash from behind. Overstreet's mouth dropped open, and a dread chilled him.

Wheeler spurred up beside him, pointing.

"Yes, Corporal," he said, "I saw them."

"What do you think they meant?"

Overstreet bit his lips. "They might mean nothing, or they might mean everything. I'm afraid they mean we've got more than just Yankees to worry about now."

He swallowed and looked bleakly ahead. "And only God knows how far it still is to Fort Bliss."

Fatigue rode heavily on his shoulders. His eyes burned from want of sleep. Soreness from yesterday's fight still lay in his bones. He watched the wheels of the wagons turning slowly—Judas Priest, how slowly—their iron rims leaving deep cuts in the earth wherever the ground was soft enough. Then his tired eyes would sweep over the range of hills to the east, searching for mirror flashes, smoke signals, any sign of Indians. A flicker of hope flared in him each time he looked and saw nothing. But always dampening it was the memory of advice a Ranger captain had given him long ago.

"There's worry enough when you see them, and twice as much when you don't."

When at last he watched the sun bury itself behind the ragged stretch of mountains to the west, he wondered how far the train had gone in two days, and knew it had not been nearly far enough. He looked behind him but knew that in this rocky land there would be little dust to warn of an approaching Yank column. Again he tried to find some sign of Indians in the mountains, but there was none.

Maybe—and he grabbed at the hope like a man in deep water grabs at anything—maybe those mirror flashes hadn't meant anything. Maybe their makers had been only a stray hunting party, now many miles away.

With dusk gathering in, he picked a camp spot near a small stream which flowed through a shallow ravine.

"We can't take any chances," he said to Wheeler. "We'll pull the wagons in a circle tonight, and turn the stock loose inside. An Indian's sharp knife on a picket line could leave us all afoot."

He sat his horse a little to one side and watched as Wheeler directed the wagons into a tight circle and had the teams unhitched one at a time.

Just as the last ammunition wagon was started into place, a cry of "Fire" cut through the sharp evening air. The Yank driver piled off the wagon and started running. Panic swept through the camp with the speed of lightning, men scattering like quail in every direction.

A horrible mental picture flashed into Overstreet's mind— the whole wagon train going up in one huge, ear-shattering blast.

"Get that wagon out of there!" he shouted in desperation. But he knew that not a man would try. Even Wheeler was running. Overstreet spurred forward, fear clutching at his throat. Smoke billowed out from under the blackening wagon sheet, and the terror-stricken mules were fighting in the traces.

Pulling abreast of the wagon, Overstreet braced himself and jumped. He almost missed. Splinters ripped at his hands as he caught hold. Fighting for breath, fear burning all the way down to his stomach, he somehow pulled himself up into the heaving wagon seat. He grabbed at the reins, pulled the panicked team away from the circled wagons and toward the ravine.

His own panic was driving at him. He could feel the heat of the blaze in the wagon bed behind him. The smoke choked him, burned his eyes until he could hardly see. Any second now flame would eat through a keg and strike the powder. He flipped the reins and yelled like a madman, fighting the team on toward the ravine.

There wasn't a chance that he would have time to unhitch that team and save it, he knew. But there was a ghost of a chance he might break the wagon loose.

Almost at the brink of the shallow ravine, he hauled back on the reins with all the strength in him, trying to pull the team sharply to the left, knowing the wagon would never make the turn. The mules pulled back. The iron wheels screamed as they gouged into the bed of the wagon and could turn no farther. Overstreet heard the coupling pole break like the sound of a gunshot, and felt the wagon heave beneath him.

For a split second he was in the air. Then he had hit the ground and was rolling and sliding across the sharp rocks, away from the blazing, overturned wagon. He heard the bouncing clatter of the team running on, dragging only the tongue and front wheels of the shattered wagon. Inches ahead of him was the lip of the ravine. In one agonizing effort he threw himself over the edge.

The whole earth seemed to rock with the force of a gigantic blast. Overstreet threw his arms over his head and buried his face as rocks the size of his fist shot out over the edge of the ravine and bounced down upon him.

Then there was only the rattle of rolling stones, the easy crackle of flames eating through what little was left of the wagon, and above it all, the awful ringing in his ears.

A voice reached out to him from the dusk. Overstreet thought he recognized it as Wheeler's. He tried to answer, but his throat was paralyzed, burning from smoke and dust. He heard a horse's hooves sliding on the rocks above him, and the scrape of cavalry boots running toward him. A strong arm clamped around him. Wheeler's voice called, almost in his ear, "Come help me get him out of here!"

Soon he was lying on his back on a blanket, and Linda Shafter once again was washing his face with a cloth. He tried to raise up, but she put her hand on his chest and gently pushed him back.

"Easy now," she said softly. "I don't think there are any bones broken, but we'll have to see. You just lie there a while."

There seemed to be just one big ache through his whole body. But looking up at her, feeling the warm touch of her hands, he didn't care.

"I guess I'm not so patriotic as I thought I was," she said presently. "I should have wished for the whole train to blow up— you with it. But I was scared for you. I almost screamed when the blast came. I thought you were caught there."

He smiled. In words measured and slow, he told her, "I don't know why you should have been worried about me. But I'm glad you were."

Her fingers briefly touched his. He reached up and caught her hand. She made no effort to draw it away.

Corporal Wheeler came and knelt beside him. Shame darkened his face. "You better pick you another man to call Corporal, sir. The honor's too big for me."

He looked down at his huge hands. "I was as close to that wagon as you was. I could've taken it out as easy as you could. But I was scared. I'm a coward, sir. It ain't fitten for me to be in charge of these men any longer."

Overstreet reached out and put his hand on the penitent trooper's big knee. "You're not a coward, Wheeler. Sometimes a man gets so scared he can't move, and it's not his fault. I was as scared as you were. If I'd had time to think, I'd've run away too, I guess. So forget about it . . . Corporal."

Linda Shafter watched the corporal walk away, his wide shoulders a little straighter. "That was kind of you, Lieutenant. I think more men would be bitter, being deserted the way you were."

Overstreet shook his head. "It takes a good man to run away then come back and face up to it like Wheeler did. Next time he won't run."

Back on his feet again, the lieutenant had Wheeler bring him the Yank who had been driving that last wagon. But the Vermont captain stepped up and stood beside the teamster.

"Don't punish him, Lieutenant. He set that wagon afire on my order. I hoped to destroy the train. If you feel that punishment is in order, punish me."

Overstreet wavered. Then he signaled for Wheeler and Vasquez to let the teamster go back to the other Yanks, huddled together under guard well inside the circle.

"Punishment won't bring back that wagon," he said. "If I'd been in your place, guess I'd've tried to do the same."

A thin smile broke across the captain's face. "And I'd wager that you'd have gotten the job done, Overstreet."

Darkness dropped over the camp like a blanket. And with it came a nameless dread that Overstreet had felt before while on a Ranger patrol along the frontier. It was nothing a man could put his finger on, but it was a strange kind of premonition that frontiersmen had learned to respect and obey. Overstreet sat leaning against a wagon wheel, in solitary council. Wheeler came and sat down beside him.

Presently he asked, "You got the creeps too, sir?"

The lieutenant nodded. "Bad."

He noticed a discordant singing across the circle. The voice cracked on high notes and worked its way back down by worrisome trial and error.

"Who's that?" asked Overstreet.

Regretfully, Wheeler answered, "Duffy. Sneaked a bottle into one of the wagons before we left the Shafter place, I reckon. He'd swap his soul for a drink. You want me to go take his bottle away from him?"

Overstreet shook his head. He had more worrisome problems to ponder. "Let him alone. I hope he gets a hangover tomorrow that busts his head wide open."

But after a while he noticed that the voice was getting farther away. He stood up quickly. "That damn fool's gone clear out past the guard line, Wheeler. You better go drag him back in here."

Wheeler hadn't reached the far side of the circle when Duffy's tuneless song broke off. Overstreet's hair bristled to the terror of a throat-tearing scream.

A guard's carbine barked. From the darkness came the quick clatter of hoofbeats. There were a couple more shots. The whole camp was on its feet at once.

Overstreet's long legs carried him across the circle and out into the darkness beyond, ahead of most of the troopers. Wheeler and a guard were standing over the crumpled body of the little man, Duffy. A long, feathered lance still quivered in the trooper's heart. Beside the dead, contorted fingers lay the shattered remains of a bottle.

After a while fires began to flicker at points all over the mountainsides. Small fires, the kind the Indians made. Overstreet watched, and his blood turned to ice.

Behind him he heard a gloating chuckle. "Better feel of your head, Overstreet, make sure your hair's still on tight. That's Bowden's Indians up there. He told me he'd get you."

There was an evil smile on Hatchet's face. "I'll have the last laugh after all, Overstreet. I'll be riding high and have gold bulging in my pockets while the wolves are fighting over your bones."

With cold fury Overstreet whirled toward Vasquez. "Hatchet's known this was coming. Throw him in with the other prisoners. If he even acts like he wants to get away, you put a bullet through him and don't look back."

He went back to his place and stood watching the fires. Impatience began its slow torture of him. He itched to move on, but it was out of the question. Ambush in this darkness would be easy, terribly easy. Besides, the men were dead on their feet. And the teams had to have rest, for even mules can be driven to death.

But there was little sleep for anyone. Lying wrapped in his dirty blanket, tossing fitfully, catching only an occasional tortured nap, he could hear other men tossing too. And from Sammy McGuffin's wagon he could hear an occasional moan. He threw aside the blanket and climbed to his feet.

Linda Shafter was up too, sitting beside the unconscious young soldier. In her eyes Overstreet could see pain, pain because there was nothing she could do.

"How long has he been this way?" he asked the girl.

Wearily she looked up at him, then back at the boy. "The pain has been getting worse the last couple of hours. It'll get worse still before it gets better, or until he . . ."

Overstreet gently put his hand on her shoulder. "Go get some sleep, Linda. I'll sit by him."

She shook her head. "I can't sleep, thinking about that out there." She pointed her small chin toward the mountains.

The lieutenant bowed his head. His hands trembled. "I'm sorry I brought you, Linda. I never would have, if I had dreamed . . .

She leaned her head against his chest. Quickly he folded his arms around her and held her. Her body trembled against his.

"Oh, Miles," she whispered, "I'm afraid."

For a long time he sat there and held her, comforting her, trying to ease her mind by making her think of other things, and talk about her family. She began telling him things.

"My mother was Maria Martin de Villareal," she said. "Her family was high in the government at Santa Fe. She died when I was ten. Dad sent me to his family in Missouri then. I went to school there, and stayed with his sister and her husband."

He told her, "I can see the Spanish in your face, especially in your eyes. But I don't hear much of it in your voice."

"You wonder why I have no accent? The children in Missouri picked on me for it, and teased me. I got tired of fighting them all the time, so I went to war on my accent." She relaxed and smiled. "I won that battle."

❖

Pacing the darkness inside the circle, Overstreet knew there couldn't be any turning back. They had to keep rolling south. Trail south and hope for the smile of Lady Luck, hope that by some stroke of fortune they might find other soldiers in grey who would help them fight through with the wagons, all the way to Bliss.

Overstreet heard Sammy McGuffin begging for water. He held a canteen to the boy's hot lips. He looked to one side at Linda Shafter lying on the ground, asleep at last. He stopped beside her a moment, knelt on one knee, and pulled the blanket a little higher around her slender shoulders. For a moment the bitter worry faded while he looked down on her face. Lightly, he touched her smooth cheek with his fingers, and a semblance of a smile came over his face.

By daylight the men were up, the mules watered, and the wagons ready to go. Overstreet wasted no time in getting them rolling.

"Wheeler," he said, "I want you to flank us on the east. Ride out half a mile—farther if you can. Pick a good man to go with you."

He hipped around in the saddle. "Vasquez, you take it on the west. Pick you a good man, too. And if either of you see trouble on the way, come in on the run."

It didn't take long for trouble to start showing up. Almost as soon as the train was on the move, Wheeler sent Private Tillery back to tell the lieutenant that a band of Indians was paralleling the train's line of march a mile to the east.

"There's maybe fifty of them, sir," the trooper reported nervously. "They ain't made any move toward us yet. Just keep up, like if they was waiting for the right time to jump us."

Soon Forsythe came back from the west flank to make a similar report.

"All right," Overstreet said. "Go on back there with Vasquez. But if you see trouble coming, hightail it back. Don't stay and get yourselves killed."

A grave certainty settled over the lieutenant as he watched the flank riders pulling away again. This would be the day.

He looked up at Linda on her wagon, then turned away as she swung her glance to him. He didn't want her to see what was in his mind. And he knew that dread was stamped plainly in his gaunt face now.

The sun had swung up almost directly overhead when Wheeler and Tillery came spurring in.

"A bunch coming in for a parley, sir," Wheeler said. "That trader, Bowden, is right out in front. He's carrying a white flag."

Overstreet took out his spyglass. With it he watched Bowden and the painted and feathered Indians top over the edge of a mountain and slant down its side, riding in slowly toward the wagons. The lieutenant's hands squeezed the spyglass hard, the way he wished he had squeezed the trader's neck, so that this might never have happened.

"What kind of Indians are they, Corporal?"

Wheeler scratched his black chin. "Comanches, I'd say, sir. Not that it makes much difference."

Overstreet started to ride out to meet the four horsemen. "Wheeler," he said, "keep those wagons moving but be ready for a fight. If I give you the signal, circle them, and circle them fast."

Captain Pace stepped up. "If you please, Lieutenant, my men and I are in this as deeply as you are, now. I'd like to ride out there with you, if you'll let me."

Overstreet studied the Yankee officer's face. Funny the way of war. Yesterday, enemies. Today, friends with a common enemy. Smiling, he touched the brim of his hat in salute.

"I'm honored, Captain. Borrow a horse from one of my troopers."

Halted at the foot of the mountain, the three Comanches sat their horses with the grave dignity of a country judge. But Bowden slouched in the saddle, greasy Mexican sombrero pulled low over his gloating eyes. The day was only moderately warm, but sweat trickled from under the broad hat brim and down his flabby cheeks to disappear in the dirty whiskers. There was a filthy smear of dried tobacco amber from the corners of his broad mouth down into the mat of beard.

He raised his beefy right hand in the signal of friendship, but a savage gleam in his eyes belied the gesture.

"Morning, gentlemen," he said mockingly. "Glad you accepted council. Wouldn't be none surprised if we was to come to terms."

He made a wicked, brown-toothed grin at the lieutenant. "Shoe's on the other foot now, so to speak, ain't it, Lieutenant?"

Knots stood out on Overstreet's jaw, but he said only, "What do you want?"

Bowden spat a brown stream of tobacco juice toward the two men. "I told you once I'd have your scalp. That weren't no brag. I meant it. But I done a heap of thinking since then. Overstreet,

I'm a trader at heart. Seems to me we ought to be able to make a deal."

Overstreet looked at the cold, chiseled faces of the three Indians, and a chill settled over him. "What kind of deal?"

Bowden pointed his chin toward the Union captain. "The way I hear it, them Yanks is pushing you *Tejanos* back, plumb out of the territory. You want to get them munitions back to your own lines to keep the bluecoats from pushing you out. But ten wagonloads won't do you any big lot of good. Why, a bunch of soldiers can waste that much just getting their guns hot. Indians, now, they could make it count."

He jerked a stubby thumb toward the Comanches. "Now, I could gather me a couple of hundred good fighting men like them almost in the time it'd take me to send up the smoke signals. Trouble is, they ain't got guns fit to shoot rabbits with.

"But with good army rifles, like them in your wagons, they could wipe out half a dozen Yankee towns. And with every town, they'd capture more and more ammunition.

"Why, just think of it, man. In a month we could have a thousand warriors of half a dozen tribes, armed and ready, men that could sweep over New Mexico like a blizzard and push them Yanks plumb back to Missouri."

An eager excitement gripped Bowden as he talked. His face grew florid, and his voice rose to a fevered pitch.

"Then your Confederacy would have the territory. It could push all the way to Californy. You'd be a hero, Overstreet. They'd make a general out of you."

Overstreet's face had drained white, and rage had thinned his lips. "What would you ask in return, Bowden?" But he already knew.

"There's riches in these New Mexico towns, Overstreet. Gold and silver, horses, sheep, and cattle. There's buffalo hides and trade goods. That's what we want. That's all we want. The rest of it belongs to you and Jeff Davis."

Overstreet glanced at Captain Pace and saw the horror in the man's eyes. He turned back to Bowden.

"There's one thing you didn't mention, Bowden. Those towns have got people in them, innocent people who don't really have any hand in this war.

"Those savages of yours would leave a trail of blood behind them that wouldn't wash away in a hundred years. It wouldn't be just men, Bowden. It'd be women and children, too, butchered like cattle."

His throat was tight. He felt a hot drumming of blood in his temples. "Sure, we want New Mexico. But we don't want it like that. I'm not giving you the guns."

He glanced again at Pace. The captain said quietly, "Thank you, Lieutenant."

Bowden thundered. "Then there won't be a one of you alive to see the sun rise, Overstreet. And we'll get the wagons anyway."

The big trader swept his hand in a wide arc. "I got a hundred warriors out there, Overstreet. They'll wipe you out like a snowball in hell."

The lieutenant's voice was grim. "Not without a fight, Bowden. And if you start shooting bullets into those wagons, you'll set off the powder. The whole train'll go up, and it won't do you or anybody else a bit of good."

Bowden leaned forward in the saddle, triumph in his thick face. "No, Lieutenant, nothing's going to happen to them wagons. These men won't use guns."

He pointed to the bow carried by one of the Indians. "These Comanches can take a short bow like that and drive an arrow halfway through a tree trunk, Overstreet. And with a running start, a-horseback, they can shove a lance plumb through a man.

"You better think it over. I'll give you five minutes."

Overstreet started pulling his horse back. "I don't need five minutes, Bowden. Let's go, Captain."

The trader stood in his stirrups and shook his fist. "I swear, Overstreet, I'll have you roasted alive!"

Then, muttering something to the three Comanches, the trader jerked his horse about and spurred across the foot of the mountain. He was waving his hand at someone up on top. Lifting his face, Overstreet saw a mirror flash.

"Get a firm grip on your scalp, Captain," he said, "and spur harder than you ever spurred before in your life."

Loping down the rocky slope, he looked back over his shoulder for pursuit. He could see it coming in a shouting feathered wave like a tide sweeping in on the Galveston coast. He kept touching spurs to his horse's ribs and fanning the mount's rump with his hat. Stones clattered and bounced from under the flying hooves.

A few hundred yards ahead of the wagon train he saw a fairly flat open space, cut across one end by a snaking ravine. Down by the lead wagon, Corporal Wheeler was watching. Overstreet waved his hat to signal the train ahead. He had to do it only once. Wheeler swung into action. In seconds the wagons were rolling as fast as the teams could pull them, the canvas covers dipping and plunging over the rough terrain.

The officers spurred into the wagon train just as it reached the open spot. Overstreet waved his hat in an arc, and the wagons rapidly pulled into a circle, the iron wheels screaming on the sliding grey rocks. Shouting men fell into the job of unhitching the teams, turning them loose inside the circle. Then hands grabbed at guns and men fell on their bellies beneath the wagons, fingering loads into place and trying to catch their breaths before the painted wave swept over them.

Hands trembling with excitement, Overstreet swung down from the saddle, let his horse go, and faced the Union captain. "Will you give me your word that if I arm your teamsters, they won't use the guns against us later?"

Pace nodded. "You have my word." Overstreet shouted orders for the Yanks to dive into the wagons and get guns and ammunition for themselves. Then he fell into a brisk trot around the circle, seeing that the men were ready.

Linda Shafter was on a wagon, straining to lift some heavy rifle cases and drop them to the ground. "We've got to build up a shelter for Sammy," she said, her breath short. Overstreet helped her stack the cases on the ground, then lifted Sammy down. The boy was groaning and gripping his fists, now talking deliriously, now gritting his teeth in pain. A pang of sympathy brought a catch to the lieutenant's throat. It looked as if the boy hadn't a chance.

"Linda," Overstreet said, "you get down behind those cases, too."

She did, without hesitating a moment. But she caught the lieutenant's arm and pulled him down toward her. "Miles," she said quickly, tears glistening in her dark eyes, "in God's name, be careful."

He knelt and kissed her. Then he was up again beside the wagons, watching the Indians close in from three sides. He shuddered to the dreadful shouting and the clatter of unshod hooves on the rocky ground. At first he could make out only the shape of the strong red bodies upon the horses' backs. Then he could see the smear of warpaint and make out the bows, feathered lances, and the buffalo-hide shields. Then he could see the features on the faces, the open, screeching mouths, the paint-rimmed eyes. And he ordered his men to fire.

The ear-shattering rattle of gunfire made him wince and close his eyes. Then, through the pungent film of gunsmoke he could see riderless horses racing back and forth in front. The Comanches pulled into their traditional circle, riding around and around the train. Guns roared and Indians fell. But arrows rained into the circle of wagons like hail from a black cloud. Behind him Overstreet could hear mules scream.

The gunfire went on and on. The ground in front of the circle was speckled with crumpled men and horses. The circling redmen began to pull back, stopping to haul their wounded up beside them. Arrows still plunked into the wagons, but no longer did they fall in the volume of the first moments.

Then at last the Comanches reined around and rode away, out of range. Through the settling dust and the rising gunsmoke, Overstreet watched them gather on a rise.

He climbed upon a wagon and counted between fifteen and twenty Indians lying on the ground.

For the moment, then, Bowden was beaten. But Overstreet's heart sank inside him as he admitted to himself that the Indians weren't beaten for good. And he knew that they couldn't be.

He climbed down again to check the damage in his own camp. He found two men dead, a Yank and one of his own. Three others were hit, none badly. Two mules were dead, and three others were so badly wounded that he had to have them shot. Many mules and horses had suffered minor cuts from the rain of arrows.

Wearily Overstreet sat on the ground, watching Linda Shafter dress the wounds of the three soldiers with deft and careful hands. There was little color in her face.

He looked away and cursed himself for bringing her out here.

Corporal Wheeler knelt beside him. "Don't reckon it would do us any good to try to move out, Lieutenant. They're scattering all around us again. There ain't a way we can move that they won't be on us like a sackful of cats on a crippled mouse."

Overstreet sat and gazed out across that awful stretch of blood-spattered rock, the heart sick in him, his clenched fist beating in helpless anger against his knee.

The cold realization worked around the circle until the lieutenant could see it in the eyes of every man. Fear gnawed at them as they looked at each other, at their officers, and at the grey mountains which stared down upon them in grim and final malevolence.

The lieutenant became aware of a movement among the animals. He arose and saw Chaney Hatchet and his friend, Corbeil, mounted. They had guns in their hands.

"Have you gone crazy?" Overstreet demanded. "Get off those horses before some Comanche puts an arrow through you."

"Don't be a damn fool, Overstreet," Hatchet blurted. "Bowden ain't wanting anything but these wagons. Let him have them and he'll turn everybody loose. That's what he told me when we were locked up together at the Shafter place."

"Get off those horses," the lieutenant spoke in measured words.

"Dammit, listen, Overstreet. They'll be on our side, fighting Yankees for us. Think of the glory there'll be in it. And if we string along with them, we'll be rich. There's gold and silver just waiting for us, there for the taking."

A grim smile came to the lieutenant's face. "Gold and silver. That's all you've been interested in since the day you left San Antonio, Hatchet. You haven't cared anything about Texas or the Confederacy."

Hatchet's face twisted. "You're right, Overstreet. I wasn't listening to the bands playing or that fool Sibley talking about glory. I was hearing the jingle of gold in my pockets. Wherever there's war, there's spoils, and I wanted mine. If it hadn't been for you, Overstreet, I could've had it."

Greedily he said, "Well, I'm getting my share from here on out. I'm riding with Bowden."

All the soldiers had gathered now, facing Hatchet and Corbeil. The two men swung their carbines.

"Everybody drop their guns," Hatchet barked. "I'll kill any man who don't."

There was a rapid clatter of steel on the rocks.

"We're riding out of here to get on the winning side," he said then. "There'll be gold enough for everybody. Who's going with us?"

The only sound was the soft voice of Vasquez, cursing in Spanish, his blackish eyes fixed in hatred upon the deserters.

"How about you Yanks?" Corbeil demanded, "The color of your pants don't make any difference here."

One Yankee stepped out. Corbeil motioned for him to grab

a horse and a gun. Pace yelled at him, but the bluecoat didn't stop.

Hatchet swung his hate-filled gaze back at the lieutenant. "Just one little piece of business before we leave here. Something I've been owing you a long time, Overstreet. I missed you once."

He leveled the gun. Overstreet's breath stopped, and he steeled himself. He shut his eyes, while the hand of fear clutched his throat.

The booming of a gun crashed in his ears, but no bullet struck him. He opened his eyes and saw Hatchet bend at the middle, then slide out of the saddle. His foot hung in the stirrup. The panicked horse jumped over a wagon tongue and stampeded, dragging the rebel across the rocks. But Hatchet never knew, for he was dead before he touched the ground.

Overstreet spun on his heel. Linda Shafter stood halfway across the circle, a smoking carbine in her hands. Sammy McGuffin's carbine, one Hatchet had forgotten about.

Even as the shot was still echoing back from the mountains, Corbeil fired a quick bullet into the crowd and yanked his horse around. Elijio Vasquez's hand was a quick blur of movement. Corbeil leaned back and fell out of the saddle, the dark-skinned trooper's sharp knife driven halfway through his throat.

In sudden panic the deserting Yankee spurred away. A crackling of gunfire followed him. His horse dropped beneath him. The blue-clad soldier went rolling, then jumped to his feet and started to run.

Captain Pace took quick aim with a carbine and squeezed the trigger. The soldier sprawled and lay still, his convulsing fingers only inches away from the crumpled body of an Indian.

Corbeil's bullet had struck a Confederate soldier. Overstreet knelt beside him but found it too late to do anything for him.

Four men dead, all within little more than the time it takes for two long breaths. Eyes burning, Overstreet turned away from the awful sight before him, turned toward Linda Shafter. He walked to her.

Her eyes brimming with tears, she lifted her trembling hands. Miles swept her into his arms and felt her hands tight upon his back. She buried her face against his chest and sobbed away the terrible shock. He stood clasping her tightly to him. For the moment, then, he was at peace.

From distant protection behind the rocky slopes, the Comanches began a methodical rain of arrows into the circle of wagons. The troopers sought shelter beneath the wagon beds. Overstreet sat beside Linda, watching the feverish face of young Sammy McGuffin, wincing to the pain himself each time the boy twisted and groaned. He beat his fist against his knee and wished to heaven the boy could go ahead and die and have his misery over, or at least lapse into complete unconsciousness that would stop his suffering.

Someone whooped, "They're coming again."

Out from behind the mountain, swinging down from the hills, surging up out of the ravine, they came riding. Their fiendish cries were an echo from the depths of hell that sent ice through brave men's veins and made strong hands quiver on the wooden stocks and cold steel of cavalry carbines. Once again hundreds of unshod hooves clattered on the loose stones, and horses and mules inside the circle screamed and stamped under the hail of arrows.

This was to be the charge that would swamp the dwindling force of white men and turn nine wagonloads of death and devastation to the grasping hands of savages.

But this time the soldiers were even more ready than they had been. Each man had a stack of rifles and carbines beside him, capped and loaded and ready for a kill. Once again there was the deafening thunder of fire and powder, the defiant shouts of desperate soldiers. Horses plunged to the ground. Indians fell into lifeless heaps or sprawled on the rocks and clawed at air and screamed their last breaths away. But the circling Comanches swarmed in closer and closer to the wagons until it seemed that they would overwhelm them like an angry flight of hornets. Occasionally one broke from the circle and tried to charge in among the wagons, only to be cut in two by a withering blast.

Fearful men cursed and sweated and jammed fresh loads into their guns and swung around to fire again. Here and there soldiers lay still, their lifeless fingers still gripping guns.

And at last, once again, the swarm of Indians lifted and pulled away, leaving more huddled heaps of dead on the barren and bloody ground.

Watching them go, Overstreet rose shakily to his feet. He looked once around the circle and shuddered. Half the command, blue and grey alike, were casualties now. Dead or wounded. Half the mules and horses were dead or lay kicking and screaming until someone mercifully put them out of misery.

Despair settled over him like a cold, wet blanket. There wasn't enough draft stock left to pull the wagons out now, even if they could get away. But he knew they wouldn't get away. Not now. Bowden wasn't through. He would try again. And the next time, he would win.

Overstreet went back to Linda. His heart swelling, he looked down at her dusty, blood-smeared face, the beautiful black hair that once had been shiny and neat, now windblown and tousled, streaked with dirt. The dark eyes that had been so alive were now dull with dread and loss of hope.

He fell to his knees and clasped her to him. "Linda," he cried huskily, contritely, "what have I done to you?"

Later he walked out beside a wagon and leaned wearily against a wheel. Closing his eyes, he conjured up the memory of his father, and he found himself whispering to him.

"Pa, Pa," he breathed in despair, "I've led all these people into this trap, and I can't get them out. Isn't there any hope for me at all?"

As if in answer, he remembered tall Jobe Overstreet standing on a wagonbed, Book in his hand, speaking words of comfort
to discouraged settlers who had been hit by an Indian raid.

"There is always hope for a man of good heart," the old circuit rider had said. "The Psalmist said that though he may fall,
he shall not be utterly cast down, for the Lord up-holdeth him
with His hand."

Pondering, Miles Overstreet decided that there might be a
way. It was a painful one, the end of a dream. He fought against
it, rejected it, yet knew it was the only course left to take.

Knowing at last what he had to do, he said to Wheeler, "Get
the men all over here."

When the men had gathered, he turned to face them. Sadness was like a cold stone in the pit of his stomach. "We can't
save the wagons," he said dully. "We're going to move out of
here."

Captain Pace stepped up in protest. "And leave these wagons to the savages, Overstreet? Is that what all these men have
died for, what the rest of us are bound to die for?"

Overstreet shook his head. "They won't get the wagons, Captain. Nobody's ever going to have those wagons."

He glanced at Wheeler. The despairing look in the big man's
brown eyes showed he knew what was coming. "Get every man
busy, Corporal. They'll grab all the food and ammunition they
can carry. Then spill powder in every wagon, enough to make
sure they'll all catch fire. Get moving."

Watching the sudden hustle of activity, Overstreet felt the
warm touch of a small hand on his arm. Linda stood beside
him. She said nothing, didn't even look up at him. But he felt
the warm understanding that passed between them.

Captain Pace faced them. "Somehow, Lieutenant, I almost
regret this. You're my enemy. But I think you deserved a lot
better."

Overstreet nodded thanks. Wheeler trotted up. "It's done, sir."

"Then take the horses and mules and make a break for that

ravine yonder. Take all the wounded with you. And take Miss Shafter."

The girl clung to his arm, her eyes suddenly wide. "Miles," she cried, "what're you going to do?"

He tried to avoid her eyes. "I'll wait till you're all clear. Then I'll set the powder afire. I'll go on to the ravine afterwards, if I can."

The girl still clung to him. "You can't do it, Miles. Miles!"

Overstreet turned to Pace. "For God's sake, Captain, take her away."

He leaned against a wagon, his eyes closed, listening to the shouting of the soldiers, the pounding of hooves, the sobbing of the girl. Then he was alone. The last man left with the wagons. Nine wagons of munitions that might have saved New Mexico for the Confederacy. His dreams came back to him in a throat-clutching rush, bitter and forlorn. He tried to shove them away as he drew the Colt from his holster and pointed it toward a black trail of powder that led to a keg dropped beneath one of the heaviest-loaded wagons.

He could hear the blood-chilling cries of the Comanches as they started to swarm down again. The sudden exodus of the troops had made them think the train was theirs.

Overstreet closed his eyes and squeezed the trigger. The pistol jumped in his hand. Flame leaped up at his feet. A yellow ball of fire darted down the zig-zag trail of black powder, dark smoke trailing in its wake. Overstreet turned and began to run, hard as his legs would go. Pounding in his ears were the cries of the Comanches, the sizzling of the burning powder, the anxious shouts of his men urging him on. The ravine was a hundred feet in front of him—seventy-five—fifty . . .

A terrific blast behind him knocked him down like a giant hand. He jumped up and went running again, only to be sent rolling once more. Half on his hands and knees, he scrambled the last feet to the ravine and dropped over the side.

Looking back, he saw that some Indians had been caught in the blast. A hundred yards from the circle, the trader Bowden was down, his horse floundering, the fat man scrambling to get away.

The fire leaped from one wagon to another, shaking the ground with the mighty roar of exploding powder, hurling flames far into the air. A wagon wheel sailed high and came down rolling toward the ravine. Black smoke billowed upward.

The powder all gone, the big clouds of black smoke slowly drifted away. There was only the thin grey rising from the crackling flames that fed on the last wood of the wagons. Soon even that was gone, leaving just the smoldering of ashes, with here and there a burned remnant of an axle or coupling pole pointing like a ragged black finger toward the sky.

Overstreet watched and blinked away the stinging in his eyes and swallowed the last of a great dream. Linda Shafter held his arm.

"I'm sorry, Miles," she whispered.

He heard a voice calling for water. It was a familiar voice that made him whirl. Sammy McGuffin.

"Please," the voice came again, weakly, "I'm dryer'n powder. Won't somebody please fetch me a cup of water?"

Sudden joy over Sammy lifted some of the deeper sadness from Overstreet. "He's awake," he said excitedly.

Linda nodded. "Yes, Miles. He was beginning to come out of it before we left the wagons. A lot of the pain has left him."

"What did you do?"

Her dark eyes fastened on his. "The only thing there was left to do. I prayed for him, Miles."

A moistness came to his eyes before he blinked it away. "I'm glad you did, Linda. I'm glad you did."

The Comanches had bunched again not far from the smoldering wagons. There were many less of them now than there had been this morning. Through his spyglass Overstreet watched them argue and gesture among themselves. Then Bowden split away from them and came riding out toward the ravine. With him rode two of the three Indians who had been with him in the parley at the foot of the mountain.

A hundred and fifty yards from the ravine, Bowden reined up. His horse had a decided limp, and Bowden leaned a little in the saddle.

"Overstreet," he shouted. "I want you. Come on out, and the others can go free."

Panic leaped into Linda Shafter's eyes. Corporal Wheeler jumped to Overstreet's side. "Don't do it, sir." he pleaded. "Bowden's lying. He'd butcher you, then finish us off anyway."

The lieutenant clenched his fists. Fear stalked him. He tried to push it away, but still it was there, lurking in the shadows of his mind, chilling his blood, putting quiver in his muscles.

He called huskily, "Is that a promise, Bowden? You won't hurt any of the rest of these people?"

Bowden shouted back, "I've given you my word. You come out, and I'll pull the Indians away."

Still the fear rode him, and Overstreet hesitated. Then, from somewhere back in time, he heard his father's voice again, saying words the lieutenant had heard years ago and forgotten until now.

"You can't expect God to make you live forever, son. But if a man believes in Him, he can die in peace."

Suddenly Miles Overstreet wanted to believe again, as he had so long ago. The fear drew back. He stopped trembling. He faced his troopers, swallowed hard, and spoke to them in an even voice.

"There's one thing I want you men to know. For weeks I hated you, the whole lot of you. I thought you were scalawags, the scum of the Sibley Brigade. A hundred times I wished you were all dead.

"But in a way I'm glad this all happened. The scalawags

and the cowards are gone now. Only the brave men are left. And whatever happens to me now, I want you to know that I'm proud to have ridden with you. It's been an honor to serve with soldiers."

He turned and grasped Linda Shafter's arms. He kissed her wet cheek, her trembling lips, then gently pushed her away.

"Pray for me, Linda," he said softly. "Pray for me."

He dropped his carbine and unstrapped the Colt. He climbed up out of the ravine and started walking toward Bowden, walking steadily, his shoulders squared. The voice of his father kept whispering in his brain. "Yea, though I walk through the valley of the shadow of death, I will fear no evil . . . fear no evil."

He watched the stony-faced Comanches. He watched Bowden. The big man was torn and bruised from being knocked to the ground by the blast. Dried blood streaked the heavy, bearded face. Bowden's hands quivered on the stock of a long-barreled old musket. His eyes glowed with hatred. The trader muttered something Overstreet didn't understand and started raising the gun.

The lieutenant stopped and stood at attention. That grey animal, fear, was trying to fight out of the shadows again, but Overstreet forced himself to listen to his father. "Fear no evil . . . fear no evil . . ."

Bowden swung the gun to his shoulder and pulled the trigger. Nothing happened. He tried again and again, cursing and slapping at the gun with the heel of his big hand. Somehow the blast must have damaged the piece. He hurled the musket to the ground, his face crimson in fury.

The Indians watched in stony silence until Bowden stopped cursing. Then one of them pulled a long-bladed knife out of the waist of his leather breeches and handed it to the trader. Overstreet couldn't understand the words the red man muttered to Bowden, but he knew their meaning.

A gun against an unarmed man was not the way of valor. A

man-to-man fight with a sharp blade to strike at the enemy's heart—that was the brave man's way.

But Bowden shrank away from the knife, and Overstreet saw the fear flit across his face. He saw, too, that the Indians had seen it, and they drew back a little from the trader. Indians had an inborn respect for courage, and an everlasting contempt for cowardice.

Bowden realized his mistake. Hands trembling, he grabbed a lance from one of the Comanches. He cradled it under his arm and spurred savagely at the soldier. Miles Overstreet stood still, watching the feathered lance streaking toward his heart. He dropped to one knee and saw triumph forge into Bowden's cruel face.

The horse almost upon him, he threw himself forward, flat onto the ground. Too late, Bowden saw the move. The point of the lance drove into the rocks. His reflexes too slow, Bowden didn't turn loose of the lance. He was jerked from the horse as if he had hit the low branch of a tree.

Overstreet jumped to his feet and grabbed at the lance. He found too late that it was broken. He got the long end of the haft. Bowden's desperate, clawing fingers grabbed up the point of the lance. The big man was on his feet again, holding the point like a knife. His thick lips drew back from his brown-stained teeth, and he looked like a huge animal closing in for the kill.

But Overstreet could read fear in the reddened eyes. And now, washed clean like Gulf sand, his own fear was gone.

Bowden rushed, holding the point out in front of him. Overstreet brought up the haft and rammed it into the trader's soft belly. He heard some of the wind gust out of the man. He jumped in to follow up his lead. Grabbing Bowden's left hand to fend off the point, he punched hard as he could into the trader's ribs. But the heavy layer of fat was like a cushion.

With a bear's roar, Bowden shoved forward. Overstreet tripped and landed flat on his back. Bowden dived after him, plunging the lance down. Overstreet rolled away. The point grazed his right shoulder and tore a long hole in his grey coat. He gathered his knees under him and kicked at Bowden. He felt his bootheels grind into soft flesh. Bowden cursed.

The lieutenant rolled over again, sprang to his feet, and leaped at the trader. His fingers closed over the lance point. Bowden was on his back. Overstreet sank his knee on the big man's right hand, grinding the flesh into the sharp rocks. Crying out in pain, Bowden let go the lance.

Overstreet grabbed it with both hands and brought it down with all his weight into the big man's chest.

He stood up then and looked away, his stomach drawn up into a knot. The two Indians gazed a long moment at the quivering trader, sobbing feebly against the death that was wrapping around him like a heavy grey blanket.

They looked at Overstreet, then wheeled their ponies around and headed eastward. Overstreet stood there watching them until the entire band disappeared over the mountain. He knew somehow that they would not return. Finally he faced around and walked back, toward the ravine, the sinking sun throwing a splash of red color in his eyes . . .

Shortly after dawn, Corporal Wheeler came trotting in from a high point where he had been standing watch.

"Riders coming, sir, about a mile and a half or two miles to the north. Can't tell anything about them."

His heartbeat quickening. Overstreet followed Wheeler to the point and unfolded the glass. "It could be Indians," he said. Then, "No, it's not Indians. They're riding in a column of twos. Take a look."

Wheeler studied the riders a moment. "It's Yanks, sir. No mistake about it. Old Man Shafter's messenger must've found him some troops."

Overstreet nodded. "Then we've got to be moving out, Corporal. Get the men ready."

In five minutes the men were saddled and ready to ride. All but Sammy McGuffin.

"I'm sorry, Sammy," the lieutenant said, bending over the boy. "We're going to have to leave you. But those Yankee doctors'll have you well in no time."

Sammy nodded. "It's all right, sir. I'm not scared any more. I've found out now there's lots of things worse than a prison. They'll turn me loose, bye and bye."

Overstreet gripped the boy's hand. "Sure, son, sure."

He stood up to find Captain Pace in front of him, extending his hand. Overstreet took it.

"It's been an honor riding with you, Lieutenant," the Yank captain said. "We wear different uniforms, and perhaps many of our ideas are not the same; but if we had more men like you on both sides, I'm sure this conflict would not last long. The best of luck to you, sir."

"Mount up," Overstreet ordered his men. Then he turned for the last time to Linda Shafter. He looked for a last time into her shining dark eyes, her lovely face. He held her in his arms, crushing her soft body against his.

"Linda," he said in a quiet, husky tone, "there's no telling what's ahead for us—how long this war will last or where it'll take us. But there's one thing certain. Wars don't last forever. When this one is over, I'll come back here, looking for you. Will you wait?"

Her answer was in her eyes. She pulled his face down to hers and kissed him. He felt wetness break along her cheek. Eyes burning, he pulled away from her and swung into the saddle.

Captain Pace had his men lined up. He ordered, "Presen-n-t . . . arms!"

The men in blue brought up their guns in traditional salute to seven valiant men in grey. Overstreet looked, swallowing down a lump in his throat.

Ahead of them lay a dozen other battles in places they had

never heard of, and would never hear of again. But as he had said, wars don't last forever. Overstreet returned the Yankee salute. Then he reined his horse around and led his six men south . . . south toward the Lone Star . . .

SHEEP ON
THE RIVER

There were two large bands of the sheep. Sprawled out in dappled blots of gray, they edged on slowly, grazing at the short, sun-curing mesquite and grama grass as they toiled gradually down toward the crooked line of pecan trees that marked the winding river. In the thin veil of dust that rose behind them, two men plodded patiently afoot. In front, two horsemen rode leisurely but watchful.

Six tense riders sat their horses atop a small hill and looked down at the moving column grimly. All but one wore boots and spurs and carried ropes tied to their saddle horns. These were not sheepmen.

The sixth rider shifted nervously on her sidesaddle and rubbed shaky hands on the long black skirt that hung down well below the tops of her high-heeled boots.

Her small face was drawn taut, and her full lips were pale. The soft brown hair bunched and tied behind her head seemed to prickle her neck.

Judy Pickett felt dread idling coldly through her as she watched her foreman's mouth harden. Fury began trembling across Nat Kilday's ruggedly handsome face.

A grizzled old puncher, hunched over his saddle horn, spoke up in a steady voice. "Just like he said it would be, Judy.

They're bringing sheep in. And they'll be running all the Pickett cattle out."

The sun had been only two hours high this morning when old Glenn Tutt had come loping into the ranch headquarters on a sweat-caked horse and brought the message that had caused the Pickett riders to strap on their guns. Almost ever since Judy had made Nat Kilday foreman a year ago, Glenn had been batching in an old sheep headquarters on the river, a place the cattle outfit was now using for a line camp.

"My coffee pot had just come to a boil when this feller came stomping in," he said. "He had a gun in his hand as big as a cannon. He told me he's a sheepman, name of Martin Schell, from back around Kerrville someplace or other. He'd bought the old Reiner sheep ranch and told me to roll my tail right out of there."

Nat Kilday had exploded like a summer storm. "You cowardly old pack rat, you mean you just stood there with your mouth open and let some bleating sheepherder run you out of camp?"

Glenn's aging eyes had lit up like flint sparks. His hatred for Kilday edged into his voice. "You ain't talking to no sheepherder right now, Kilday. Any time you think you can whip me, just try it. And as for Schell, he didn't look like any sheepherder I ever seen before, neither."

Judy hated fights in any form, and she had quickly stepped between them. She couldn't really blame Glenn for hating Nat, even if the hatred did come out of jealousy. After all, Tutt had worked for her father for almost twenty years. But after Hank's death Judy had given the foreman's job to younger Nat Kilday, who hadn't been on the place a year.

Glenn was still a good cowhand, even if age was drawing him up, and even if he did take off for a big toot now and again. How could you tell an old codger like that he just didn't have the ability it took to run a spread like the Pickett ranch?

Best thing to do was send him off to batch in a line camp
where he wouldn't always be tangling horns with the foreman.

Now the whole ranch crew sat grimly together on a hilltop,
watching a little of the Pickett spread start to break off and
pull away from them.

Judy's mouth was dry as her troubled gaze settled on Nat
Kilday's hands expert handling a six-gun, spinning the cylinder.
He was methodical about it, as he was about everything. There
was the merest trace of a smile on his lips, as if somehow, he was
glad this was happening. She wondered desperately why it was
that the prospect of a fight always did this to him. She wished
Nat would say something reassuring, or even touch her hands
that felt chilled despite the warm summer sun. He didn't. He
seldom did.

"But we don't want a fight, Nat," she managed to say. She
had said it before. "There must be some other way."

He flung a sharp glance at her. "There ain't any other way to
handle a sheepherder. I thought you learned that when Otto
Reiner killed your dad."

He hipped around in the saddle to see the cowboys. "All
right, now, let's teach them hill country Dutchmen to stay
where they belong. Scatter them sheep to hell and gone!"

He raised his rope-calloused hand and brought it down in
an arc. Cowboys socked spurs to their horses and plunged
down the hill. Judy held up a moment, wishing she could call
them back. Then she spurred her black-maned dun after the
cowboys.

Down in front of the sheep, one of the two horses swung its
head around and nickered. The two riders quickly pulled away
from the flock and loped out to meet the Pickett men.

Judy's breath came hard. Her heart thumped heavily. Why
had the sheepmen come again? Just when she had thought
Nat's fighting blood had settled, they had returned to fan up
again the one thing she dreaded most in him.

The cowboys pulled up a few feet apart in a formidable line. Judy caught up to them and slid the dun to a halt. She sighed in relief as she recognized one of the two oncoming horsemen—Sam Booth, the sheriff.

Sam and the other rider drew rein a few feet in front of the cowboys. Judy glanced quickly at the second man, who was tall and weather-browned. Surprise made her swallow hard. So this was Martin Schell!

She had expected to see a greasy, bearded man with grimy old clothes, floppy hat, and worn shoes. But Schell was young, maybe just on the far side of thirty. His plain working clothes were much like any cowboy's, and he sat his horse like a top hand.

The biggest surprise was his face. Who was the fool who had told her sheepmen looked meek, like their sheep? Martin Schell's stern face looked as if it could have been carved from a Llano granite quarry. The determined glint in his gray eyes was hard as any she had ever seen in Nat Kilday's.

Sam Booth's silver badge glittered briefly in the sun as he looked at Judy and touched his hat brim. There was a grave droop to the full, graying mustache that helped balance his long, broad nose.

Nat Kilday's voice had a razor edge. "You're a long way from town, Sam. This ain't none of your affair."

Booth never glanced at Nat. Like Glenn, the sheriff had always had little use for Kilday.

"A fight's always my business, Judy," Booth said, answering Nat indirectly. "You better take your men back home. Martin Schell has bought this land. The law's on his side."

Nat's voice was brittle. "If somebody was to put a bullet through you, Sam, there wouldn't be any law."

Booth jerked up his shoulders and lashed a furious glance at Kilday. "There won't anybody on the Pickett spread kill a lawman while Hank Pickett's daughter is still running the place."

His eyes cut back to Judy and seemed to bore through her. "You are still running the ranch, ain't you, Judy?"

Her cheeks tingled and flushed warm. She knew it was common gossip that Nat Kilday was the real boss now. Folks said it wouldn't be long till he would marry Judy. Some already called it the Kilday ranch.

She looked down at her saddle horn in embarrassment. Nat meant well. He was fighting for her. It hurt her to say anything that might anger him. But it looked like she had to.

"He's right, Nat," she said uncertainly. "We can't buck the law."

Nat angrily slapped his big hand across his leather chaps. "Your dad took hold of this land when the Comanches left it. He fought for it, and he died for it. Now you're letting some foreigner slip in here and take it away."

Martin Schell edged his horse forward. The sheepman's rigid face was darkening. "Listen here, Kilday. I was born here in Texas, the same as you. My parents left the old country because they didn't like to have soldiers bossing them around. I don't like to be bossed, either.

"I bought this land from Otto Reiner's widow; I'm putting my flocks to graze on it. And I'll keep it if I've got to bury half of the Pickett crew!"

Judy's breath caught short as Nat's hand edged down toward his gun. She reached over and grabbed it. "Please, Nat, we'll find another way. We're not fighting now."

Nat sat firm, knots of muscle swelling in his broad jaws. "I could shoot him right where he sits."

Schell leaned forward. His cold eyes hinted that he wished Nat would try it. "You wouldn't find me as helpless as Otto Reiner was, Kilday."

Nat snarled, "That was a fair fight. Everybody knows."

"Everybody knows just what you told them, Kilday. You were the only witness—or you think you were."

Judy flicked her gaze to Nat's face. For a split second his

eyes widened, and his chin drooped. Then he regained his composure.

Judy closed her eyes, remembering with bitterness that day a year ago. Otto Reiner had bought the river land from the state, after Hank Pickett had run cattle on it free for years. Angrily Hank had scattered his flocks, chased off his herders. But Reiner was a firm little man with a wife and three kids, and he stuck like a grassburr.

Judy had been able to see defeat ahead. She had pleaded with her dad to give in, to stop bucking the law. Finally she had talked Hank into buying Reiner out. Nat had argued vehemently. Give in now, he had stormed, and Hank would have a dozen more land-grabbers on his neck. But Hank had made up his mind to keep it legal. He and Nat had ridden off together toward the sheep camp on the river, still arguing.

Hours later Nat had come back, bringing Hank Pickett's body tied across the saddle on the ranchman's big roan horse.

Reiner had been out back of a barn, building a rock corral the way Texas hill country settlers always did, Nat explained. The minute the two men had ridden around the barn, panicked Reiner had jerked out his gun and started shooting. Hank Pickett had died without a chance. But Nat had killed Reiner.

The next day Reiner's widow and three children had bleakly started back toward the Kerrville hills, taking what was left of their flock with them. As she buried her father, Judy had hoped all the trouble was done. But here it was, starting all over again.

Schell sat facing them, his face rigid as the Texas hills. "It's customary in this country for a man who owns land to be able use some of the free range around him. I've got more deeded land now than you have, Miss Pickett. So I'm pushing your cattle off everything as far north and east as Wingate Draw, and I'm putting my sheep on it."

That was like a stick of dynamite going off between the two groups of riders. Judy gasped, hardly believing her ears.

Even Sam Booth's mouth dropped open. "See here, boy, as long as you stay on the land you've bought, I'll stand up for you. But when you go to crowding folks off free range, you're on your own hook."

Nat Kilday stood up in his stirrups and shook his hard fist at Schell. "The day you try driving Pickett cattle back across Wingate Draw, that's the last day you'll live!"

He roughly yanked his horse around and jabbed spurs to him. The cowboys strung out behind Kilday.

Judy held back, a big lump of fear thick in her throat. Her hands trembled. Now it had started, and she wouldn't be able to stop it.

Sam Booth was still muttering. "You'll sure split your britches, boy. What chance have you got—you, two sheepherders and an old woman?"

Schell never answered. Judy couldn't keep her eyes away from his face. It was proud and defiant—like old Hank Pickett in some ways. Like Nat Kilday, even.

"We've been using your place as a line camp," she said to him. "We still have some gear there. Will you let us come and get it?"

Schell's gray eyes intently studied her. She looked down uncomfortably.

Shortly he answered. "We'll take everything of yours and pile it up. We'll let one man come get it. One man in a wagon. And he'd better not bring a gun with him."

She glanced up at him again. He was still staring at her. She felt approval in his gaze.

"I couldn't trust one of my cowboys not to start a fight," she told him. "I'll come for it myself, in the morning."

Martin Schell tipped his hat to her, then turned his horse around and started back toward his sheep. Sam Booth sat his horse.

"Judy," he said unevenly, "I didn't know it was going to turn out like this. That boy Schell has got some kind of a hate that's driving him on. I have to protect him on his own land, but there's no law covering the free range. About all I can do is wait for somebody to get killed."

Topping the last rise two hours later, Judy started her dun down a dusty, crooked cow trail that snaked through the stunted mesquite. At the foot of the long slope was the cluster of small frame and rock buildings and corrals that stood as the only monument to Hank Pickett. Brown smoke curled upward from the bent chimney of the cook shack. Down in one corral two punchers were roping out the night horses, to be used in gathering mounts again next morning.

Judy looked vainly for Nat. He must be in the bunkhouse, sulking because she had not stood behind him all the way. She unsaddled and walked to the four-room "big house" in which she had grown up. In the corner of the front room was her father's big, rough, homemade desk. Still stuffed up in one cubbyhole was the sheet paper he had studiously scrawled his figures on, when he was trying to decide what he could afford to offer for Reiner's land. He had tried force and it hadn't worked. At Judy's insistence, he had turned to a peaceful settlement.

But, she thought sadly, that hadn't worked, either. Was it really worth it, so much bloodshed for so little land, when there was so much more land available?

Eventually the cook stepped out and clanged the gong on the cookshack porch with a metal strip of wagon tire. Judy combed her brown hair, then stepped down off her porch and walked to the cookshack, long skirt rustling. She took her place at the head of the big, rough table. There was a tablecloth on it, a result of her influence.

She quickly noted that Nat wasn't in his place. All the other cowboys were in. She listened carefully but could not hear his footsteps anywhere. He wasn't coming, that's all there was to it.

Worry began to pinch at her. She ate only a little, and hardly tasted that. Shortly she pushed away from the table and stepped outside. Her gaze swept quickly over the raw plank corrals, across the big yard, and back to the frame barn. Nat sat there at the barn, on the front step, bent over some task.

Quickly Judy strode out to him. He was polishing up his .45. He gave her a quick glance then sharply cut his eyes back to the six-gun.

"I didn't mean to make you angry, Nat. But I don't want anybody to get hurt."

He sat still for a minute, digesting that. His jaws moved a little. Then he jerked his head up. His eyes were fiery. "This ranch'll get hurt, and hurt plenty. I thought you'd have sense enough to see it."

He rose to his feet and stood there stiffly, his face dark and angry. "You know what'll happen if you let this sheepherder get by with running a sandy on you? There'll come another, and another and another. First thing you know, we won't have any ranch left.

"You won't have anybody to blame for it but yourself, because you were too much of a coward to fight for the land your dad died to keep!"

Judy's temper left her like a blast from a shotgun. She swung back her hand to slap Nat, then lowered it. "I still own this ranch," she told him, seething, "and I'll decide who fights, and when. If that doesn't suit you, then maybe you'd better head for town."

Her skirt swirled as she spun around and walked briskly back toward the house.

Perhaps ten minutes later she heard someone knocking on her front door. Wiping the angry tears from her eyes, she called, "Come in."

It was Nat. He stood shamefaced, hat twisted in his big hands. "Look, honey," he spoke quietly, "I'm all rattled today. So much has happened."

He bowed his head, like a schoolboy apologizing for mischief. "I didn't know what I was saying to you a while ago. Please give me another go at it, Judy."

Her anger evaporated. He had made her mad before, and he had come to her before in just this way. Sometimes she got a feeling he didn't mean it. But she couldn't help herself. She had always given in.

"Look, Judy," he continued, and he stepped closer to her, "I need you. I've asked you before, but I'm begging you now. I want you to marry me. Right away. Tomorrow."

Almost before she realized it, he had his arm around her, pulling her to him. Her blood warmed quickly and she struggled against herself. She made herself pull away from him and turn half around.

"I still don't know, Nat," she said. "I think maybe I love you. But sometimes I wonder. A girl has to be sure."

For an instant anger flared in his face. Then he swallowed, and it was gone. In its place was a thin smile. "Sure, Judy. Sure, you're right about that. But I'm going to keep asking till you say yes."

She stood in the door and watched him go. The excitement in her slowly died, and doubt bobbed up again. He was the only man who had ever made her feel this way. But then, he was the only man who had ever had the chance. Her father had been plenty strict about the attentions she got from men.

Even after her father's death, no one had ever paid her court except Nat Kilday. Sometimes she suspected that he made sure there were no others.

Next morning, while the cook was still up to his elbows in soapy water and dirty breakfast dishes, Judy got old Glenn Tutt to catch up the wagon team and help her hitch them. She popped the reins and headed off down the dim trail that led toward the sheep camp.

She reined up when she reached the hill from which the

trail wound down into Wingate Draw. She shuddered. Something about the thorny tangle of mesquite brush down there had the grim suggestion of violence.

A light breeze swept across from the other side of Wingate Draw, from the Pickett range Martin Schell was claiming. It brought with it the faint sound of bawling cattle.

Judy jerked her head up quickly and turned her ear into the wind. Her heart skipped. Schell had meant it. He must be rounding up Pickett cattle and getting ready to push them across the draw.

Just three men, Sam Booth had said—three men and an old woman. She thought fleetingly of the Pickett Ranch crew. Half a dozen riders and Nat Kilday. Schell must be crazy!

She flipped the reins and started the team into a brisk trot down the rough trail that snaked across the draw. Maybe now that Nat wasn't here, she could try talking some sense into the sheepman. Chances were he wouldn't listen. But the memory of Otto Reiner was still strong. She couldn't let that happen again.

A mile and a half or two miles farther on she began to see Pickett cattle moving slowly but steadily toward the draw. She saw no riders, but she could tell pushed cattle when she saw them. How could Schell be so confident?

It didn't take her long to find out. A rider moved slowly toward her, pushing some bawling cattle along. For a moment she thought it was Schell, but as he drew closer she knew it wasn't. The man was a stranger. The gun on his hip looked as if it really belonged there. Four hundred yards down to the left Judy could now see another rider.

Her heart sank. Nothing dumb about Schell. He had hired some extra men to see him through his trouble. And he had done a first-rate job in picking them. Suddenly she felt foolish.

Pretty soon Schell came loping around to meet her. Watching him, Judy realized he was winning.

He was taking the range her father had claimed. He had guns to hold it, if she chose to fight.

Schell pulled his horse to an easy stop as she reined up her team. "No gun, I see," he spoke in a friendly manner. "You kept your word, Miss Pickett."

"And you kept yours," she answered coolly, pointing her trim chin toward the cattle moving toward the draw.

He grinned suddenly, like a man caught on a joke. Trouble was, this time the joke was on her. But somehow his grin was contagious. He hadn't looked yesterday as if he could ever show humor. Now Judy felt a strange desire to grin with him.

"I'm sorry there won't be any men at the camp to help you load your things in the wagon," he said. "Papa Lehmberg and Fritzi are out with the sheep. The rest of us are pretty busy right now, as you can see. Mama Lehmberg's there, though, cooking for us. She may be able to help you."

He smiled, tipped his hat, and was gone. She watched him and felt a thrill ripple through her. A sheepman! He had the manners of a knight from Sir Walter Scott. He was a far cry from the type of enemy she had expected.

The line camp had changed a lot from what it had been a few days ago. Glenn Tutt was a fine old cowhand, but any place where he lived by himself soon came to look like a boar's nest. This one had. Now the sheep people had cleaned it up. All the trash was gone from the yard. Way out back a pile of ashes, gradually blowing away in the easy wind, showed what had happened to it. In front of the house was another stack, unburned. It was Glenn's warbag, bedroll, and other equipment, and all the Pickett gear that had been in the barn.

Judy drew up beside it and stepped down. She started pitching the stuff into the wagon. Suddenly she became conscious of a big woman standing in the door of the crudely built little house, drying her hands on the clean apron that spanned her broad middle. The portly woman stepped out into the yard and cautiously approached Judy. The breeze fluttered a wisp of gray, pulled loose from the knot of hair tied behind her head.

She looked Judy over thoroughly, like she would a horse.

Finally she smiled. "Well now, so you are Judy Pickett. You do not look like you would come riding on a broomstick. You are quite a *schones madchen*." Judy wasn't quite sure what the words meant, but she knew they must be complimentary. She smiled uncertainly.

The old lady picked up an extra saddle and heaved it into the wagon. "I am Mama Lehmberg," she said in breezy friendliness. "Come on, I help you. We get through quick, then we have some coffee."

There wasn't anything to do but agree. Minutes later she was in the line shack sipping coffee strong enough to float a horseshoe and listening to the talkative old lady. Mama Lehmberg was comparing her new home to the Kerrville hills.

As Judy started to leave, Mama Lehmberg forced a half-hearted promise from her to come back again, and often. Judy flipped the reins and circled the team back toward the ranch trail. Guilt began to tug at her. So this was the enemy she had to cope with! A lovable, talkative old woman, and a young sheepman who might be a fine friend to have under different circumstances.

She wished they could be common, greasy old sheepherders, the kind she had always heard about, the kind she now doubted existed except in the eyes of cowboys. At least then she would be fighting only the sheepherders. The way things were now, she would probably end up fighting not only Schell and his group, but also herself.

The bawling of the cattle became plain a long mile back from Wingate Draw. They must be getting close to the brushy deadline.

She was only a quarter of a mile from the draw when the shooting started. Dust from the gathered herd still lay heavy in the air and she could not see far ahead. She didn't have to. Nat had found out somehow about the cattle being moved, she thought desperately. She should have realized he would have watchers posted. Now he would be at the draw with the

Pickett cowboys, ready to turn back the cattle and whip three sheepherders.

Her breath came short, and her hands began fumbling. Nat wouldn't know until too late that Schell had foreseen trouble, and had brought along men who knew how to use their guns.

Heart thumping wildly, Judy lashed at the team with the ends of the reins. The wagon jostled and bounced, but it covered country fast.

Far ahead she could see Pickett cowboys spilling over the brow of the hill and quartering down through the brush, guns drawn, to hurl the cattle back. For just an instant she glimpsed Martin Schell at the head of the herd. Hat in his hand, he made a sweeping signal with his arm.

Gunfire rattled from all around the herd. Loud shouts went up, and Schell's riders suddenly began to push the cattle hard. Judy's heart froze as she realized what was happening. They were going to stampede the herd across. Nothing the Pickett riders could do now would stop this frenzied tide of running cattle. Hoofbeats rumbled. Horns clattered. Schell's men rode hard, yelled loud, and kept their guns barking. Brush popped loudly as the vanguard of the herd struck a mesquite-clogged draw.

Judy's team was still running hard as it could go. Choked by fear for what might happen to the Pickett riders, she let the horses have their heads. Only when the wagon hubbed a fair-sized mesquite and tipped half over for a breathless moment did she realize the panicked horses were out of her control.

She sawed desperately on the lines, but the horses plunged on. The wagon bounced dangerously.

Up forward one rider saw her danger and came spurring out to meet her.

Dead ahead a big mesquite loomed. Choking, Judy jerked desperately on the lines to pull the team to the right. Seconds before the collision, she knew she hadn't pulled far enough. She felt the thorny limbs clutch at her and rip her skin as the left front wheel of the wagon smashed into the thick trunk. She heard the coupling pole snap like a gunshot and felt the wagon flip. She hit the grassy ground shoulder first. The pain cut through her like a lance. The loose saddle struck her on the head.

Next thing she knew someone had an arm around her shoulder and was trying to lift her up.

"How bad hurt are you?" the man asked tightly. Groggily she realized the voice belonged to Martin Schell. She tried to make some kind of answer but could only mumble. She struggled for breath.

Schell lifted her into a sitting position and supported her with his knee. He slapped her back, helping her regain her breath.

Breathing again, she managed to open her eyes. He was leaning over her anxiously, his arm again firm around her shoulder.

"Anything broken?" he asked again.

She shook her head. It ached a little. "I . . . I don't think so."

He tried lifting her to her feet. Pain wrenched again through her shoulder.

"My shoulder . . . I think maybe it's sprained."

Looking about her, she could see the wrecked wagon and its contents scattered for fifty feet. The frightened team was gone. Looking at herself, Judy found her blouse ripped in a dozen places by the mesquite thorns. She could still feel their sting.

She realized with embarrassment that her bare skin must be showing through the torn garment. But the sheepman was being gentleman enough to pretend he didn't see it.

Martin Schell said, "Mama Lehmberg ought to wrap that shoulder up for you. Think you can ride horseback as far as our camp?"

She looked up at him. There was none of the hardness in his face that she had seen yesterday.

"Maybe I could," she answered. "I could try."

Schell's horse stood ground-hitched. The sheepman led him up to Judy. Arm around her shoulder, Schell lifted her to her feet. He helped her find the left stirrup and boosted her into the saddle.

She had to pull her long skirt high so she could sit astride. She couldn't help blushing a little. It was seldom in this country that a man got to see even a girl's ankle, much less her leg almost all the way to the knee. But again, Schell politely gave no indication that he saw anything out of the ordinary. Quickly he swung up behind her, back of the cantle, and spurred the horse toward the sheep camp.

She noted that the shooting had stopped. She could still hear the clatter of hooves as cattle scattered out on the other side of the draw.

"What's happened back there?" she asked with sharp concern.

Schell chuckled. "Oh, your men saw how many men I had, and realized there wasn't any wool grease on them. So your side backed off. Easiest way in the world to keep things peaceful. Just carry the biggest club."

Judy didn't laugh. After all, they had been her own men. But she could see humor in it. Nat would be boiling like a wash kettle by this time, getting himself fooled by a sheepman. Thank God there hadn't been anybody hurt.

Nobody but herself. Her shoulder ached with every step the horse took, though Schell tried to keep him in the easiest gait possible.

Schell's arms were around her, holding her in the saddle and also holding the reins. She tingled inside as they brushed her own arms. Every once in a while a jolting step would make her fall back against Schell, or make him lean forward against her. Each time a warm spark would glow within her.

This was what she felt each time Nat got near her. She had thought it was love. Now she didn't know. She wished she could know.

The ride lasted almost an hour, a painful hour. But she felt a little sorry when it was over, and Martin Schell's strong, firm hands lifted her down in front of the frame line shack. He called Mama Lehmberg.

The old lady appeared in the doorway. Her mouth fell open, and she almost dropped the pothook she carried. She exclaimed something Judy couldn't understand and ran out to help Schell take the girl into the house.

Briefly Schell told Mama Lehmberg what had happened. The big woman clucked sympathetically, at the same time feeling skillfully of Judy's shoulders and back, hunting any broken bones. Finally she waved her hands and shooed Schell back toward the door.

"You go away now," she ordered. "No place for a man. You come back in a little while."

Schell stood a moment with his hand on the doorframe. "I'll go catch up the team. I'll have to take you home in our wagon."

His face held a tenderness she had never seen in Nat's, Judy thought, and a seriousness she had never seen Nat show except when it came to ranch matters, or a fight.

Mama Lehmberg kept up a continued stream of talk as she helped Judy take off the tattered blouse. She treated the stinging thorn scratches and bound the shoulder tightly with strips of clean cloth torn from an old skirt.

She had known all the time there would be trouble, she said. She had seen it in the wall eyes of the fractious team. A girl should be more careful. No place for a girl anyway, running around all over a ranch. She ought to lean back and let the menfolks take care of things. That's what menfolks were for.

There was no end to it.

"Mama Lehmberg," Judy broke in, "I don't like to see men fight. Why do they always have to do it?"

The old lady frowned and threw up her hands. "*Ach*, fighting. It is always in men's heads." She winked at the girl. "Our Martin came here with much hate for the Pickett ranch. But now he likes you, I think. So maybe you say to him, 'You use this land and I use that land and we help each other don't fight any more. There is so much land. You don't use it all, we don't use it all.'"

The old lady shrugged apologetically.

"Look, *madchen*, I don't always talk too good. Maybe it makes no sense, what I say to you?"

Judy's heart was warm. She broke into a broad smile. "Mama Lehmberg, you make more sense than anyone I have talked to in a long time." She caught the surprised old lady and hugged her.

When the wrapping was done, Judy ruefully picked up the tattered blouse and held it up to the light from the open door. Mama Lehmberg laughed. "You wait. I get you one from me. It will cover everything."

It did. It fit Judy like a tent, but she managed to fold it and tuck it into the waist of her skirt.

As Schell brought a rattling wagon up in front of the house, Judy caught Mama Lehmberg's big hand. "Don't you worry," she told the woman. "I'll have that talk with Martin. There won't be any more fighting."

The old woman smiled and kissed Judy on the cheek. Judy hurried out the door.

Schell helped her up onto the plank wagon seat, then took a long, amused look at the baggy blouse, demurely pinned up just below the throat. "If you'd been wearing that this morning, those cattle would have been a lot easier to stampede," he chuckled. His arm brushed her again as he flipped the reins at the team. She felt the same warm tingle.

When they were well away from the house, Judy questioned him carefully. "You came here hating the Pickett ranch. You were wearing a chip on your shoulder as big as a fence post. Why?"

The levity left his eyes, and his face became set again, much as it had been yesterday.

"I didn't hate you. I didn't exactly hate the ranch, either. But I hated Nat Kilday, and the way I heard it, he all but owned the Pickett ranch."

He looked levelly at her. "You see, Otto Reiner was my brother-in-law. When Kilday shot him, he left my sister a widow, with three kids and what little was left of a flock of sheep two hundred miles from home.

"I mortgaged my sheep and sold what cattle I owned—every hoof. I scraped up enough money to buy the land from her. I came here determined to take it, and as much more as I could get. And I came ready to kill Nat Kilday if I ever got the chance."

Nervously Judy squeezed the slim fingers of her left hand. "Reiner shot my dad, Martin. Dad had gone over to buy him out. But Reiner never gave him a chance to talk."

Schell stared at her, slack-jawed. "Buy him out? You mean your dad was actually going to buy Otto's land?"

Judy nodded. "Nat only shot Reiner after Reiner had killed Dad."

Martin sat quietly a moment, mulling over what she had said. When he spoke, his tone was grim. "You've had no one's say-so on that but Kilday's. Someday, when the time's ripe, you'll hear a different story."

He quit talking then. He sat straight, holding the reins tightly, looking directly ahead. Covertly Judy watched him. Here was a man unlike any she had ever known. He was sure of himself, firm, determined. In those ways he was much like her father, or like Nat Kilday. Yet he was different from them, too, different in a way that stirred her pulses.

She remembered the thrill of his arms around her as they had ridden to the sheep camp. She found herself wishing he would hold her again.

Mama Lehmberg's words kept coming back to her. After a while she leaned forward on the wagon seat.

"Martin, I don't want us to fight. We don't really need the range this side of Wingate Draw. There's more we can use, I guess. I'd like to call off this war between us."

His eyes widened. His lips parted as if he was going to speak, but he didn't. He pulled the team to a halt and turned half around, facing her.

"Do you mean it . . . really mean it?" She nodded, swallowing. His mouth dropped open a little more. Shortly he managed to ask, "Why?"

Judy had to strain for the words. "Well, it's just that you're so . . . so different from what I expected, I guess," she said haltingly. "I had looked for some kind of greasy, thieving sheepherders like cowboys have always told me about. I didn't realize they were folks just like us.

"Mama Lehmberg's kind and sweet, and you're—you're—"

She felt warmth flood into her face. She swallowed again, looking directly into his softening gray eyes and catching her breath. She felt his hand close on hers. Drums throbbed within her as he folded his arms around her, pulling her to him. Her bruised shoulder ached, but she didn't care. She trembled to the warmth of his kiss.

Numbly she realized that this feeling was one Nat had never given her. If there was ever real love, the marrying kind, this must be it.

After a long moment he released her, but the thrill of the kiss clung to her, made her head whirl. She sensed that he had started the team moving forward again. She leaned against his arm, eyes closed.

Moments later she heard hoofbeats approaching. Opening her eyes quickly, she moved over to her side of the wagon seat. Coming down the trail toward them, from the direction of the cattle ranch, were half a dozen men. In the lead were Nat

Kilday and Sam Booth. Behind the sheriff and the foreman were bent Glenn Tutt and three watchful strangers—part of Schell's men.

Judy's breath came short. Nat must have seen her leaning against Schell's shoulder. He might have seen more. Guilt stabbed her. She wished she could have found an easier way to let him know.

Martin Schell sawed on the reins as the riders pulled up. Sam Booth spoke quickly. "You all right, Judy?"

She nodded and told the sheriff briefly what had happened. As she talked, she could see the sullen anger splotch Nat's face.

Booth said, "I been looking for trouble here, so I camped down in the draw and waited. When the fracas was over, and I got both sides together, one of Schell's men told about seeing you wreck the wagon and seeing Schell take you on his horse.

"Kilday here thought you was kidnapped. So we was on our way to the sheep camp to see about you." He pointed a thumb at Schell's riders. "With escort."

Judy smiled the best she could, nervous as she was. "Thanks, Sam. And you won't have to camp in the draw any more. The trouble's over. I've just told Martin—Mister Schell—that he can have the land on this side of the draw."

Judy saw Nat's face fairly explode "Judy," he roared, his face like a beet, "you've gone as loco as a sheepherder yourself. Not an inch of this ranch is going to any land-grabber while I'm still here!"

She struggled to hold down the surge of anger that burned through her. Nat never would learn that it was still her ranch, not his.

"Look, Nat," she said evenly, "that's the promise I've made, and we'll keep it. I'd like to have you with me. But we'll keep it with you or without you!"

That sobered him quickly. "Have it your way, Judy. But you'll come to regret it. That sheepherder won't be in this country long. I promise you that."

He jerked his horse around, dug spurs into him, and pushed toward the ranch.

To the sheriff, Martin Schell said, "Since the fighting's over, Mister Booth, I'll let my extra men go back to town tonight. We won't be needing their guns."

Booth rubbed his whiskered chin. "I can't say I'm sorry to hear that, son. A keg of powder's dangerous to keep around close to a firebrand."

He pointed his chin meaningly toward Nat Kilday. "He's the firebrand I'm worried over, Judy. What about him?"

"I think I can handle him, Sam," she said.

The sheriff frowned. "I hope so. But wouldn't place any bets."

Schell lent her the wagon and rode back home double, behind one of his men. Grizzled Glenn Tutt tied his horse behind the wagon and drove Judy to the ranch, stopping only to pick up the wreck-spilled gear. The whole way she thought of Martin's kiss. Was that to be the last of it?

Tutt let her out at the front of the barn and drove around back to unhitch the team. Nat Kilday stepped out of the barn.

"Judy," he called quietly, motioning with his hand. "I want to talk to you." Somehow she wished she could have missed him. She walked reluctantly toward him.

He stepped back into the barn. "Judy," he said, half apologetically, "I know you don't like what I said today. I was thinking of you, honey—just you."

Feeling the anger begin to rise again, Judy turned to go. Nat caught her shoulder.

"Wait, Judy, please. I couldn't help seeing what I did this afternoon, you and Schell together. I don't know what came over you. But I tell you he doesn't care about you. He'll just use you to help him get his hands on Pickett land."

Nat gripped her shoulders so tightly they ached again. "I've asked you a dozen times to marry me, Judy. You've always put me off. How patient can a man be?"

Roughly he pulled her to him. She struggled to get away. "You're going to marry me, do you hear?" he said loudly. "You're going to marry me!" He tried to reach her lips with his.

Angry tears rushed to Judy's eyes. "Nat, please. Please!" She caught hold of his big hands and managed to pull them loose from her shoulder. Jerking back out of his reach, she whirled around and ran out of the barn, sobbing. Through her tears she saw Glenn Tutt standing there, openmouthed and angry, the collars and harness on his arms.

She didn't stop running until she got into the house and threw herself facedown on the bed.

It was her own fault, she rebuked herself bitterly. She had let Nat fall in love with her. She had done nothing to discourage him. Maybe she had even encouraged him a little.

Now she knew that she was in love with another man.

She didn't go to supper when the cook rang the gong. She waited until all the punchers had left the cookshack before she ventured over. Halfway there, she stopped dead. Over at the bunkhouse Glenn Tutt had a saddled horse standing. He was tying his few rolled blankets behind the cantle. On the ground was his small warbag. He was leaving!

Judy ran across the yard to him. She saw that his face was bruised, and one eye was blackened.

"Glenn," she cried, "what's happened to you?"

He just grunted and went on tying his blankets. "Got myself fired."

Judy protested, "You can't be. You take your stuff right back and stow it in that bunkhouse!"

He looked at her gravely. "Ain't right sure I want to stay, with Nat Kilday here." Her eyes widened. "Nat did that to you?" He nodded.

"But why, Glenn? Why?" He grunted. "I seen too much a while ago, I reckon, and then I got to talking when I might ought to've been walking."

Tutt stopped tying the blankets and frowned at her.

"You really been thinking serious about marrying Nat?"

Judy flushed and averted her gaze from his stern eyes. "I'd just as soon we didn't talk about it, Glenn."

The old man's brow knitted. "All right then, but if you are, maybe you better ask yourself the same question I just put to Nat, before he hit me. Is it you he really wants, or does he just want the Pickett ranch?"

With a quick catch of breath, Judy bit her lip. She didn't look at him. "That wasn't a fair question, Glenn."

He retorted, "The way I got it figured, it's a damn fair question!"

She stood without a word, half numb. Finally she managed to say in a strained voice, "You unsaddle that horse and turn him loose, Glenn. You've been here twenty years. You're not leaving now."

She turned and walked quickly back toward the house, forgetting supper, forgetting everything but a confused maze of faces—Glenn's, Martin Schell's, Nat Kilday's, Mama Lehmberg's.

Most of the pain was gone from her shoulder next morning. The thought of facing Nat again while this uncertainty still plagued her kept her away from the cookshack until the crew had finished breakfast and headed for the barn. On her way to eat, she tagged one of the cowboys and asked him to rope out her horse and Martin Schell's team for her. As an afterthought she told him to wait until Nat was out of the way. She didn't want to have to explain to him where she was going, or why.

When she went to the barn a little while later, the puncher had her horse saddled and the team hitched to the wagon.

"Where'd Nat go?" she asked him.

"Oh, he gave us all something to do around close here this morning. He went riding off yonderway, kind of toward the sheep outfit."

She thought of Nat's fight with Glenn. "What did he tell Glenn to do?"

"He told him to go with us. But the old coot saddled up and went trailing off a little ways behind Nat. He was acting mysterious as a Ranger after a horse thief."

Judy frowned. There never was any telling what was going on in Nat's mind, and it would take the patience of Job to keep up with old Glenn.

But any worry she felt soon faded with the thought of seeing Martin Schell again today. No use trying to kid herself that she just wanted to take his wagon back. All night long she had dreamed about him, remembering his warm kiss, and imagining a hundred more just like it. She yearned to be with him again, to find out if the warmth had lasted with him, as it had with her.

Tying her horse behind the wagon for the return trip, she put the team into a solid trot on the sheep camp trail. Her desire to see Martin made it seem as if it took her half the morning to get to Wingate Draw, cross over, and follow the grass-crowded ruts down to the sheep camp by the river.

Mama Lehmberg met her at the door. "Ah, my friend Judy. I have coffee on stove. We drink some?"

Judy smiled. "Glad to, Mama Lehmberg. I brought Martin's wagon and team back to him. Where is he?"

"Martin? Then you didn't come to me. For shame!" the old lady said in mock severity. "Papa and Fritzi took the flock to the river. I think Martin went after."

Judy found Martin sitting in the shadow of his bay horse on top of a hill and gazing at a flock of dirty-gray sheep, scattered loosely over a quarter-mile area of abundant short grass. Way across yonder was a herder afoot.

Schell was so absorbed that he didn't hear her. She was within fifty feet of him when his horse turned its head around and forked its ears toward her. Martin looked about quickly. Joy washed into his face as he saw the girl.

He seemed to be struggling for something to say. "You heal quickly," he finally grinned.

Judy's heart leaped. Yes, it was there all right, the same soft look she had seen in his eyes just before he had kissed her yesterday. She swallowed.

"Hello, Martin. I . . . I . . ." She managed to get a grip on her voice. "I brought your wagon and team back."

"You didn't have to. But I'm glad you came."

A long, uneasy silence came between them. Judy knew he was thinking pretty much the same way she was.

She motioned toward the grazing flock with her hand. "I guess that's a wonderful sight to you, Martin."

He gazed proudly across the flock. "Sure is. All fine Merinos, as good as gold. I'm up to my ears in debt on them. But I wouldn't swap places with anybody now."

"Who's the herder across yonder?"

Martin smiled. "Oh, that's Papa Lehmberg. Fritzi, his nephew, has another band over about a mile west of here, along the river."

The thought of Mama Lehmberg brought a happy feeling to Judy. "The Lehmbergs must be fine people."

"They are. When I was a boy, I herded for Papa Lehmberg. He taught me most of what I know about sheep. Trouble was that he never could handle his money the way he could handle sheep. So now he's working for me. But we're all happy about it."

Judy looked off to the left. A good way down there, a ewe had left the band and was ambling determinedly off by herself. On the far side, Papa Lehmberg had seen her. But it would take him a long time to get around this far.

"Let's go head her back for him, Martin," Judy said.

Martin took something out of his pocket.

"We'll head her, but there's no need to go down there to do it."

The object in his hand was a slingshot.

"Always keep a few rocks in my pocket," Martin said.

"You'd be surprised how many steps this thing saves a sheep-herder."

He whirled the thing a moment, then let the rock go. It sailed down toward the ewe. Hitting the ground, it skipped along the grass almost under her nose. The ewe stopped suddenly, jerked up her head, then turned and trotted back toward the band.

Martin grinned. "When I was a kid herding sheep, I used to get a lot of my own meals with this thing. I could bounce a rock between a rabbit's ears at a hundred yards."

Watching the ewe hurry back to the band, Judy laughed. Martin laughed, too. They looked at each other. Their laughter died away. Once again Judy felt drums throbbing within her. Then she was in his arms again.

She didn't know how long they had sat there together on the hilltop. Two hours, anyhow. Maybe three.

Martin was saying, "You know, Judy, I've been thinking. I won't really need your range this side of Wingate Draw. I was just taking it to spite Kilday. There's better sheep country down the river, free for the taking."

It was then that the gunshots came. The sharp, slapping reports drifted in over the warm, noon breeze that came lazily from the west.

Martin jerked his head up as if he had been prodded with a needle. His face suddenly turned cold and hard. "The sheep! he exclaimed. "Fritzi's band!" He flipped the reins over his horse's head and lifted his booted foot for the stirrup. He stopped then and turned to face her. His gray eyes were like steel.

"All my life I've used Judas sheep to lead my flock where I wanted it to go. I never thought I'd have one used on me."

He swung into the saddle and spurred west, toward the river.

The shots still came, but Judy could hardly hear them for

the hot rush of blood pounding in her ears. "Martin!" she called frantically. "Martin!"

Tears stinging her eyes, she managed to get onto her side-saddle and race after him. She had no idea what was happening. It was none of her doing. He had to know. He must believe her.

Pushing down the hillside that led onto the pecan-studded river bottom, she managed to blink away her tears. What she saw sickened her. Down there cowboys were scattering sheep, riding horses over them. One was running them into the river to drown, slapping his rope against his chaps and yelling, "Hu-cha! Hu-cha!"

There was no doubt whose cowboys they were. They were hers!

Martin Schell plunged into the band, his gun out. The cowboys promptly quit chasing sheep and spurred in toward him. In only seconds he was surrounded. He never used the gun.

Spurring down off the hillside, Judy saw someone drop a rope around Martin's neck and lead him toward the big pecan trees. Shock turned her stomach over. They were going to hang him!

She pushed recklessly into the band of boogered sheep. She tried to shout, but her throat was tight with panic.

Right in the middle of the riders was Nat Kilday. He saw Judy coming and yelled something. Two cowboys jerked their horses around and quartered out through the sheep to head her off.

"You've got to stay back, Miss Judy," one of them said, grabbing her horse's bridle reins. "You mustn't see this."

"Why are they doing it?" she cried. The puncher answered gravely. "Glenn Tutt was killed this morning. Shot in cold blood. Never even had his gun out of the holster. Schell did it."

Old Glenn dead! Grief stabbed through Judy. She buried

her face in her hands. But Martin couldn't have done it. He just couldn't have. "I've got to see Martin," she cried. "Let me go!"

Swiftly she pulled her horse's head around, jerking the reins from the cowboy's hand. She touched spurs to the dun and plunged forward before the man could stop her.

Nat's face was dark. "You shouldn't have followed us, Judy. This ain't going to be pretty. I told you you shouldn't have let this sheepherder stay."

She protested desperately. "Martin wouldn't kill Glen. I know he wouldn't."

Nat was grim. "I saw it myself, Judy."

Judy's blood turned cold. Icy needles prickled her face. She could feel the color drain out of it.

"I was going to scout this side of Wingate Draw this morning and pick up any of our cattle that drifted back over," Nat explained. "For some fool reason Glenn had followed me, so we went on together. We heard shooting. We rode to it and found Schell killing some Pickett cattle that had drifted onto the range you had let him have.

"Knowing we had caught him, he whipped out his gun and killed Glenn with the first shot. I tried to fight back, but my gun jammed, so I rode back to the ranch as fast as I could and got the boys.

"Now we're going to finish Schell right here, before that long-nosed Sam Booth can get hold of him and save his sheepherding skin. You better head back for the ranch, Judy, right now."

Judy hesitated. It just didn't ring true. She looked at Martin, still sitting in the saddle, his face battered, his gun and hat gone, a rope around his neck. There was a trace of fear in his gray eyes, but there were pride and defiance in his strong face. It wasn't the face of a murderer.

"When did this happen, Nat?" she asked.

"A little over two hours ago."

Two hours! A cold chill went through her, made her shiver. It was a lie!

"I was with Martin two hours ago, Nat," she said flatly.

Nat's eyes widened. Red splashed in his face. "I thought you were at the ranch I . . ." Suddenly he was wary, like a man cornered. "You must be wrong, Judy. You've got to be."

Martin spoke up quickly. There was the slightest tremor in his voice at first. His tone swiftly strengthened as relief washed over him. "She's not wrong, Kilday. But you are—about a lot of things. I couldn't have killed Tutt. But you said you saw it. So you must have killed him yourself."

Nat suddenly had his gun up, covering the whole group.

Realization struck Judy, cold, hard, painful. "You've always hated Glenn, Nat, and he's hated you," she said, her voice trembling. "He followed you this morning. You pushed some of our cattle across the draw and started shooting them to give you an excuse later for running Martin out of the country. But Glenn caught you at it. You had to kill him.

"That made it even better for you. You got rid of Glenn, and it gave you a fine chance to get Martin lynched."

Nat's eyes burned. He waved the barrel of his pistol. "Everybody drop your guns. Try to stop me and I won't be afraid to shoot any one of you," he spat out.

As guns and gun belts plunked down on the matty grass of the pecan bottom, Nat started backing his horse. He whirled him around and spurred him savagely. The horse broke into a run. Cowboys swiftly dropped to the ground to pick up their guns.

In an instant Martin had the slingshot out and a rock in it. He whirled it a second and let it go. The rock made a soft, whirring noise. With a dull thud it hit the middle of Nat's back. The foreman jerked, dropped out of the saddle, and rolled on the ground.

"Grab him now, quick," Martin shouted, "before he can get his breath back!"

Almost before Nat could move, the cowboys had him.

Dismounted now, Judy felt her knees give way under her. She fell to the ground, sobbing. Martin put his hand on her shoulder.

"It's pretty hard on you, I know, Judy, coming all at once. So I'd better tell you the rest of it now, and get it over with.

"It wasn't Otto Reiner who killed your dad. It was Nat Kilday. He wanted the Pickett ranch for himself. He figured one way to get it was through you. But it wouldn't work as long as your dad was alive.

"Kilday thought there weren't any witnesses that day at the sheep camp. But there was one. Otto's oldest boy had been out hunting rabbits with a slingshot. He saw your dad and Kilday ride up to Otto, there behind the barn. He saw Kilday shoot Otto without giving him a chance. Before your dad had gotten over the shock of it, Kilday shot him, too. It was the easiest thing in the world then to put the blame on a dead man, like he was going to do to me here today.

"And if Otto's boy had told his story, who'd have taken the word of an eight-year-old kid against that of your foreman?"

Martin patted Judy's shoulder comfortingly. "Well, with your dad gone, you owned the ranch. The next thing for Kilday was to make you lean on him, then fall in love with him. Eventually, he figured, you'd marry him. He would have the Pickett ranch and a good-looking wife, too. He was fighting me because he considered the Pickett ranch to be as good as his already. He couldn't stand to lose any part of it."

Judy wiped at her tears with a handkerchief. She felt Martin take his hands off her shoulder. "I guess I'd better head for town to get Sam Booth," he said.

"No, Martin," she called softly, "one of the cowboys will go. Please stay here with me. I need you."

Tenderly Martin folded his arms around her again. "I'll stay as long as you need me, Judy."

Judy smiled through her tears and leaned her head against his shoulder. She would need him always. She was sure of that.

About the Author

ELMER KELTON (1926–2009) was the seven-time Spur Award–winning author of more than forty novels, and the recipient of the Owen Wister Award for Lifetime Achievement. In addition to his novels, Kelton worked as an agricultural journalist for forty-two years, and served in the infantry in World War II.